A WINDOW ON THE DOOR

A WINDOW ON THE DOOR

A NOVEL BY

JAMES WATSON

Illustrated by the Author

PUBLISHED BY JAMES & MEGHAN WATSON AT THE
GREEN GATE PRESS, 425 AUSTIN AVE, WACO, TEXAS

© COPYRIGHT 2015 BY JAMES WATSON

All rights reserved, including the right of reproduction in whole or in part in any form.

This book is a work of fiction. Names, characters, places, and incidents are products either of the author's imagination or are used fictitiously. Any resemblance to actual events or locales or persons, living or dead, is entirely coincidental.

PRINTED IN THE UNITED STATES OF AMERICA
By Litho Press, San Antonio, TX
10 9 8 7 6 5 4 3 2 1

ISBN: 978-0-692-51020-9

for my beloved
Meghan
and the rest of the Watson Seven, indominatable.

A WINDOW ON THE DOOR

Time present and time past
Are both perhaps present in time future,
And time future contained in time past.
T.S. Eliot

Suffering is one very long moment.
Oscar Wilde

There is a ditch that flows around the fields of the prison,
and it carries the irrigation drainage and the chemical fertilizers away,
and from it the ground squirrels and the jackrabbits
drink in their seasons.
The horses sometimes, too, but they have their own cisterns.

And the waters are the same that you have drunk,
and in all the seas,
flowing from his side and over which he brooded.

Time past.

Hold the cup over the edge.
I can just baaarely fill it with my arm out straight, straight.
Sharp corner on my elbow. Push the handle and turn it off.
Carry the cup from the bathroom. Turn off the light over my head like Daddy told me.

The tiles of the small entryway are brown and dappled pale sky gold by the morning light through the window on the door as the boy kneels carefully, balancing his watercup, and sits. His legos and lego men arranged before him on the floor cast long black shadows, becoming huge and lifelike. He glances up at the bright door, then lowers his head again.

Over here is where the bad guys are, with the black helmets.
Here this is a river between them.
And so the good guys are sending out spies to the river. To check out what the bad guys are doing.
Its nighttime, and so . . . Okay, see the good guys are laying down. On the edge of the river. And they can look over and see the bad guys castle. And they can see . . . these guys on top of it are walking on top of the castle.
Okay. So then, the bad guys are talking. About what theyre going to do. And the good guys are listening.

He reclines on his elbow, ancient face and wondrous eyes close to the lego men. He moves them with gravity, bestowing on them their true mass.

There is a crashing and thudding sound, and muted cries.

The boy freezes, holding a woodsman suspended in the air.

A loud bump on the wall! It makes me stop real quick.

Oh, its just Daddy in the garage. Hes moving something big or using one of his Tools.

It goes again then it stops.

I look at the window on the door. Its like a hole full of light on the door. And I know the window will get dark if Daddy is coming in.

But its bright and theres nothing there.

Book I: *A Summit.*

AH WELL, YES. With a priest, of course, that's a tricky question, he said. I was last stationed at San Remo, a hundred miles or so southwest of here if you're not familiar, at the end of a mostly empty farm road out from San Antonio—more or less all Germans from three families though they don't know it and that was a hundred and eighty years ago anyhow—deeded by Austin himself and lived on by those same three families all that time, with of course the odd mercantile man in and out, marrying occasionally and et cetera. I was there six years. Long enough to know the brewmaster well, and to learn more about their history than they. Of course most folks won't want to hear they're married to their third cousin, and one can appreciate that. Though the church does permit it, you know. But I've been up here now for twenty-two years this autumn. My people are in upstate New York though I never knew them except my mother. But to answer your question, I suppose by now I'm mostly Texan, for what that's worth—and I tend to think rather a lot . . . But now then, what can I do for you? Ah, I see. Well.

Here the priest's voice lowered from a pitch just over the general soft din down to nothing, even the cadence of it indiscernible. In an adjacent booth, a young man sat alone. Leaning back on his seat he lost even the tremor of the voices in the wood, and he smiled gently down at the moon goddess grinning up at him on his coaster. Her weird eyes distorted in the bottom of the rimpled tumbler. It was happening now. The booths in which they sat, back to back, were two of several arranged on the wall of the barroom of the old restaurant. Wood paneled and groined and floored.

Numberless unshriven confessions had been made in that room before the priest's time, silently by blood-stained leathern frocks bellied up to the barcounter, or spilled in soft tones down the beards of old mindblown cusses communing in dark corners with no one but themselves. The young man waited a few minutes then heard a soft Amen, and Thank you, Father, and the sound of scooting and thudding as the guest behind him left the booth quietly. He realized he had been holding his breath. He looked down long enough for the footsteps to reach the front door. On his table were a small stack of books and a thin brown notebook that was open before him, with markings which from above appeared to compose a map. He pushed his glass to the corner of his table, wiped the dew of it, and folded his napkin against it.

Well hello there, Jonathan! Getting much in the way of work done?

Some. Over your racket.

The priest was peering around the back of the booth. Well I take offense at that, he said. I accept no money, and rarely a drink. He smiled. And that only from them I think it will do some good to give it. Racket.

I meant the noise.

I know what you meant but I can't imagine it was so loud. Though it can get dicey with the older parishioners.

I just had to sit through the whole goddamn history of Texas.

Well then you're welcome, and I suppose I can conscience extorting a fee from you. The priest left his booth and slid into the bench opposite Jonathan dropping his purple stole beside him. In the interest, so to speak, of your eternal soul.

Ha. Thanks. And how's the raleigh?

Oh, rolling along. Rolling along nicely. I will say though that those gators are overrated. Two flats just this month. He sighed. And then, I've been coveting this nitto quill for a few weeks. Which of course I don't need.

Probably not, said Jonathan.

Ah, but a beautiful nickel headset would no doubt serve to . . . lift my countenance, so to speak—as I rode along from job to job. And that could be no harm to the ministry.

Jonathan laughed. Well, aren't we just full of it, father.

Ha ha. Naturally. I guess I mean simply that it's beautiful and that's enough. And how is . . . the priest looked at Jonathan's notebook upside down . . . how's the garden coming along?

The younger man turned his notebook around to the priest, who squinted. There were boxes drawn in rows, and labels in tiny architectural print. Butterleaf, beans, flour corn, russet, red, tomatoes, spinach, bell, habanero, pumpkin, others.

Hmm, well. So you're interplanting and that's good. Cornfield beans. Good. And this is the plot . . . he looked up, furrowing at the ceiling . . . northwest of the parking lot? Morning sun? Okay, well.

I was thinking of bringing the water down from—Jonathan pointed—here, off the roof, and then catching the runoff from here, too.

Hmm. I'd say you'll want to start your drip up here, said the priest, squinting. And then you should have . . . well, you'll want your beans up top here for the water, and then zig zag your line down, just like this, all the way to your cucs—and is this a prickly pear? While he spoke he traced a line slowly with his finger through the boxes on the page.

I'm thinking margs in a year or two.

Bless you son.

I didn't say for you.

Ah. Then your sins be retained.

Thanks.

At any rate this should work. But have you thought of peas here? Easier than these beans.

I hate peas.

Okay.

Can I get y'all something more to drink? said a waitress who had appeared at the booth. Father, you having anything tonight?

Yes. My work is done.

We'll get two more of these devil's backbones, said Jonathan. And this one's mine, he said, circling the table with a finger. I owe Father here.

Okay. I'll have those right out.

Well thank you, Jonathan.

No problem. I do owe you, after all.

They fell silent for a moment, looking at the open page. Journeymen of life who have made maps and charts of the other's interior landscape, but who at moments such as this, in the lull of things, are content to leave the territory unobserved.

Jonathan had arrived in Texas in early March of that year, as the teeming Spring was rushing in. Like the priest three decades before him, he had come out of the north, though not like him from the hamlets of New

England. A land burnt by the winds of history and early wizened. No, Jonathan had found his unlikely way south from the pioneer northwest, touched by the infinite sky and still raw with wilderness. Mountains where men do not rule. No wars to speak of, and nothing truly old save the earth itself and the quincentenary trees. The ancient peoples of the place who had roamed down from Alaska and British Columbia and walked amongst the wet towering trees all but gone, leaving no sign but their mute place names. Champoag, Mollala, Tilamook, Snohomish.

But even the afterfolk who had staked the land and supposed they settled it, hairy anglo saxon godless protestants, still held in their blood the memory of foot travel over the continent and therefore of the land, and they were pagan under the misty skies. A mushroom and lichen people. A beer and coffee people.

In that land Jonathan, skinny and quiet and growing old by the minute, had worked at a smoothie bar. Blending loud fruit smoothies in a strip mall with a little parking lot in front of it, next to a dentist office and a mediterranean store. It backed to hills of shrouded mansions glowing golden through the drizzle behind enormous dark fir trees. People bought the smoothies, he thought, as brightness to shore up against the continual gray. He lived with his mother and two younger sisters in a little second story apartment at the foot of those hills. It was his last year at the school aptly and horrifyingly called public, and he was seventeen.

He first knew he was going in late February of that year. Felt it like a hollow, somewhere just below his collar bone. He was closing the smoothie bar with the assistant manager named Lindsay, who had short diagonal hair. She was in the back room, though he knew she could see him small and gray in the security camera as he mopped the front of the store, getting a jump on it because it was a quarter till ten and almost no one came in at that time for a smoothie, especially not in the cold wetness of a February Tuesday night. The windows were black, speckled and streaked with bright rain smear reflecting the signs in the parking lot, orange and yellow and green.

That day the customers had come through the store like characters in his dreams. They said things like: I'll have an epic size passionberry blitz with protein and immunity. And can you guys sub extra sherbet for the bananas? And double blend it. Oh, okay, he would say, in his big yellow t-shirt, black apron and nametag. And can I get a name for the order? What do you want my name for? You can just write down Martha. I don't want my name in the computer. Or actually just put down a number. Four. No, wait, seven. Can I get an extra boost? Did your prices change?

But now there had not been a customer since nine o'clock and Jonathan was double-mopping the floor because the a.m. manager Derek had walked in that very afternoon (according to Lindsay) and had said Who dragged a dead body through here? The stickiness, not the smell, Jonathan afterwards learned, having inquired of Lindsay, and he had remarked to her that in this case orange pulp or a leaky sherbet were the more likely culprits and Lindsay, who wasn't all bad, had giggled though it wasn't very funny, and though she was serious, really, about doing very well in what she saw as the first step in her career as a successful businesswoman, which in her mind meant, vaguely, slim gray pant suits and eating and drinking little things at sidewalk cafes on busy downtown streets while people walked quickly by and she checked her phone or met with an improbably handsome representative of some foreign firm of indeterminate business, also in a slim gray suit. Nevertheless Jonathan mopped on and did not mind it, because it meant that he was alone and was completing a task with a verifiable end.

It was on this perfectly ordinary night that he had first said it to himself, as he rounded the corner with the wet mop on one row of tile: I'm going. For though he had felt it before (just below his collarbone), now he knew it somehow, and he said it aloud, softly to the mop, as confirmation or ratification: I am going. Though he did not know how it could be done.

Jonathan looked up, out into the room. Anything good tonight?

The priest laughed. Ha ha. Never gets old.

Well, you could change the names, you know. Spice it up a little.

Ha ha. You put my soul at hazard. But unfortunately, sin is rather boring.

Ha. I doubt it. You should write a book. Where only you know . . .

Ha! Actually, sometimes I yawn right in the middle of the prayer.

That's not rude.

Never during the absolution, though.

I'm relieved to hear it.

The priest paused for a moment. You know, on the other hand, anybody who is any good—and they're rarer than you might suspect—is good in their own particular way. Our dear Fyodor had that backwards. When someone finds his way to goodness . . . well that's often *quite*

peculiar. Like a maimed dog when it learns to—
 Tolstoy.
 —what?
 Anna Karenina. Good families all the same. You've got it mixed up.
 Oh. Well. You know I'm only recently of the learned, so to speak . . .
 Anyway. I'm sure it's fascinating. Goodness and all.
 You'd be surprised.
 Ha. Well, probably I would. But anyway are you getting the nitto or not?
 Well, all your ribbing aside . . . and I suppose all ribbing is a side—my back really could use an inch or two at the bars. Posture.
 And it's beautiful.
 Yes, and it's beautiful. The priest, in his simple black, was looking at his hands. Speaking of which . . . prickly pear, eh? What does Jane think of your layout there? He pointed at the penciled garden plan in the notebook.
 Ha, and there it is, said Jonathan.
 Just then the waitress returned with her tray. Heeeere you go baby.
 Thanks.
 Thank you ma'am.
 Okay, anything else right now?
 That'll do it.
 Yes, thank you.
 The priest looked down for a moment and then raised his pint glass, To you, Jonathan.
 To you, father. And to sin. In all its boredom. They took a sip.
 So, said the priest.
 Yeah. So. I don't really know. It's kind of a weird thing in the end, I guess. You know.
 Yes.
 But I guess if we leave off my feelings in the matter, it's not that complicated.
 Hmm. Love often is though, I'm told.
 Well. Let me get warmed up a little, I guess.
 They sat for a moment, at bay, and Jonathan looked at the pitted pine floor boards and the black reflecting front door and the hostess stand and the back of the hostess who if one thought about it was a human, a woman girl, and then away at the gratingly bright round window of the swinging door to the kitchen wherein fluorescence showed every bacteria-laden stainless steel surface and every pockmark on face and hairthinning,

and then he buoyed himself up from the sucking mire of impression: from the sucking mire of the infinitude of impression at every moment if one let oneself—and he said:

So you lived in New York. That's news. How come I never knew that. What? Oh . . . the confession.

What was that like? Different than here.

Well, that was a very long time ago. And it wasn't The City, as they called it. He bounced two fingers in the air. He took a drink and seemed as if he would stop.

But Jonathan remained silent, like listeners to storytellers will.

Well, it was somewhere rural, continued the priest, leaning back in the booth. Like here. Of course everywhere is like everywhere, now more and more. The priest took his first long tilt from his pint. But there it was colder and back then the people there were less friendly on the outside. Maybe they still are. I haven't been back. But they're probably better underneath. Or at least, whatever it is, you know it's really there, he said.

This isn't bad, said Jonathan.

No. Brewed thirty miles from here. In Blanco, said the priest. He went on. When I remember New York—I grew up there—I think of Dunkin Donuts. That's what comes to mind. Lit up bright places in the middle of snow at night. And also just the snow itself—at night in the forest. It glows a little bit. You could see where you were going without a light. I used to take long walks through the forests near our house. And if there was just a little bit of moon, you could see fine to walk in the snow. And it would be so quiet. I remember scaring up foxes. And skunks—they'd waddle on ahead of you, and you would just stand stark still. And I remember—it seems so foreign now—near autumn there would be corn roasts. Apple oriented gatherings. He smiled briefly at Jonathan and then closed his eyes again. Mother and I would get in line where the grills were lined up. And we would take our corn from the piles. And I would always sense what she was thinking or feeling, and I think she knew that. Living in a new town and mom worked at the bank. It's weird to think about now. But people were solicitous. You know.

Yeah.

They were. Dad was pretty much gone by then. I must have been . . . Oh, let's see. I was probably seven.

Jonathan, listening, had been looking at the table. He looked up. Why did you do that?

What?

If that happened then you know exactly how old you were. I mean, don't you?

Ah yes. Thank you, Jonathan. Forgive me. Habit. To speak of it like that. It was the week before Christmas that he finally left. In second grade. And I remember the corn roast earlier that autumn when I first knew something was coming. Mother and I had come alone. And we were both probably a little shy. And I sensed it in her though she didn't show it at all. There was a pastor . . . or I think that is what he was called. And damned if he wasn't friendly. Tall. He leaned over and smiled at us. He smiled at Mother. And so of course I wanted to tear this guy's face off.

Easy there, father.

He chuckled and glanced around. Ha. Well.

I'm sure he just trying to be nice.

Nice. Yes he was. Nice. Which was not what I needed. But at any rate it was uncharitable of me to say. I am speaking through my second grade memories. No one got divorced in those days. And I remember that year at Christmas, my mother took me to Vermont. We drove there. She was a valiant woman. And you never think about it when you are a kid but somehow I knew even then. And Dunkin Donuts is what was open all night back then. So we stopped, in Massachusetts, I think, at this little Dunkin near the turnpike and nothing else, except sometimes headlights, and the trees on the highway were black and the sky was pink from some town lights and we sat at a tall counter and I remember there were just two policeman there and they tried to give me stickers like badges. But I was so scared. But she was very strong, and small. She took the stickers and gave them to me later.

The priest talked, and Jonathan listened, his head bowed slightly to the table. The priest suspected that the interiors of other souls were like his, cavernous and housing magnitudes, though undoubtedly with their own accidents of architecture. Even as he spoke of the snow and the bright light of Dunkin Donuts in winter in Massachusetts when he was seven years old, he was feeling other memories of the snow. Most keenly of a gray and cold morning thirty years ago now, when for the first time at age twenty six he had driven the two hours he would afterward drive almost every Saturday to visit a man named Moochie in the Attica State Correctional Facility—a man whose nickname he did not at the time know, but who had, seventeen months prior, been incarcerated consecutive sentences without parole for manslaughter in a case involving a four year old boy.

Jonathan knew nothing of all this. And he thought of hard, bright things: bleachwhite asphalt under live oaks and the welcoming toughness of life in Texas. And the itch of work. So when the priest finished his recollection, and drifted to a stop like a sled in a snowdrift, Jonathan nodded down at the table meaningfully with the slow cadence of one who had been listening, but who had been seeing as well his own history play before his eyes.

When it was one minute to ten, Lindsay came out from the little back office, carrying the register drawer past the walk in freezer and dry storage, and the long closeout register tape billowed behind her like a train as she walked. Alright, let's get out of here. She and Jonathan clocked themselves out on the touch screen and then they stood very still by the alarm so as not to set off the motion detector while it armed. Standing close together. He could feel, just, the warmth radiating from her bare arm. What am I doing here. She punched in four digits to the alarm, beep beep beep beep, and then the warning chime started and they turned off the lights and walked quickly to the glass front door. Outside, Lindsay turned the big key two revolutions and gave the door a hard yank.

You need a ride?

No, I'm walking, said Jonathan, but her face was already awash in the ghostly pale blue from her phone. Okay have a good night she called over her shoulder without looking back.

He walked home and the streetlight mist turned to a soft cold rain. The same rain that had veiled the douglas fir saplings on this hillside half a millennium before. The black hill rose to his left, dotted with warm lights. Huge houses ensconced like the lodges of some endor retreat. The sheer size of them gave him a thrill of electric possibility, as if the dove face of a princess might appear on some sill and look down at him. But he turned right and walked downhill to his apartment complex lit by a buzzing orange lamp: Greenwood Plaza carved in relief on a wooden sign from the seventies with silhouettes of coniferous trees.

Hi sweetie pie. How was work.

Oh, just dandy.

I covered a plate in in the fridge.

Oh okay.

His mother in a gray bathrobe and big light blue glasses sat on the dark green couch under lamplight from a sidetable. A Reader's Digest condensed book next to her and a magazine open on her lap.

Meet any girls?

Tons.

You shouldn't count them by weight.

Ha ha.

And anyway I don't want you to just take up with some chick that gives you her number at work.

Okay Mom. He found the plate and took the saran wrap off and put it with a clink on the microwave turntable. Beep beep beep hummm . . . He sat down on the far end of the couch.

Who'd you work with? she asked.

Lindsay was closing.

She seems nice.

She is nice. How was work for you.

Oh. She curled her lower lip thoughtfully, setting her book aside. Another day, another . . . well more than a dollar I suppose. Teensy more. Linda the Hun was out sick. So of course everyone was a little . . . gay?— did I just say that? It came so naturally. She smiled halfway and laughed through her nose. But I guess it's the right word for it. What else would fit? Lighthearted and sort of bouncy? Who says that?

Geesh, mom.

Sorry. Anyway. You know. I guess it sucked, pretty much. But I did have some fun little inside jokes with Jo. So that helped. I mean she's fat but hilarious.

I didn't know they were mutually exclusive.

Anyway. It was fine. I've got to take Sparrow to early practice tomorrow. Can you stay here till I come back to get Ruthie for school?

Sure.

Are you sure?

Yeah.

Really?

Yeah.

Okay. I'm about to pack it in. I just wanted to stay up to see you. Did you walk?

Yep.

I guess that's why you're all wet.

Yep.

Okay. She stretched with little fists and a yawn and stood up. Well. G'night and make sure you lock up. Love you sweetie.

Okay. I will. Goodnight.

She turned to the hall with the bedrooms. Her shoulders seemed so narrow from behind.

Oh, said Jonathan.

What?

Um. Real quick. I've been kind of thinking.

Sigh. And after all my precautionary tales.

Yeah.

Thinking about what.

You know, about the next thing and stuff.

Okay.

And . . . I'm kind of thinking I'm going to move somewhere and work. And make some money before I think about college. Not rush it.

Okay . . . like close to here?

I don't know. But I mean . . . I just . . . I think I'm going to do that.

Okay, she said, seeming smaller. Well. Let's talk about it tomorrow.

Okay.

Goodnight.

The microwave beeped and he ate his late dinner on the couch.

The priest had first visited Moochie at the Attica State Correctional Facility on a dark snowy biting morning when he was twenty six. On the way to the prison, he stopped at the Tops Pharmacy in Bath, New York. Five thirty in the morning. A slow hour behind him, and at least another in front. The plows on the eighty six had just run. The parking lot of the pharmacy was black and slushy with salt. He wasn't a priest yet, then, and he wore jeans and the red zip-up sweatshirt he had worn almost every day for two years so that it was near to coral. Also he had a long dark beard that had been growing for as long as he had been wearing the sweatshirt.

Can I get a pack of Marlboro, he asked the cashier at the Tops Pharmacy.

Sure thing, man. Freezing as tits out there.

What?

Freezing as tits out there.

Okay. Yeah.
Here you go. Dollar eleven.
Oh. I'm sorry, I don't . . .
I got your penny.
Oh. Thanks.
Sure thing, man. Stay warm.
Okay. You too.
I will.

The bell tinkled on the glass door. His tennis shoes crunched on the sidewalk snow and he hunkered down into his little bronze volkswagen which he had kept running. The belts under the hood made a sewing machine whir in the little engine bay. A styrofoam coffee cup in the well of the emergency brake. There were no cupholders.

He drove north on a slaky black river with plowed white banks that wound on in front of him, his hoary crusted headlamps showing the dark glittering trees indigo and silver as he took the curves. Once, a pair of bright animal eyes reflected back to him. Halfway up a bare black tree, snowless, overhung by larger trees. A coon or an owl.

He turned west and came to the village of Warsaw, New York, his last stop before Attica. Cars were just now slipping out of the dark residential lanes at dawn into the single main avenue. Creaking old towncars, one by one, picking their way over the bumpy unplowed snow with dull yellow headlamps, then turning into the little alleys between buildings. To clerk cells, cook lines, janitor closets. While a mile away the doctor, lawyer, judge, or factory owner slept or stood on his porch in slippers looking for the paper that the snow had delayed.

He turned off the main street and went another block to where there was a circle drawn on his map and he stopped in front of an old chapel in the american gothic style whose steeple was large and white and as tall as the chapel was long. There was a lightbulb out and he could read half the sign: St Michael the Archangel Cat. He eased his car close against the curb and got out.

The air was softer here and the flakes came down now one by one, huge and delicate. He stood just outside the aurora of the streetlamp and listened to them brushing through the blackness silently and no other sound. Coming into existence suddenly as they glid through the lamplight. Winking out when they left it for the dark.

The yard of the church and its shrubs bore undisturbed white mantles. He walked crossways over the lamplit snow and mounted the steps to the arched door. He pulled the oak weight of it, leaning back. A front of warm air gushed around him as he crossed the threshold and then he was in and he let the door come heavily and quietly to.

Inside it was dim and silent and smelled of old damp stone and plaster. He walked through the narthex and through the doors propped open at the back of the nave. He put out his right arm as he entered and without looking dipped his whole hand into the font and touched himself thrice. His dark beard glistened with droplets in the light of a bank of candles on his right, wavering under an icon of the archangel.

He was alone in the church, softly echoing down the center aisle to the crossing, his eyes fixed not on the crucifix in front of him but on the gold tabernacle to the left, dull gleaming under the red light of a glassed candle. Between the transepts at the crux of the church he stopped and looked up. He bowed. A twisted wooden effigy writhing on the wall. Then he turned his eyes once again to the tabernacle and gathered himself and strode toward it.

When he reached it his hands came up at his sides as if in questioning. As though he were a driver behind a windshield asking silently what in the hell another pilot across an intersection, in his own hermetic universe, was thinking. And in the half light his hands were trembling. And then suddenly as if he had not known he would do it but as though it were the most natural thing in the world he began to punch the solid metal tabernacle. It rang mutedly like a stuffed bell. His fist became bloodied. By this time tears joined the droplets of holy water caught in his beard and finally he stopped. His arms hung at his sides and now his head, too, and all the while he had not uttered a sound. Then he looked again at the tabernacle and its little door, and said like an agonized lover But I know youre in there. I know youre in there.

He left the church and sat in his volkswagen for a few minutes, since it was early yet for visiting hours. He wiped his hand with a white paper napkin from the floor, arranging and pressing down the flaps of skin on the cuts until they stopped oozing.

He watched as the snow slowed then stopped around the little car and a thin cataract of pale fire through the trees shone under a low break in distant clouds. Then he started off, his front tires slipping for a moment as he pulled away from the curb.

After eating the microwaved plate his mother had prepared for him, Jonathan scraped what remained into the garbage can since there was no disposal, rinsed the plate, and then put it in the sink for the morning's load.

He went over to the oak rolltop computer desk in the living room and opened it quietly. He got on to craigslist. Where can you live? Where can you go to just live? Billings Montana. Cheyenne. Ogden. North Platte. Missoula. Logan. Bismark. Fargo. Grand Forks.

And what can I do? he said quietly aloud to himself. He looked at the job categories. Arch/engineering. Food/bev/hosp. General labor. Customer service. What can I do?

He continued around the country. He clicked on his home city. Portland Oregon. Real estate. 3 bedroom 1.5 bath. 1240 sq. ft. An investor's dream! Hardwoods underneath all the carpets. Dishwashwer. Cute backyard. Central heat. Two and a half hundred thousand dollars. A quarter million.

He sighed and typed in Alaska fishing. He had heard people talk about that. And I guess they have to feed you anyway and put you in a cabin. He read through some forums. Some helpful posts and some angry. All of thses people on hear are all just a bunch of posers If your a real worker your not on these sights, your out there on the boat. All a bunch a momma's boys Canydasses. But overall, Jonathan thought, the fishing route didn't seem very probable and anyway it was late in the year to try it. And if you thought about it it was just more smoothie making. Except manly and dangerous and you were trapped on a boat.

He thought about maybe selling his bicycle that he hadn't used in years, and taking his little savings too and buying a big external frame backpack and some boots. And maybe a rifle. Though he didn't really know how much those cost. And walking the public lands of the Oregon territory. Here to the coast, nothing but forest and mountains. Living on . . . elk? He clicked on REI and wilderness survival sites. But he knew enough about survival from living close to the bone with three females in a rich town to know that it wasn't a game and it wouldn't really work. And anyway what was the point? You were just as powerless living off the land by yourself as anywhere. More so maybe. And he wanted to love and to mate as much as any other quiet rawboned seventeen year old saxon boy. He went back to craigslist.

And then scanning down the list of conjoined republics, lonely places and populated, he clicked on Texas.

Yes. There had to be corners of that place left.

Endless grass and rock fields and white highways boring a line into the horizon.

He didn't know the names of the towns. He opened google maps in another tab and looked at a satellite view as he clicked on the various towns on craigslist.

Dallas/fort worth. No. No.

He looked at the barren west of the state. No. A place for megalomaniacs. Universes unto themselves.

Life. Life would be found somewhere in the middle. A green ridge ran southwest. Flanking Austin it ran down to San Antonio.

San Antonio. A dusty bright sounding place. Latin but dispassionate, like an infinity pool he had once seen in a National Geographic Traveler magazine. A direct encounter with the globe. The horizon.

It meant to him men, real men of diluted Spanish ancestry, who quietly laid away pesos or dollars for decades to provide for their unknowing families. Who died instead at thirty six years old fighting with a broken bottle someone who turned out at the last to carry a small revolver and pressed it into his ribs. Bang bang through a lung. Gasping in an alley of San Antonio, where Cortes rode gleaming awfully against the sun. Dying alone in a dusty alley at three in the morning. Having just come from a latino stripper joint that was as much a whorehouse as anything if you had the money, and thinking as your last thought how what little you had managed to put away would never be enough, and it would only be maybe a year before she took up with another. Who worked at a car dealership maybe and she wouldn't even mourn you that much when she would find out you had come from that place when you died and she wouldn't know how much truly you had loved her and had done everything for her. And you are twitching hopelessly on the pavement and all youre trying to do is get the ticket stub out of your pants and stick it down the gutterdrain by your head where you lie but you cant manage it. You cant, and you die there, and thats your last feeling. Shame and terror.

Texas. Yes.

He zoomed out and scrolled up the ridge. Wimberly, new braunfels, san marcos, driftwood. The devil's backbone, it said. And then, there. West but not out of the reach of the larger cities north and south. In a little cultural eddy. Or so it seemed from the green and brownish map satellite image. Ventana. The name looked breezy like italian. Ventana. But hard. It was a small sized dot. A few dozen miles north and west of San Antonio. The same south and west of Austin.

I'm moving to Ventana and I'm going to work for my living, he whispered aloud. Every cent. And not smoothies.

Real estate for sale by owner. Fixer upper special! 2800 sq ft $36k OBO. Bring all offers! A house for . . . like a car, he thought.

Skilled labor. Granite counter installer.

Sales/Biz Development START TODAY, GET PAID TOMORROW! Advancement bonuses of $100k, $200k, and mid six figurees. (From home.)

Cust service rep, inside, 8.50 to start.

General labor. Oil derrick hand. Competitive Hrly DOE.

Yes, he thought. Oil derrick hand. Hand. I'm a hand on an oil derrick.

One year contracts. Will train the right personel.

So what you do? I work in oil. Derrick hand. Oh, really? Yeah. Lots of climbing around. Like a ships riggin. Ycant be scared of heights! That a fact. Yessir. Ha ha. How long you been in. Well, bout two years. Hell, it aint always easy, but the money caint be beat! Well hello there, darlin. Aint you a sight for sore eyes after a long week up in the works.

He closed his eyes and then shut down the computer. He slowly lowered the rolltop desk cover. He shut off the kitchen light. He checked the front door lock. He thought about school in the morning. Stuff he had to do for that. Stuff he wouldn't do. School. He chuckled to himself, now a working man.

He pictured himself stepping into rough carhartt overalls and grabbing a blue speckled enamel cup of coffee from his counter and facing the day. Facing every day. He imagined the sun.

At the first light of cold dawn he pulled away slowly from St Michael the Archangel's and started down the final road to the prison. Ten miles later when he turned there was no sign for Attica off the two lane country highway except the street sign: Dunbar Road. If you were headed there then you already knew.

The road was unplowed and he sloughed side to side as he gained the crest of the little hill through the trees. Then he was on a level stretch of road cut in the slope and he crawled along the south flank of the main block. The wall loomed above him on his right. A false gray horizon. Forty foot of sheer concrete a half mile long with turrets on the corners and at the midpoint. A mathematician's snow castle.

He turned right at the southwestern corner and came to a small parking lot naked in front of the west wall, with the central guard tower overhanging it. There were three other cars there already but no movement.

He stopped his car. He did not pause after the long drive, but methodically unbuckled his seat belt without looking up. Like a first time high diver not daring to stop. He took off his cheap watch and set it on the passenger seat. He unzipped his sweatshirt halfway and began unclasping the small crucifix and then stopped and left it on. He reached onto the back bench seat and retrieved a carbon copied form: *With little exception anyone can visit an offender, as long as it is during visiting hours, the visitor has proper identification, and the offender agrees to the visit . . . The introduction of contraband to the facility is ABSOLUTELY PROHIBITED. The Superintendent may deny, limit, suspend, or revoke the visitation privileges of any offender or visitor if the Superintendent has reasonable cause . . .*

He tossed the paper back on the seat and, with a hasty adumbration of the cross, opened the door and stood up into the hard morning. He turned and pushed down the doorlock and closed the door and set his keys on top of his front tire back in the shadow of the wheelwell and stuck his hands into his sweatshirt pockets and trudged with his head down toward the towering gate, his white breath streaming around the edges of his red hood.

Inside was a bare gray room. One row of chairs along the back wall. A long counter fronted by thick glass. There was a desk behind it and an officer chewing a bearclaw and holding a newspaper up away from his face. He didn't look over but spoke, still chewing: Name.

Donald Rumley.

Identification.

He slid his drivers license under the divet in the counter. The visitation supervisor glanced at it and the list in front of him.

Inmate.

Collangelo. Byron Collangelo.

The supervisor turned, and leveled his eyes with the hooded face before him. Relation?

None. Just . . . visiting.

Friend?

Um . . .

You his attorney?

No.

Cleric?

No.
Then the visit is personal.
Yes. Personal.
You a criminal?
What? No . . .
It's a felony to plan criminal activity with a detainee behind bars.
What? I'm just visiting.
Okay. The supervisor seemed satisfied and set his bearclaw down and licked his fingers and whizzed the license back through the aperture and began to rifle through an accordion file. Collangelo, collangelo, collangelo, he muttered.

The word became abstract to Donald. Something you could roll around in your hand.

He ain't in here in my desk file. The supervisor sighed. When's the last time you seen him?
I . . . never. This is the first time.
Okay. DIN.
What?
What's his DIN.
What's that.
Department Identification Number.
I . . . don't have that.
The supervisor rolled his eyes and began to get up off his padded vivyl swivel stool and both he and it groaned. You mean to say didn't you ever ask him?
Um . . . I've never talked to him.
What? How long he been in here?
A year and a half.
And you never seen him yet? Some friend.
I've never talked to him before at all.
Like never in your life never talked to him?
No.
What the hell you doin here, then?
Visiting him. I have permission from the judge, and he . . . the prisoner has okayed it too.
Well okay then I guess. I'll just have to go and fetch his file up from the archives. You hang tight there.

He turned and hitched up the back of his trousers decisively by the tooled black patent leather belt, jingling the cuffs and keys and clacking the long wooden baton in the process. He breathed heavily as he walked off with his thick arms swinging out around his girth. He turned at the door as he left.

What the hell you wanna talk to him so bad you ain't never talked to him before now?

The beard, shadowed by the faded red hood, seemed to vanish up into darkness. He killed my son, he said.

Donald waited in the sun by the open door of the volkswagen. The bronze paint close to new. Doing well for himself at twenty four years old. It was parked in the white clean driveway of a small ranch house with a two car garage. A spring day. The garage was closed.

C'mon buddy. Can you get the door? Okay, come on. Let's go.

Out of the little house ran a boy. He stopped and turned around and leaned into the front door to push it to, his head hanging down between his hands stretched out.

Once it latched he turned and sprinted toward the car. He looked down, watching his feet as he ran, swinging his arms in big motions.

Over here, buddy. This side. The child got in. Okay. Closing, said Donald. He closed it and walked around to the driver's side.

Okay. Let's see here. Over your head and behind your back. Scoot over a second. Click! Okay fella. Let's hit it.

Daddy.

Yeah.

Where we goin.

The store, remember.

What store.

Hardware store.

Oh.

Did you need to get anything?

Mmmm . . . the boy looked out the window. I dont know. Can we go to Haps?

Hmm . . . we'll see. What do you want there?

Ummm . . . gatorade?

Hmm. We'll see. I've got to get a few things for the garage first. You wanna help me with that?

Yeah!

Okay. And then we'll see about Haps.
Okay.
The man looked at the boy every once in a while. Stealing glances. The boy looked ahead or out the window. He began to hum to himself.
Daddy? He said still looking out the front.
Yeah?
What are you working on today?
It's a cadillac. A type of car.
Oh. What are you doing to it?
Well, on this one I'm making it go faster. And also I'm fixing the transmission. That's the part . . . between the engine and the wheels . . .
I know, Daddy, he said cheerfully, still looking ahead. Like on my bike. Like the chain, right Dad?
Yep. That's right buddy. Good memory.
How fast can it go?
Well . . . hmm. Good question. Faster than it did before.
A hundred?
Ha ha. Well, yep. At least a hundred.
Yeah, the boy said evenly in affirmation. Then he went back to humming. Peering over the dash at familiar trees and buildings and signs. The father turned into Ace hardware and into a spot. He wiggled the stick in neutral gently, and then gave the parking brake a precise ratcheting yank. He unclicked the boy's seatbelt. There you go buddy. Okay. Now hang on for a second. I'll be right there. He went around and opened the door and let the boy scramble out, shielding him from the anarchic expanse of the parking lot.
Hiya Joe.
Hey Bruce.
And hows the little consiegliere, huh? said Bruce the storeclerk, smiling forcefully down at the boy. The boy made a half smile, not looking at him, and slid just behind his father's leg.
Ha ha ha! I think I made him nervous. It's okay, kid. You've got some time to start thinking about business! You've got some time. Plenty of time. You got any girlfriends yet, huh kid? I bet you got lots, right? Ha ha!
Oh, he's alright, the father said. Look, Bruce, you got any of those stainless adjustable hose clamps? Just the generic multi pack ones. With the different sizes. Pep boys is closed today. I can get by with the hose I have but I need some clamps.
Yeah. Sure thing Joe. Aisle eight most of the way down. He waved his

arm. You doing another job for Michael or what? he said in a lower voice.
I'm just working on a car.
Oh, okay. He nodded and turned back to his register and clipboard where he had begun to take inventory of the fasteners. He took a pencil stub from behind his ear and began scanning the paper and still looking down at it he said But you ain't planning on using them little screw clamps on his wastegate or something, is you?
Well Bruce, the father answered, starting off toward aisle eight holding his son's hand, I'm not a [ ] idiot you know. Turning and mouthing the fucking back at him over the unknowing head of the boy.
Ha, ha, said Bruce.

In the morning Jonathan stayed at the apartment with his sister Ruth while his mother took his other sister Sparrow to beforeschool woodwind practice. Oboe. He helped Ruth with the heavy gallon milk for her cereal. He asked her if she had any homework left. He roughly pulled the hood of her jacket out from where it was caught between her hair and her magenta backpack.
The door opened and his mother came in.
Ohh . . . she exhaled and came in with the loud rustling and commotion of coming in out of weather. Thank you for staying, Jonathan. Ruth, you ready to go?
I guess so.
Wonderful. Jonathan. Thank you. I'll take it from here.
Okay.
Ruth, go into the bathroom and brush out that side of your hair, she said squinting and tilting her head and demonstrating with splayed fingers. Ruth turned without a word.
Scraggly little darling isn't she? Do you have everything you need Jonathan?
Geesh mom.
I know, I know. But really. Anyway. I'm running. Oh! So, this whole going away business last night. What's that about. Hmm? She put her fists on her hips and looked down the length of her nose at his face half a foot above hers.
Oh. Let's talk about it later. You're trying to get out of here.
No. I want to know now.

Okay.

Well?

Well what do you want to know.

Why do you think you have to leave. She lifted her eyebrows even further. Why not just stay here if you want to make money. Free rent . . . Let me tell you, buddy pal. Can't be beat.

It's not just money, mom.

What is it.

Geesh mom. What do you think? Seriously. You want to talk about this now?

She sighed. I know. I guess I'm just saying couldn't you . . . find something around here?

Well. I don't think so mom. I think that's kind of the point.

Yeah. Well don't think I won't hate you for it.

I know mom.

And you sure as hell better call me once a week. That's a good compromise. Yes. Once a week. And it will be on Sunday afternoons. She was pointing an emphatic finger up at him. And you'll tell me what you did that week. And you'll tell me if you've started liking a girl or something. And you'll tell me about your job. And . . . she was crying as she spoke.

He didn't say anything. Then he put one arm around her. I'm not leaving yet. I've got to see about school and stuff.

She sniffled. Ha. I guess so. School. Are you still in school? That's right. So, where you going to go?

Well. I'm . . . I'm kind of thinking of Texas. There's some jobs there I could do.

She nodded, wide eyed at how inevitable it now seemed.

You can have any of these, Donald said to his son. These ones up here.

This one?

No, that's a sugar drink. Here, here, or here, he said pointing through the glass door.

Hmmm. Blue.

Okay. Go ahead. He opened the door and the boy reached up and grabbed it out. Okay, and here you go, he said, giving the boy two quarters. They walked up to the front of the little store. Okay. Put it up there. Okay, now put your money up there.

Anything else for you sir?
That'll do it.
The italian cashier put the gatorade in a plastic bag and slid three cents and a tiny receipt to the edge of the counter for the boy. The man and the boy walked out, the father holding the door for the boy. They walked down the street hand in hand, the boy swinging the plastic bag from his other hand.

It was sunny and the fruitless pear trees bordering the street were white. Droop petaled flapping bridal gowns drunk on the breeze, delicate and sweet and rank with the spring.

The road wound up a little hill. The house was on the left. They reached it. The bronze volkswagen flared with the sun on its corners.

They stopped and sat on the tiny front porch, awash in light. You want me to open that. He did. Here you go. They sat down in the concentrated sun, on the single step of the porch. Keeping them warm in the cool spring air.

Dad.
Yeah.
How long will you be my dad.
Well. Forever.
Okay.
Dad.
Yeah.
What was that man talking about.
What?
At the store.
At the hardware store?
Yeah.
Oh. He was just joking around. Just kidding.
Oh.
You should slow down on that. It's going to be all gone.
The boy lowered it from his lips. His mouth was blue. Who's Michael.
Who? Oh . . . well. You remember when those two cars came a couple days ago?
Mm hmm.
And they left one of the cars here?
Mm hmm.
That's Michael's car. That's the cadillac I'm working on.
To make it go faster?

Yeah. And other stuff.

Okay.

The breeze picked up. He looked down the street. He looked up the street. He centered himself here on this porch. This house. He owned this house. He had worked since sixteen at the garage. Then he had started working on his own at nineteen. Maybe money slipped through his fingers. But he knew his way around a motor. The manuals all memorized. A preternatural diagnostic intuition and an artisan's precision.

Dad?

Yeah.

Why is mom still gone.

What? Well. She . . . what made you think of that?

I don't know.

Well, buddy. He looked out over the street. She's . . . you know mom is . . .

Will she come back?

Well, buddy. You know . . . mom loves you very very much. You know that. She's like . . . you remember She-ra?

Shela?

Yeah. Mom is like Shela. She's out . . . mom has missions to do. You know? He-man and Shela don't always do everything together. She loves you very much. But she's going to be gone doing her missions. He stopped. He looked at his son. Okay? Does that make sense?

Yeah. Okay.

Good.

But you'll always be with me.

Yeah.

Okay.

The afternoon was drawing in. Early spring and a chill in the darkening air. He thought of the crazy girl he had met six years before, who would become the boy's mother. Both of them eighteen. Met her at some Binghamton place after work. With a gaggle of shiny black plastileather girls wearing big permed hair. New York girls. All trilling in unison. But she, even as she trilled along, mocked herself as she did it, though the others of course did not notice but he did, and he looked over and gave her the slightest nod and lifted his drink. They were both in on it. The big joke of it. That the rafting trip had a surprise ending. And there were so few, really. She did not talk to him nor look at him again all the evening but just as he was about to leave and he was sliding a five under his glass she maneuvered so that she was the closest to him with her back to him and she put out one hand behind her and held him by the waist so he sat down. And in a minute or two when the other gagglers were occupied in another direction she took a napkin and quickly wrote her number and didn't say anything but looked up squarely into his eyes with her lids half down and not an expression on her face.

She had introduced him to Michael's people. She had never wanted the boy after she found out. And one horrible morning he had stood in her doorway. No. No.

Well. Let's get you in for your nap.

I'm not tired.

I know. But a nap will feel so good.

Can I play legos in my room.

Well. Why don't you take a little nap first. And then I can set up your table in the hall.

Okay.

Does that sound good?

Yeah.

Okay.

They walked into the house. The door was a widening black portal in the sunlight. Then he shut the door.

The supervisor returned with the file from the archive room. He had brought with him a deputy sheriff. The sheriff was smaller than the supervisor. Compact and intense. His service revolver was pitched forward.

Now look here, began the supervisor, slapping the file down on the counter and leaning over toward the plate glass. I seen the history of this detainee. I read the notes and everything. And I seen the order from the judge. But I'll tell you what. I'm the only one runs this place here and I'm responsible for the safety of the folks inside and the deputies and the guards and so forth.

Donald had been watching the supervisor's pendulous gut sway just over the remains of the bearclaw and its crumbs and napkin, numbly, but now the supervisor straightened up and hitched his global pantwaist in the front, tugging his dark polyester pants up into his crotch.

D'ya get my drift, he said, with his thumbs in his belt leaning back and looking over at the deputy who continued to stare darkly at Donald.

No.

The supervisor looked significantly at the deputy. Hmmph. Well I'll spell it out for you. You ain't gettin in that visiting room, and you ain't seein Moochie.

What? Who's Moochie.

Ha. Your prisoner. He flipped open the file and tapped it with a finger. A mister Collangelo. Goes by the name of Moochie. That's how we know him in here. You ain't seein him. Ain't happening.

Why not?

Well why do you think, buster?

Excuse me?

Why do you think?

Donald looked into the supervisor's eyes, and then into the deputy's, and then back to the supervisor's. He looked old in his hood. What do I think? What do I think, he began slowly, now looking down. What I think. Well. On your little counter there is a signed court order from circuit court judge Rupert McGlanshon. And the granting of visitation rights, within the bounds of the law's parameters, devolves solely onto the authority of the prison warden. In your case Jim Conway—with whom additionally I have both spoken and written. Call him up. Go on, wake him up. It's seven twenty on a Saturday morning. In his state-funded warden's mansion. Just up the hill. I don't really give a shit. About you or your googly eyed friend here. I'm here to see that fucking monster you got back there. And you can bitch and throw your not inconsiderable weight around. But it doesn't change shit. Buster.

The supervisor blinked at him. Then he looked over at his deputy. Then he looked back at Donald. After a while he said Well Jesus Christ you don't have to be an asshole about it. God, son.

He sat down on his groaning chair and flipped the file back open. Just don't start anything. That I *am* warning you about. I been here since sixty seven. I lived through the riot. But two of my partners didn't. And you have your reasons but I'll tell you what, I've got mine. And ain't nothin like that going to happen again on my watch. So don't go incitin nothing. Shit, son. No need to bring my weight into it. He began looking through the file again. Okay, just have a seat and wait your turn. We'll bring you back soon enough.

I'm not saying she was thrilled. Jonathan laughed. The barroom was warm and seemed closer and it was filling up. From his vantage he could see an older foursome laughing occasionally and uproariously. The kind of couple-friends who have in common the raising of teenagers. Or empty nesting. Or caring for ailing parents. Their meeting serving as an oasis to their cold, careening, sattelitic journeys. A moment to let down the lifelong stamina. At another table was a new young couple twirling their fingers together and laughing secretly. And then the usual group filling up the barcounter line. Black men and women loudtalking down the row to familiars on the other end, leaning back on their stools around the backs of silent construction mexicans who would shortly be leaving after paying cash.

Ah, well. I can't imagine it would be easy.

No. But I do call her every Sunday. I think in some ways we're closer than we were. In the important things. But God, father—sorry—the woman's a little crazy. I sometimes honestly get a little nervous for Ruthie and Sparrow. I mean, not really. But man.

Two weeks before he flew down, he had called the number on the craigslist ad. Ventana, Texas. An empty space on google maps. General labor. Oil derrickhand, Buck & Liddell Energy Corp. Will train the right personel. Full ben. and sick pay. Called using the business voice he had cobbled together from memories of his father taking calls on the long corded handset. Take initiative. Be proactive. The few things left him by way of concrete instruction about this world. A flimsy few tools against all this inchoate vastness. His father was what would have been called a traveling salesman before that title universally soured some time in the middle twentieth century. Hawked big corporate label printers, then CAD software to engineers in the nineties, and now was a gun for hire or so he had labeled himself last Christmas. For venture startups. And so Jonathan said to the manager who answered Yello! at the number on the ad: I'm heading down there to Texas and I fully intend to start a career in oil. Proactive.

Okay, well, that's fine son. Fine. You got any experience? His accent cut through the connection sharp and dusty. As if he were saying fan holding his nose and Jonathan almost laughed because people didn't talk like that in real life.

Well . . . in that industry, in particular?

Yep.

Well . . . no. But I'll be the hardest working hand you have.

Okay, well, fine. Fine. Show up on the fourteenth. And for those of y'all make it through, y'all'll need a drug test. But we compensate for that.

Alright, said Jonathan, sounds good. I'll be down there. Looking forward to working with you.

He heard the hesitation on the other end of the line. Oh, okay. Take care now.

He walked out of the Austin Bergstrom airport and into the white hot air. A blue jansport backpack and a cheap brown duffel from target that his mom had bought for his journey. He took the airport shuttle to a shopping mall where he would catch a greyhound to Ventana. He walked across the lot. Couldn't believe the bleached hardness of it. Even the st augustine grass in the medians seemed too hard to walk on, like spikes. And the small liveoaks with emerald dragon scale leaves, shiny and bristling against the sun.

And so he sat for an hour in the bus station, diesel hot, with seventies glass doors and one little color tv up on a wall, and around him the dried effigies of marlboro men with their boots sticking out in front of them and one blowsy loud and massive black woman mounted over a vinyl covered steel chair bellowing at two frowzy craze eyed children taking breaks from coursing around the room to jump on either end of a huge stuffed deployment bag in light desert camo. I'm finna kick both yo asses! Pop pop comin out that bathroom in one minute you want him to whoop you? Her eyes got huge like a sea tyrant's. I swear . . . she growled low and long.

The stop in Ventana when he reached it wasn't a station but just a covered area with two benches and a few empty parking spots. The bus roared away and behind it a roiling wake of silence. There was no one around. The stop was next to a shell gas station kiosk with no customers on the outskirts of town. He planned to go immediately, proactively, into the offices of his new employer, and so after the bus disappeared he went into the outdoor restroom stall adjacent to the gas kiosk and changed into the bib overalls he had bought for the job from walmart. Cheaper than carhartts, stiff and vivid brown orange with newness. And a plaid wrangler shirt he had found at goodwill. He removed the tags. He tucked the shirt in and put the unfamiliar straps of the bibs over his shoulders and squinted down high on his chest as he worked the metal keys into the hasps. He bent and folded his t-shirt and jeans back into the duffel and emerged from the stall like some rodeo clown farmer staring out with solitary self consciousness.

    He knew the direction to the town from the ride in but the highway did not head there on either end and so he said Well, I guess this is it, and he slung the duffel slantwise over the backpack high on one shoulder and pushed down the roadside barbed wire with one hand covered in a sleeve, and awkwardly straddled it and was over.

He faced the tawny open pasture, the fence behind his back. And suddenly he was in Texas.

He walked through the fields directly toward the town. Like a released prisoner, down the middle of some mainstreet at noon. Once he saw a black bull shimmering sixty yards off and it spotted him too, raised its head and gave a coughing roar, then stood stock still, but Jonathan edged slowly sideways and away, and the bull lowered its head and continued grazing. On the far end of the fields Jonathan came to a dike dense with shrub trees and he pushed through them and emerged into the town.

Eighteen months before his first trip to Attica he stood in a disused closet off the dining room of Michael's small mansion in the suburban hills outside Vestal, New York. Oddly columned like a plantation manor. He had arrived three hours earlier bearing two armfuls of groceries in brown paper bags and wearing a Weis Markets uniform. The white maid on duty had opened the back door for him and said Oh . . . Mrs Clooney had her order in yesterday. But Donald had flashed a smile in his still young dark beard and said sheepishly, Well, I think the packers missed a few things, so here I am! Oh, well, she said, I can take those for you. Don't bother! he said. Just show me the way. So he had followed her to the kitchen and glimpsed the bodyguard who was stationed by the front door on a chair reading a comic book, and had unburdened the sacks onto the island counter and then had said I'll show myself out and strode off purposefully toward the back door. Looking back and seeing he was alone, he opened and closed the back door, pausing for his simulated exit, and then got quickly into the hall closet.

The office, resting on cinderblocks, buzzing and clacking with the AC unit on its side, was nestled in a small lot between two brick warehouse buildings halfheartedly reclaimed for retail. Gravel and dirt with tufts of grasses. The converted doublewide just fit across it and was half shaded.

    He paused at the perforated iron steps and unloaded his duffel and backpack to the ground. Better not to look like a vagrant. He didn't wait longer to collect his thoughts for fear someone was watching. Go in strong and you won't get hurt. He looked at his feet and walked up the steps and pulled the flimsy door, which in its lightness flew open too quickly, and there he stood in the doorway, blind for a moment in the darkness.

    Um hi can I help you.

    A young woman's voice that he couldn't locate in the gloom.

    Uh . . . yes. He was letting his eyes adjust, just standing there. When they did he realized that they had settled unseeingly into the eyes of the voice, which without expression were looking back into his own. Wells colorless in this light but extending perhaps to the watery center of the world. He stood on the threshold.

    Yes, he said. I have an interview. Tomorrow. I just thought I'd come by and introduce myself. Beforehand and everything.

    A slight quizzical look came into the eyes, and though they remained fixed, he knew they took in his overalls and his plaid shirt and he wished he had worn anything else and was conscious of the sweat and a little pungency from the sun in the still air of the office. Tomorrow? she said.

    Yeah, just . . . I was thinking since I just got into town I'd just say hi to whoever's doing the hiring and everything. If they're here and everything.

    Her brow wrinkled almost imperceptibly and she said slowly and kindly, Okay, um, well. The super isn't normally here. Except for the group interview. He works out at the towers. But . . . I can put your name down. And tell him you came by?

    Oh sure. Sure. Yeah. Perfect, he said proactively. Go ahead and just do that.

    Okay, she said, peeling a single lavender post-it from a stack in her lap drawer. And . . . what is it?

What?

Your name.

Oh. Jonathan.

She waited, and then said, Okay . . . Jonathan? Alright, I've got it. She stuck the post-it to her desk with a maternal slap of finality.

He stood there. She smiled with her mouth closed and he turned and walked out into the bright day.

See you tomorrow, she called after him, and he turned and saw her eyes just as the door closed.

And so it came about that after several months of planning Donald found himself hiding in the hall closet of the man he hated. Still wearing the Weiss Markets grocery uniform. He had a Colt 1911 in one pocket, from a pawn shop in Binghamton not overly fastidious in regards to its log book. An extra mag in the other pocket, though he knew he would not need it. Light blue pinstriped overalls and a short sleeved button down white shirt and a cheap newsboy cap. He had watched Michael's house for several weeks at different times of day through binoculars from a little park a quarter mile away. He would pretend to watch birds if anyone came. He had an audubon guide tucked under his notebook. In the notebook he recorded the times of every arrival and departure at the house. And besides the information he sought, he noted the meetings at the house of several groups of men connected to Michael's business, some known to him and some that he had only suspected. After a few weeks of observation, he decided that early afternoon on a Friday would be the best opportunity for entrance. The two kids not yet home from school. He must not think about them. He tried not to. The wife and mother to the children out playing tennis every Friday at that time. Unsuspecting from all he could tell of how her husband's business, nominally engaged in plumbing distribution, managed to fund the house and cars that she enjoyed. She came back each week with her sweater around her neck.

So on this Friday he had left his bronze volkswagen rabbit parked on a street which could be reached by a path between two houses a block away. Earlier that day he had felt an unaccountable need to wash the car and polish the wheels and tires. Then he changed the oil and checked the tire pressure. Like a favorite treat for a dog before it is put down. He folded the Weis Markets uniform on the passenger seat. He had stolen the overalls with the embroidered chest badge from a hook by the bathrooms near the back receiving area of the store. Rolled them up quickly and walked out of the store with them under his arm. Now on this Friday he had gone back and purchased the groceries from the store to bring to the rear door of the house. Things, mostly, that he knew had not been delivered on Thursday because he had glassed the delivery boy from the park and had seen celery tops, carrots, and milk.

 Four hours later he sat in the closet. The thin bar of vertical light from the gap of the door striped over his left shoulder and chest. He watched shapes come and go through the crack. The kids. The mother. Fussing at the maid. He sensed the maid knew more than the wife did. The kids shrieking and playing and being sent out to the backyard. The bodyguard lumbering to situate himself at the back door to watch. Ronnie, the mother called him. Donald sat in the closet with the gun held loosely between his drawn up knees, the safety off but the double action hammer uncocked.

 He did his best not to think but when he did he forced memories before his mind and did not question his course.

 Finally after the maid and the cook had set dinner and Mrs Clooney had said Thank you Lupita, that will be all for today, and, Barb, I'll need you after dinner, and after Mrs Clooney and the children had been eating for twenty minutes, Donald heard Michael come in the front door.

 Alright Ronnie. Thanks. Get on outta here.

 Thanks Mr Clooney. See you tomorrow.

 Okay Ronnie. Then later: Geez. You guys can't wait a few minutes, you gotta start stuffing your faces?

 Well where were you? The kids were hungry.

 Excuse me?

 Why are you so late?

 Excuse me?

 Mikey, she whispered harshly. Barb is still here. I'm just asking what kept you.

 Work, whaddya think, he said just as loudly, though his voice had changed when Mrs Clooney had mentioned the maid.

 Gracie, why ain't you eating up? he said. You don't like what Lupita made? A pause. What? What are you looking at?

 Mikey . . .

 What? I pay that woman good money.

 Mikey.

Shut up with the Mikey already! he suddenly yelled. There was a pause. Danny boy. What you crying about? Eat your fucking dinner. This is all a bunch of bullshit, he said to himself and stabbed his plate with a loud clink and began eating.

It was quiet for a few minutes, and Donald knew that the time had come. Barb the maid, silent, was most likely in the kitchen to his right and the family was to the left. He stood up and shook out his legs in the closet. He checked the heavy forty five once more. He patted the extra mag in his left pocket.

He waited a moment longer. He felt as though there would be some sudden and clear sign, and he would know it was time. In front of a precipice overlooking water and knowing you can jump. But no reason to pick this moment. No reason not to. And so you turn off your thinking mind, and step off.

Donald closed his eyes. Buddy. Buddy.

He opened the door with his eyes closed and stepped out.

In short, everything happened like this: He walked into the dining room and everyone looked up at him stock still and they really did have their mouths gaping open.

At first they didn't recognize him and then after that Michael kept trying to say something, and Donald just kept shaking his head and holding his hand out. Donny! . . . Look, Donny . . . Michael was saying. But Donald kept shaking his head, and he said I just need to talk to your daddy for a minute. Come on outside with me, Michael. Donald saw the wife and the kids' mouths moving, but he didn't know if any sound was coming out. Donald and Michael went out through the back door. On the way Donald called back Stay in that room. When they passed Barb in the kitchen, who was crouched down in a corner behind the island, Donald said You'd better get in there with them.

He felt like he was walking on automatic stilts and he said to himself Why is everyone looking at me so funny but then he laughed when he remembered that he was holding a gun out in front of him. When they got outside to the backyard Michael turned around and said, Look Donny. Man. Come on, man. What are you thinking. Are you fucking crazy. Look. I'm real sorry about what happened to your boy and everything. You know I never meant for all that to happen. Shit. That guy Byron's fucking crazy, is all. We didn't know. I swear on my kids' souls.

Do you? Donald asked.

Donny, I never was even going to let him get hurt at all. I just didn't know. I was just going to scare you. We thought you had turned snitch on us, and . . .

Then Donald said in return, It's always been no kids. That's always been the rules. From the beginning of fucking time. No kids. I mean . . . you have two kids.

Michael was quiet for a minute.

And then this happened. Donald said: Well I brought you out here to kill you. His voice was strange.

Michael's mouth was moving open and closed.

I've been planning it for a lot longer than you think. I realized nobody's going to touch your fucking pervert inside. And anyway he was always just your little bitch. Youre the one. But you know what? You know what I realize right now? I could make you lick my fucking balls right now.

He looked up at the night sky.

But who gives a shit. I don't know why you fucking people care. Why you even do this stupid shit. You know, there's a lot of other ways to make money. And there is nothing in this fucking world like holding your little boy's hand. God . . . youre such a blind little . . . I want . . . At this point he looked at Michael like a stray dog. I want to tell you to go inside and learn to get on with your life. Right? Love your kids a little better. But I know. Ha. If I let you live you won't do it. No matter what you say here. Everything in this life is just pure fucked up, is all. And you . . .

He shook his gun at Michael's face a couple yards from him. He turned to the side and was looking up at the sky which was dark now. There were stars and orion was overhead. He was thinking about how long those stars had been right there, in that place in the sky. The vikings had seen them. The greeks had seen them. And then he saw in the signs above him his own foolishness.

For Michael had put his hand into his suit coat and taken out his own small pistol.

And Donald, though he did not know this, suddenly whirled around and shot Michael two times.

Michael's revolver went off the same moment as Donald's first shot but it was too late, for his cheek was already stove in by one bullet and his throat flayed by another and he fell crazily to the ground and kicked on an axis around the back of his head like a frog pinioned by a nail and shortly he was still.

The next morning Jonathan arose in The Sandman. A squat yellow weekly rate motel, scratchy sheets and a cathode ray tube and parking spots four feet from his door. The weekly charge added up to four fifty a month, for which he thought he could hardly rent a room.

His three shirts were on the unremovable hangers, his shoes underneath, and his underwear, socks, and t-shirts folded inside the brown duffel bag open on the ground next to the shoes. Everything, right there.

He was wearing the orange brown bibs again, but a different longsleeve work shirt that was at least gray this time. He had made the bed and he sat on it now, holding the application and a resume and looking them over intently. Under the References heading were the names of his high school principal and Lindsay the assistant manager from the smoothie bar where he worked back home. Women. Females. Did that matter? Everything suddenly looked so fragile on the page. But craigslist had said will train, no experience necessary. He nodded fiercely in the empty room and said Proactive aloud to himself and then stood up and patted his pockets for his room key. He looked once more front and back at the papers in his hand.

This time when he reached the street in front of the gravel lot of the cinderblocked office it was filled with pickup trucks and ratty imports. Jonathan walked steadily forward. There were men lounging against the brick walls or sitting in their vehicles listening to southern rock or country or generic metal. They wore jeans and black tshirts with classic rock bands or energy drinks on them, and skateboarding shoes. A few had well worn work coveralls and boots, and they were the silent ones. Most of the men were smoking and absorbed in their phones. None held any papers. Jonathan was fifteen minutes early. He walked into the lot and leaned against one of the surrounding brick walls. With nothing to smoke and no phone he studied the ground in front of him and occasionally looked over his papers as if there were something to remember there.

At a few minutes after ten the trailer office door swung open and a stringy man in light jeans and pull on redwings came out and squinted on the top step with his thumbs in his beltless belt loops. His ash gray carhartt t-shirt was tucked into his jeans.

Alright. Well, thank y'all for comin out today. We're fixin to begin shortly. The way this is gonna work is Jane here is gonna come out and call y'all's name, and y'all'll come in one at a time for your individule interviews. Basically we'll just ask you what experience you got and what outfits you worked with and if you got any holdups on your applications. Maybe half a dozen of y'all'll get callbacks s'aftrnoon and we'll have the second round tomorrow. For the two spots. Course you'll have to pass a drug test if'n we offer you the position. Othernthat, I think y'all all know the drill here. Thanks again and good luck to all y'all.

    He disappeared into the gloom and the young woman whom Jonathan had talked to the day prior emerged into the white light and stood there with a clipboard, and the paper on it flapped and whipped in the small wind and she spoke in a voice that Jonathan could tell was measuredly sure of itself. Alright first up is . . . Bolton. William Bolton . . . Her profile, high boned and straight, showed blood that was american before the first conquistador clinked up the Brazos river, and her mouth and cheeks were soft and brown. A woman. A woman. She seemed altogether a falcon to him. Wary and hidden but somewhere was an aerie amongst the rocks and there would she let her steel pinions rest and riffle in the sky. I'm Billy! the man piped up from a corner of the lot, and then scissor kicked up from the gravel where he had been sitting and beat the seat of his faded black pants as he approached her on the steps, his other hand up in conciliation and a dogged eyebrow smile. That's me, he said again.

    One by one they went into the dark hushed coolness. Jonathan stayed where he was. The oldest man there, and the only one who appeared to be over forty, sidled up to him, smoking.

    I hear Buck and Liddell's a good rig, he said.

    Oh yeah? Said Jonathan.

    Yeah, start you at twenty six, mebbe twenty seven bucks.

    Yeah?

    Yeah, that's a fact. My old lady's on me for benefits and stuff and everything. And I hear after three months they put you on *in*surance. No one else was talking in the courtyard, and the short man's conspiratorial voice carried around the masonry.

    Wow, said Jonathan.

    Yep. The man pulled out his cigarette and spit into the gravel in the sun between his feet and then replaced it it with satisfaction. Yessiree benefits after three months and like I said the old lady's on me these days. These times, you know. He squinted up out of leather cheeks into Jonathan's eyes. Rheumy perfect blue.

    Oh yeah. Totally. Yeah, said Jonathan.

    I been in and out of rigs my whole life. He leaned back next to Jonathan with satisfaction. Bred to it. My old man was an oil man. I finished school and stuff and everything though. He looked up at Jonathan significantly. But I got myself up on a tower and into a paid position a – s – a – p. If you know what I mean. As soon as possible.

Yep. Well. That's what I'm aimin for, said Jonathan.

That's good. That's good. All this college bullshit excuse my french but I aint never seen nobody make no more money off it. Just a bunch of wasted time. I got up on the diving board as soon as I could. Up there youre just sittin on money. You see it comin up ever day unnerneath of you. Buckets of it. Just . . . money comin up outta the ground. Its beautiful's what it is.

Well. That's why I'm here, Jonathan said, and looked around, looked down at his papers. No one seemed to be watching them, but he knew they all could hear.

Well. Good. That's the way I was at your age, said the sage, nodding. But it's not all just the money and everything. Sure there's that and don't ever lose sight of it. But it's the beauty of it all. Youre touching the bedrock foundation of everything. Aint nothing runs without oil. Not a thing. Every good thing in this life comes outta what we do. I been doin this my whole life and I only come out this way because my last rig dried up and the owner's son had him a . . . his voice lowered and he said the word like a foreign borrowing . . . an affair with the secretary and she sued when he dumped her. Because *conflict of interest*. He raised his eyebrows at Jonathan and tilted his chin up for full effect. Conflict of interest. He leaned in again. Because she was working for them, he explained.

Oh I see.

Yeah. So that brought me out here. I was down in Waller County over by Houston. Let me tell you, you ever get the chance to work for Rinkel Onshore you walk away from that chance. He gave a single slow nod at Jonathan. Y'hear? Walk away. Them Rinkel brothers is trouble. I worked for em better part a eight years come april and I left with nothin. So I know what I'm talkin about. He spat a stream in the gravel. What all outfit you say you was with before you come out here?

Oh, well. Jonathan glanced around the company, who remained still. I haven't really worked in oil before.

Ain't never . . . well. What you *been* doin?

Oh. You know. Odd jobs. Finishing up school.

You a Lobo?

What?

Ventana High.

Oh. No, I just came down here for the job.

Robert Cochran! Jonathan looked up and saw Jane on the top of the steps like wisdom crying at the city gates.

. . . I said, where you come from?

Jonathan turned back to his companion. Oh, Oregon.

Texas is somethin, huh?

Yeah. It's nice. Really nice.

You know, you're in the devil's valley here.

Oh really. Jonathan was still trying to stop talking, but then he said, What?

Well, that's the devil's backbone over thataway . . . the man pointed like a prophet past the blue haziness of some distant hills. So I suppose you could say we're located in his hinderparts! He wheezed at his own joke, holding the cigarette out to the side.

Oh. Yeah.

You know, there's a story about this valley. Oh, prolly fifty years ago now. Some folks seen a young girl runnin on all fours with a pack of wolves in the moonlight. Butt necked, he added quietly, looking around. Seems she been raised by em. Part Injun. My conjecture bein she was the daughter of someone had *lain* with an Injun. Who didn't want the evidence running around to Sunday School. Well, soon after, some of the local red folk from the mission seen her eatin a fresh killed billy goat—just scoopin the flesh from the carcass with her nails and eatin it blood and all. Which is against scripture. Anyhow, they captured her next day and locked her in a room of the church. And what do you think happened? He paused. Jonathan just shook his head. That night she set to hollerin and howlin like a wolf, and sure enough the whole pack run yappin and growlin into the village. Surrounded the church. The padre was obliged to unlock her and push her out the front door. Never seen again.

Wow, said Jonathan.

Well, ceptin twenty years later when some feller saw her in a meadow givin teat to two little wolf pups.

The names were called in succession, and presently Jonathan's conversationalist left him with a two fingered salute. When he exited the trailer a few minutes later he winked at Jonathan and went to his old brown chevy cavalier.

Then Jane, standing on the step with the wind catching some loose hair, called his name. She looked more intently at her clipboard and panned the crowd evenly.

Okay, right in here, she said. He followed her back into the dark.

"The next morning Jonathan arose in the Sandman Motel."

Well John, how you doin.
Good, thank you sir.
Well fine, fine.
I go by Jonathan.
Oh, well. Do ya now. Okey doke, let me make a note of that. He looked at Jonathan over his reading glasses then elaborately made a note at the top of the application page.

Jane, who was sitting over at her desk to the side, said, Oh, Mike?
Yes.
This is the guy I was telling you about. Who came in yesterday.
Okay. Thanks Jane. He looked back at Jonathan's application. Jonathan saw that it bore the lavender post-it on the front. Says here you ain't got no experience.

Um, not in oil precisely, no.
Well, how you expect to work here?
Well . . . Jonathan searched for proactive words. The ad said no experience necessary. Will train. And I . . . well, I learn quick and I work really hard.

Well everone here works hard, son. Hmmm. No experience at all. Hmmm. He was shaking his head down at the paper. I don't really see how I can help you.

Jonathan felt the beginnings of panic in his throat. Well . . . I talked to you on the phone two weeks ago. And, I explained my situation and everything. I'll be the hardest worker you have here.

Oh, I got no doubt of that. No doubt. But you see the position I'm in. I got twenty guys out there been up in towers and down wells they whole lives.

Well. With all respect sir, I came down here just for this job. The ad said will train . . .

Oh, that's in a manner of speaking. Shoot. No experience at all. I'm not sure what you expect me to say. This job's for a derrickman. How long you think it'd take me to get you up and runnin? Look, youre young. Whyn'tcha go work with your daddy or uncle at their place or somethin for a few months and get em to at least sign off on you. Write a letter. Somethin. Find some sidework on a rig.

I came down here from Oregon. You didn't say any of this on the phone.

Look, son. He took off his glasses. Your application shows no experience at all. None. I cain't help you. I'm sure you'll find something.

Thanks for your time. The manager went back to looking at the next application on his desk.

Jonathan sat there, staring at the him. He could see Jane out of the corner of his eye scribbling at something on her desk with a studied attention. Jonathan stood up slowly and turned his back on them and walked out without looking back, letting the thin door whack itself loudly closed.

He walked through the silent men. The driver of a lifted truck was playing syrup country, and Jonathan glared through the windshield. He stalked through the town like he was looking for a fight, past antique stores and for lease signs and little clothing boutiques with no customers then away from the downtown strip and down the road back to the Sandman Motel. He unlocked the gaudy red door and flopped down on the bed.

He lay there until the afternoon.

Then he sighed and sat up. He changed out of his overalls and put on jeans and a different shirt. He smoothed his hair in the mirror and walked out of the motel room and into the sun. Hot and bright. The heat on the ruined asphalt.

Crossing the street he entered the parking lot of a mexican restaurant that he had seen on his way back to the hotel. Before he went in he glanced up at the sign. He sighed. The Sombrero. Indeed. He pushed open the front door. Inside, lurching mariachi beats and the smell of mesquite wafted up to him, and the mexican girl at the front desk with shiny black hair parted and swooped to the side and kept there with a fuchsia plastic ring glanced him up quickly from foot to head and said with an invisible smile at the corners of her mouth How many?

Oh. Actually I just wanted to see if I could get an application.

The invisible smile surfaced into a suppressed smirk.

You can fill it out there. She pointed to the little bar and then bent over and retrieved a single page application and gave it to him along with a pen.

Okay. Thank you.

He felt her watch him as he walked to the bar and pulled up a stool. When he had finished it and had drunk the water the bartender had brought him he returned to the hostess stand. I'm done.

Okay, I can take that.

Actually, would you mind if I talked to a manager real quick?

Well . . . I can see if he's available.

Okay, thanks.

I'll just take this to him.

Okay.

He stood by the desk and waited. Occasionally he saw the furtive glances of waitresses and bussers as they went about the semblance of their duties in parts of the restaurant where they could see him. Some white, some mexican. It was the afternoon lull.

Presently the manager came out, holding Jonathan's application.

Hi, Jonathan?

Yep.

They shook hands.

Well, tell me a little about yourself. What brought you down here? Your school and jobs are a long ways off.

He was redhaired and seemed to have no eyebrows but pulled off kindness in spite of that.

Well. I thought I had a job lined up at the oil rig. I'm here to work.

Mm hmm. He was studying the application and then looked up. Well, a lot of people don't know it, but serving is pretty hard work. When we get slammed, and you're running in five directions and folks are yellin at you . . . You think you can handle that?

Yes sir.

Well, you got a good application, and we need people right now. And you got a good handshake. So you're hired. Talk to Angelina here about getting your shirt and apron. Come in tomorrow at a quarter of four and we'll start gettin you trained.

Okay. Thank you very much.

Yep, see you tomorrow.

Angelina got him his apron and shirt Jonathan walked out and back to The Sandman and that was that.

He stood over the body. The gun was yet in his hand and his ears stuffed with ringing. He was breathing and staring at the half of Michael's face that was still recognizable saying, No, no, no, no over and over again to himself. The crushed pumpkin look of it. Irrevocable. Entreating the spirit to return to the body. The parts of the skull to knit themselves together. He was weeping though he did not know it. No, no, no, no. As if once his mind lost its hold time itself might turn back three minutes and unmake what it had wrought. He didn't look at the house and he willed them to stay in the dining room, his hand held vaguely up to ward them off. He wanted to throw himself at their feet. Please no. God, no. No, no, no, no.

As he and the priest sat quietly in their booth for a moment, Jonathan looked out across the room, and there, at a little table in the corner, sat Jane and Nate. He hadn't seen them come in. Eating late night curly fries and drinking sodas. He looked quickly down at the table in front of him. After all these weeks. Here of all places. He wondered whether she'd been the one to suggest it to Nate. He took stock quickly of how much he'd drunk.

    Some minutes later they came over, and Nate started talking to them. Jane stood next to him, but Jonathan didn't look at her.

    . . . you know, we're really just trying to make a space where people can, like, connect with God in a real way. You know?

    Yeah, said Jonathan. He was listening as Nate warmed up. Jane stood at his side.

    . . . and I mean, I feel like it's filling a void in this town. He looked up for confirmation. We really emphasize genuineness. You know?

    Totally, said Jonathan, twisting his pint glass slowly in both hands.

    So we're doing this new coffeehouse thing on Thursday nights? And it's been pretty awesome. I mean the Tuesday night college gathering has been great, but we've been sensing a call to really immerse ourselves in the community. You know? We're meeting in one of those warehouses on Second Street?

    Nice, said Jonathan.

    Yeah. It was totally abandoned, so we're just renting it real cheap. It's just totally raw. Like, concrete and beams and stuff. I've kinda gotten to know the owners and everything . . .

    Oh. Cool.

    Yeah. It's been a total blessing. We have students that come all the way out from Austin. We do just real low key organic worship . . . acoustic, congas and stuff.

    Wow. Nice.

    Yeah. And we have this one banjo player that comes sometimes. Ricky Lawson? He looked at Jonathan and the priest for recognition. He plays for the Corduroy Minstrels. From Austin? He tries to make it out on

Thursdays. When they don't have a gig.

Jonathan noticed the way Nate relished the word gig. Yeah, well. That's great. I'm glad it's going so well.

Yeah. Nate paused and then went in. You know, you should really come out some time. He looked with a kind expression at Jonathan. I know you came to the college night out at New Life that one time, but I think you'd really like this. It's totally chill. We just have a speaker share from his heart a little bit, and then we just have some great music. And it's right near here. Downtown. Jane and I would love to see you there.

Oh. Well, I appreciate that. But Thursday nights I hang out with Father here. I wouldn't want to take his only company from him.

You go ahead if you like, Jonathan, the priest said quietly with a smile. My parishioners are company. And besides, I can always use the time to pray.

You know, you'd be welcome too, sir, said Nate. It's really laid back.

Oh, said the priest. Well. That is kind of you.

Anyway, said Jane. It doesn't matter.

Jonathan was still looking down at his glass but he knew Nate must have glanced at Jane then.

How have you been, Father? she continued. I haven't seen you in it feels like ages.

Oh, I'm quite well, thank you Jane. Advent starting up soon, you know, he said gently.

Yes, she said.

I do love this season.

Yes.

After six weeks at The Sombrero he crossed the street one hot Thursday afternoon with his black apron folded under his arm. Cinco de Mayo.

The nights were always crazy, but he had been warned Cinco would murder him. My god, dude! You have no fucking idea, they had said.

Sup Jonathan. What it do what it does.

Hey.

Hey Jonathan.

Hey Rachel.

Where you at?

Jonathan walked into the pungent darkness from the hot bright May and was leaning over the plexiglass map of The Sombrero on the hostess stand, with borders and names drawn with dry erase markers to show each server's territory for the night. The lifers were in their usual expansive domains. Every restaurant has one or two of them, roped in decades ago by the cash and the frenetic social intercourse of a busy night's work. When you're slammed it's like drugs or a little death as you stand outside yourself for those few moments and maybe that's what had caught them and chained them to this artificially intense engagement with humanity. And the cash at the end of every night feels more like money than waiting two weeks for a number printed on a check. Or at least they imagine it thus. And so they never leave, even as the social high fades with their aging, and they see in the faces of the younger servers the reflection of their own smirking mortality. The reflection that waiting tables was supposed to obliterate.

 Um . . . I'm in section fourteen.

 Oooo . . . wow. We're neighbors, said Rachel. You gonna make fucking baaaaaaank. She slid her arm around the small of his back and side hugged him.

 I've never been there.

 Ha. Good luck. She walked away with a smile over her shoulder.

 Damn, brother, said Miguel.

 Yeah.

 On Cinco?

 I guess.

 Shit. You need anything you hit me up.

 Thanks.

 Jonathan went into the back room adjacent the kitchen and tied his apron into a floppy square knot behind his back to prevent prank loosings and checked his book for paper and his row of black gel pens lined up with their clips over the edge of his left apron pocket. In the book he had complete change for a twenty. Like a soldier checking his straps and bore, waiting for the causeway to lower. He walked into the bright kitchen. Already they were yelling.

 Queso grande!

 Let's run some food people! My window's already packed.

 Quick like bunny. Quick like bunny!

 Hey, on those enchiladas, the lady actually wants them half queso and half chile con carne . . .

 *Teek*et!

 She just told me!

*Teek*et!

She just fucking told me! I already put in the order. Can't you just do it?

The torpid old cook behind the window, with three children in Mexico whom she hadn't seen in the flesh for six years, shook her head and clucked but she put the wasted order on the overhead window with a clank and started the re-do enchiladas.

Hey, these enchiladas dead?

Si.

Dude. Jonathan, you want some of this?

Jonathan was punching in his numbers to the touchscreen and clocking in. Sure. He joined Carl, white with spiky hair, and dug in with a spare fork from a cup of them on the stainless steel counter.

It felt like a ship's galley with the bright lights and being the center of the rolling and bucking restaurant floor outside.

Rachel came back into the kitchen and put an order in the computer with rapid touches almost faster than the screens and subscreens could change and then grabbed another fork and started eating too.

So when you going to go out with me.

Ha. Well.

Seriously. You come to this town. You live all alone. I could show you what's fun to do in this town.

Rach . . .

Okay, okay. But you don't know what you're missing.

She left, tossing her fork into the bus tub and Carl watched her go and then said, Dayum, boy. I mean . . . you don't hafta like her an shit, but she just *throw*in that pussy at you, man.

Jonathan didn't say anything.

Carl turned away and put his iphone in a plastic drink cup laid sideways on the steel counter. It made a little phonograph. He started the music. Megabass pfiffed out. A tough little voice declared: Ball so hard motherfuckas wanna fine me. That shit cray. That shit cray.

Ben the manager who had hired Jonathan walked from the back office and down the kitchen line.

Jonathan.

Yes sir.

You see where I put you tonight.

Yes sir. Thank you.

Oh, don't thank me. Look. We're gonna get ass raped tonight. Cinco, to start with, and we're doing two dollar frozens. And you got a big top at six.

 Okay.

 Sorry, but it's gonna be a pretty shitty big top.

 Okay?

 Yeah, pretty sure it's all Canadians. And it's one of their birthdays.

 Hmm. I don't mind.

 Oh, I know. That's why I put you there. But I'm just sayin, it's probably gonna get a little wild, and you're gonna have other tables too. You think you can handle it?

 Since the moment Jonathan had sat up on his bed six weeks before in The Sandman Motel after his unsuccessful bid to work at the oil rig, something had changed inside him, and he had decided to make all future decisions with a reckless boldness, if an affirmative answer could in any way be backed up subsequently by dint of work. He had taken a menu home to The Sandman that first night, and spent an hour in memorizing every item on it, with ingredients and prices. He had come in early the next day and practiced the touch screen system, off the clock, until the logic of it became intuitive to him. After the first week, he had created an organizational system to collate side duties: refilling drinks, rechipping baskets, staggering the timing of appetizers and salads. He tweaked his system the following week and began to aim for perfection. And then one day during his second week, as he walked up to the restaurant from his shabby room across the street, he had stopped on the sidewalk and said to himself, looking up at the comical purple and green lit sign with a picture of a big hat: I'm going to be the best fucking waiter in this place. He didn't know why he said it but it became a tacit mantra that played in the back of his head while he worked. To never apologize to a table. To never need to. And so when Ben had said You think you can you handle it Jonathan had replied, even though he knew what was in front of him—though he saw clearly the hell through which he would pass in the next few hours—

 Yes.

 Okay then. Good. Ben walked back up the line and began worrying Manuel the side cook, who did the quesadillas, the deep-frying, the queso, and the sides for the fajitas.

 Jonathan peered through the windows of the swinging kitchen doors out at his section. He looked at his five tables, three of which would be added to two from Rachel's adjoining section and put together for the twenty five top coming at six. Canadians.

His first table was being sat. A old retired looking white couple. Which could go two ways. Stingy, dried up, and Texan. Or quietly generous and Texan. To him this seemed to describe the bivalent nature of the thing: there was about this land something so parochial, so hatefully cultic on the one hand, and so . . . large on the other. As he observed them, he whipped a chip basket liner from the container and laid it precisely in the basket, then with one motion scooped the basket through the chip warmer and shook off the excess. He dipped two bowls of salsa and held them in one palm overlapping each other like Beau his trainer had showed him. Then he took a breath and steeled himself for the performance. That had been the last lesson he had learned as he constructed his myth around himself. And he had had to learn it from Beau, a Ventana native and a sort of godfather to The Sombrero. He had thick black hair. Could have been a young disney Davy Crockett reincarnated as grinning waiter. He never rushed. No one ever rushed him. But he got all the best tables and took care of them. Jonathan had been more than competent within a week, but the master performance, like all true art, required something more. An unhurriedness—urgency, yes, but one must feel, and more importantly, must *seem* to feel, that one has all the time in the world. Beau had never walked quickly, never beat down the tiles of the floor with his frightened running stride like some servers. He had never tossed a messy scoop of chips into his baskets, had never tapped his foot in panic waiting for the bar to fix the margarita machine, had never spoken in the usual high pitched and desperate tone at the kitchen when there was a rush. He did things at their timely times.

So Jonathan approached the table and began. His first movement was often quiet, like an unexpected adagio at the start of a symphony. Unexpected and therefore louder than a shouted Hi I'm Jonathan and I'll be taking care of you tonight. He set the chips on the table and then the salsa bowls.

Hi folks. And how are you doing tonight?

I need a bowl of queso. She didn't look up out of her menu. It wasn't malice, but the unthinking blindness of one long used to accepting the necessary services of those who serve.

Alright, he said quietly. And what can I get y'all started with to drink.

Water with lemon, she said with the aggression of a lifelong teetotaler.

Me too. The old man's voice was soft like the silt that collects in roadgutters after a rain.

Alright, I'll get those right out for you, and that queso.

And a couple more bowls of hot sauce, she called after him. It sounded like bowels and he nodded curtly back at her as he walked away.

Jonathan had that old two top, and then a young couple with a carseat in a sling. Then Jennifer the hostess began blocking off his section for the big top coming at six. The bussers put napkin bundles at the places and chip baskets and salsa bowls for every three. He told Rachel who was adjacent him and two of whose tables he was commandeering for the group that she could start taking over his two wallbooths whenever she wanted and if she needed anything before the big top got here to let him know and she said she would but he knew she was more than sufficient to her tables and he didn't think she would need anything.

And then they began to arrive, spectacular. Women of twenty stone mincing on platform heels and bringing with them a trailing aura, jangling with bangled ear and wrist, flowing in shimmering polyester and carrying history august in their wake. He didn't know why it felt this way. They were black. But hadn't there been black people in Oregon? Not really, he supposed. Not many. And mostly islands engulfed in the surrounding suburban sea. He sensed an unspeakable reverence welling up in him and felt simultaneously that he ought not to feel anything remarkable at all. But he did.

He finished up the couple with the baby and gave them the check and his best genuine thanks, and grabbed the cash from the old two top who had left stiffly some minutes ago. Five bucks on eighteen for an unexpected thirtyish percent though still it was a slow start to the night.

He went into the bright kitchen to close out his check and prep himself for the maelstrom that was looming. As he was tapping in his tip and clearing out the two top Carl walked up close to him at the computer. He could smell his cologne.

Damn. That sucks man.

Oh, it's fine.

Naw man. Tell me you're at least gonna grat it. They gonna get *shit*faced, so at least they're spending money. Not that its worth it.

I'm not gratting them.

What? You crazy? You know you're not gonna to make any money on them.

Oh, it'll be fine. Anyway, if they don't want to give me their money I don't wanna take it.

Dude. You're gonna make like five bucks on that table, and they gonna get like half their food comped. Ben'll put a twenty percent grat on that table right now you know.

Oh I know.

Dude, you know you can hide it, right? You just print the tickets and then reprint them and the grat doesn't show up on the tip part. So they'll have no idea.

Ha. Thanks. I'm just gonna go with it.

Carl shook his head walking away. Shit man. Fuckin canadians. Good luck.

Jonathan went out to greet the table. No quiet symphony opening here. About eight of the party had arrived, still all women. He began. Hoping perhaps to run fast enough to stay ahead of the wave that was about to chase him up the shore.

Hey everyone. How y'all doin tonight? Alright. I'm gonna come around and start taking drink orders. And let me know if youre going to be by yourself or if youre with anyone.

He leaned over the woman nearest him, with his notepad and pen to take her drink order, but then he heard . . .

Scuse me. *Scuse* me. *Sir*. An authoritative matron in crimson commanding one end of the long table. He went over to her, feeling the waters suck out to sea in anticipation of the roller building on the horizon. She placed her hand on his forearm like a padded shackel, and spoke patiently to him like a fractious child being given its last chance at church.

Ima need a parple margarita. She paused. No salt. Pause. Suga ona rim. She raised her eyebrows. *No salt*. She was ticking the items off on the fingers of her free hand. And a tableside. No jalapenos, extra tomatoes, and mush it up real good. I don't like the chunks. An then *she* gonna need, she said, pointing to a younger woman in satin black looking away from the table with pouty annoyance, a *straw*berry.

Okay, said Jonathan. Sounds good. And are you two together...?

What? She looked suspicious, as if he were trying to take something from her. She just need a strawberry, she repeated.

Are you two . . . gonna be on the same tab, or . . .

She looked down and to the side and made a face like he had said something obscene and answered with quiet disgust, What? Naw.

Okay, he said, trying to sound upbeat and proactive and writing something in his notepad. Really just scribbling in the corner.

No limes, the Pouter muttered without looking at them.

What? yelled the first woman. What you say?

No limes! the other one yelled back and stole a quick angry glance in their direction.

Alright. Sounds good, Jonathan said, quickly writing what he could. Then the others began to rouse themselves, and he knew he would be submerged.

Donald couldn't look away. He found himself examining what had been Michael's face. Or still was. His one leg torqued under his lower back and the other straight and natural out in front of him. His remaining eye was open. Like in movies. But Donald watched the bloodshot feather lines drain away as the pressure died with the fibrillating heart until the white was truer white than ever in life, making it almost blue. And the skin looked papery against the sudden jagged gore. And seeing down into the cranium, inches under the exploded eye. And the mouth below, unchanged. The lips hanging there as they had in life, terse in seeming concentration. He could see them talking. He could remember them smiling and making coarse jokes. He saw the stubble on the upper lip and he remembered in an instant, unbidden, the scratch of his father's jaw on his own cheek when he hugged him as a child and their faces touched. He wept.

Jonathan tapped furiously at the screen, looking up and down at his pad.

The iphone gramophone spoke over the scene in the kitchen: I never see the whips niggas be claimin they drivin. I guess entertainment means blatantly lyin. Fake it til you make it. I've driven those toys, been in the wars, in the streets, cops kickin in doors . . .

You gonna be a whole minute? said Kristin, lined up for the computer in his peripheral vision, tapping her foot, freckled redhead, crook-toothed, sardonic and kind.

Well, maybe like point eight.

Huh?

Not quite a whole.

Huh?

I don't know. Probably like fifty seconds more. He found his place in his pad and added another subdivision to his table. Nineteen women and four men and twenty one tickets.

Okaaaaay . . . said Kristin.

Jonathan let her leave confused. Through the kitchen door he could hear his table above the others. Explosions of hard laughter, shouted punchlines, insults sent from one end of the table to the other.

He punched the send button and whipped his pad closed and shoved it in the center apron pocket and grabbed a big tray from the stack under the stainless steel counter and walked out of the kitchen leaning forward. He straightarmed the rightside swinging door and turned the corner to the bar and slid his tray onto the barcounter. The bartender Romeo was tending to customers seated at the other side of the enclosed rectangle. Jonathan watched his ticket still emerging with ratchety scratches from the little dot matrix thermal printing machine. It was about a foot long. He realized he was bouncing his knee up and down against the bar.

He could see his table from his position. He wasn't sure if they had spotted him yet.

But then he saw the Matron holding up an empty chip basket and shaking it at him with a patient look. She used it to point at the other chip baskets on the table, one by one. He nodded with a smile and held up one finger. Her face said now. He looked back at Romeo, nephew of the owners of The Sombrero, with his thick black shoulder length hair, goatee, and vest, providing impeccable service to two college girls from San Marcos State. He realized that he was doomed. Romeo . . . he called over his shoulder, nodding at his ticket that had just finished printing. Romeo looked over, up-nodded him, and went back to talking to the girls.

Jonathan quickly grabbed new baskets and brought them to the table.

Nobody looked at him while he exchanged them, but kept talking, and then a woman yelled from the other end of the table Where them dranks at? and a man close by, hunched over the table, said without looking up We tharsty, and then kept saying it, We tharsty, every few seconds like a mantra. He was statuesque and shimmered in a loose maroon shirt unbuttoned half way. His skin was of one perfect sateen bolt, and his shoulders and back seemed hugely powerful under the silk.

Alright, Jonathan said, looks like your drinks are just coming up at the bar, and I'll be right back with those . . . he saw Romeo just turning away from the girls to snap his ticket and hold it up expertly and begin pulling handled tumblers for the two dollar frozens and stemmed tureens for the large margaritas. Jonathan strode away from the table and tossed the used baskets in the pile and ignored the fading chorus of We tharsty behind him and went up to the bar. He waited until eight drinks were ready and then limed them and put straws in them and loaded them up symmetrically on the tray, lifting it and testing it for its center of gravity. He turned back to the table with it raised high over his shoulder.

And just then he saw, walking behind his big top and led in procession to his one remaining booth by the hostess, a middle aged man and woman and behind them a young couple. And he saw that the young woman was Jane, from the office of Buck & Liddell.

Oh shit. Just as she looked in his direction he looked down at his big top and started placing drinks. Luckily We Tharsty's purple margarita was on the tray, and when Jonathan put it down in front of him still balancing the tray on his right palm the man shoved a one dollar bill into Jonathan's apron, and said like an axiom of the cosmos You take care a me, I take care a you, and began sucking down the drink.

Thank you sir, said Jonathan.

The man said again without looking up, You take care a me, I take care a you. Jonathan moved on before it became a new mantra.

He put down the last of the eight drinks still with his back to the newly sat booth and headed to the bar for the next round. He clattered his tray onto the counter and then stuck his head into the kitchen and said, Rach! Hey, Rach. Is there any possible way you can take that four top booth I just got sat? It'll be easy and a good table. I'm in the weeds with my big top . . .

The plastic iphone gramophone was blasting tinnily into the wrecked kitchen: I tell the hoes all the time: Bitch, get in my car. Bitch, get in my car. Carl was bobbing his spikes and dropping plates onto his tray and mouthing along to it. Ooooooh . . .. old school classic baby, he said.

Sorry sexy, said Rachel. I'm runnin right now. Can Maria or Carl do it?

Oh . . . no worries, said Jonathan in growing despair.

He grabbed a chip basket and salsas and went to the bar and circled the remaining drinks onto the tray and turned to walk to the booth. He set his jaw and said to himself *Best fucking waiter in this place*, and then he reached the booth and smiled and set the chips and salsas gracefully down while keeping the laden tray aloft and perfectly still. And how are y'all? he said calmly without the slightest hurry.

We're good, thanks, said the woman. How are you? The older man just smiled.

Jonathan said, Great thanks. Oh, hi, he said to Jane, who was looking down at her menu but then looked up and he could tell she had already recognized him.

Oh, hi, she said.

Good to see you again, he said offhandedly.

You too, she said. He saw for the first time in the incandescence of the hanging lamp that they were a perfect green gray, starred and swirling like a hidden tidepool sheltered by brown rocks.

Mom, Dad, Nate. This is Jonathan. He applied for that derrick opening last month, she said.

Hi Jonathan, said the man. Tom Liddell. Nice to meet you. He nodded with a smile.

The woman just smiled.

Nice to meet you, too, Mister Liddell. Ma'am. He nodded in place of a handshake since he held the tray still.

Nate was still looking down, reading his menu carefully.

Well, I'm going to run and drop these real quick, but what can I get you started with to drink?

I'll have a small frozen margarita, said the woman with a mischevious smile that creased her face in a hundred beautiful ways.

Jane's father ordered whisky and a longneck back and then Nate looked up and said, Oh, sorry. Um, sweet tea, please.

Just water, Jane said.

Get whatever you want, said her father. It's on me, he laughed.

Well. Okay. A merlot or something.

Okay. Um, sorry, Jonathan said, but can I take a look at your ID?

What? the same perplexed look he had seen in the trailer office.

I'm her dad, laughed Tom Liddell.

And then Jonathan remembered that Texas law allowed for minors drinking at restaurants with parents.

Oh. Right. Sorry. Yeah. I'll be back with those in a second. Actually, I'm taking care of this large party here, so I'll have my bartender bring them out to you. And then I'll be right back with you.

His right shoulder had begun aching but he hadn't shown it and he turned back to his big top and deposited the rest of the drinks. Over the continual din of the packed restaurant, and the localized conversational bazaar at his table he yelled, Alright, I'll be right back to take y'all's order . . . his voice was drowned and he let it die out and he made to leave quickly, but then he saw We Tharsty gesturing to him, low and furtive. Jonathan went over and saw the empty stem bowl in front of him.

Spahdaman, he said.

Jonathan just raised his eyebrows.

I'ma need me a spahdaman. Then the man looked up into Jonathan's eyes for the first time. He was hiding under a cloak of quiet amidst the crescendoing noise around him. Making him and Jonathan somehow brothers. His temples around his eyes drew back with an unsmiled smile. You Tobey Mac-gwar, he said. Ha. You Tobey Mac-gwar. Jonathan didn't wait for the contemplation to deepen but grabbed the empty glass and said, Sounds good, I'll be right back with that spiderman.

You Tobey Mac-gwar, ha!

Jonathan went to the bar and said, Romeo. Romeo! The bartender turned around from where he had resumed his conversation with the San Marcos girls. Jonathan motioned him over intensely. He came over. Look, Jonathan said, I'm about to put three drinks in. But I've got to get that big top's food order. Can you just run these drinks when they come up?

What? I've gotta cover the bar . . .

Look, it's just that booth over there. Just one little tray. Seriously, it's important. Can you do it?

Fine. Yeah. Whatever. That booth?

Yeah.

She's hot.

That's her boyfriend.

So? She doesn't care. What is she, like Mexican? Indian?

How would I know. I gotta get this food order. Thanks.

Okay, okay. I'll do it. I'm gonna talk to her though, he added.

Whatever. Thanks.

Jonathan leaped into the kitchen and wildly tapped in the four drinks then rushed out to begin taking the long order from the big top.

Finally Donald just sat down crosslegged by the corpse and released the magazine from the 1911 and removed the round from the chamber and pressed it back on top of the stack and left the gun racked open and placed both of them side by side on the ground next to him where he sat in his baggy pinstriped grocery overalls. He waited.

He had planned to run down the hill to his volkswagen through the sideyards in the dusk and drive away. But now it did not matter much. Now that the momentum of his revenge had taken him out over the edge of the cliff and he saw that below him it fell away to nothing. He had not felt the revenge pleasure that was his due. Not for one moment had he felt it. In a horrifying instant he saw that the fat bullets winging into the neck and face of a man had taken his son from him when he did it. For he sensed that his boy could not follow him in this and he felt utterly alone, and in his aloneness, then, it seemed that the dying and kicking Michael was as near kin as any he had and Donald felt that he would gladly have exchanged postures with him, and all he wanted was his boy and feeling the soft little hand in his and hearing oh God his voice still raspy and smoky with newness and all double-u's for l's and the solid little manly back of him and his tawny crown. And God oh god his tiny narrow man shoulders. And it was in panic that he thought maybe this would take even the memory piercing and joyful sad of him away, and no, that . . . no could not . . .

And so he waited by the body, for here is where it happened and he would not run. For fear of losing something there forever. And he wondered would the wife come down from the house, and if she did what could he do but sit there and look at her dumbly? And did she have any idea what it was her husband did? And had she heard, whispered perhaps in the hall with the bodyguard, what had happened to Donald's son? And her kids—oh god, fuck me, fuck me, his head moaned. He would kill himself for that daughter, and for that son whom he had glimpsed only once in the dining room. And he said even aloud quietly to himself oh yes he did love you, he did, and he was so proud of you and he was a good man underneath it all and just . . . something had gone wrong at work and someone's son was killed and then . . . that man he did this to your dad but it was not your dad's fault and don't think about how he was yelling at you at the end, he loved you he did and it wasn't your fault and everything's going to be okay and . . . willing these thoughts toward the boy he had never met, and the girl. And if he had known to pray, this is the shape his prayer would have taken.

When he was a little boy once, he had hurt a neighbor kid, and the boy had run off, and he had just stood where it had happened waiting for a parent to come and scold him and while he waited he picked up a rock on that cold winter day and was scraping his forearm with it, for when they would find him, doing penance without knowing and without instruction.

Finally he heard the distant sirens and after a while the whoosh of revving police V-8's ascending the hills through the neighborhood until they came to a stop with screeches in front of the house above him and the sirens still going. He sighed but he was glad it was all over now and he felt light in the simplicity of it. He wondered whether when he died he would see his boy, and then he thought, You just killed this man. You just killed this man.

Lights flashed from the street through the windows of the house, and he listened to the sobs and the children's repeated shrieking again and again, and he heard it as someone watching a scene. The sirens stopped but the lights continued and there were crickets on the hillside in the darkening air.

Then they came down the hill, two and two, dark forms around either side of the house and past the swimming pool phosphoring in the night under the moon. Donald just stayed there. They all had their revolvers out glinting dully and he saw one of them start when he spotted him. Donald slowly put his arms out sideways at full length, with the bare palms open and facing them.

Don't move!

Get down!

Lay down on your stomach!

Don't move!

Very slowly Donald leaned forward, and with his hands still out straight from his sides he tumbled gently onto his chest and face.

Stay right there!

His wrists were violently torqued behind him and the cuffs ratcheted on.

The hell is he wearing?

Faggoty mechanic getup.

Then suddenly, Hey, Donny! one of the cops said. Don, it's me. It's me, Robby.

Oh, hi Robby. Donald's face felt puffy and it was half buried in the manicured lawn with the other cop on his back. His eyes were scratchy and hot, and in his ears was a high pitched whine.

Hey Duncan, let him up a little bit I can talk to him, now you got him cuffed. The cop called Duncan released some pressure from Donald's neck and back.

What the hell is going on, Donny?

Well, I . . .

You kill this man?

Hang on, said the other cop. Give him his Miranda's.

Geesh. Okay. But first, look, Donny, off the record . . .

Detective!

Okay, geesh. Donny, look. You know you don't have to say nothing, right? And whatever you say someone could use in court, yada yada yada.

Now. What in the godawful hell is all this. Yeesh. You did a number on this guy. Michael's face it was true had ballooned and contorted with the massive inner contusion. The skin had stretched taut and purple now, and the gaping hole in its midst, with the flower of red flesh, was like the spread womb of death.

God, Detective, said Duncan.

Sorry. Look Donny. Talk to me.

Yes I killed that man. Donald was suddenly calm. I put the gun right there on the grass. His name was Michael.

Okay, yeah, that's what I thought. I spoke to the, uh, bereaved up at the house. Yeah. This guy is Mikey Clooney, aint he?

Is he?

That's what I'm asking you.

Well, it's his body.

Huh?

It's his body. It . . . it was him.

Funny guy.

Hey Detective, said Duncan. The DB's got a gun too. He still had his knee on Donald's back and he was pointing to the body six feet away.

Alright, gimme that here, said the detective. Okay . . . he took the small gun and flipped open the barrel and sighted the empty hole and pulled the release and the five remaining rounds fell out of the cylinder into his palm with little clickings against each another. Then he looked at the lawn and quickly found the spent casing and said, Okay, one rounds been shot outta here. Don. Look. Don. Did he shoot at you?

We shot at the same time. I came here to kill him. But then I decided not to. And then . . . Some grass was getting into the corner of Donald's mouth.

Geesh, Duncan! Let him up, wouldja?, said the detective.

Duncan got off of Joesph's back and he rolled on to his side and sputtered out the spear of grass that had stuck to his lips. I decided not to kill him. But then I turned around to shoot him and he shot at me at the same time. He just missed.

You didn't miss though, said the detective. Whoo! He chuckled. Alright, well, looks like self defense to me. But we'd better bring you down to the station anyway. Write it up all air tight.

Self . . . Donald started. Robby. Look. He squirmed with his arms behind him on the ground to look more fully at the detective. I came here today to kill him. He was the one, when . . . you know.

Look Don. From me to you. I ain't doin you no favors. This guy was a mob boss. Small time compared to up in Buffalo. But still pretty much runs the business here and Binghamton. Pure liquid slime. Simple. And I was in on the case with your boy. That's as shitty as they come. He paused. Sorry. But anyway, we're just lucky Mikey pulled his gun on you. Look. You say you decided not to shoot him. Fine. Okay. Good for you. And then you turn around and shoot him the same time he squeezes one off at you. Sounds to me like your spidey sense kicked in. Sixth sense. Self defense on the basis of premonition is what it looks like to me. Plain and simple. But anyway, come up to the car. We're gonna take you in. Duncan, help him up and come with me in the car. You two. One of you wait here till the body baggers show up. The other guy go hang out with the screamers in the house and get their statements. Tell them what happened down here. Mikey pulled a gun and shot at our boy here and that's that. Help him up, Duncan. Donny, come on. Get up.

Jonathan. He heard his name called inexorably from some distance.

Jon-a-*than*.

He was hurrying around the table, filling chips, delivering extra tortillas, scoops of sour cream.

Jonathan.

He went over to the corner where the Matron and her court were huddled around a small pile of pink and red and blue shiny boxes and crumpled wrapping paper.

Jonathan. He felt his name like a handle protruding from some part of him. And then some other woman, who had just learned his name from hearing it called, said without interest: Jonathan, you *fine*.

He addressed the Matron and her corner. Hi ladies. Yes ma'am. What can I get for you.

The other woman answered, Yo ass, on a plattah! and laughed unsteadily and tried to look into his eyes.

Shut up, Jasmine. Don't mind. Don't mind, said Matron to Jonathan, shaking her head slowly with her eyes closed and her fingers on her temple. We gonna need some sopapillas. It her birthday, she said, pointing to the empty seat of a woman who had disappeared. Journey. She in the bathroom. An Jonathan, she said, leaning in close, can you do like somethin to embarrass her real good.

Like dance, said the Pouter who was now smiling at him with that same pout, but with smiling eyes.

Jasmine chimed in: Like dance, *you* know . . .

Shut up, Jasmine, said Matron. Jonathan. Can y'all come out and sang to her and stuff?

Yes ma'am. Absolutely. Totally. I'll try to get a bunch of the other servers out and everything.

Yeah, yeah. A'ight. And can you do, like, a candle . . .

Yeah, we do one on like a little cake.

Yeah, okay, she said.

Okay. Yeah, Jonathan said. I'll get that out in a few minutes when she comes back.

As he walked away from the table, he scanned it quickly, and however improbably, he saw that it was caught up. Just then his booth's food was coming up in the window so he refilled a sweet tea and brought the food out. He served Jane's mother and then Jane and then the men, from the left, properly, and with unhurried smoothness, taking pride in details no one would notice at a place like this. Last he put Nate's refill in front of him and took the glass.

Oh . . . thanks, said Nate.

Pleasure. Alright, enjoy everyone, said Jonathan with the slightest nod. And turning to walk away, he caught just the edge of Jane's eyes. Like passing gravitational fields, no thread stretching between them but mutual imprint on some unseen plane. No less palpable for that.

He was printed, and processed, and he sat in the green holding cell of the Vestal jail for two hours. His belt and gun and the pinstriped oversuit and his watch were locked away somewhere. Donald had tried to make very clear that he had planned everything. That he had intended to kill Michael. That he had gone to the gun range. Practiced. That he had watched Michael's house.

It was very late now and he fell asleep on the concrete bench.

He woke to Robby the detective tapping on the barred door. Donald was cold and sick.

C'mon. You're outta here.

Donald sat up and rubbed his eyes. He had slept very deeply but he had not forgotten anything.

Look, Robby...

Donny. I'm not gonna tell you again.

Donald stopped.

I'm not chargin you with a crime, said Robby. I know you never woulda hurt a fly. I know you never will again. Mikey shot at you. He's a dirty mob boss. Probably half a dozen homicides we know he did. Or had people do. You got mixed up in it. And it was his goon . . . he paused, and looking at Donald, chose not to bring it up again. Anyway. Donny, this stuff's over. That's it.

Donald sighed. How is this . . . how is this . . . He meant to say how is this possible, how is this going to work? He finally said, I just want to say, just because we played ball in highschool, Robby . . . Look, I am not afraid of the consequences of what I did.

Donny. Shut up. What you did was defend yourself against a mob guy that had your kid killed and shot at you. You wanna confess, St Marys is thattaway a few blocks. He gestured easterly in the windowless room. Though I gotta hope father ain't awake at four in the mornin. Ha ha.

He unlocked the door and walked Donald to a desk and gave him a plastic bag with his belt and watch and gun. Here's all your stuff except your getup. The overalls was stolen, obviously, but since they ain't worth anything, I'm just gonna drop them off at Weisz next time I'm there, said Robby laughing.

Donald almost vomited when he saw the gun.

Yeah. Might wanna get rid of that.

At the front door Robby said, You wanna wait an hour I can give you a lift home.

Thanks. I need to walk.

Robby thumped him on the back and walked him outside.

Donald took a few timid steps into the night.

Six servers stood with Jonathan and he was the seventh. Happy happy birthday, we wish from us to you, from all your big Sombrero fam, we hope you're happy too! Olé!

They clapped rhythmically. Jonathan announced to everyone in earshot that it was Journey's birthday, and would everyone join in wishing her happy birthday. Afterwards the other servers all rushed back to their sections. Rachel stood next to Jonathan and brushed his arm when she clapped. The Liddells looked on bemusedly. Nate was still eating. Jane tilted her head slightly and crinkled about the eyes.

Jonathan placed the dulce de leche cake slice down in front of Journey and she blew out the candle and the Matron smiled and mouthed Jonathan a serious Thank You. Jonathan smiled and nodded back to her. He pulled from his apron pocket the twenty one tickets he had printed and methodically and swiftly placed them with a little crease in front of each person without error. Then he took Jane and her family's plates and the empty beer in front of Tom Liddell. He slipped the ticket in front of Tom and carried the plates away.

When Jonathan came back out he saw Jane and her family walking away from their table. He sensed somehow that Jane knew he had returned, but she didn't look over and she put her arm around Nate and leaned her head on him and laughed at something he said. Well fuck you too, thought Jonathan. But Mr Liddell glanced over and gave Jonathan a brief nod and a wave. Jonathan nodded back. At the table he saw a hundred dollar bill under a glass. He paused and calculated and looked up to see the front door swing closed.

Donald stumbled out of the Vestal police department and walked around for an hour in the cold night.

It was spring but the nights still cut you with chill, and he was shivering and spent. He didn't know the neighborhood down by the Susquehanna in the old part of town, but when it was near dawn he turned a corner and there was the church.

He didn't know if he had ever been in a church. Two weddings maybe. But on movies people went into churches and . . . they went in there and just . . .

The dark hills rising above the patchy spring mist of the river were outlined against the sky just graying over the cross. The sign said Our Lady of Sorrows. Our Lady of Sorrows. He stumbled and jogged toward it and pulled open the big door and went halfway down the center aisle and fell down and he lay there and it was warm, and he fell asleep on the floor of the church dark and soothing like his mother rubbing his back when he was young and afraid and daddy was gone and he would sleep all alone in his tiny attic room and daddy was gone and she turned on the nightlight and he heard her singing.

That night Jonathan made over two hundred dollars in tips. After Jane and her family had left, the Matron had stood up and said A'ight y'all. Na I want y'all to all git in yo pockets and pull out yo dollar bills an yo qwahtahs. Don't be a bunch of niggas. Missa Jonathan hyuh taken real good care of us. An we gonna take good care of him.

We Tharsty, looking down at the table with a smile, resumed his You take care a me, I take care a you verse with gusto. He rose, up nodded Jonathan, and gestured him over. Then he palmed him a twenty and gave him a half embrace with his left arm and said, A'ight. A'ight.

When they finally left, less steadily than they had come but not less regally, he found in the middle of the table a crumpled pile of ones and a few fives and stacks of coins that added up to seventy three dollars.

The servers were astounded, and Carl said That's the first and last time that's ever going to happen.

After closing, Ben the manager went around to the rockstar servers who had been there all night and said Hey y'all, Romeo is making drinks, whatever y'all want on the house, and they all sat around The Sombrero's little bar after they had cleaned up their sections and most of the lights were out in the restaurant and they laughed at their customers and told horror stories and then walked out into the warm night. Some of them were going to get late night wings, but Jonathan said Have fun and that he was going to head home.

That night Rachel had come to his motel door and knocked softly and Jonathan had let her in without saying a word and without turning on the light.

Donald sat in the midst of the concrete universe of Attica, in the half darkness on the bench against the wall. The cinderblock at his back was cold with the winter. It was silent in the room but the dim white fluorescent light buzzed on the ceiling. He touched the pack of Marlboros through the outside of the pocket of his red sweatshirt. He didn't smoke and he didn't know if these would be the right ones.

Minutes later he heard the boots of the supervisor coming back down the long corridor, echoing and multiplying.

Welp. I guess youre gettin whatcha asked for. Come on.

He snagged the manila folder off his desk and put it under his left armpit and hitched the back of his pants with his right hand and started off the way he had come. Donald walked behind him.

Now, he said, slightly out of breath, You seen the rules. No contraband, no . . .

Oh . . . I have these. Donald reached in and pulled out the unopened cigarettes. For a gift.

Hmm. Okay. Well that's fine, just you can't smoke em in the visiting area.

Okay.

He walked on. Donald couldn't tell but it seemed they were going gradually downhill. It was getting warmer. They went through two different doublelock enclosures.

Then the supervisor turned a corner, and Donald after him, and there he was.

Sitting on the other side of thick glass with a little hole. His hands manacled in front. Looking off to the side. Like a face prepared to meet the faces it knows are coming. Comely profile. Light brown hair falling mid neck. A sandy beard. From this angle, shining kind eyes and thick brows.

He turned to look at Donald, and his eyes spoke pity. Then he looked down at the counter on his side of the glass and nodded at his hands.

Well I'll just leave you two be, laughed the supervisor. Thirty minutes maximum but you just come to the gate when youre done. He chuckled as he left and his black rubber soles slapped the concrete corridor and his belt jingled, receding.

There was a metal chair on Donald's side of the glass. There were four visiting booths with windows. No one else was there. All the walls were gray. Sealed concrete gray, dull lustrous. Artificial light. Dim. There was a single tiny scrap of white paper under one of the other chairs.

Donald looked at him. He wore a forest green jumpsuit with a white V of t-shirt underneath. Clothes laundered by launderers who do only that. Clean and trim. Silence all around except sometimes echoed noises from far away. His throat was clean shaven and Donald saw the place where the beard started.

Donald looked at his eyes. Downturned lids, with long curling lashes. He was still nodding slowly and his mouth frowned with understanding.

Finally Donald swallowed and said, Look, so. He paused. Look, so . . .

He sat there and he couldn't keep up with the images and was paralyzed. Natural politeness and reticence at a time like this so crazy and insurmountable.

Then, instead, the other man spoke.

Well, I'll start. He let out a breath through his lips like this was a long time coming. When I heard you were coming down here. I mean, I hope you can appreciate, just really, the sort of—what that can mean to a guy like me, locked up in here. And just, I hope you know—I hope you know that words will never . . . from my end, I know words will never . . .

Donald glanced up, expressionless. The young man across from him met his eyes at that moment through dog eyebrows like someone who had just glanced up too. His mouth might have moved in the slightest hint of empathy. Then he looked back down at his hands and he opened and closed them.

Well, so I won't say anything. And look at me, talking. I just . . . He looked off to the side with self conscious deprecation and gave an ironic and white half smile at the wall.

Donald felt dizzy. He felt a strange aching.

The man turned his head back toward Donald. He took in a shuddering breath with his eyes closed like he might cry. Donald still couldn't move or talk.

You should know. Your son. He . . .

Like a man dreaming, with paralyzed legs and lungs and suffocated voice, Donald tried to will himself to move. His legs beat helplessly through a viscous air. But no, not this. He suddenly jerked bodily, and jumped up, clattering his chair on the floor behind him and he pounded the metal counter on his side once with both fists and said loudly NO.

The concussion drifted away down the corridor. Donald heard himself breathing.

Don't say a fucking nother word about him. Don't you ever open your fucking mouth about him . . . I am here to fucking forgive you but if you ever mention him. If you ever say one . . . I will find a way. I will find a way. I will find a way.

The face across from him lost none of its empathy, looking up through bunched brows like a loyal kicked dog, and started nodding again and looking down at his hands again.

But then he looked back up, and his face had completely changed, as if it had lost the animating, acting force, and the eyes were dead.

Okay, he said.

Then he sat there, looking down and to the side like a child.

Donald picked up his chair and gently righted it and sat back down.

They sat for a while.

Then Donald said: How old are you.
What?
How old are you.
The other man put a face on like he was thinking.
Um . . . twenty five?
You know, you're younger than me.
He didn't look up.
Do you know my name?
He nodded.
Did you know . . . his name?
He didn't move, but his face might have winced.
You know, it will never go away. What you did. My mind still . . . three years later . . . you know I can't make it stop? Like maybe I'll wake up . . . It will never go away. You're going to rot in here. Youre going to get older and older. Youre going to get ugly and old in here. If they don't kill you first.
He paused.
But it's the same for me. It's no different for me. And my memory of him is fading. Here his face spasmed but he controlled it. Every day he's still getting taken from me. You don't know what he was like. No one even remembers what he was like. His voice didn't change, but his eyes glistened. I'm the only one. There's no one I can talk to about him. Donald looked down. The man across from him still looked with dead eyes to the side.
Donald stood up, slowly this time, carefully sliding the chair back.
Then he said these things, like evenly spaced, dispassionate rifle shots: Here are some cigarettes. I don't know what you smoke. I'll be back next week. I forgive you.
Then he turned and walked echoing up the long corridor and he never looked back, and the air thinned and grew cooler and the supervisor, grinning and about to talk, stopped abruptly when he saw him and led him out, unlocking the doors as he went and didn't say a word as Donald walked out of the the guardhouse and into the soft brightness of the winter morning.
Donald walked to his car and knelt down behind it hidden from view and put his face in the snow.

Rachel left early the next morning. Jonathan received two phone calls that

Sunday. They were the first two times his motel room phone had rung. It was loud and jarring. The first phone call was from his mother, whom he normally called in the early afternoon.

Hello?

Hi Jonathan. It's me.

Oh, hi . . . uh . . . sorry I haven't called yet.

It's fine. It's just, it's already three here now, so I thought I'd call you.

Okay. How's it going?

Oh fine. Just folding laundry. Sparrow's taking a nap. Ruth is reading some dumb book or other in her room.

Okaaay.

No, seriously. Before, she *was* into this series with a girl who trains dragons. Not like any of this new stuff. I mean like it was older and the reading level is higher. And where the girl is a loner but finds her place when she meets her first dragon. I'm all for it. All for it. But that's not what I'm talking about. The last few weeks she's been racing through these books called like The Facebook Princess series or something. Or like facebook queen or whatever.

Hmm.

They're like Nancy Drew but like lots of selfies and I don't know if there's crimes. Maybe like middle school mysteries. Like who's trying to sabotage the winter dance or whatever. Actually probably not winter dance. That's too—you know, real life. Actual bodies and hormones swirling around a sweaty gym and all. Probably it's more like who's using some fake account to tweet gossip about the other girls. I don't know. She just like lays on her bed for hours reading them and unfortunately I think they're up to like twenty five of them now.

I'm sorry.

Yeah. Can't keep up with the ghostwriters.

I think she'll survive.

Yeah but I was stricter with your program.

And look at me now.

Hah! Well nobody's bragging about you, buddy boy. But I console myself that it's just a phase.

What?

Oh, stop it. You know. All this, work a real job see a real paycheck shtick. The novelty wears off, believe me.

You're a joy.

Anyway, I don't think your program hurt you all that much.

Well. Besides that, I read a lot of crap, too. When I was a kid, you know.

Well, the crap back then was honester. Campier.

Back then? You mean, like, what? Five years ago . . .

Oh, shut up. How are you.

Fine. Epic night last night.

You make any money?

Best night ever, actually. Over two hundred.

Wow. I should give up my lifelong passion for medical records and wait tables. Like Robinson Crusoe. Ishmael. It sounds so romantic.

You're too old.

I'm not aging any faster than you. And what do you have to show for it?

Hmm. Good point. How about you?

Well, I guess I always hoped my firstborn would amount to something. My redemption. But anyway let's get back to cynicism and euphemism. It's too early in the day for honesty.

Yeah. How far along are you?

Oh geesh, buddy boy. I've had a couple whites.

Are we talking glasses or bottles?

Thanks for the sharp parenting thar, feller. Let's focus on you. For all you know I'm still trying to drink off raising you. Quite a debt, there. You hooking up with any girls yet?

Hooking up?

You like any girls?

Yeah. Yeah I do. But that's not going to work out.

Okay. Sounds like a quitter to me.

She has a boyfriend. Like a . . . has dinner with her parents boyfriend.

Okay. So what's the hold up?

Mainly that, mom.

You used to be so creative.

Anyway, I'm doing fine. I'm actually saving like two thirds of my money.

Wow. How do you feed your children?

Cereal and presliced cheese. How about you? Oh wait.

Zing. Anyway. Look, you know girls like a guy who can save money and stuff, right? And you're a good looking kid. You're so friggin tall.

I'm not actually that tall, mom.

Well, from where I'm standing.

Anyway. She seems happy, so.

Oh no.

What?

That sounds like love.

Anyway. How are things.

Oh, fine. We're getting used to the different household around here. To be honest I think Ruthie misses you the most.

You need to chill out on her, mom.

God, I know. She just . . . irks me.

She's like you.

Yeah but like the annoying parts that I hate.

Mom.

I know. I know. I'm not an idiot. I get it. I'm trying. I'm getting better. But Sparrow is so easy for me! I'm trying to find some other way to . . . connect with Ruthie. Instead of just, you know, tearing my roots out in her general direction. Gosh. Soon she's going to be like thirteen . . . fourteen . . .

I'm pretty sure she's nine Mom.

But it goes so fast. Or at least that's what the old people used to always tell me. When I pushed you guys around the grocery store by myself. Enjoy it, they said. They're gonna grow up before you know it, they said. And I was all like, Bring on the speed, people!

Wow. I can't believe I don't have a more positive outlook on life.

Oh. You turned out fine.

I know.

You hear from your dad recently?

No. I don't think he knows I'm in Texas.

You didn't tell him?

Well, let me see. I'm not sure when that would have come up last Christmas.

You should see him.

Why?

I don't know.

Anyway, mom. I was up really late. I need to do some laundry before tomorrow.

Okay. Yeah. Monday morning comes quick.

Yeah.

Well. Take care of yourself, Jonathan. And I mean that. Don't let any . . . any . . .

I won't Mom.
Okay. Well, talk to you next week.
Yeah.
Okay.
I love you Mom.
I love you too.
Bye.
Okay, bye.

Jonathan cleaned up the room and made the bed and put his few clothes into the duffel to take to the coin washers at the far end of the motel and then the phone rang again. He sat on the bed for a second, looking at it. She must have forgotten something.

Hey, he answered casually.
Oh, hi. Jonathan? This is Tom.
Tom . . .
Tom Liddell. Buck and Liddell.
Oh, I'm sorry, I thought . . . I thought someone was calling. Sorry sir.
Oh, no problem. Look Jonathan?
Yes sir?
I'm looking over your application.
Okay.
Well, I guess you know you're not qualified at all to be a derrickman. But that's not what I need. I'm looking for someone to do . . . a variety of things for me. Invoicing, accounts receivable, and writing some stuff up. Some basic analysis, too. Guys up in the tower do good work, get their job done. But they're not sending any e-mails for me.
Okay.
How come you're not headed to college, son? Your school record . . . you could go just about anywhere.
Oh. Thank you sir. I'm just . . . I just wanted to make sure that's what I wanted to do. And I just wanted to . . . work.
Well. Good. So I'm offering you a job.
I appreciate that, sir.
And?
Well. The thing is, I have a job. You know, at The Sombrero.
Okay . . .
It's just, my manager hired me right when I got here.
I see.
I just . . . I owe him.

Oh, I understand. You don't have to quit there if you don't want to. I'm thinking I need you maybe twenty, thirty hours a week. You can do everything in the mornings.

Oh. Well.

I'm gonna start you at twenty seven an hour. Same I start my derrick hands at. That work for you?

Yes sir.

Okay. Can you come in tomorrow morning at eight?

Yes sir.

The office where you interviewed.

Okay.

Alright. I'll see you then.

Okay. Thank you sir.

Oh. You're welcome. See you then.

Okay.

Oh hang on.

Yes sir?

One more thing. You'll be back and forth at the towers and the office. And sometimes Austin for permit stuff. You'll need a ride.

Yes sir.

Time Past.

Okay. Now the good guys are crossing the river. Swim swim swim. The bad guys dont see them yet. Okay. Now, uh oh! The bad guys are looking over the wall. The good guys hide here . . . under the wall . . . That was close.

His face is creased in childlike concentration, head sideways to the human plane of the lego men. He slides the green and brown woodsmen close by the little table in the entryway that serves for the enemy's castle, on which are arrayed a legion of gray and black stronghold dwellers. The good in this small world having apparently nowhere to call their own.

The shadows of the lego men are long. The sun is at that angle it shines at for hours and hours in childhood. Whole afternoons. Years.

Okay. The bad guys are going back . . . They say We give up. Theres nothing there . . . And then the good guys jump up and—

Suddenly he looks up and there is something blocking the bright window on the door.

Daddy! he calls.

I get up, to show daddy the world I made. I love you daddy and daddy puts his hands on the window on the door and his face in the middle of his hands, to look in . . . why does daddy's head look like a horses head? Its not daddy that's not daddy its a horses head! and the boy screams and starts running back into the house and he hears the door break open behind him and big footsteps big big steps and he screams Daddy, Daddy, Daddy!!!

Some history.

The barroom where Jonathan and the priest sat those many nights was the oldest part of the old timber and plaster house. Over the course of a century and a half, the restaurant had sprung up around that room, which had stood since the beginning. There was a wide riverstone fireplace at one end, and tall wooden booths along one wall; while opposite, the old barcounter itself spanned half the length of the room and those seated on its stools would have their backs to the warmth of the fire when it was kindled.

The establishment had opened as a stagecoach inn just after the Texi-ans had taken the rule of the land from Santa Ana and given it to the United States of America (though not of course before galloping it around the pasture for a decade on their own). The original house was built in eighteen thirty eight by a longhorn rancher called Barnabas Mason, who had missed the alamo on account of a lost courier, to shelter his family of eleven, until his daughter Rachel, who was the youngest, took it over with her husband Jim Muldoon, who was Irish. Jim purchased the aging Masons' holdings and sold off the land and the two thousand head of andalusian cattle to German Catholics who founded several villages further west over the next fifty years. Fit cows that would calve every nine months and fifteen minutes, or so Jim had boasted to the silent German buyers. Rachel Muldoon was the prototype of that particularly Texan beauty: a drooping lily child with an extravagant mouth and a large convex forehead. An early wilting flower. Her distant granddaughters, spread across the state a hundred years hence, would someday float down the nearby river from San Marcos on monster truck innertubes or scream to the warriors of a new battle in new stadiums. Rachel it was who gave the idea of an inn to her husband Jim. After the properties in land and beef were liquidated, they built the inn to serve the trade that passed through from Bexar County and its seat at San Antonio. The mayor-aldermen of that new and booming old mexican town wrote to Jim and promised improvements to the roads and tracks that led in and out of Ventana, which at the time was a frontier junction with no name.

 The building was situated in a little dell, and behind it a short slope down to a tributary of the Blanco River. At that time it was brushwood from the house clear to the water with a little footpath cut through it for fetching. Now there were concrete bordered peastone paths winding down to the creek, by which minivan roadtrippers and their children would feed the ducks or the turtles that floated in the green water. The dusty track that had passed in front of the inn was now called Main Street, though in truth the building was on the outskirts of town just before that road lost its named prominence and went twisting up into the hills as any other farm to market road.

 In Rachel and Jim's time the upper rooms of the inn had served as guest apartments for travelers between San Antonio, Austin, and the farther reaches of the new republic to the west. The proprietor and proprietress lodged, with their two daughters, in the largest of these rooms, a hanging curtain separating the two beds. Below, in the daytime, Rachel supervised the three black cooks named Moses and Latham and Lydia who were not slaves by denomination but who nevertheless lived in common in a low outbuilding forty yards from the house behind a grove of cottonwoods closer to the creek, while in the evenings old Jim Muldoon poured drinks from kegs and bottles behind the bar, and managed the company that would gather in those days from the surrounding ranches and gins. He wore garters on his sleeves with conchos engraved of Irish pastoral scenes and it was an unlikely tradition that would be continued into the next century. From the beginning he was in the habit of inviting the town's fiddlers and singers to play for coins to the company, and by the time he died, just after emancipation, he had managed to secure an upright piano that was in those days kept in tune. It is now dusty and forgotten under a canvas tarpaulin in a maintenance closet.

 Branching off from the old main barroom were two later additions. Immediately to the right as one entered was a door leading to a larger dining room with newer tables and booths and a corrugated tin roof that faced the street. At the back of the old room, left of the fireplace, another door had been cut leading to a screened sunroom with a sloping ceiling and two levels separated by a few steps, going down almost to the creekside and with big windows facing it. On Sundays a late lunch crowd would fill the whole place, and girls in dresses and boys in khakis and seersucker (their blazers kept by mothers inside) would squeal and run up and down the little creekside boardwalk throwing stale bread saved by the kitchen for that purpose to the ducks and fish and turtles.

During prohibition, before the additions had been built, Jim and Rachel's grandson Robert Earl Muldoon had run a speakeasy on the second floor by opening up the walls of the guestrooms to make what passed for a club, the town being far enough from Austin or San Antonio that the illegal hooch lubricated for the most part only the workings of the immediate municipal social scene and engendered none of the mobster drama of eastern bootlegging. The mostly German and Irish population of the town shared little of the anglo-protestant hysteria over liquor, and thus their resistance to the federal mandate was of a quiet and invisible kind. Nevertheless, on the day that the twenty first amendment was ratified, Robert Earl drove his Model T truck forty miles northeast to Austin to stand in line on the courthouse steps to receive his liquor license. The fifth of december nineteen thirty three was warm and Robert never put up the canvas top of his truck. He arrived early and was near the front of a queue that soon reached halfway down the block. Many hispanic, Italian, and Irish Catholic storekeeps were in line, and the court clerk that distributed the licenses was a white haired baptist who examined the five dollar bills or bank cheques distrustfully. But Robert received his license and drove home in triumph. The original document was still framed above the renewed and current one.

After Robert, who was the last of the family proprietors, retired and sold the establishment in nineteen fifty four, it passed from owner to owner. Interstate thirty five when it was finished in the sixties did much to divert traffic from the town, and the inn came near to closing in the eighties before the final enterprising owner bought it. Dan Makowsky reimagined the place as a nostalgic Texas landmark, and paid for magazine ads and billboards at the two joints of the highway to the interstate, north and south. Soon he had built the first addition and expanded and refurbished the kitchen. The walls began to fill with old Texas photographs. Of the original homesteading family, of Jim Muldoon, of bootleggers, railroad men, real cowboys, pretend cowboys, a senator, a sherriff, beauty queens, comanches. A pit on the side of the building smoked barbecue, though the place was no brisket mecca. The second and final addition was built in nineteen ninety two and a few items of trinket memorabilia were sold from the hostess counter: clear plastic keychains with photos or drawings of the place, fat wooden pens burnt with the name, bumper stickers.

But the old barroom remained much as it had stood when Barnabas Mason framed it out as the center of the original farmhouse. The floor was laid with eight inch unlapped ship planking brought from New England after the War of 1812, upon which Barnabas Mason had begat nine of his eleven children, and onto which had strode in the year eighteen and seventy a black railroad hand named Ned Richard with a brace of pistols and screamed May this great democracy be fucked forever more! and had shot them both off at nothing in particular. After a pause and a silence in the smoke, the men present had then killed him with knife and ball. A second man had also died that day when a bullet from one of the men's rifled guns had passed through Ned Richard's shoulder and lodged itself in his throat. He was a bystanding itinerant presbyterian preacher on his way to see the indians holed up in Big Bend. On this floor as well had stood the boots according to popular legend of Jesse James, Sam Houston, Stephen F. Austin, and by some accounts Robert E. Lee.

And down to this very day locals still gather in the old room to eat huevos rancheros and toast in the morning with coffee or to drink down a friendly pint at quitting time. Square backs in jackets of canvas duck, tan or green lined up at the barcounter in winter. In summer and spring and autumn double yoked plaid western work shirts with sewn pen holders or salt stained denim. Mexicans and whites and some black farmers. Couples in the booths. All joined, whatever their internecine feuds, in the unspoken and congenital knowledge of the mesquite hills and the scree and the little gray pastures of the land.

Book II: *A Party*

THAT SPRING was one for work, and the work spilled into days and weeks and became the summer. All that time he saw a vision. It played again and again in front of his eyes when they were closed and even more when they were open. He was in a park as a small child and he was with his mother. His father was there too, indistinct at the far reach of his sight. Suddenly he was on the edge of the playground and he heard children's voices and he looked up and a baseball was rolling slowly toward him and it came to rest at his feet. He saw the nearest boy coming toward him. He bent down and picked up the ball and he could still remember how brown it was, and how hard the raised red seams, and how perfect an object it was to pick up from its nest in the grass and the dusty clippings, and how real it felt in his hand. And he threw it to the boy approaching him and it bounced and dribbled to his feet and he bent and picked it up and flashed a smile and thank you and ran back to join his friends.

Jonathan learned his new job quickly. Mostly Jane taught him. Sometimes Tom Liddell or Mike showed him things to do at the towers. Inventory of drill spares, estimates of scrap, taking numbers of all sorts from Ralph the engineer—a blade of a man with a sunburn that might have been hereditary. Jonathan suffered little of the normal hazing that is the lot of new roustabouts and mud hands, being placeable on no ladder and therefore on no man's bottom rung. He appeared out at the field from the office a couple times a week and asked intelligent questions when necessary to get his job done. He had realized, also, that he truly gave no fuck what anyone there thought of him, and he stayed out of their way. The foundation of respect. Everyone assumed he was older than he was and soon he would be a fixture. He continued to work at The Sombrero three nights a week and now he found, in the short lifecycle of a waiter, that he had become one of the old and experienced.

Early, early in the morning, Donald awoke in the close dark of the church. There were no candles here save the red flame at the front which shed no light to illumine anything. The stained glass by now was faint with the morning, and the wooden pew backs just glinted. The only bright places in the church were two high windows on either side of the crucifix, on the wall of the apse at the front. Between these windows hung the wooden man. Smaller than some church crucifixes, light colored and literal looking. He lay there, on the slick tile floor. The feel of morning incommensurate to his deed. He felt, lying there, a sudden kinship to the cartoon lacquered man above him. Almost apologetic in its oaken pristinity. Hiding in its retailed bosom the secret of all suffering.

    The door opened behind him making an azimuth of white that washed out the comfortable darkness. Loud unthinking footsteps stopped suddenly, and the encroaching light halted. All was still.

    What's going on here?

    An old voice, echoing weakly. Its first words spoken this morning.

    Donald rolled over and sat up shielding his eyes.

    I told you people before. This isn't a place for you to sleep. The shelter's on Pine and Fourteenth. The voice unsure of itself.

    I . . . I'm here to confess. His voice, timid, echoed loudly in the church. To . . . make a confession.

    The priest was white haired and bent. The hair combed over his large ears. He looked full at Donald on the floor.

    What?

    I need to confess.

    But . . . confession's at four, the priest said plaintively.

    Four . . . four today?

    Yes.

    Well. Can't I do it now?

    Well . . . But what if everyone did that? Why on earth are you on the floor?

    I . . . fell asleep there. Not on purpose. I came in late last night. This morning.

    Well . . . can't it wait?
    I don't know. I guess so. I . . . I guess I don't know.
    Well, you're young. You're not dying are you?
    What? Donald answered, startled.
    I said you're not dying are you?
    Dying? No, I . . . no.
    Well then it can wait. Come by at four. That's when confessions are. You can just think about it till then. Examine your conscience.
    Okay.
    Alright. Well, I'm going to get things ready for the day here. You're welcome to stay and pray if you want, but it's only . . . he looked at his watch under his black shirt cuff . . . Why it isn't even seven yet. Why don't you go on home.
    Okay. Donald got up stiffly. He put his forearms on his thighs and bent over. Okay. I'm going. He massaged his stiff lower back.
    We'll see you later today.
    Okay.
    The priest turned and ambled away.
    Uh . . . sir?
    Yes?
    I . . . really would like to . . . to confess as soon as possible.
    The old man had not really seen Donald yet. Anymore than one saw a body on a bench somewhere. An appurtenance to squalor. He sighed.
    What's on your mind, son?
    Well. I killed someone last night.
    The priest's eyes widened, and he whistled through his teeth. He paused a long time. Finally he said, Well. Let's get that taken care of then. He turned toward the sacristy. Jesus, he said, looking up with his hands outward as he walked away.
    Um . . .
    Yes?
    Where do I . . .
    Oh. Just meet me in the confessional. I don't suppose you need a screen at this point? He pointed off to the side.
    Okay.
    Donald opened the room. There was a board across half of it. A mesh window. There was a padded thing for your knees in front of the screen. In a few moments the priest entered, this time with a sober face that had

absorbed the news it had received, and with a purple stole draped over his shoulders. He motioned to a chair and he sat in another one that was behind the dividing board. Donald sat.

Well. You better not be joking. He stared at Donald, and then he knew he wasn't joking. He sighed and made the sign of the cross. Donald mirrored it clumsily in reverse.

I . . . so . . .

The priest sighed: Father, forgive me for I have sinned . . .

Okay. Father forgive me. I have sinned. I, uh . . . I killed a man last night. I . . . he had, a little less than two years ago. He had someone else . . . come to my house. And my boy. My son. They . . .

Hold on. How long has it been since your last confession?

What? I never . . . this . . . It's my first time.

Oh. Are you a Catholic?

Well. No. Not specifically.

Are you a baptized Christian?

Well, no . . . I mean, I'm not sure.

Have you been baptized?

No.

Oh. The priest tossed his stole onto the back of his chair. Well. Then we can't do this. He stood up.

What? Wait. Donald felt the dam of his confession straining. He held out his hands impotently, as if to hold the priest down in his seat.

Come with me.

The man shuffled away. Donald followed him. They came to the front door and Donald didn't know if the priest was going to throw him out, and that would be that forever. But he stopped at the little concrete sconce by the door with a glass bowl of water in it.

Kneel down.

Donald did.

Both knees. Okay. Now. You want to be baptized?

Well . . . yes.

You know it will make you belong to the Church now. To Christ?

Yes.

You know what that means?

Well . . .

That's okay. You don't have to know too much. Hold still. He held his sleeve back with one hand and cupped the other and dipped it in the little bowl. I baptize . . . oh. What's your name?

Donald.

I baptize you, Donald, in the name of the Father . . . he sloshed some water onto Donald's head . . . and of the Son . . . more water . . . and of the Holy Spirit . . . more water . . . Amen.

Blinking through his wet hair Donald said Amen as if it were the first thing he had ever said.

Okay, he said as he watched her. Faded linen long sleeve shirt too big for her like a tunic and she was thin like a deer. The sleeves rolled up loosely. He felt reverence seeing her at her work. Why a falcon, and why now a deer? Not, certainly, that he felt she was somehow parseable or limited but rather that he sensed when he leaned close to her desk as she showed him the accounting software or when she smiled with half of one eye that he was verging however improbably on a universe wholly other, infinite and yet contained in this woman's body—irrevocably separate, and yet the film between them somehow vanishingly thin, so that he felt keenly the alien strangeness of his own soul and its glory.

Okay. He said again as she finished.

He sat back down at his own little folding table desk across the trailer. An older computer with Windows and next to it a metal in and out tray. I'm going to finish these up and then go check in with Ralph for the numbers.

The numbers?

Yeah.

The numbers? Her voice and her eyes smiled at him.

Yeah. The numbers I need for the things.

Ha.

He didn't smile back.

You could . . . ya know. She wiggled an imaginary phone at her ear.

Why did her smile make him ache. Well . . . you probably think so. But there's some things I have to check out for myself, too.

Mm hmm.

You don't know what goes on out there. But trust me.

Mm hmm.

Anyway. I'll probably just take the bus home from there.

Oh. Okay. Well. Have a good night.

You too. He went back to the papers in triplicate in front of him.

Ten minutes later he got up and put a legal pad and some folders into his blue jansport and slung it over a shoulder. Okay. Well. See you in the morning.

Oh. Hey. Real quick, she said.

Yeah?

She looked down at her desk, hesitating. He wanted to say it's okay it's okay. She said, So . . . there's a thing for my church tonight.

Okay.

It's on Tuesday nights. And me and boyfriend go there. Nate. You met him at the um . . .

The Sombrero. Yeah.

Yeah. Anyway, it's tonight at seven. It's like a college age group.

Okay.

I was wondering if you'd want to go with us?

As she said it her face crumpled slightly and he saw then that it had been an effort and he wanted to take her narrow shoulders up in his arms and kiss her forehead and tell her yes anything but then he remembered me and my boyfriend go there and this is a good deed youre doing.

Hmm. Thanks. We'll see. I worked last night at the Brer and I'm pretty tired. Where is it?

It's at . . . New Life Community. If you take the forty six out of town for like five or ten minutes it's on the hill on the right. You can't miss it. It's pretty big. But no pressure either way.

Okay. Hmm. Does the bus go out there?

The airconditioning fwoomed on and clacked up to speed until it hummed.

Oh, I don't know. No, probably not. She looked truly disappointed. Oh! We can pick you up. Can we pick you up?

He imagined Nate chauffeuring him around with Jane, his girlfriend. Well. What exactly is it?

Um, it's just like for college students.

So is it like a church service?

Well, kind of I guess. I mean, it's not formal or anything. And you can just sit there. I mean, it's not like anything weird or whatever.

Are they trying to convert me?

What? No. She said it quickly.

Oh.

Well, I guess that's not true. Yeah. I suppose they . . . we do want people to meet Jesus. It's a relationship.

Okay. How do you know I haven't met him.

"The doves went in a come and-go chorus. What did who *say?*"

Oh, I don't. I'm just saying.

I'm just joking.

Well. I'm just trying to be upfront about it. Look, I'm just inviting you to this thing, okay? I go every week.

Okay.

Okay?

Yeah. But if they're not trying to convert me, I don't want to go.

If they're not?

Well, I didn't come down to Texas to fuck around. He smiled.

Okay . . .

Sorry. Anyway. Yeah. Thanks.

Okay. So where at. To pick you up.

Oh. The Sandman. He saw himself, with satisfaction, handing an envelope to the motel landlord every week. A hundred dollar bill and a ten and a five.

The Sandman?

Yeah, it's a hotel. A motel. Across from . . .

Oh, across from The Sombrero.

Yeah.

You live there?

Well, for now.

Okay. We'll get you at six forty five.

Sounds good.

He grabbed his things and started for the door of the trailer. He turned with his hand on the latch. Jane? She looked up and he knew that was the only reason he said it. But then he just said Thanks and walked out.

That night Nate said, Hi Jonathan. Jane's told me about you. Jonathan and Jane. Ha. You two should be best friends. I'm Nate. Nate Williams. He stuck out his hand from the front seat, twisting around. Nice to meet you officially.

You too.

Jonathan sat in the back of the cab of Nate's pickup on the driver side. He could see Jane's cheekbone and the architecture of her nose.

They drove out of town. It was the first time Jonathan had been out of Ventana since he stepped off the greyhound two months before. They rose amid the surrounding limestone, pink with the sunset, and drove some distance up into the hills. Then ahead in the lee of one of the highest was a large building. It was underlit by lamps hidden in the low shrubs. Like a luxurious convention center or business park. It gave him a low inanimate thrill. High on one side, seemingly carved out of the concrete in a helvetican type, were the words: **new life community**. The words, lowercase and offset on the wall, were unassumingly sophisticated. Nothing too religious could happen here.

But why then, after all, had he said yes? For how else could he try this out? Get to the root of things? He had come to Texas to get to the root of things. And if there was anything to be found, he wanted to find it. But there could be no epiphany here. No weird people, even. And becoming suddenly aware of the invisible social net into which he was walking, he felt a moment of panic, as he used to feel walking into new places with his mother and sisters in his poor clothing. But no one knew him here. And where he lived now he paid for. He belonged to himself.

Hey Nate! said one of several bearded boys, soft about their outlines, who were emerging from large black glass doors that wildly reflected the hillside and the lowering sun.

Buddy.

Whats up, mah brotha.

Dude. I need you in my life.

There were back slappings and hugs. I need you in my life was wearing long cargo shorts and sandals and he did a slow rocking hug dance with Nate.

Hey guys, this is Jonathan.

Oh, hey Jonathan. How's it going.

They all shook hands with sincere eyebrows.

Hey, glad you could make it.

He works with Jane. At her dad's company.

Hey.

Hey.

Well come on in, guys. We've got some *toight* coffee going tonight. You gotta to try this roast, y'all.

Hey. You guys sitting anywhere?

Inside was comfortably lit with wall lights. Dozens of boys and girls were milling around. Some with paper coffee cups, almost all of them thumbing their iphones. There were many sets of doors leading from the foyer into the big auditorium, all of them open. Inside were expensive upholstered folding chairs in rows. It was dark. The stage at the front was lit with many colors. A wraith in jeans and a white v-neck was bent over a pedal board tweaking something on the body of his guitar and his hair fell over his face and then he stood up and whipped it back and he seemed to look up the aisle right at Jonathan.

  Everyone began pouring into the auditorium and they found some seats near some of Nate's friends and Jonathan sat on the end of the row next to Jane. The light dimmed and a synth chord faded in and the silhouetted band walked out and began stepping on pedals. All of them looking at the floor. The main singer nodded his head back at the drummer who began a driving beat and then he turned back around with his guitar and the other musicians all started too. There was a beautiful girl with a microphone still nodding at the floor. The music swelled and then cut out completely except for the synth chord, which floated over them all as the main singer suddenly stood to his mic and began singing.

  In this place.
  In this place, God.
  In this place.
  Come into this place.
  God we need you
  Oh we feel you
  God we feel you
  In this place.

  The drums and other instruments returned right on time and Jonathan wondered if there was a metronome going in the wires that trailed from their heads to the belt packs under their shirts. The white v-neck man he had seen was the main singer. His hair fell over one half of his face. He closed his eyes at the ceiling and let his guitar hang from his neck with his arms out at half mast like he was feeling the wind on an arctic bowsprit all alone. God we invite you now. Be in this place. May your spirit reign here. As we stand here, may you empty us. May you fill us. And I invite you, he said looking out at the crowd, to enter into worship in this place. We are glad you are here. We have come to worship our great God and Savior. Amen?

  Most of the crowd had their arms loosely up toward the stage, and there were murmurs and shouts and a female throat screamed with erotic desperation and the music picked up and went into another verse.

  There was just the one song, and it coalesced into a contemplative refrain that went on for several minutes. In the quiet moment Jonathan glanced over and Nate had one fist raised fiercely to the ceiling and the other on his heart.

And then Jonathan saw Jane, who seemed small, and her palms were turned up but her arms were at her side and he saw tears on her cheeks and her eyes were closed and it was in that moment that Jonathan understood something and said silently, I will love you forever.

As the synth chord continued, Jonathan, with his eyes open, saw a blond man with a bible come on to the stage from the side behind the musicians. The man was nodding his bowed head as the song ended. The singer resolved the progression and then prayed in the same fashion he had begun and then said Amen.

Amen. Amen, the blond man said. Everyone sat down. He was young. He greeted everyone. He said how are you guys doing tonight and then repeated it with a joke like a summer camp to make them respond more loudly. He moved his hands and smiled.

Then he was telling a story like a spell about a man who had a skin disease. He had gone to a prophet. And the prophet had told him how to get better. But he had held on to his pride, and he wouldn't do it. Just a little easy thing, but he didn't have faith. It didn't matter that it was dipping seven times in the Jordan or sticking his head in a toilet (everyone laughed) the point is that he didn't believe. You know what faith is? It's knowing that the thing you're hoping for is going to happen. It's feeling sure about that. It's—here, turn with me to the book of hebrews. Hebrews eleven. This is the hall of faith people. I know all you texas boys out there are wondering will Jedwayne Percy be inducted next year (laughter) but what we all should be thinking about is how we can be in God's hall of *faith*. Everything is about faith. You know, way, way back, Luther put down his foot on this issue. Faith. Everything by faith. Let's read what it says here. Now faith is being sure we will get what we hope for. It is being sure of what we cannot see. God was pleased with the men who had faith who lived long ago. Think about that. Are you sure you will get what you hope for? Of course we have to hope for the right things. But think about it right now. What are you dreaming? He paused. What is that one thing. Picture that. Are you sure you're going to get it? In your mind, in your heart. It's really the heart, isn't it? You might not see with your mind any possible way that it can happen. But I can do all things through Christ who strengthens me. And nothing will be impossible with God. So it's not with your head, but with your heart. Do you feel like it's going to happen? Or do you doubt that it will happen?

Some of the boys and girls were taking notes. Many had their iphones out and were reading the passage online or maybe doing other things. The man up front didn't seem to mind. It fit into the atmosphere. The auditorium was dark except for the diffused colored lights dappling the man's head and body.

After a few minutes, he said, But what's this really about? He paused significantly. There was a palpable shift as people sensed the climax approaching. You know, bringing it back to the guy in the old testament. Naaman. He paused. Just a dusty old king thousands of years ago. What does he have to do with us? He has everything to do with us. Remember, it doesn't matter what the thing was that God asked him to do. The point is that he didn't believe it.

As the blond preacher began to swell the sermon to a close, Jonathan felt the words that he was saying drop away. It was as if he were conducting music or shaping a waterjug out of wet clay. He built the monument and began lifting it up. The watchers were rapt. And then he held it, invisible, aloft, as he intoned into their gaping mouths And maybe you're here, and you hear what I'm saying but you say to yourself I don't think I've ever really believed. Sure, I've gone to church—look at me now! But if you were to be really honest with yourself you'd say I've never truly given my heart to Jesus. Deep down inside. I've never let go of the things in my mind that are holding me back. What will she think. What will he think. I'll have to stop doing that. And maybe youre sensing right now that this is the time. This is the time to just let go. Stop fighting it. Do you feel that still small voice knocking at your heart? Maybe you feel a little uncomfortable right now. Thats okay. Thats the Holy Spirit, and hes knocking patiently. Youre thinking, Ill do that later. I want to have some fun first. Ill wait until Im older. Until Im married. Until I have kids. Well, it goes on to say in Hebrews: if today you hear his voice, dont harden your heart. Today is the day of salvation. Another significant pause then he said And so as I close would you pray with me? Would you all bow your heads and close your eyes, and as the band comes up, let me pray over you. And as they all bowed, Jonathan, seeing yet the sculpted thing in the hands of the preacher, sensed that he lifted it up over their lowered heads, and somewhere far away a bell chimed clearly, and the prayer that the man prayed was the pulse of that bell: Dear Lord . . . Oh, Father God. I come before you now, and I just . . . I thank you for these people. And I thank you for what you're doing here on Tuesday nights in Ventana Texas. And God I just pray that if there's anyone here who's hearing your voice . . . would you just convict them God? And would you just give them no rest until they open their heart to you. And now, with every head bowed, I'm going to pray over you, and if this is the prayer of your heart, go ahead and pray with me. In the quietness of your heart. God's not so concerned about your words but about the posture of your heart. Dear Lord. I know that I am a sinner. I am sorry for my sins, and I ask you to forgive me. Jesus, will you come into my heart and make me the kind of person you want me to be. Thank you for saving me. Amen. There was thick silence, and he waited a few moments. And if you prayed that prayer, you can know that when you die, you are going to heaven to be with the Lord forever. I would encourage you to talk to someone about the decision youve made. Maybe the person who brought you. Maybe one of the pastors or a friend. You might not feel any different now, but something has happened inside of you. Something eternal. That is what faith is. That is faith.

He put his head down and walked humbly off toward the back of the stage, turning off the belt pack of his wireless mic as he went. The band had materialized and stood holding their instruments while the celebrants in the auditorium breathed freely and many of them smiled. The tone of the room had changed. The ceremony was done, the vows said, the sacrifice made. They had ushered in the new covenant. The energy had not dissipated, but had gathered itself and become a universal hum. They were quiet, reverent, but something had been accomplished up front and they all felt it. They began to rise as the main singer stood up to his microphone.

Amen. Amen, thank you for that word, Ryan. Wow. I don't know about you guys, but that was convicting. Thank you for that. And now we're going to worship, and I would just invite you to worship however you feel led. If you want to kneel, that's fine. If you want to stand. Whatever. Sing. Whatever. There is communion available in the front and the back at the tables if you feel led to worship in that way tonight. Or if you just want to sit quietly, that's fine. However the spirit leads. And would you join me now. Let's sing this together.

> Your breath it takes me through the desert
> Without a home, in the wilderness.
> I breathe your Name and I'm undone
> I breathe your Name, and I am . . .
>
> Standing, standing. God I am standing in
> Your mercy, your mercy now, oh oh oh

Standing, standing. God I am standing
God I am standing in your grace.

Your fire it takes me through the trial
When I'm scared and all alone.
I feel your fire and I'm undone
I feel your fire, and I am . . .

As the preacher had been praying, Jonathan had seen himself with an old anchor hook in his hand and he was trying to cast it onto a whale and when the hook would land on the whale it would pass through it like smoke and the rope would still be in his hands but there would be no weight on the other end. And Jonathan prayed the prayer with the preacher, and then he repeated it twice and then suddenly he saw the baseball rolling toward him with his eyes closed and he picked it up and it was more real than whatever he had been trying to pray and he opened his eyes and kept them open.

Okay. Now bring me your cup, said the father, standing at the sink under the light with his sleeves pushed up.
    Okay.
    The boy brought his yellow plastic cup from the table.
    Okay, right there. He pointed with the wet brush at the counter next to the sink. The boy stood on his toes and lifted the cup up.
    That everything? Donald asked.
    Umm . . . he craned his neck back to the table. Yep.
    I see something else.
    Umm . . . Oh! he laughed high and clear.
    Yep. Mr Fork.
    The boy laughed again. He retrieved the fork from the table.
    Trade ya, the father said, and took the fork and held out a small damp rag.
    The boy wiped the table. Donald finished the dishes and dried them and put them away.
    How's the table coming.
    All done.
    Good enough.
    Donald turned on another light in the kitchen to sweep and the boy

left the rag on the table and disappeared into his bedroom to work on his legos. After sweeping Donald turned off the overhead light and then tugged a small curtain to cover the window in the kitchen. Then he opened the freezer door and took out an empty pizza box and pulled out a wad of cash from his front pants pocket and stuffed it into the box with the other bills and some receipts. He felt for the thousandth time that he should count the money. Manage things better.

When he turned around he saw the boy's head around the hall doorway. He was hanging sideways from the doorframe with a smile.

Hey buddy. What's up. He tried not to sound annoyed.

The boy was swinging side to side and said something quietly with a smile at the floor.

What?

Can we have a dance party.

Hmm. Donald looked at his watch. He sighed. He looked back at his son. First put on your pjs and brush your teeth and remember to go potty . . .

Before he was done saying it the boy was running back to his bedroom. Donald turned back and saw his own reflection dimly in the dark window through the thin drapes. It gave him an uneasy feeling of being a kid playing pretend adult games.

The boy came thumping back into the kitchen.

Ready! he said, shirtless and treading on the bottoms of his pajama pants.

Okay. Alrighty. Hang on there. Let me roll those up for you. Okay. There you go.

The boy skipped into the small living room. Donald followed him.

Okay. So what do we want.

The apple one!

Hmm. Some Beatles, huh?

Yeah!

Okay. Only two songs tonight.

Okay. The boy nodded in serious agreement.

What do you want first. Donald was pulling the album from a built in dark wood shelf. He pinched the edge and set the sleeve aside and held the record between his palms and slowly spun it end over end.

Ummm . . . Hey Tsood!

Okay. Okay. Classic. You know I should count that as two. Alright. Let's see here. What side is that on . . .

The inside apple!

Okay. Inside apple. Donald set it down on the Technics turntable and flipped a chrome switch on its brushed nickel face. It hissed. He lowered the clear plastic lid gently. Then it began.

They did a sort of slow scarecrow dance with stiff legs and arms out at the shoulders, laughing, facing each other. When the drums came in, the son shrieked Louder! with glee and the father obliged. The speakers were large wooden cabinets with tweed covers on either end of the low table that housed the turntable and receiver.

Now the father and son joined hands and did the scarecrow dance together, jerkily careening side to side. Then the father swept up the boy and spun him around like a ballroom dance.

And then they got to Make it better . . . better . . . better . . . better . . . BETTER BETTER *AAAAAHHHHHH* and the father took the boy's hands in his, and began to bound him up and down to the ceiling in giant half-time leaps to the na-na-na's, and the boy felt like he was leaping over the mountains of the world, and the father upheld him, and it seemed like the song would go on forever and ever, world without end. But Donald could not lose himself in it this time.

Well, so. Now. First we make the sign of the cross. Good. No, left shoulder first.

Donald and the old priest were back in the confessional, Donald's hair still dripping. Okay, good. Now you say, Father forgive me for I have sinned. And then, it has been . . . and you would say how long it has been since your last confession. This gives Father an idea of where you're coming from. So you say this is my first confession. Go on.

This is my . . .

Father forgive me . . .

Father forgive me. I have sinned. This is the . . . my first confession.

Okay. Good. Now go on.

How do I . . . should I start with the—you know, do I start most recently?

No. Start at the beginning. The old priest yawned. Donald saw his teeth were bad. Sorry. It is early even for me.

How far back.

All the way back.

So . . .

Whatever you remember. You can group sins together. I have sinned in pride often throughout my life, you could say. For example. In lust. In envy. And then any specifics that stand out to you. And approximate number of times. If applicable.

How long should it take?

As long as it takes.

The sun had set and night had leaked up from the ground to the east with stars, while westward the rim of the world glowed yet in the gaps of the toothed hills. Jonathan walked out of the building. The air outside in its evening was warm and embraced him after the chilled false air inside. The building that housed the church would be ugly on the hillside but for its linear and planar integrity: a rectangular prism, setting off with mute logical idiocy the living and riotous limestone and cactus and shrubtree and metalgrass and the small liveoaks rattling soft in the breeze that wended down the cooling hillside. Every white rock of gravel beside the sidewalk and each stalk of gray grass on the far side of the road overlooking the valley seemed to him the gift and surety of life. He ached for work. He ached for something that would make him a part somehow of that rock and that blade of gray grass. Of the hill itself and of Texas.

Nate and Jane were caught in saying goodbye to friends in the foyer. The twilight shone big amber blocks on the walls. They all hugged each other and Nate repeated the waddling slow dance of manly affection with I need you in my life. Jonathan stayed close to the doors outside, and then they came out. The hill was far from water and higher than the surrounding land so that no toads burped, but the cicadas sang softly their summer song in the rattling trees. Jane and Nate were holding hands in the afterglow. Jonathan turned sideways and started walking toward Nate's truck, after giving them a half wave. Jane looked at his eyes but he lowered them to the parking lot. They got in the truck and Jonathan clambered to the small rear seat and Jane said You should sit up front, but Jonathan said Oh, no worries, and he was already there and buckling his seatbelt. Jonathan wanted to be quiet and he stared at the glowing line of sky drawn taut behind the jagged hills and then Nate said—

So, what'd you think?

Jonathan was silent a moment. What do you mean?

I mean . . . just, what'd you think of it?
Well. What part.
I mean, just overall impression. Anything interesting to you.
Well. It's stuff about God.
Yeah . . .
So I guess it doesn't really matter what I think about it.
Okay. I just mean, what do you think . . . like for you?
I don't know. Why?
Just curious.
Okay. I don't know.
Okay.

They drove in silence. Jane glanced back and Jonathan met her eyes.

They drove on down the hill. Lights twinkled through the dark humped treetops below them. As they fell through the hillcountry the horizon was lost and it was dark. They passed oldfashioned service stations closed for the night with one white fluorescent light over their bay doors and abandoned and routed gray farmbuildings on the outskirts of town with darkness between them. Crazily looping bugs discovered like window lechers in the sudden headlights. They slowed as they came down out of the hills to the main strip. A few bars and restaurants on the one main street through downtown, vertical electric signs on the old buildings, sidewalks overhung by awnings softly lit. People were walking on both sides of the road and down the center of the road. Little clusters through the warm night air. Kids from the community college or San Marcos students, mexicans with their families groups of black women and some white middle aged hippy couples and gothy highschoolers, and the town's one visible homeless man grizzled with sunburnt forehead and amazed eyes strumming a guitar next to his dog. Jonathan saw the doors of bars stood open with wooden doorstops, and could hear music as they got closer. Thumping dance beats with blue light inside or the offkilter crash of bad live bands.

Okay, so it's off of eighth, right?

Yeah, said Jonathan. And then, as he looked at the living and the moving street and smelled the sewage and all manner of foods and the gasoline and the perfume and the bodies, while Nate tapped the steering wheel of the big pickup impatiently as he slowed for a laughing and unknowing gaggle crossing slowly in front of them, Jonathan felt suddenly that this was gloriously *it* and he said: Actually.

Yeah?

Actually would you mind just letting me off here? I'll walk the rest of

the way.
  Oh, okay.
  And thank you for bringing me.
  Oh. Yeah. Sorry if it was like weird or something . . .
  Jonathan looked at Nate in the mirror. No, no. Thank you. Really. I know it's very important to you guys. And so thanks for . . . well. Thanks.
  Oh. Any time. If you want to go next week just let us know.
  Okay.
  Right here?
  Yes. This is perfect.
  Okay. Can you make it out?
  Yes. Thanks.
  Alright. Have a good night, Nate called.
  I will. Thanks again.
  He stood on the curb and waved and Nate pulled out into the street and Jane smiled and waved back through the cab windows and then they were gone.
  Jonathan passed into the crowd.

Anger is powerful. Like a flood of water held back by a dam.
  She just . . . when she would put him in between us. It made me crazy. Like . . . I just wanted to . . .
  Did you ever hit her?
  No.
  Okay. Still it's right to confess it.
  Okay.
  Now . . . let's see, what about stealing?
  Donald paused for a long moment. I've never stolen anything in my life.
  Wait a second. The old man seemed to sit up straighter. But you said you did work for the mob around here.
  Well, I just did work for them. I wasn't a heavy or something. They were paying *me*. I wasn't taking anything from anyone.
  The priest didn't say anything.
  I just worked directly for them, continued Donald. Fixed their cars. Worked on their cars. Stuff like that. And they would tell people to bring their cars to me to my garage. But I do good work. It wasn't stealing.

You benefited from *them*.

Well.

You know half this town owes money to the mob. Maybe more.

Well, I guess people borrow it. They owe it.

Owe it? Owe it to the mob.

I mean . . .

They little white haired bent priest stiffened. Son, I've been here at this parish forty years now. When the mob comes in to a place . . . When they came in here. You think any mom and pop dry cleaner wanted to be involved with them? You think anyone is beholden to them of their own free will? They can make things so people *have* to be their slaves. That's what it is. The priest in his growing anger began to sound like his past in Brooklyn. That's what it is. You think that's anything other than enslavement? The guy with more power making things so the other guy has to owe him? Or work for him to feed his family? You think that's anything other than enslavement? Whether it's the guys in white shirts down in The City, or the small fry bozos up here. His early morning voice was raspy as he almost shouted it. Jesus. Hates. Usurers. His watery red eyes were enkindled with blue flame, and in them Donald saw dimly the memory or vision of a stone weight around his neck. And if you work with them—if you profit because of their enslavement of others—you're as guilty as they.

I . . . I'm sorry.

Confess it!

I, I . . .

You helped steal from the weak!

I confess it.

Jonathan watched the taillights go. Then he walked slowly down the street. Further up were the offices of Buck & Liddell, where he had first washed ashore in Texas, pale and untried. The street was transformed, now, with humid electric nightfulness and he felt at home in it. The warm air lifted him. He felt it around his ribs under his t-shirt and he closed his eyes. Behind the city sound and the amplified guitar echoing down the brick street and the occasional snare and exultant voices he could hear the crickets still drifting in on the breeze. He put his hands in his pockets and walked on.

Two girls were striding down the sidewalk toward him amongst the crowd, leaning on each other and laughing, their legs each of them crossing over the other with every step in their low cowboy boots and the front pockets of their jean shorts lower than the frayed hems and the white denim strings like little beaded veils on their brown thighs.

Hey. *Hey*! they said.

He stopped.

You remember us?

Uh . . .

The Som*brer*o, duh. They laughed and leaned on each other. He tried to peer through all their makeup. His soul keen for any shred of life.

You're new here.

In Ventana?

They nodded.

How do you know.

Oh, *we'd* remember, they said, looking at each other. In this small ass town. They laughed. We're back for the summer. They were wearing big San Marcos t-shirts cut into short loose tanks. Swimming bras peeked around the edges of their shirts, and from their navels hung tiny bejewelled chainlets. We are fucking *booooored*. You wanna hang out with us?

Oh, okay. Sure. But he felt even as he said it the quiet and sympathetic night loose her hand from his and retire to her inscrutable place amongst the more distant stars.

The girls came around him and put their arms through his elbows and suddenly he was walking with them. Do *not* tell us your name, they said. Don't fucking tell us even if we fucking ask you! they laughed. They passed doors on the sidewalk and he felt his credit with passerby rise and the three of them looked into the blue lit club and the girls said Eww and they walked on until they came to a country bar with rockin country music coming out, and the stomp and hoots of line dancing, and they said Come on! and pulled him in. A man in black with a black vest brought them light beers and he only asked for Jonathan's ID which luckily he still had—bought for seventy bucks from a guy in highschool, a million years ago in Oregon, and never used until now. Seventeen going on twenty two. Jonathan paid for the beers with cash from The Sombrero and as a server he knew how to tip and how to do it well and he took pride in that. Then the girls said Let's dance! and Jonathan said, Uhh . . . you guys go ahead. Are you fucking *ser*ious? they said and rolled their eyes at him but with smirks and then they went out and danced together looking at Jonathan and sometimes at other guys in the place. There were real cowboys there, too, and they danced with intensity in their ballooning cowboy cut jeans, staring down their dates with hard-earned lust. The two girls came back flushed and tilted their longnecks to the ceiling and drank off most of them and then said Let's get the hell out of here. This is fucking stupid. All these country guys in here. *God*. They walked out and resumed their places in his arms, and now that it was the second time they were familiar and they leaned their heads on his shoulders. One had brown and one had light hair. They started guessing his name—Jack, Billy, Mark, Matt, and then Bruce (*Bruce! Ha ha*), Richard, Dick, is your name Dick?, Phil . . . Don't fucking tell us! they said. They walked up the street but there wasn't much more to the town. Up ahead, well past the lights and alone under the waning moon which had risen and hung silently over everything was a building sheltered under the black hills outlined with stars. Between it and them was a dark church with a steeple. What's that place? Jonathan said, pointing to the building beyond the church. That? Some old ass bar. Just like . . . random people go there. Like old people and mexicans and the priest from that church and stuff. To Jonathan it shone under the dome of the sky and he knew where the night had gone. I . . . think I'm going to go check out that place. What? they shrieked. Are you fucking kidding me? But they were laughing at him. Okay. Whatever Tommy. Ha ha! They each hugged him for a long time. Hang out with us again! Yes! Oh my god, the other one said, and she had taken his palm and was writing on it. Call us or text us or facebook us, okay? Facebook us, okay? Oh . . . sure, he said. Actually, I don't have a facebook. What the fuck? they said. Ha ha. You *are* like an old man! Ha. You'll fucking love that place then, the other one said. Jonathan said: ha, maybe I will. Don't forget us! they said. Okay. I won't. Bye! they said. We love you! Yeah, we love you . . . Ryan! It's Ryan, isn't it! Don't fucking tell us . . .

They walked off arm in arm, their other hands up, wrist-waving in salutation, and their hips swaying in time. Brad! Jake! Ha ha.

Bye, he said quietly, and then turned and walked into the dark towards the mysterious, unsigned building at the end of the street. He passed the church on the other side of the road and he looked at the steeple pallid in the summer moonlight and walked another couple blocks to the lighted tavern and there was a wooden wheelchair ramp to its door and on the landing were two men in shorts and rafting sandals.

Well if Perry has his way we won't *pay* anything, sure, but we won't *get* anything either. You can say goodbye to . . . I don't know, to decent schools or whatever. I mean, that's where taxes go and . . .

Yeah but the thing is . . . hang on. The thing is if you think about it every dollar . . . hang on . . . every dollar that goes through the government. I mean, you might as well launder it. It comes out the other side, like . . . I mean, if the *businesses* got to keep that instead—how you doin?

They cordially noticed Jonathan and resumed their talking and Jonathan pulled the old doors and went in. It was dim, and noisy but not sharply. A warm cacophony flowed over him. The hostess looked up and said Just you? and he nodded, and she said You wanna sit at the bar? and he said Sure and she handed him a menu and he walked over there. The light was golden and he looked over and he saw that there was a fire burning in the hearth. Not enough to heat the room so it felt good even in summer. He found a stool at an empty place and looked at the menu selfconsciously.

What can I do for you. The barkeep was middle aged with a silver handlebar.

Well. Honestly I was just looking. I'm not sure yet. What . . . do you have any recommendations?

Well. You like whisky? His voice was very deep, like the final infrabass note of some crazy gospel quartet.

Umm . . . Jonathan hesitated and then said Sure.

Well, I've got a single malt from up in Waco. Balcones. Best stuff in the world.

Waco? Okay. Let's do that, Jonathan said. Umm . . . with coke?

The barkeep squinted. With stuff like this you should just do a little splash of water or nothing.

Oh. Sure. Yeah.

Jonathan was prepared to pull out his ID but it was never requested and the barkeep turned and found a bottle at the top of the mirrored wall and then a tumbler and he inspected it and gave it a slight polish with his towel and then expertly poured the liquor and took a shot glass and poured a small amount of filtered water after it into the tumbler. He slid a napkin into place and said: You wanna close this out or start a tab.

When he drank it he closed his eyes and after the initial lip-numbing there passed in front of him places he had never seen before. Or at least the feelings that went with those places, and time.

How is it? said the barkeep in his deep voice.

It's . . .

Exactly! Ha ha, laughed the barkeep with a low thrum. It's somethin else. Made under a bridge, up in Waco. Seventeenth and Mary Street. Nothin else there except hobos. Everything abandoned and then they set up shop in an old—oh, I think it was a machine shop. And now they're beatin the world. Beatin Scotland. You know I'm Scottish.

Oh?

My ancestors. Came over in the eighteen eighties. Clan Buchanan. He puffed out his chest for a moment in a sort of physical salute, and then deflated and went back to polishing a row of highballs. So what do you do?

Jonathan wanted to just sit there, but he contented himself with watching the company behind him in the bar mirror and submitted to conversation.

I'm with the oil rig.

Oh? Is that right.

Jonathan heard a loud and round laugh, and looked in the bar mirror and saw behind him in a wooden booth, seated across from a old man in ruined jeans, a priest. Or at least Jonathan knew he was some sort of clergy from his black pants and shirt and white collar. The priest was laughing, apparently at a story the other man had just finished. He slapped his hand on the table. Wheeeew! He said. His stein was mostly empty.

That a good gig?

Oh, it pays the bills. Jonathan didn't know why he said that.

Well you know, I'm always on the lookout for something. Jonathan didn't say anything, but the barkeep didn't need any encouragement. I went to film school for a while. My teachers said I have a really good eye for the camera. But the industry's just a bunch of old cocksuckers. Old boys club. Don't want any young blood. So I saw I wasn't going to break in there and I cut my losses. Then if you can believe it I went to culinary school for a while in Detroit. I've been talking to the owner here about letting me redesign the menu. Put in some seasonal fare. He glanced at Jonathan to see if he knew what that was. Then I was in the army for twelve years. That was good. Regular pay and cost of living. I was over in Desert Storm you know. He looked at Jonathan. But I guess you're too young to remember that. Best days of my life, I'll tell you that. Best days of my life. Had to strap myself back into civilian life, though, and that was a bitch. A lot harder than army life, I can tell you that. Man, I wish they'd let me reenlist. He leaned on the bar now. I actually went down to an actual recruiter and tried to get back into Iraq but they said I was too old now. I don't care what this one's about. But I sure do miss driving around in a hummer. Carrying your M40. Brings out the best in you. Everything's real simple. Real simple. You ever imagine what it'd be like to be a knight? Just ride around on a horse and fight when you had to, and love the woman you loved?

Yes.

Well that's what I did. I'd do anything to go back. And I'll tell you what else. The only friendships you can ever make in this life are in the army. Guys who'll die for you—

—So sorry to interrupt, Gary. Truly I am. Hi there. The priest slid quickly onto the stool next to Jonathan and glanced briefly at him with a nod. Bucky and I are going to require a pitcher of something cold and cheap, he said, turning back to Gary the barkeep.

Oh, alright, Father. He turned around to the taps.

Gary talking your ear off? said the priest loudly enough for Gary to hear.

Aw, back off, said the barkeep in his deep voice.

Oh, we were just talking, said Jonathan.

Don't be so polite, buddy, laughed the tipsy priest. It's a pathology. Don't enable him.

You want your beer or not, Father.

What I mean is, you'll never meet a more hospitable and interesting conversationalist. And good looking. And employed.

Here you go, Father.

Well, I'll leave you two to it! The priest glanced at Jonathan and his eyes were smiling, and he walked back to his booth balancing the gently sloshing pitcher.

He's a character.

Yeah?

Don't you know Father Donald?

No. Is he some kind of minister?

Ha! Hardly, laughed the barkeep.

Oh.

I mean he's the priest at the parish, continued Gary. Right down the road from here. Holy Trinity. Comes in *here* pretty regular though. Sees folks that wouldn't step foot in that place. Kinda funny to me that a priest has to go out on the town to track down his congregation. Tells me something ain't right there. *Catholics*. Me personally I can't stand with their theology. I'm not too religious. But all this *Mary* crap and *Pope* crap and *praying to saints* crap. That ain't in the Bible. My background's Baptist, so I got my head on straight. But even there, a lot of Baptists add on stuff to the main thing. I've left a number of churches on account of them adding on stuff. He puffed up again with pride and nodded. That's what it comes down to. You've got you, and you've got your Bible. Just you and God. It's simple. It ain't about religion. You know the priest over there—sometimes he has people do their confessions there in the booth. He shook his head and wiped the counter. No sir. No sirree. Just you and God. He considered for a moment, looking off. It's like being American, he said. Then he turned back to Jonathan and said, Did you know Texas is a country?

Jonathan had been watching the priest and his companion in the mirror. They were now somber and the priest was talking to the other man slowly and intently, and the other man was hanging his head.

Wait, what? Jonathan said, and Gary went on.

Yeah, Texas is the only state that's a country. You know what that means?

Jonathan thought of several things.

It means we can secede any time we want and Obama can't do shit about it.

Oh.

Yeah. We're a republic. We could just vote and that'd be it. The Republic of Texas. Wouldn't that be the day? No more fed shoving their northern bullshit down our throats.

Oh. Like what?

Like what? Like what? Like . . . well, you seen the stuff the kids learn in school these days?

No, I guess not.

They're teachin them about *sex* in elementary school. *Sex* to elementary kids. And evolution. And *condoms*, he finished with a face twisted in the saying of it.

Oh. Yeah. But wouldn't the rest of America stop us? I mean, stop Texas?

They couldn't! Y'see, when Texas allowed ourselves to become part of the US back in the eighteen hundreds, our constitution said explicitly . . .

Gary had his elbows on the bar, and was gesturing expansively with his hands, which were large and matched his voice. He wore a white shirt rolled up past his elbows, and a brown vest, and bands on his sleeves with little engraved ovals for clasps. Jonathan drifted away, and concentrated on his whisky. Despite being a Tuesday and late in the evening the barroom was filled, and he was amazed at the panoply of human: black, white, mexican, old, quiet, loud. A spike struck evenly through the strata of the soil, with no one to say which layer was deepest.

. . . and I'll tell you what. Texas is the only state could do it, too.

Oh yeah?

Yeah. You think Cali*forn*ia could survive on its own? New *York*? Those places are worthless except that people made it expensive to live there so people want to. And they pay poor people just to be there. If you're poor in those places you just sign up and they give you food and a place to stay and you can go to the doctor anytime you want for free. More than I got! But those places would fall down in six weeks if they went out on their own. Texas, we got oil. All the oil we need. And people make their own way here. Nobody pays for you to go to the doctor. You do it yourself. And you take pride in that. But you said you're in oil. So you get it.

Yeah, I guess I do.

What you do for them over there?

Well, I do some accounts receivable, invoicing. Keeping track of some inventory. That kind of stuff. I'm actually working on some analysis right now that's going to take me a week or two more. But I think it will really—

Oh, so you're not actually on the rig.

Well, I go out there about twice a week.

But you're not actually getting your hands dirty or something.

Well, I guess I don't try to.

I'm just sayin.

What?

Oh, I'm just sayin. They're the ones doing the actual work, if you think about it.

I have.

What?

I have. Thought about it.

Oh, I'm just sayin. You make money off of them, all of you in the office. But they're doing all the work and you're making money off of them. No offense.

None taken.

I'm just sayin.

Jonathan was quiet for a second, and then sat up straighter and stretched. Say, speaking of which. Since I do actually make it out to the rig sometimes. I've been needing a car. For now I take the bus or try to catch a ride with someone. But I've saved up some cash. So how do people find a used car around here? There's nothing on craigslist.

Well, you can go into a lot. And most of them will do your financing right there.

No. I want to buy it from someone. Just directly from someone.

Well. I guess you could drive around town and look for cars with signs on them, or . . .

Alrighty, Gary. We're *quite* finished. The priest had come out of nowhere and resumed his seat next to Jonathan. Jonathan looked back at the booth and the tattered man was walking out the front door. So how'd you two make out? asked the priest. I've got the whole thing, Gary.

Gary turned to the computer to print out the ticket.

Oh, just dandy, answered Jonathan.

I've got your ride, answered the priest.

What?

I've got your vehicle.

Okay . . .

Motorcycle.

Oh, I—

Technically more than that. A game changer. A piece of history. A steal. And beautiful.

Oh, well, I . . . thanks. I mean, but I don't . . . I've never ridden a motorcycle.

Ha ha! The priest leaned back on his stool laughing, precariously. Well no one has. He looked back at Jonathan. Before their first time, I mean. Naturally. That's the way it *works*. Anyway, this is a great deal. You got seven hundred and fifty bucks?

Yeah . . .

Perfect. Meet me tomorrow morning at the rectory. Say . . . oh, eight. I'll take you out there. He's a friend, more or less. Farmer. Goes to the parish. He's got a beautiful little seventy two C B three fifty sitting out there that he just told me he's selling. Only nine thousand miles on it. Who knows when it was last kicked over. Of course, he wants two grand. But I'm gonna go out there with you and you're gonna buy it for seven fifty. Just dust it off and it's gorgeous. The carbs'll need going through and the rubber's probably got dry rot, but—

Ha. Thanks. I mean . . . hang on. Seriously, though. I have no idea how to ride a—

The priest broke in: What do you think *youtube's* for! You'll be fine. Anyway, I'll go with you. I'll bring it back to town.

Well—

The priest laughed. Okay, great. So eight? See you there. The priest counted out bills and laid them evenly on the ticket Gary had brought and then he bowed and strode out into the night.

When he was gone, Gary shook his head and said Crazy sonuvabitch.

Good thing he tips good.

Is he serious?

Gary shook his head slowly. Yeah. He sure is. You know, he used to be a mechanic or something before he was a priest. Or that's what I heard someone say once. And I seen him get cars started out in the parking lot for people. Out of thin air. Like magic. Like sorcery's more like it. Ha ha. Weird thing is he rides around on that bike of his all the time though. I mean on a *bi*cycle. That's what he goes around on. All over town. Visits people. With a basket on the front of it. Ha ha.

Hmm.

But if he says it's a good motorcycle it probably is.

Hmm. Well we'll see. I'm done here.

Alright.

Gary took his tumbler and then printed off his ticket.

Jonathan took cash out of his pocket, and when Gary came back and Jonathan was counting out money, still looking down at the counter he said, You think any of those guys knows where to dig?

Gary pursed his lips and said What? in his deep voice.

It takes the geologist, said Jonathan. He felt his voice begin to waver, talking to a man. He looked down at the money he had earned in his hands, and breathed once, and then went on. He has to learn where to drill. How long do you think that takes? I don't know how to read those instruments and figure it out. Do you? How much money do you think it costs to put the equipment at a site? I mean, is one of the guys with a shovel going to say, Okay, now I run the place. It'd be like, where to, buddy? No. And you think it's just guys out there lifting heavy shit and getting dirty? You think they know how to make it all work? How to plan ahead and keep everything going? Like what I'm working on right now. I've been looking at the waste slag that's processed through the post drill line. I've seen some numbers that have changed in the logs over the past ten years. And from that, I think I've figured out how to add in twenty percent efficiency from the front end. You know what that means? Well, it means the guys with the shovels aren't saving anyone a couple million bucks by next summer, Gary. Here you go.

He left his money with a generous tip on the counter in front of the older man and walked out of there.

The confessional was grown warm with the morning outside. Thievery and hate they had traversed. Avarice, hubris, sloth and lechery. When it came down to it, Donald said simply Last night I killed a man named Michael. Michael Clooney. A man who had two kids. I killed him because two years ago he came to my house with his guys, and they were threatening me over something I didn't do and they were using my son and they wouldn't believe me and the one . . . Donald had held his exhausted composure until now . . . and one of them . . . he did things to my son and my son died. Then he wept. And the priest was silent and then he said: God forgives you for your sins. He forgives you. The priest was silent again for a long while. Finally he said, I have nothing else to say. He raised his right hand over Donald's bowed head. God, the Father of mercies, through the death and resurrection of His Son has reconciled the world to Himself and sent the Holy Spirit among us for the forgiveness of sins. Through the ministry of the Church may God give you pardon and peace, and I absolve you from your sins in the name of the Father, and of the Son, and of the Holy Spirit. Amen.

One day, as Jonathan was packing up his blue backpack to walk home from Buck & Liddell, after Jane had already left, he had an idea and he stopped and went over to the row of tall brown filing cabinets that took up one of the end walls. He scanned them for a minute, then opened two drawers and began rifling through the folders. There were normal files, and then there were binders stuck into hanging folders. 1994 – 1998 OBM Log. Shaker Reports. He inspected some of them. He took two out and put them in his backpack and locked up the trailer and walked home. Later that night he read through them both.

Tom Liddell told his wife that he would smoke the brisket himself. Ginny had shaken her head but not resisted. And when, at four forty that morning, his phone played softly Willie Nelson and Ray Charles singing Seven Spanish Angels it was the first thing on his mind as he sat there on the edge of their bed and turned off the alarm and the day rushed slowly in on his waking memory. The brisket. Rubbed already and aged, too, having sat in his basement refrigerator for a month, until, finally, he had sprinkled the cumin and coriander, paprika and black pepper, salt, chili powder, brown sugar, garlic powder, cayenne pepper and thyme all over its oil wetted surface and patted and spread it until the meat was russet brown, evenly, from point to flat. And then came the other waking feeling that even after several weeks still felt new: a stormcloud looming behind his conscious thought, descending and resolving itself until, until . . . Dying. Dying. Pancreatic. Democratic. Automatic. He rhymed it to beat it. He calculated and remembered four months left and at the same time he thought: twelve hours makes it five in the afternoon, plus an hour to hold. Get the smoker started and go from there. One thing at a time. And without addressing the question directly in his mind he decided that for one more day he would not tell her. One more day yet within the circle of the warm and the living: the bright circle outside of which were the untrustworthy sea, black and impassive, along with those innumerable elderly, mute in their nursing homes, and the friendless or dying—pitied, loved even, in a way, but held there, politely, firmly, by the smiling uncompromising eyes of those inside the ring: pushed, even as they looked at you, out of their ruthlessly surviving minds.

His lower back where it connected to his butt hurt in the mornings and he smiled as he walked, bent, and said *That's* just age. *That's* just age. Smiling as he walked softly down the hall with its familiar hundred-year old creaks, past the bedrooms, all empty now except little Jane's. Not little, of course, but still he could hardly see her without seeing the shivering nine year old in an oversized black t-shirt with a horse's head on it and the words Reno Nevada in neon green. Shivering there, tiny on her chair, in the Methodist Children's Home office lobby while Tom and Ginny signed the final papers. Ginny had gone over to her and gently put one arm around her and the child hadn't moved or looked at her, and then Tom had taken off his blazer and draped it over her shoulders and he felt as it he were adorning a tiny granite statue, and she had turned her head ever so slightly away from him.

Down the stairs he stepped gingerly, and then walked out the back door off the kitchen into the morning air, warmer than the house even at this dark hour. He felt as though he had been saying goodbye to the old farmhouse or to certain trees as much as to his friends or family (and them only in his mind, since he had spoken not a word to anyone and had forbade Dr Haryana from doing so)—saying goodbye to that pebble exposed in the concrete there, important because he had always noticed it; to the firepit he had built in the first years they had lived there, when he was in his thirties and the older three were still young; to his favorite poplar, alone on the far edge of the rise, that would toss in golden salutation every evening but was pale and still now—in short, saying goodbye to those silent, watchful things which, now that he was leaving them, seemed as much a part of him as any living soul, and more sympathetic for their silence. He lit the smoker and piled in some mesquite chunks cut from a dead tree in a lower field. Then he went back inside and down to the basement.

There was something satisfying about the huge brisket. The heart barricade of a living steer. Big enough to feel like raw material. A hunk of meat. A construction project. Thirteen pounds, this one. Ordered from the Czech butcher two months ago, carefully chosen. It was the kind of thing you wanted to slap softly, to feel its resistance. He lifted the saran wrapped baking tray out of the old refrigerator in the basement and felt its heft. Its precariousness. Ribs he had mastered, whole turkeys for thanksgiving. But brisket remained some small token of adventure. One couldn't manhandle it. It had to be coaxed, and there was a real risk of failure.

He walked up the stairs and out again to the patio, checked the temperature on the smoker, placed the brisket on the grill, and got on about his day.

Donald took to visiting the old priest at Our Lady of Sorrows in Vestal New York every Saturday morning at the same time he was first discovered lying there on the tiles. Or at least first thing, if not so early.

The old priest was prone to a silence that resembled resentment in the morning. Donald started bringing coffee. Though he restrained himself, he couldn't help asking question after question. In Donald's enthusiasm, the old priest began to feel reflected the heat of his own young faith. After a few weeks, the old priest told him that he should attempt to make recompense to families in town that had been harmed by the mob's presence in their life. Donald considered, and then began calculating how much his house and his 1968 fastback would bring on the market, and who would need the money most. Then later on, the priest told Donald that he should visit Byron Collangelo, the murderer of his son, in the Attica prison where he was held, and forgive him. Or begin forgiving him. Donald said that he would not do that.

Jonathan walked to the rectory from the Sandman early the next morning. It was most of a mile getting there. There were some cars on the roads. He walked through the heavy, humid, dove-filled summer morning. There was a man with a large black lumpy trashbag over one shoulder, shuffling down the road like a runaway kid fifty years in the making.

At five minutes till eight he opened the screen door of the little brick house and braced it open and knocked on the door. It was dark inside, and he waited a while before knocking again. Finally he pounded one last time and then turned away slowly and walked down the steps to leave.

Hey. Over here.

Down a path on the side of the house stood the priest, with his black sleeves rolled up past his elbows and a wrench in one hand. He was standing next to a single car garage shack and was waving Jonathan over with his other hand.

The garage, set apart from the house, was small and old, indeterminately white or yellow. Behind it was a very small garden, and a wire enclosure with two black chickens who were stabbing at the ground. Jonathan went around the corner where the priest had disappeared and came to the open overhead door.

Inside was well lit, and cavernous. It seemed bigger than the building itself could have supported. From the rafters long wooden shelves were hung by perforated strap steel. On one side a narrow workbench ran the length of the structure. The walls were covered with tools and a pegboard grid of blue plastic small parts bins.

Leaning on the workbench there was an old black bicycle with a wire basket. In the basket was a red plastic gas can. In the center of the garage was an old truck that had been backed in, with its hood facing the door. Most of it was covered with a cloth tarp, but it had been thrown back as far as the cab revealing the engine bay over which the priest had resumed his position with his back to Jonathan.

What was your name again? he asked without turning around.

Jonathan.

Father Donald. Pleasure. He lifted a blackened hand and waved it over his head. Almost done here.

Jonathan walked around to the fender and waited. What are you doing?

Oh, nothing. Don't use the truck much, so I normally disconnect the battery and such. The fuel lines. So it doesn't get gummed up. When I remember! Just takes a second to hook it back up.

They were silent while the priest finished.

Okay. The priest straightened up and put the socket back in its place on the wall and dropped the ratchet into a tray on the workbench and then pumped some goop from an orange dispenser, rubbing his hands together and then wiping them with a small towel which he tossed into a five gallon bucket in the corner.

Ready? With one motion he flourished the tarp off the truck and draped it over an arm, then tossed it on the workbench in a heap. Wait out front while I pull out. There's no room over there.

The truck cranked a few seconds and then thrumbled to a steady idle. The priest leaned over and rolled down the passenger window. As he pulled out he called Grab that gas can. The birds grew louder over the new commotion in the still morning.

Jonathan grabbed the can from the bicycle basket and put it in the bed of the truck and got in the cab, closing the door with an old metallic clunk.

Alright. Here we go.

The priest pulled slowly around through the yard, between the little house and the garage on a drive worn in the grass, and bumped gently over the curb and onto the empty street.

You brought your cash?

Yep.

Okay.

They drove through the town and what little commuting traffic there was, and then took a road that headed south and skirted the small lake before turning out west.

They were quiet in the truck. It was an old truck with a blanket on the seat. An intimate metal atmosphere. Like the control room of an antique submarine.

Far out in the country they passed a blue pickup stopped in the shade with a mexican couple selling watermelons and Jonathan wondered if anyone else would pass them that day. The woman wore a flat cotton printed dress and the man wore dark bellbottoms and a paisley western shirt and a hat and cowboy boots and they waved solemnly to the priest and the priest lifted his hand over them as they passed.

They turned off the empty two lane highway and onto a white packed limestone road that went straight toward the visible edge of land and disappeared at some low dark hills. It passed between lurid green fields on either side, with trees spaced along the roadside.

When we get there, just let me talk to him. The priest had both hands on the wheel for the gravel.

Does he know we're coming?

Oh, yes. He paused. More or less.

Wait a second. He doesn't know we're coming? Did he say he would sell the bike to me?

He's a farmer. He's up. He told me he was selling the bike. I'm his priest. We have every reason to be here. And I told him I'd find someone with whom he should place the bike. I'm just saying let me talk to him first. Work things out.

They bumped along for some time raising a white cloud behind them.

These are all his fields.

It's huge.

Yes it is.

They finally reached the main buildings on a slight rise. At the back of the compound was the original old Texas farmhouse, surrounded by red oak and cottonwood. There was a galvanized windmill in the sideyard feeding a watertank. All the other buildings were newer beige industrial structures. There were three tractors parked in the open gravel lot between the buildings and the priest slowed to a stop in front of them as the dust caught the truck and washed over them.

Alright. He got out and Jonathan did too and there was a neat and serious mexican man walking toward them from one of the buildings with his jeans tucked into his boots and a green workshirt with a logo emblazoned on it tucked into his jeans.

Yes Father?

Buenos dias. Como va.

Todo esta bien.

Escucha, estamos aqui para ver a Bob si esta aqui. Esta aqui...?

Si, esta aqui, pero no estoy seguro de donde esta, padre. Que...?

Oh, el sabe que estamos llegando.

Bien. Dejame ver.

The foreman pulled a clunky radio phone from his belt which beeped to intercom and then a voice said Yeah from the other end. He had turned his back to them and they could just hear.

There is the father here to see you.

The priest?

Yes.

What's he want?

He said you expected him.

Oh. Okay.

The radio beeped again and the foreman put it back on his belt and said He will be here. Then he nodded slightly and said Father and walked briskly back toward the buildings.

Presently a short white man with white hair emerged from behind the farm house. He was convex all over and had shiny black alligator cowboy boots. His face was burnt and creased and wore an expression of continual amazement, of living always at the mercy of the weather.

Hi Bob.

Hey Father.

They shook hands.

This is Jonathan.

Hey. Bob Carswell. Pleasure to meet you.

You too.

What can I do for y'all?

We're here about that old CB.

Oh. I guess I haven't run it by the old lady yet. I'm just thinking about it.

Now, Bob, I've got a young man here who's working out at the rig who needs some transportation. Why don't we just go ahead and get this taken care of. Get it off your hands.

Well . . .

Let us at least take a look at it.

Well. Okay. You can take a look at it, I guess. But I haven't touched it in years.

They walked over to one of the near buildings. The farmer bent down and raised the overhead door with a rhythmic thack thack thack. In the rear, behind old comealongs and pull behind mowers, wooden barrels, boxes of nails and coils of fencewire, stood some handlebars and one mirror poking out from under a blanket. Bob picked his way gingerly back to it and removed the cover.

When they got it out into the light it was dusty and brown all over. To Jonathan it looked like a relic. There was a cobweb from the tank to one footpeg.

Stored dry?

Yep. I left the oil in there, though.

Jonathan, would you grab that gas from the truck?

Sure.

You gonna try to start this thing?

I guess we'll see.

No way it'll start. The old farmer pushed the skin on his forehead back with his thumb and finger. It's been twenty years since it was ridden regular. Robby was the last one to ride it before he went off to college and he graduated in ninety two.

While Jonathan was getting the gas, he looked back and the priest and the farmer were talking. The farmer leaned back and put one hand on his head. He was shaking his head.

When Jonathan returned, the farmer spoke to him.

Son, this is a classic motorbike. I get it cleaned up and runnin, I can sell it in Austin for two, maybe three grand. It's only got nine thousand mile on it. Your slick friend here says I should sell it to you for four hundred. You understand there's no way in heck I'll do that. You wanna take it as is, I'll give it to you for twelve hundred. Save me some work. But anyway, it ain't gonna run without some work. So father says if he can get it runnin in under five minutes will I sell it to you for the four hundred. And I says to him that that would be a miracle and he ain't no miracle-workin priest. He laughed at the priest. A good padre, no doubt. But not raisin-the-dead good. Ha. But anyway, it's a wager I'll take. Because it ain't gonna happen. Sorry son.

Jonathan didn't say anything.

The priest released the catch on the seat and flipped it up, and then bent down and opened a small secret looking comparrment on the side of the motorcycle and produced from it a toolkit in a rubbery envelope. He gently tugged and removed two thick wires sticking out of the sides of the engine, and then fitted a large socket over the exposed nubs and quickly took the spark plugs off. He inspected them. One of them he scraped with the flat of a screwdriver like a dentist, and then gently tapped the end of it on a rock and replaced both of them in their caverns. He left the wires off. Then he removed two metal plates on the side of the engine, and again scraped something inside gently. Then he took a wrench and put it in the exposed generator housing and very gently began turning it over counterclockwise. Just audibly there was a whoosh, fwoom, whoosh, fwoom as he went. Satisfied, the priest put the wrench aside, leaving the covers off. Then he plugged the wires back into the side of the engine.

He stood up, starkly black against the white gravel and the sun, with powdery dust on his knees from kneeling. He jiggled something and then lifted the tank entire with little black hoses dangling like goatish entrails from the train. Disemboweled thus, the motorbike to Jonathan now looked like the prehistoric skeleton of machine itself: beautiful and menacing.

Over the dark hills to the west tall violet clouds were roiling up from beyond the horizon, and a cool swift wind had begun.

The priest disconnected the little battery and then pulled out a black plastic box and laughed. Ha ha. Looks like your bike has been offering hospitality to the least of these. He tilted the black box and deposited an ancient rat and its bedding onto the gravel drive. Ivory toothpick ribs. The priest then pulled a flattened paper gas station funnel from his pants pocket, and gingerly poured thimblefuls of gasoline into the exposed carburetors. He glanced at his watch and smiled quickly at the farmer. He straddled the machine, high up in the air on the pegs. Then he caught the kickstart with his right foot and plunged it down. There was a liquid rumble of air, but nothing else. Well . . . said Bob the farmer with a grin, and then the priest kicked it again and there was a violent roar and a popping. The priest gave it a few low revs and then took off around the gravel court, standing on the pegs over the denuded motorbike, carving a fissure as he slid to turn, and then racing back straight at them, black shirt and pants flapping in the wind with the storm over his back and his white collar gleaming in the eastern sun. The engine choked and died as he reached them, and he coasted to a gentle stop.

Well then. I'll get this loaded into the truck, and I'll let you two handle the paperwork.

Tom watered the flowers in the small planter he had built twenty years before. He soaked the roots of the climbing bean hyacinth. Forty-one years. And yet all the years since then, he thought, colored with her the way a rose blush wash lies behind the opaque black Japanese brush strokes and   Are those hyacinths not draining or am I watering them too much?   English accent, saying What are you, an American? asking such a question, and with so much smile, and in such a city at such a time, how could you not fall in love with her?   Ah, need the corn yet and had Ginny said get watermelon?   how could you not   Oh Jane, he thought. Yes, it's your day. Little Jane. And he wondered to himself is that a cult she goes to? The modern building outside of town. Or just . . . overenthusiastic? And who will this Nate turn out to be?   With that low, English voice how could you not fall in love with her? I mean there's a reasonable question. How could you   Oh yeah watermelon. But also: *not* corn. Not corn this time, that's right. Let's do asparagus and then corn*bread,* we had said. Who's going to do the cornbread?   I mean, after all this time . . . going to meet her? In death. Was that true? Would they recognize each other? There's a thought to have. Sitting here watering hyacinths. Wendy. And it's okay that not given in marriage, not given . . . but any sort of memory? Funny how such ardor over time muted itself into dulled sadness layered under years and years of varicolored sediment of grief and joy.   And Ginny. They loved each other. An ornery twisted root of a thing.   How distant and how close two people could be. Take one's arm—did one consciously think, This, here, is my arm? These hairs, these folds of skin, this curved ulna poking out at the wrist. The same bones you were born with. Though not really. Every cell and molecule replaced.   What then remains? Ginny the quiet cheerleader in white and gold. He tried to picture her in high school. But all that remained were the vague feelings and images of an orange water cooler and the smell of chalked grass and the electricity of a humid Texas autumn Friday night and the angsty malaise of puberty and an uneasy feeling as if one is being shuffled courteously along down railroad tracks with a nodding herd of shaggy cow.   And now, really, we would be so old and different. Wendy and me. Not the seventies anymore. Even the clothes unrecognizable. Ha ha Oh dear God mustache and collar length hair oh . . . ha. Wondered what you'd look like as you got older. If you had lived   Often wondered That dog   Often wondered how beautiful you'd stay and in what waysFucking BombFuckingBombFuckingBomb it went in his head like a melody   Dammit Chase. You dumb old dog, I . . . Tom called out, Chase! C'mon. Chase. C'mere. Chase!

Tom wrapped the hose in big coils onto the wall loop and walked back into the garage as the morning light gleamed suddenly from between two trees and Chase sprinted after a low flying dove.

Donald sold his small house and his sixty-eight fastback and with the proceeds he went one by one to the households to whom he felt, after some consideration, he ought to attempt to make some amends. He gave each of them an envelope of two thousand three hundred dollars, which is exactly what it came to, split six ways. Four of them understood and took it without much comment but perhaps some gratitude and forgiveness in their eyes. But two refused in fear and Donald repeated that if they did not take it he would give it to catholic relief services but one still refused and the other took it but shut the door immediately in his face. How light he felt. All that remained was his bicycle. After he sold the house, he went back one last time at dusk and let himself in through the side fence and walked to the little clump of trees where they had played for hours. There, hidden in the trees, still stuck in the ground after two years, were the crossed hilts of two swords, one big and one small, made from scrapwood, plunged into the dirt one autumn as a pledge of eternal fealty. He squatted there in front of the swords and he promised he would never forget him. He promised everything.

He would sell the Volkswagen too, but for now he needed it. For after some months of meeting with the old priest, Donald had announced to him that it seemed there was nothing for him in this world but to join the older man in priesthood. They were friends enough now that the older man laughed when Donald said it, balancing the coffee that had been brought to him, as they sat in the last pew with the morning coming in through the two big windows up front. But when he saw the earnestness in Donald's face, he said softly, Well. It's not an easy life. But I think it's good. Then they talked for a while about seminary, and discerning a vocation, and the steps it would involve. But to Donald it had the calm conspiratorial feeling of something already planned and certain. Of course, said the white haired priest solemnly, there would be one condition. He straightened up in the pew. As priests we are all christs. In a small way. It will be your special penance and purgation to forgive your son's killer. And to serve him.

And so Donald would need the volkswagen for some time yet.

The storm had broken and it was raining torrents. Jonathan watched the way it made undulating sheets that had their echoing counterparts in the exploding ground. The cabin of the truck was dry and warm.

Well, that will give the bike a bit of a bath, I should think.

Will it . . . will it hurt anything?

On the bike? No. Or I should say: it won't put it in worse shape than it's already in. I know I managed to get it going—which was a bit of luck, to be honest—but it'll need new points and plugs and battery. With moisture, the points are the thing. But the very first thing you'll want to do of course is get that oil out of there and rebuild the carbs. I'll admit that I probably shouldn't have let it run as long as I did. Showing off, no doubt. But after you have the carbs off . . .

How do . . . I mean, where do you . . .

The priest looked at Jonathan briefly. The rain thundered on the metal roof.

Well. Right. One thing at a time. You'll want to find a manual. Google it. Someone will have an old one for sale.

Okay.

They unloaded the bike in front of Jonathan's door at The Sandman. They got very wet. Jonathan balanced the back of the bike as the priest carefully rolled it down the two by eight he had brought in the pickup for that purpose. The front tire slid briefly on the slick wood as they wheeled it down. Whoa. Whoa. Jonathan saw that the bike, washed in the rain, was a tawny golden color, candy flecked. Then they had it out and the priest parked it under the four foot overhang in front of Jonathan's red door.

Lucky number thirty six, eh?

Well, it's the one that was open.

Alright, well I've got Mass in twenty minutes, so I'm not going to stay. I look like a wet rat. He turned to go.

Um . . . sir? said Jonathan, and the priest stopped.

Yes?

Thank you very much.

Oh, of course.

The priest trotted splashing around to the truck's door and jumped in. When he had backed and turned, he opened his squeaking window before driving off and called out over the roar of the rain You know, of course, that I'll help you with whatever you need.

Jonathan was about to say Okay, thanks, great—or something. But as he lifted his hand his throat closed and he just waved and nodded.

Later Jonathan walked the few blocks to the Buck & Liddell office. He had toweled off his hair and wore the thin rain jacket he had brought from Oregon.

When he got there, Jane said, Where have you been?

Oh. Just taking care of some things this morning.

It's after eleven.

Okay.

Sorry. I was just wondering if everything was okay. And since you don't have a phone.

Jonathan closed the door behind him and took off his jacket and laid it on the floor near the door. The rain was a low drum on the trailer's roof.

Oh. Sorry. I was taking care of the vehicle situation.

Oh. So what'd you get?

Just . . . well, I ended up buying a motorcycle.

What?

Yeah . . . to go out to the towers. And other things.

I didn't know you even knew how to ride a motorcycle.

Oh. I guess I figured I'd learn how.

Wait . . . you bought a motorcycle and you don't even know how to ride one ?

I mean, I know how to ride a bicycle. And I know how to drive a car. So . . . ?

So I figure it's basically a combination.

Okay so I assume you're joking.

No, seriously. I mean I'll practice in a parking lot first or whatever.

Oh. Wonderful.

Ha! You're worried.

No no.

There was a boom of thunder.

Well. How's your morning alone with the invoices been?

Oh, you know. Riveting. Look, I feel like I should say goodbye to you or something.

Ha!

I mean, it's been great sharing the office suite with you and all . . . she waved one arm slowly and expansively around the trailer.

I'll be fine.

Oh, of course. I'm sure you will. Make sure you leave your blue backpack to me, and . . . well, I guess that'll be the only thing on the will.

Whoa, whoa. Listen. You're forgetting my whole wardrobe. Stored securely at the Sandman facility.

Oh, right. But I'll have to liquidate that, since I have no use for it.

Well, you could use some of the t-shirts for, like, art projects...

Oh, but you have to leave me that secret brown notebook! Since I'll be your only surviving heir it has to go to me.

No way. That gets burned.

Well, only if the lawyers get to it first. I'll chase the ambulance.

Nice. Thanks. And anyway, you're not my only surviving heir.

Oh, I see. I see how it is. Who'd you write into the will? Some secret lover in Zimbabwe?

I . . . Zimbabwe?

Well. You know . . . yes, Zimbabwe!

Well, her. Yes. But then also I should leave something for my mom and sisters.

Oh, right. Of course.

Though you're right they probably don't need the backpack, so I'll make sure that there's a line about that for you.

Well. Please get it done before you start experimenting on that thing.

Ha. Don't worry. I'm going to take thorough lessons from youtube first anyway.

You're gonna watch *videos*? No comment.

What?

Besides, you don't even have a phone or a computer. To watch them on.

I'll go somewhere . . . and print them off.

Print off the videos?

Yeah.

Okaaaay.

Actually here in the office so I don't have to pay for paper.

Well I won't report you.

Yes! You're in on it.

Well, also I'm pretty sure these computers don't actually get on the internet.

What's the internet?

Ha.

Plus, you know, you're assuming. You're assuming that a long life is my goal at this point.

Don't joke like that.

What? I'm just saying. There's a quantity quality equation I'm working with here.

Don't even say stuff like that. I had a second cousin who died on motorcycle.

Did you know him?

Her. And no. But still. And anyway, if you don't even know how to ride it, how'd you buy it? Where is it?

Just then the door opened and Rafael, the mud supervisor came in. He was wet and steaming in his boots.

Escuse me, he said to Jane.

He talked quietly in spanish to Jane and Jonathan caught a few words and then Rafael gave her a form and then walked back out into the rain. The damp of his boots and clothes left the smell of dirt and wet iron in the office. Jane was already typing quickly. Occasionally her right hand would fly over the number pad. When she was done she leaned over and put the form on one of many sorting trays.

You speak spanish?

Yeah.

Jonathan nodded. Cool.

A lot of people do in Texas.

Yeah. How did . . .

Well I'm sure you can tell I'm adopted.

Oh. Yeah. I guess I didn't . . .

Know how to ask. It's okay.

How old were you?

Like nine. She looked at her screen with apparent interest when she said it. I grew up speaking spanish and english.

Yeah.

In Nevada.

Oh, wow.

Yeah. My mom was half Shoshone. Is. Dad was Argentinian. He was a dealer at a casino.

Wow.

Anyway. There's my history.

How'd you meet Nate?

Oh. We went to school together. He graduated last year and I just finished. She looked at Jonathan. Wait, when did you... ?

Yeah. I just graduated. Kind of. I had plenty of credits before and so when I decided to go to Texas I talked to my vice principal and got my degree. I didn't walk or anything.

Sad!

Well.

I can't believe you didn't walk!

Well, I think on the day I would've I was actually working at the Sombrero. So. Win win.

No way! Did you think about it?

I don't know. No, probably not.

C'mon. That night.

Well, I don't know. I guess I thought about it a little. Like, how it was weird that everyone was graduating like they were supposed to and everything, and here I was in Texas of all places. Working at some random mexican restaurant. Like, you know, right now the valedictorian's getting up there. Right now everyone's having to sit through Mr. Beekman shaking every single person's hand . . .

That must have been so weird. Did you have a girlfriend or anything?

Ha. Not really.

Oh I see. Running from love.

No. Nope, it wasn't that.

What was it?

Running from . . . the rain. They both looked out the little window and laughed.

Also I knew Nate from church, too.

Uh huh.

And . . . by the way. Jane looked at her desk. I just wanted to say. About college group last night . . .

Seriously. No worries.

Well. I'm just saying. I'm imagining it from your perspective and everything.

Don't worry about it. Thanks for taking me.

Okay.

They worked for a while in silence. Jonathan listened to the messages on his blinking desk phone and took notes in his notebook and then called them one by one and crossed them off. Well, sure, we offer terms but there's a one and two percent if you decide to go ten thirty instead of cash. Hi Ryan. Yeah, we're gonna go ahead with that gooseneck sleeve. No, we're doing fine now. Just don't want to get in a bind. Yeah. No, just the one. Unless there's a discount. Oh. Well, if you can make it seven percent I'll take em. Okay. Great. Thanks. You too.

You sound so old on the phone.

Ha. What?

No, I mean, you know. Like a full fledged adult.

Oh. Okay. So like the rest of the time . . .

Ha ha. No, I just mean . . .

I know what you mean. You sound the same on the phone and real life.

Real life?

Or whatever.

I know. I can't ever act. Or be anything different than like, what I'm feeling . . .

I'm not acting.

Well you sound different.

Maybe I'm acting now, and that's the real me.

Ha. I don't mean acting like bad.

I know. I guess I probably sound like my dad on the phone. He used to work from home a lot. Jonathan thought for a second. You know, you have to build up an image in their mind. So they know that you're confident. A business voice.

Jane had her hand over her mouth and was nodding but her eyes were laughing and then she started laughing. A business voice?

This is an important concept.

Okay. She laughed.

They were quiet for a few moments and then she said, Okay, tell me everything about Oregon.

And they talked and talked and the rain went on.

Tom finished his morning chores. The watering of the purple bean hyacinth and all the rest of them. The little bit of weeding here and there; the cutting of a few handfuls of blackfooot and some of the lavender for mason jars on the table; feeding Chase with a metallic clatter that broke the morning stillness. He went back in and pushed the button on the coffee maker. Then he went out to the smoker and adjusted the temperature. He added some mesquite from where it was soaking in a bucket near the grill. He flipped the big brisket with two big tongs, gently, so as not to disturb the formation of the bark. He set a timer on his phone to go off every hour so he would remember to check on it. It was cooler than most August mornings, and he would almost have said to himself, aloud, that This night will be perfect. But he sensed parties of this kind, though he would not have been able to say it, could not be looked at directly, lest they vanish.

After Donald visited Byron Collangelo the first time, he went every

Saturday. Brought him Pall Mall instead of Marlboro, not because Byron smoked them but because they counted the most in trade. He brought licorice for him too because he did like that. The fat visitation supervisor came to recognize him and over time to be friendly with him. Donald never remembered saying much to him. But somehow he became his first unlikely convert. Told Donald every week that he was heading to mass the next day. Couldn't stop smiling.

Later on, during the nominal prison reforms of the early nineties, Byron, who had been in some five years and whom Donald never called Moochie, was scheduled to be moved to Texas to a medium security facility west of San Antonio. He had demonstrated exemplary behavior while at Attica, and had also been gang raped several times. It was during this season that Donald was beginning to apply to seminary and so, with the blessing of the old priest at Our Lady of Sorrows in Vestal, New York, he enrolled at St John's Catholic Seminary at the Mission Concepcion in old San Antonio.

Donald was prepared to be deeply moved when he said farewell to the priest, but the old man had lived through many partings, and treated it as a long expected thing, and could speak only of practical matters. Have you got your ticket? You're sure Sister Margaret is driving you to the station? Pointing at his suitcase: Is that all you're bringing? Do you have swim trunks? It won't be all books and prayer, you know.

But then, when Sister Margaret had showed up as promised in her antique Oldsmobile, he had grasped Donald about the shoulders at the last minute like a boxing coach and cleared his throat, sniffed severely and said, Take care, work hard. And then he had simply turned and walked slowly up the stairs into the church.

Donald and the priest wrote letters back and forth. And then during his second year at St John's the old man, content and full of years, died at last.

Later that afternoon, when the rain had stopped, Jonathan carefully wheeled the bike over to a corner of The Sandman lot, near the overflowing community trash bins, where there was a spigot on a pipe sticking out of the ground. He washed the rest of the barndust off. He couldn't help but stand and look at the machine. Then he wheeled it back to his room. On his walk home from work he had bought a tarp at the small grocery and bait store, and it was spread out on the floor in the entryway of his room. He unplugged the TV and moved it and the little armoire into a closet to make room. He went back out and looked around the empty lot and then pushed the bike over the threshold and into the room, centering it on the tarp. He strained and got it up on its center stand, and closed the door behind him.

He knew he shouldn't, but he turned the key fob hanging from the ignition. The controls were simple, though unfamiliar to him. Nothing happened with the turn of the key. He gingerly tried the foot brake before spotting the kickstart lever. He flipped it out and then stood up as he had seen the priest do. He drove his leg down and swore. The lever stopped halfway and jolted his bones. He tried it again less certainly, and it happened again. The third time he got it around, and he heard the whooshing sound he had heard when the priest had done it. He kicked it again. Nothing. He kicked and kicked. One time, there was a single loud pop. The deep sound, emanating from the bowels beneath him, hinted at a latent power and gave him a false hope, so he kicked for a while longer, until he was out of breath and sweating, and his right shin was bruised both from the kickstart lever when he slipped off it and the engine casing he continually grazed.

He sat back on his bed, looking at the bike. Fuck you, he said.

He looked at his old black digital watch. He got up and walked back to the office trailer. When he opened the door Jane was just picking up her shoulder bag.

Oh, hey! she said.

Hey. So . . . okay. He sighed. Do any of these computers actually get on the internet?

Are you serious right now?

He didn't say anything.

She laughed. I can't believe you don't have a phone. Like a real phone and not your janky hotel one.

Okay okay. Come on. I need to figure something out.

Come here. She beckoned to her chair. She pulled out the laptop that she used to e-mail sometimes. Jonathan sat on her chair. It was still warm. There was a cardigan on the back of it, because Jane would get cold in the trailer. The whole area smelled faintly of her. She leaned over the desk, wrist cocked backward as she used the mouse on the laptop. He looked at the skin of her forearm near her wrist, smooth and brown. Made of rows of cells. And he thought: what is skin? What is skin.

Okay. Get whatever you need, she said. Then she took her bag and went and dropped herself into Jonathan's chair with one leg tucked under her, and began to twist slowly side to side.

So . . . whatcha doin.

Jonathan sighed.

Mm hmm . . . ? she said.

I'm trying to figure out some stuff on the bike.

Any regrets?

No.

You could be driving around town right now. In your new car.

Hmm.

But you'll be much cooler.

Stop it.

She laughed. Okay.

Jonathan googled 1972 CB350 manual. He found something even better than he hoped. A PDF of the factory shop manual.

Okay. How do I print from here?

Go to the wifi. Make sure you have what you want pulled up, because it will switch to the printer and won't be online.

Okay.

It's almost out of paper. How much do you need.

Well . . .

What.

It looks liked a hundred and seventy nine.

She barely paused. Okay.

Okay?

She got up and put a ream in the printer.

Go for it.

Once it started she sat back down and Jonathan closed the laptop and handed it to her and she put it in her bag. They sat there while the printer whirred and spat out leaf after leaf. The clouds had broken outside and the crumbling downtown strip was steaming in the afternoon and the steam was shot through with light.

So now we're accomplices, she said.

You should get out now. Pin it all on me. I'll take it to my grave.

She smiled. They were quiet for a moment. She was looking at her knees, and she brushed them off. And yeah. You're probably curious. Yeah. It wasn't a good situation.

He was sure he knew, but he said, What?

My adoption.

Oh. Yeah.

Things weren't so swell in Nevada.

He was quiet.

She just said, So.

Yeah. He nodded at the ground. He was about to say I'm sorry but he felt his chin wrinkle and he just kept looking at the ground.

The printer stopped and Jonathan got up and grabbed the papers out. A whole manual. It seemed like a miracle to him. He turned to Jane. He took a breath. But all he could do was look in her eyes and he hoped that was enough.

See you tomorrow, she said, with her smile.

Hey Tom.

Bubba.

What do you know.

Same old same old. Hey, you got any of those candles. You know. For like . . .

Oh, like them ones with the pictures on em?

Yeah.

Yeah. Sure thing. Come back thisaway. Aisle two. By the cleanin supplies.

They walked over there.

Whats the uh . . . whats the . . .

Oh, Jane. Tonight. Celebrating her graduation. And starting off at college.

Oh really! Shoot. Didn't know she was goin off to college. Ain't she workin for you?

Yessir. Just community college, for a year at least. I think she's as scared to go as I feel.

Yep. I can imagine that. That all you need?

Yessir. Thanks Bubba.

Don't mention er. See you real soon.

Alright.

Jonathan had all the pieces neatly arranged and spread out around him.

The bigger ones on the tarp. The smaller ones were on the wooden chair that he had pulled over from the room's anachronistic writing desk. How cozy he felt, in his room, with the two lamps turned on, with the bike and the manual and the dark window enclosing it all.

He had bound the manual in a three ring binder bought at the pharmacy on his second walk home. On many of the pages were greasy fingerprints, now digitalized and immortalized. From how long ago, who knew? And was that man still alive? Was he bald now, or a grandfather? Jonathan pictured a long line of men swearing at their bikes, and then taking a swig on their budweisers, and then getting back to it.

He had changed the oil, and cleaned out the centrifugal oil cleaner, which was something. It was like building legos again. The directions felt the same, with more words but still plenty of pictures, in the black binder spread open on the bed. He was trying to set the timing and he had gone back and forth, back and forth, and couldn't seem to make it work. He had taken the right rear turn signal off to use as a test light. He looked at his watch again. Eight twenty four and he was no closer and he hadn't eaten. He sighed.

He got up and walked out and locked the door. It was still light and he walked most of a mile to the rectory. When he got there it was dusky and he could see that the windows, draped, were lit.

As he approached the front door, he heard music coming from within. Loud enough that he thought there must be a party or something going on. But there was no one around. He paused, and then went forward.

He raised his hand to knock on the door, and he saw through a curtain just askew the priest inside, alone. The priest was holding his arms out awkwardly from his sides to some imaginary void in front of him. His legs were stiff and he was dancing. The music was old rock and roll. The priest was making slow jerky circles in time to the music. Jonathan stood there, mesmerized. Then he turned around and walked back to The Sandman Motel.

It was almost a year after Donald had moved to San Antonio that Byron Collangelo's transfer was finally effected. His only known relation was a grandmother who had married a second husband late in life and retired with him to Uvalde. The husband had been a foreman in a nearby peanut drying plant forty years. The grandmother, when contacted, said yes she knew who Byron was, and so he had been shipped down by train to San Antonio and then trucked to the Dolph Briscoe Unit in Dilley, Texas. An hour's drive north of Piedras Negras, Mexico. The bus drove south through the night and just as the sun came up Byron saw a sign that read: Welcome to Dilley, Texas, "A SLICE OF THE GOOD LIFE."

After that first night, Jonathan went back regularly to the old barroom where he had met the priest. Most Tuesdays the priest was there.

    Jonathan would talk to him, when he was alone, about the particulars of his restoration. Often he would see him hearing confessions in the booth, and it seemed to Jonathan as if it might be just more mechanical work to him: the priest's hands out, gesturing quietly as if he were setting the bones of a soul. The only difference being the open handed cross he would make over them at the end. Jonathan wondered whether that wouldn't help the bike, too.

    He had ordered several parts online using Jane's laptop and her debit card and then paying her cash, since he still had no bank account. It felt intimate. He bought the other more generic parts with cash from the Pep Boys in town. His checks from Buck & Liddell he would cash every two weeks, and add to the growing collection of paper money he kept in neat stacks in one of the drawers of the writing desk. And besides, Jane was happy to do it.

    Then one night, in hot early summer after Wednesday's evening mass, the priest showed up at The Sandman. Jonathan opened the door, and there he was with a sixpack under one arm, and a bundle of tools in the other.

    Okay. So I don't know about you, but I'm sick of hearing about this thing at the bar. Just sitting here in your living room. Or your, ah, *room* room.

    Yeah.

    I want to hear it actually going.

    Yeah. No kidding I—

    —you need to be out acting foolish on this thing in the summer air.

    Hey. You're preaching to the . . . well, I don't know if you guys have choirs.

    Well. The priest considered. We don't really. At our little church at any rate. Sometimes at Christmas.

Oh.

So. Where are we?

Well . . . Jonathan looked around at the room. I got the new points in the mail today. And I picked up a new battery on the way home. And I think the carbs are good to go. I had them off and boiled them and dried them and sprayed them out and everything looks clear.

Okay. Well let's get your points on and your timing done. My recollection is that things were a bit retarded.

The priest rolled up his black sleeves.

Okay.

It means the timing was behind.

I know what it means.

Okay. I brought my light and a feeler gauge.

The priest set the sixpack down on the desk. Help yourself.

They got down to it. Amid the mutterings and hmm's they eventually started talking.

So. I've heard about your mother (he peered at a tiny screw). And Sparrow (he adjusted his reading spectacles). And . . . Ruthie, right? Where was your father in the picture? The plastic tarp crinkled as he rolled slightly, on his side by the bike.

Oh. Well. Not much in the picture, I guess. Jonathan was sitting on the edge of the bed, watching the priest at work. That's pretty much what everyone says, right? But it was weird. I mean obviously everybody gets divorced. Like almost everybody. But with other kids it was like this huge deal and then whatever. With us it was like . . . well, not like that. My dad, honestly, he just kind of faded away. Like, he traveled a lot anyway, to begin with. And it seemed like he was gone more and more. And then one time Sparrow was like When's daddy sleeping here next? and my mom was just like, Well, it appears your father will be living in Phoenix for the foreseeable future. That was exactly what she said. I remember it. And that's exactly how she announced it. God. That woman. Honestly it's the kind of thing she would do. I was going to be a freshman in one month. So at least I was changing schools and not everyone would know me already. I know some time after that they got officially divorced but I didn't know much about it. My mom would confide in me and stuff but they kept that hidden. Honestly it didn't change too much, so I didn't notice really. I don't know if I minded or not. Sometimes I think I was really angry. But you know. Sometimes it was just nice. It felt like not having any parents at all.

I see, said the priest. But he was intently eyeing the alignment of some marks near the new contact points they had installed. There! he shouted suddenly, and then: I think that's everything. I'll let you button it up. Nothing too tight on the cases, remember. They're aluminum.

Okay. Jonathan bent down to put the covers and other surface components back in place. The priest went and twisted a beer.

So. Where is he now?

What? Jonathan didn't know that he had heard anything he'd said. Oh. Well. I think he's actually in Texas. Austin last I heard.

Hmm. Not far from here.

Yeah. Jonathan was looking back at the bike now, and spinning a screwdriver. But frankly I don't really think about it, he said.

Okay. The priest was quiet and watched Jonathan work. And then the priest said, Frankly?

What?

You said that. Frankly. People don't say that. You talk like someone who's read books. But you're not in school and you work at an oil rig.

Oh. Well, not that school does anything for you. But yeah. My mom had this Program.

A program?

Yeah. The whole time we were in school. Our Program, she called it. We had a list of books. Not like YA fiction or something. Like philosophy. Russian novelists. Plato, whatever. She was kooky.

Well. There's a blessing, the priest said as he reached under the bike for a bolt end on the other side.

Ha! A blessing, said Jonathan.

Would you know, said the priest grunting as he reached under the bike lying on his side, I don't think I read a single book until I was preparing for seminary?

What?

Yes. Not one whole book. My mom didn't have time to read to me. And as you know, one can skate through school easily enough. And being too bookish certainly wasn't the thing to be at my high school. This was the late seventies. And I started working very early. Yes as a mechanic. And I guess I spent too much time dreaming about cars and women. He looked suddenly embarrassed. Well, that was before I was a priest, of course.

Jonathan smiled. And then he laughed. He realized suddenly that they were friends. Well. I'm sorry to hear that. About the books. But I guess I don't mind so awfully much about the mechanic bit, given my present circumstances.

Ha! It's not all about you, answered the priest. Anyway. I made up for lost time during my first year in seminary. In San Antonio. I was a hermit. One or two books a week, on top of what we had to do for class. He pushed himself up to sitting, and scooted away from the bike.

You know, said Jonathan. With my dad. It's like . . . I can't help it. I feel so much, like . . . I don't know. But I guess I just hope he's like the best fucking salesman in Texas.

The priest nodded. He stood up and brushed off his black pants, front and back, and set the wrench he had been using next to Jonathan's other tools. I understand. Well, for better or for worse, I think we have a runner. Let's find out, shall we?

Yeah . . . oh, I don't have any gas.

But of course! I've got some right outside in my basket. I had a feeling we'd get this going tonight . . .

They went out there and Jonathan looked over the bicycle for the first time. It was locked up to a pipe running vertically on the outside of the building. The bicycle was black with thin pinstriping on the tubes and said Raleigh, and Nottingham England in gold letters. The gas can was in the front basket, and Jonathan saw a wicker basket strapped to the rear rack with a leather belt.

You could have brought this in, you know.

Oh, I know. Force of habit. I don't usually wheel it into people's homes when I visit, you know.

What do you do when you go around? On your rounds. It's like an old doctor.

Oh, normally I'm just bringing the sacrament to homebound folks. That's what the basket's for.

Like, you bring the, the . . .

Yes. I the bread and the wine around in my little wicker basket.

Okay.

And also oil. I pray with the sick.

Well. It seems like a nice bike. Old, right?

Thanks. The priest was casual but Jonathan saw how he touched the leather seat lightly, and the top tube, and the cork grips when he said, Nineteen forty nine. Three speed. But that's all you need around here. At the time these were real workhorses. Last you a hundred years if you take care of it. He grabbed the gas can and went back into the room. Okay! he said exultantly. Let's take our lives in our hands! You want to start er up?

Well . . .

You should. You should be the one to do it!

Okay. You might have to talk me through it.

Okay. You re-connected the new battery, right?

Yep.

Okay. So hop on. Good. Okay. Now. You want your choke on. Right here. Pull it up. Good. You should only need it for twenty seconds or so. And we'll undoubtedly have to adjust the idle, et cetera, after we get it going, but that's later. Okay, now turn on the ignition. The key. Good. See your neutral light there? That's good it's working. Those go out. Okay, now check this thing over here. This is your . . . it's like a kill switch. It just cuts off power to the plugs, so. For now, just make sure it's in the middle. Okay, ready? We can test out the starter, but really you should kick it over for the first time. Okay, you know how to kick it? Okay, give it a go.

The priest smiled and did actually make a small sign of the cross over the bike, and looked up to heaven with a grin and then stepped back.

Jonathan kicked it once and it came alive. It seemed very loud in the room.

Ha! There, you see! The priest opened the door quickly. There, you see! he was yelling. Bring it outside!

Jonathan bumped it down off its centerstand and backed it out the way it had come.

Well, this is as good a time as any, said the priest over the motor note. You know the way it works? Just take it to the end of the parking lot and back.

Jonathan pointed the bike down The Sandman's strip. He had his feet planted, then he deliberately squeezed the clutch in his left hand and clicked his left foot down with a solid clunk.

Good! Now easy. Take it easy. Don't give it too much throttle. Just eeeeaase off the clutch.

And with a lurch and a jerk, Jonathan was off. Once in motion, the bike smoothed out. Jonathan looked down at the ground moving under his feet in the glow of the parking lot lights. He looked at the golden tank underneath him and the headlight like a joyous figurehead cutting the new air. He couldn't stop smiling. It was like riding a bike but it went by itself.

Yes, yes yes! he heard the priest shouting behind him.

Tom bounced gently in his truck as he flew over the packed gravel that made the final quarter mile to the towers. It makes you wonder what one life amounts to, Tom heard himself thinking. Sometimes lines like this would repeat themselves and he knew how tired was the phrasing of it but still it was the kind of thing that would play over and over. Everyone he knew getting on with their lives. Not the funeral, not the mourning, not the times (rarer with each passing week) they would speak of him, at first desperately or sadly but more and more by happenstance, when some quirk was brought to mind by chance in conversation (Remember how Tom used to—laughter), but the return to simple, normal days without him. The life that would be built without him. Nothing would stop. All would go on. It made him sad to think of himself in the third person. But then maybe he would be fixed in their memories as a relic of the good times. As his friends faced true old age, long, long after he was gone. Thinking back to old Tom, who had it lucky. Checking out at, what was it? Sixty four years old? Still a young buck. Probably still out chasing tail! Ha ha. Remember when he . . . Not Ginny, though. And that would make her more and more alone, like him in death. He ached when he imagined her undone. Completely unmanned. Never the same. Each creak of the house. The trick to get the dishwasher to stay shut. And too late in life, perhaps, to remarry. Not that he wouldn't want her to. But he knew the way of the world and who could see the jewel under the aging body? Would he, even? Perhaps some lonely widower. Ginny and he had often joked about When I'm gone. And he had said Well, it'll be time for you to cash in on your young man candy. Heck, you'll be better off with me dead than alive. Joan Baez was on his truck stereo. Music he would have been ashamed be discovered with when he used to listen to her long ago in high school, aching with first love for Ginny. You some sorta hippy? Faggy hippy. Ah, Texas. Walking ten miles at a time down empty dirt roads under thunderstorms from some imagined indifference. Not knowing, then, that they never saw you do it. Never knew the private sufferings endured for their sake. It did no good. Better to take action. Of course Ginny and he hadn't joked that way as much in recent years. They were getting old. Five year observed survival three percent. Five year observed survival three percent. It had a quick jazz rhythm to it. An underhanded syncopated brush stroke beat. For the thousandth time, he went over the accounts in his head, re-checked that the life insurance was paid up which it was. Everything in order. He thought back to the last time they had made love, before he knew, and he wondered suddenly whether there would be any more times. It's just cancer. Not catching. Ha. He would feel something squeezing him near his stomach and he would

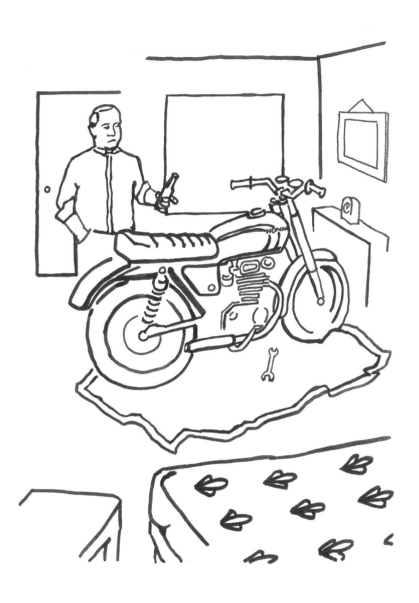

"I want to hear this thing actually going."

sit stiffly. Time squeezing him. Like the small, implacable mass in his abdomen that would grow, dumbly and blindly, like a retarded strongman, until it choked out life. He imagined a tendril creeping its way up, up, like a tapeworm from his pancreas (where exactly . . . is that?) into his throat. Felt it tickling. Down his ureter. And he knew he must accomplish it before he grew too weak. Mr Liddell, I'm very sorry to say we've found a Mass. A Mass. A Mass.

He pulled into the gravel lot. The two towers above him in the morning mist. It makes you wonder what one life amounts to. And none of them realizing the most significant fact about it all. That he was already there, paralyzed with his eyes open, watching them trundle to the end. It makes you wonder what one life amounts to.

There was one close call the first day. As he made a righthand turn onto the road out of The Sandman parking lot he tensed and gave it too much throttle, sending him on a line towards the opposite lane just as a truck was bearing down. He didn't lean enough. The truck went by just before he veered across the line. Jonathan's chest tightened. The truck horn dopplered fiercely by. And then, when he made it back into his own lane, he laughed.

He used to rip through the gears one after the other. He bought some cheap sunglasses so he didn't worry about bugs torpedoing his eyeballs. He would find roads that were straight and pointed westward or nowhere and no one on them and he would lean back with his right hand just resting on the throttle and the hot wind pushing him back, embracing him, with his eyes half closed.

    So. You like music.
    Is that a question?
    No. I mean, it's an opener.
    Why do you need an opener.
    Okay, whatever. You want to go to a concert? It's in Austin.
    Okay. Yes.
    So, I've told you about my friend Raiden, right?
    Um . . . let's see. The Jew. Liked you for a few years in high school.
    Yep. Well, he's at UT. Well, kind of. I don't know. He's like a total

genius. I think they let him go there for free and he works with some of the professors. In physics or something. He's technically like a sophomore but I think he's already graduated or something. He's on his own program.

Okay . . .

Yeah so. Anyway, he lives right over sixth street. And have you ever heard of The Labradors?

Yeah.

Well he knows the bass player and he's going to have like a pre party at his place on Friday. They're playing at Stubbs.

Okay. Yeah. Is Nate going?

Yeah. We can give you a ride, but he'll probably want to leave early . . .

Oh. Thanks. I'll probably just ride up there.

Ugh. On that thing? She nodded her head at the door where the bike gleamed in the sun and dust.

Yeah. On that thing.

Okay. Well I'll give you directions. I think people will get there at eight and stuff. Nate and me'll probably get dinner first.

Alright.

The ride over the hills from the southwest was glorious. Racing the sun down, then dropping into the dark basin of the big city like some invisible eagle.

Raiden lived in a penthouse off sixth street in Austin. There were many rooms, and a ladderlike staircase that went from the kitchen to a rooftop patio, garden, and bar. Everything was lines and white and concrete. A deep bass throb shook everything, and the melody over the top of it was anarchic and cranial.

Three of the five Labradors were there. Even though he had never seen pictures of them, Jonathan could tell who they were. They looked as though they were performing a drama that unfolded over the course of four decades, opening on the turn of the century and with final curtain at Pearl Harbor. Two were bearded and tweeded, and one was shaven and slick. Jonathan afterward learned that shaven and slick was the bassist (*upright*), and the others fiddle and keys respectively.

The house and patio were filled with people. Jonathan arrived late enough to ensure that Jane and Nate would be there. He was about to knock, but then resolutely opened the door and walked in. Jane was nowhere to be seen, and so after some purposeful milling with a furrowed brow, he made his way casually to the rooftop. That's where he spotted the Labradors, standing coolly in one corner, silently, and occasionally laughing to themselves.

Jonathan sidled over to an edge of the building, looking down casually with his hands in his pockets, and then decided there was nothing for it and walked over to the bar.

Behind the bar was an almost unattractively handsome young man, blond in a chartreuse tuxedo jacket, skinny plaid pants and no tie. He was thin, and his hair flopped over one eye occasionally. He had a boston shaker going over one shoulder.

Well I think you need some of this.
Oh . . . sure. Yeah.
Summer in Texas.
Yeah . . .
No, I mean that's the name of the drink.
Oh. Right.
You've never had it so don't pretend.
Okay . . . well I wasn't going to.
I know.
Okay?
You have the look of a man who has recently drunk Balcones.
What? How . . .
Looking for a man who has recently drunk milk.
What?
Sorry. Movie turrets. But seriously. The single malt is good—great even—but not gonna lie . . . naganna naganna—naganna work here anymore . . . as a whole (he whispered behind his free hand with a furtive glance at the crowd on the roof) a teensy overrated. Teensy. I mean, the brushfire . . . bonfire, what's it called? . . . *brimstone*. That's right. I mean. Soak some water in your campfire. Drink. There you go. *Brimstone*.
I . . . what . . . ?
Say what one more goddamn time. I dare ya. I double dare ya. No, I mean, there's peaty—he bounced the fingers of one hand in the air while he poured with the other—which, incidentally, is a synonym for shitty. I mean literally. Peat is just like, shit and stuff, fermented on the bog.

It's used for cheap fuel. Why in the holy hell would you want to drink that?—but so anyways there's peaty, but then you have whatever the hell *Brimstone* is. I can just see the thirty-five year old whisky connoisseurs holding it up to the light. *You* know. Twenty pounds overweight. Cuffed selvedge. Chinstrap but no chin. I detect notes of . . . of . . . That's shit youre detecting, Sherlock.

Jonathan didn't have anything to say.

Well. Anyway. Here you go. He placed the cocktail glass precisely on an embossed black napkin in front of Jonathan. There was an almost invisible gray RB on the napkin.

A bit much? Yeah. Probably. You're right.

No, it's really good, it's . . .

No, not the drink. I mean the monogram. I mean it's horrible, right? But selfconsciously. Not ironic. Does that make it okay? Probably not.

Jonathan just stood there sipping the drink with his eyebrows raised.

I know the drink's good.

Yeah, thanks, I . . .

Yeah. Blah blah blah. So you're here with Jane. That's nice. Technically, of course, I mean that you're here *at her behest*—but then aren't we all, in some sense? He paused a beat, looking out over the skyline with affected gravity. Only Nate is really here *with* Jane, in the strict sense, but that never mattered so very much to her. Or to you, I take it. Don't get me wrong—I've no doubt it kills you, etc, etc. Martyr, etc. But still, there's something of the whole marry the sister so at least you're still connected somehow and you can still love them from afar bit going on, yada yada yada.

Okay. Hold on.

Oh, right. Yeah. So you're Jonathan. Sorry. Raiden Bartholomew. He held out his hand.

How the *fuck* . . .

Don't worry, you're clean. He put his hand in his jacket pocket and cocked one eyebrow and looked about the patio suspiciously. Then he looked back at Jonathan with a perfectly calm and friendly face.

Anyway. Enough of that, said Raiden. He tossed the shaker in the metal sink behind him. I haven't pried too much. But I am curious whether you came on the honda. I'd love to see it. Classic. And at some point I'll show you mine. When I get a break from hosting. He looked back at Jonathan. Oh! Right! So how do I—not to mention *why*?, etc. Yeah. It's true I do physics and stuff, sure. But then, all of life is physics if you think about it, isn't it? But really I'm doing information theory, etc, obviously.

Cryptography, to put it very crudely indeed. So I just checked stuff out a little. Don't be alarmed.

Okaaay . . .

Anyway. Let's not belabor the point. You don't really mind. And now you don't have to feel awkward anymore. You know someone here now. Or someone knows you, at any rate. So.

Alright. Well then.

Yeah.

Okay. So, what do you . . . I mean, how do you . . . Jonathan gestured at the rooftop.

Oh. Right. So, *yes*, I *am* employed. I don't actually own this, though. Just renting.

Oh. Okay. I'm employed, too, but . . .

Well, I do a few things, you know. I've made myself valuable to the right people. With deep moneybag strings. Or whatever.

I should meet these people.

Ha. No. You're doing fine. Raiden made a fake embarrassed look: I mean, I as*sume* you're doing fine. Besides. These people are pretty . . . *particular*. Though not, it seems, particular enough. You know, that big . . . um, *warehouse* outside of San Antonio?

No . . . sorry.

Oh. I though everyone knew by now. I think it was leaked somewhat recently. Wikileaks or no, I'm not sure. Not that I give a shit. I mean the money's good, etc etc, but I don't pretend to love what we do overall. I mean, I guess I console myself with the fact that it could be done worse—or by worse people. But anyway, I don't think they love me so much either. But they can't really do without me . . . He opened his arms to the party on his roof . . . So here I am.

Jonathan took another sip. What's in this?

Ah, now there *is* an interesting topic. It's a whisky based drink, of course, and I used a good one, but it doesn't really matter so particularly much in this case—you wouldn't be able to taste the difference. It just needs to be a smooth canadian. And I'm loth to admit there is in fact sour apple pucker in there. I hide the bottle. I really do. And pour it out of a carafe. An opaque carafe. And cranberry juice. Not cranberry cocktail. Real stuff. But what you're getting is the cucumber and jalapeno. Muddled and strained. Summer in Texas. There you go. There's some pepper and cilantro, but hard to catch.

It's really good.

And naturally I've no intention of reporting you.

What? Oh right . . .

Yeah. Happy birthday in four months, by the way. I could recite your driver's license number to you if you like. But then we're getting into the creepy zone.

Already there.

Yeah so. Back to our topic. Raiden was rinsing the shaker and other dishes in the sink. Sure. It's true. I liked Jane. From February of eighth grade year until about the end of sophomore year. Or I should say I was in love with her. Technically I don't know if there's really any other way to be. But that was back when I was still capable of liking *people*. Like human beings and stuff.

Okay . . .

Yeah. I know. It sounds weird.

Jonathan raised his eyebrows.

Okay. *Is* weird. We'll save that for later. And yes, there will *be* a later. For now, let's blow this popsicle stand and head down to the garage. I've got to show you the Ronin.

Just then the three rooftop Labradors had sauntered up to the bar.

Hey man. Could we get some beers.

Oh certainly.

Raiden turned his back on them and grabbed a liquor bottle, a two liter of some soda, and two plastic cups. He walked out from behind the bar and said This way! singsongingly to Jonathan. Jonathan followed him.

Hey . . . so . . . said Prohibition Era.

Oh, yeah, they're in the fridge.

Okaaay. Aren't you the bartender? asked the newsboy.

Yep.

Jonathan followed Raiden down the stairs and back into the kitchen. Everything was closer and more frenetic and the music went on, mechanical hammers over the liquid beat. Raiden grabbed a tray of hors d'eurve from a passing waiter all in black. Thanks, Chris, he said loudly so he could hear. Yes sir, said the waiter.

Push that, would you? Raiden indicated a small silver button on a wall. He nibbled a steamed muscle from the tray delicately with his lips. In a few moments the light wood paneling of the wall opened and they stepped in and went down.

Private elevator, Raiden explained. Then to himself, Heh heh, are you sure?

What?

Sorry. Tommy Boy. Reason I picked this place. Directly to my garage.

Wow.

They descended six floors.

When the door opened again it was to a flat gray prism. The concrete floor was stained and sealed, and the walls painted to match. There was a lone metal cabinet on wheels to one side, all white. In the center of the garage was the bike. It confounded Jonathan's eyes. He saw the wheels, but at first he didn't know which end was the front. It was a chaos of planes and angles, like a mechanical dragon. There were hoses and plates. Every surface was smoke black.

There were only going to be forty seven of them. All numbered. But then this is number zero which doesn't count and so there's actually forty eight now. I commissioned it specially. Okay, anyway. He seemed embarrassed and impatient. So, I wanna see the CB.

Oh . . .

Come on. Raiden pushed something with his elbow, still holding the cups and bottles. The garage bay door opened revealing a dark street. He walked out as the door was closing again, and Jonathan went behind him.

He stopped and sat on the curb. Here you go. He poured some from each bottle.

Jonathan tasted it and made a face.

Ha. This is the best ever. Don't tell me you don't like it.

Umm.

Vodka and diet Dr Pepper.

Okaaay . . .

Ha! Look who's a snob now. There is no more pleasant drunk to be had, at any price. And believe me, I've canvassed the competition.

Okay.

Raiden poured himself a second one.

They walked down the alley to where Jonathan had parked a block or two away. They could hear the bang and crash of sixth street, and smell the foodcarts on the warm breeze. The capitol loomed invisible in the night to the north on the hill. They walked in silence through the electric southern city air. Raiden was stooped, with his hands in his plaid pants pockets. They came to the bike.

Oh . . . wow. Beauty. Nice.

Raiden walked around it slowly and took it in. He looked closely at several parts.

Want to take it for a spin? said Jonathan.

Oh, thanks. No no. Raiden patted the seat gingerly. But we'll have to blast around together sometime.

I won't be able to keep up.

I know. It's okay. It'll be fun.

Yeah.

They started walking back. They could just catch a saxophone strain squiggling from the frontside of sixth. They passed dumpsters. Suddenly a bent black man appeared from behind one of the dumpsters. Hey brothas. I'm tryin to get me in a shelter. You got a dolla or somethin?

God no, said Raiden. Get away from me.

Jonathan was shocked.

Fuck you, mothafucka! said the black man.

Hang on, said Jonathan. I've got something.

Raiden walked on ahead without looking back.

Mothafucka, the man muttered.

Um, okay. Um, how much is a shelter . . .

The man muttered, Shelter twelve dolla . . . look man, I'm tryin to get me a sammich at *Mac*Donald's.

Jonathan had some of his money in his pocket. He pulled out a twenty. Um, is this enough.

Yeah man, yeah man. You got any mo? He took the twenty quickly from Jonathan's hand and stuffed it in his pocket.

Well . . .

Look man, I'm tryin to hep out my baby sista. She in the hospital. *Cancer*. Man, how much you got.

Well, I need some of it for gas to get home. I'm gonna give you twenty.

Twenty five. Man, my sista, she in *rill* bad pain, man. And I aint et in two day. He looked up and counted on knuckly, chalky fingers. Naw, man. Fo day. I finna get me—listen brotha. I made it up. I call it the MacGangbanger. You take a big mac, and a chicken sammich, and you open it up, and you spread apart the meat, and you put the chicken inside there. Mmmm . . .

Yeah?

Yeah man. Lemme tell you. That shit more hearty than fuck, man. More hearty than *fuck*, man.

Yeah. Wow. Look, all I can spare is twenty, or I'm going to run out of gas on the way home.

Aww . . . man . . . The man looked at Jonathan askance. Look, just fi mo dolla.

I would if I could.

The man shook his head. For *rill*, man . . . and turned his back and walked away.

Jonathan jogged to catch up to Raiden. He was walking with his hands in his pockets, stooped once more.

Uh . . . what was that all about, asked Jonathan when he reached him.

What?

I mean, you kind of freaked out on him a little . . . You know him or something?

Know him? *God* no.

Okaaaay . . .

What?

I mean . . .

Look. I'm not an idiot, said Raiden. Okay? I think I've made that sufficiently clear. I think I feel like most people do. I'm just being honest. What would you do if like a . . . cockroach walked up to you and was like, Gimme twenty dalla bro?

Well . . . like can this cockroach talk?

No, like a normal cockroach.

Okay.

You seen any of those yet, by the way?

Oh, yeah. There were some in my room when I first moved in.

Creepy as hell, man.

Yeah. Especially at first. They're huge.

Yeah.

Actually, the first night I was in my room at The Sandman I woke up because I heard something moving across the floor and I thought it was like a rat or whatever. Turned on the light . . .

Yeah.

Yeah. Cockroach. Huge.

So, what would you say?

Well. I mean that's not fair. That's like a bug.

What's the difference?

Come on. I mean . . .

Yeah?

Well, that guy was a person.

So?

Well . . .

Well what? What possible use is that guy? How is it possibly better that he exists rather than the cockroach? What good does he do?

Well, I don't know . . .

None. Zero. One hundred percent drain.

Drain on what?

Raiden hesitated for a second. On like . . . I don't know. I don't want to say society, but like . . . you know, everything.

Well. I hope I'm useful.

That's not what I mean. It's not like a measurement. I mean it's like . . . that guy's not even barely human. He just goes around like an animal trying to feed himself every day.

I don't know. That's how I feel.

What?

Like I'm just trying to feed myself.

You've got plenty of money.

Well. Still, like. It seems like that's what everyone's doing.

Oh, I don't know. Maybe you're right. Honestly people like that just make me want to hate them.

Why?

Go*dammit* Jonathan! I don't know. Allow me the use of my heavily medicated emotions. Look. I'm kind of just feeling out what I think here. He talks to me, I feel like kind of nervous or violated and gross. So that's how I react. I call it honesty.

They were quiet for a bit, and then reached the closed garage. They sat down on the curb and Raiden poured another round of his drink.

I guess this isn't *too* bad, said Jonathan.

See? It grows on you. Pretty soon it's all you'll want.

Hmm. Jonathan was quiet for a moment. You know, my family is poor. My mom. She does everything she can.

Look man, that's not what I mean at all. I don't even believe what I'm saying. I'm just talking because I feel something. Don't listen to me.

Okay, said Jonathan.

Well fuck. Now you make me think I should go apologize to that little cockroach.

No, no . . . I mean. I don't think we could find him anyway.

No, yeah. We can. C'mon. I know where he stays.

But I thought you didn't know . . .

Yeah yeah yeah, I don't *know* him. But I've seen his little nook. Calling over his shoulder, he said, He has a cell phone by the way. C'mon.

Oh, I . . .

Look, you fucking Samaritan, said Raiden, stopping. This was your idea. You're sure as hell coming with me.

Okay . . .

C'mon. He stalked off the way they had just come. Then he yelled, Baris! *Baaariiiiis*!

Baris?

I didn't name the cockroach.

They found him in the alcove made by two concrete pillars of an empty warehouse. He was sitting crosslegged on a sleeping bag, thumbing away rapidly on his phone. His face, deeply caverned, was underlit by its glow.

Baris! My old friend, said Raiden when they found him.

Fuck you want? he answered. And then, The fuck you know mah name? You mothafucker . . .

Yes, yes. That I am, in every non-literal sense. I deserve that. Look. I owe you an apology. Consider it given. The thing is, you make me uncomfortable. Et cetera. But anyway. There. Consider it said.

What?

Nevermind. I'm saying that I am sorry that you were on the receiving end of my underdeveloped emotional response. It comes out like you saw. My profoundest apologies.

Baris just looked at him. Finally he said, *Gim*me somethin.

Well shita*lo*! She has emerged. But of course.

Raiden reached into his plaid back pocket and grabbed a money clip and unfurled, and then tossed, three hundred dollar bills so that they floated down onto Baris' lap.

Daaaaaaaamn, brotha!

Quite.

Baris jumped up, stuffed the bills into his pocket, and then hugged Raiden around the neck, hopping on his feet while he did. Aww, man, I *love* you.

Yes, yes, said Raiden, standing stiffly. Okay then, enjoy your evening.

Aww, you da *best*, man. Shit, you *both* the best. Lawd Jesus, he said, closing his eyes and raising his hands over them, bless dese men in your Spirit, Lawd Jesus, Kingdom God Father. Watch over dem, Lawd Jesus Kingdom God Father and . . .

When Baris finally opened his eyes, Jonathan and Raiden were gone.

As they approached the garage once more, Raiden said, Would you know I was a Christian for two years?

What?

Right? I know. Well. Love will do that to you. He shuddered as if he was talking about a disease. You should be careful.

Look . . .

Oh, blah blah, your secret's safe with me. I won't tell her. He sighed. Anyway, so yeah. I actually was pretty *involved*. It wasn't any trouble to learn a few songs and play electric for the worship band. Say that ten times. Worship band. A traveling covered wagon with a menagerie of folk aboard, giants and dwarfs and bearded women and . . . like, cripples or whatever.

Cripples?

Yeah. And on the side it says worship band. And giants! *It's not my fault being the biggest and the strongest. I don't even exercise!*

Got it.

Finally! Anyway. And I really meant it all. But then . . . He trailed off and was looking at the city and took a drink from the plastic cup.

Yeah?

Then I woke up. That's all.

They were quiet again.

Well, I suppose we ought to head up. Host this thing.

Okay. Sure.

Don't worry, Jane's there, said Raiden, looking at his phone.

Did she text you?

Jealous?

Just asking.

Well, you should get a phone. Oh! But first I've got to start up the Ronin for you.

Oh, sure.

Raiden pushed something on his phone and the garage door opened once more. Okay. Raiden bent over and fiddled with an invisible switch on the bike. A sleeping worm's eye sprung open and shot rays around the garage. Then Raiden pushed a button on the right side handlebar. The bike awoke like a nightshift factory manufacturing lightning. When he revved it, it screamed liked a god, and Jonathan felt some urge to hide. Raiden shut it off.

Wow.

Okay, let's go upstairs.

Okay.

They got back in the elevator as the bay door closed on the night.

Here, let's do another round real quick.

Why not?

Utilize what we've got, as it were.

I'm a fan of the utilization.

Raiden poured them out while the elevator went up.

What's this called? said Jonathan.

Oh! It needs a name, said Raiden.

Um . . . the cockroach!

Yes! To the cockroach. Here you go.

Well, it looks like a cockroach. And it tastes about that good, so. And why diet, bee tee dubs?

Shut up. This shit is amazing. And the calories, that's why. Pound that shit. You're about to see your soulmate.

Fuck you. She's not. She already has one. But yes. It tastes better all the time.

You have saved the best wine until now!

Yeah, I don't . . .

The fucking *bible*, man! *Jesus. I'm* the fucking *Jew* here!

Is there a movie of that?

The elevator glided to a stop. Raiden stood up straighter and adjusted his collar. Alright. Game face, man.

The door opened, and they strode out into the party like roman magnates. Raiden, of a sudden, was all smiles, and each guest felt as though he were somehow an irreplaceable part of it all. The dr pepper and the vodka vanished and there appeared in Raiden's hand an oldfashioned champagne goblet. The speakers now, invisibly from somewhere, dropped dance remixes of eighties pop hits and brazilian samba. The place throbbed and you felt like you had to yell, but when you talked to someone it was like there was no one else there.

The faces came and went in front of Jonathan, like images through a melting pane of ice. Suddenly huge. Disappearing. Leering, smiling, gone. And then there were Jane and Nate! Hey Jane! Hey Nate! he heard himself saying from some distance. Why isn't Jane smiling. Nate looks nervous. Hey Nate. Dude. Man. *So* good to see you, brother. Hey. Welcome. To our little party!

Our little party? said Jane.

Ha ha ha! Right? said Jonathan. That was . . . silly of me. Rai raidens been showing me around the place and all. We had a nice little chat with Baris. Baris. Have you met him? No. No. No. You wouldn't have.

You're totally drunk.

No . . . no . . . no. I totally see what Im saying. And thats totally reas onable. Jane. But I . . . like I totally see myself. I know youre all like . . . he's act ing different. But my mind's like . . . totally in control. Im totally seeing myself right now . . .

It seemed like Jane and Nate walked off. But then there were so many people crushing around him who could tell? And then later someone was holding him up by the arms and they were all dancing and he thought it was the macarena and he was being very very funny and he could tell because everyone was laughing and the big cold room was turning, turning slowly, and the music was the only thing holding him up.

Much later in the night, it seemed, he found himself outside retching into a bush and somehow Jane was there.

You stupid idiot. You stupid idiot, she kept saying, but then she would pat him on the back and say You okay? You okay? and Jonathan kept looking around for Nate but the lights going in a line down the street made his head swim and they left trails when he moved and he kept trying to lie down on the sidewalk and then he saw the steps leading up to Raiden's house going under his feet and then the last thing he remembered was Jane taking his shoes off his feet and he fell asleep in a spare room.

Tom gently eased the steaming brisket off the grate once more with the two plastic spatulas. He turned it, letting the weight carry it over. He took drippings from a tray underneath and basted the new topside. Smoke poured out around his shoulders, and his torso made a vertical shadow on it that danced as the coils went up in the morning light. He went back in the house.

You grab the votary while you were out, honey?

Yep.

Will you drink any more coffee.

Nope.

They orbited each other in the kitchen. How could one keep the flame in front of one's face? Grant another person his full and other humanity, season after season.

Jane said Nate's coming. And she invited that new kid from the office.

Oh yeah? Jonathan. Good kid.

What's with that.

Oh nothing.

Hmmm, said Ginny as she took her oatmeal from the microwave. You know Jane's not real sure of herself.

Well.

You getting flowers like you said? asked Ginny.

I remember. I thought I'd cut some. A few big jars on the table. And . . . he turned toward the window and looked out. He centered himself on the poplar, steadied himself, and said, And I was thinking maybe a bouquet from the grocery store? For graduation?

Yeah. That's a sweet idea.

Okay. I'll grab that after.

Here. I've got a coupon for the HEB.

Okay.

She knew better than to ask if she should check on the brisket while he was gone. How much of marriage was like that, she thought—the marking out of borders and neutral zones; questions that would not be asked again; the knowing when to let things be. When to hear out, and when to interrupt. The irreparable hurts to try to forget. And, she thought to herself, she had arrived at the perfect equipoise of give and take. Stiff leather broken in the truer for that. She sensed his distraction, and that this formal remembrancer of Change had put him in a mood that was, if one looked closely at it, nothing more than sentimentality. He was thinking, no doubt, of the girl he had known who was killed when he was over there in the service. Oh yes, she knew about that, though she had never told him. Their black neighbor Marcus had let it slip one time early on. Wendy. It was a nice name. But there wasn't much to it, in the end. Did he think Ginny had never had her own attractions? Her year-long flirtations? Neither of them, she knew, had ever been unfaithful in the technical sense. But did he think she was too boring for that? Could he not imagine that Francis, for example, from college, had come to her dorm room late one night and confessed his love? That she had been tempted to throw her arms around his neck? But there was a comfort in coming up against the well worn, shiny contours of their harnesses. Like old pack mules chafing gently, familiarly in their common yoke.

Ginny rinsed the coffee mugs and whipped a towel through them briefly. She fidgeted, waiting for Tom to go. The fine gears of her domestic

173

clockwork slowed by the influence of his presence.

You think there's enough people coming? he said. Tom seemed to shuffle to her. So strong, so impressive to so many in this town. But would say things like that. When what he meant was . . . who could tell? Some primary color of emotion, finger painted on his mind in bold outline. He felt, perhaps, the smallness of this flag for the marking off of time's passage. Or the way that you could never communicate your love to children so that they felt the depth of it. For if they did, they would surely fall over stricken, with a low idiotic moan . . . well. But to see a love like that for what it was would make you weep.

There'll be plenty, Tom, she answered with annoyance, setting the carafe upside down in the drainer.

Well.

She wanted him to go. What did he want? For her to assuage some inarticulable anxiety in his breast? That was it, she knew. To tell him what to do next? To offer him something to eat? She would have been marching off this very minute to the laundry room to put the table cloths in the dryer. For though he might see the major strokes of the thing, there were a thousand small details that went into the throwing of a party that slipped by him without his knowing. For it to work. She knew that to his mind merely smoking the brisket counted as doing the main thing. Mowing the lawns, trimming the hedges. When they could have catered in better barbecue and had it delivered and then dropped it on a nice platter, done. And then maybe some year they'd pay someone to tend the grounds. Some year when Tom was immobile, she thought with a huff. But Tom wanted to do it himself—no matter that they had the money now; no matter that it took him hours. He thought these things affected no one but him, when why couldn't they see, men, that hours doing one thing—even a necessary thing—meant hours not doing something else? Would it be such a feat to drive into Austin for a dinner and shopping once in a while? To get away from the smallness and backwardness of this town for a breath of fresh air? Not to mention that now that the kids were all but gone Ginny could imagine living in a new house, in some subdivision in the hills outside the city. Actually having a place to shop where somebody's sister or cousin didn't know the style and size of the undergarments she bought. But Tom loved this land. Like it was his own family. And she would admit it could be beautiful in the right light, though a severe sort of beauty—anyhow when the trees on the eastern line were full enough to hide the McGowan's trash heap of a property. Tom said they were just country and they saw things differently but to Ginny orderliness was the universal and apparent axiom of creation, and its trespassers inexcusable.

Alright, said Tom, still slouching there. Well, I guess I'll go grab those flowers. And pick up drinks. He was screwing up his face to think. And, anything else we need?

She raised her eyebrows and lowered her forehead at him.

Oh. Right. Cornbread. You good on butter and honey?

Yep.

Ginny turned back to the draining rack and started putting them away.

Ginny?

She wheeled around.

Love you, he said as he turned his broad back to her and walked out into the hot day.

Jonathan awoke in a white room with a white bed and a simple white nightstand. He sat up and the room moved. He put his head in his hands. At the end of the bed he saw his shoes and socks neatly beside one another, and there was an untouched glass of water on the nightstand.

Squinting at the floor, he shuffled out of the room, barefoot.

Hey, said Raiden when Jonathan reached the kitchen.

Hey.

Sorry about last night.

Oh . . . no. No worries. My fault.

Well. I do feel bad. Have some aspirin. Raiden pointed to a large bottle by the filtered water dispenser emerging from the countertop.

Yeah.

Raiden was wearing top and bottom pajamas, in a dove flannel. There was a newspaper on the breakfast bar in front of him, and he sat crosslegged on a stool.

Coffee?

Um . . . not right now.

Okay.

I think I'm going to try to get going.

Okay. I would like to talk more sometime. Certainly not this morning.

Okay.

You didn't get to meet Eowyn.

Eowyn?
My girlfriend.
Oh, like in . . .
Yes. That's her name.
Oh.
Anyway. I'll text you.
I don't have a . . .
I know. You should get one. Just a prepaid nokia or whatever. More secure than a smartphone, anyway.
Okay.
I'll text you when you have it. We need to ride.
Okay.
Anyway, I'll leave you be. If you decide you can handle it, there's a lovely coffee bar a couple blocks away. It's called Teh Coffee.
The coffee?
Yep.
Okay.
Towards so co.
Okay.
Anyway. I had fun last night.
Me too, said Jonathan, as he shuffled out of the kitchen to retrieve his shoes.

He walked down the street toward his bike, and decided to go to Teh Coffee. He started up the CB and parked in front of the shop. It appeared to be made out of discarded pallets, painted an unattractive blue. A five foot tall typewriter had, apparently, burned words into the side of the building: teh coffe. The wall ended before the word did.

The tables inside were made of concrete slabs bolted onto tree stumps. Jonathan put his Jansport on one and went up to the counter.

The coffee was very good.

He took out his thin brown notebook and wrote some things in it. Things to do and also things he thought he had learned.

20 June
[ ] Prepare findings re. obm, etc. for Tom et al. — set

    date for meeting? Tues?
    [ ] Look into petcock— o-ring? new, etc.
    [ ] . . .

A shadow came over his shoulder.
    Hey man. Sorry man. Hey, is that your bike?
    Yeah.
    Aww, man. That's just . . . so fucking authentic, man.
    Oh . . . thanks.
    No man, really. Like . . .
    His friend came up next to him.
    ... Real as *fuck* man.
    Yeah. Real as fuck, said the the first.
    Oh . . . Thanks.
    They both had mustaches on their faces. Big nietzsche ones that they had started growing early on.
    You mind if I ask where you got it?
    Um, it was just really old. It belonged to an old farmer outside of . . .
    Aww, *shit* man.
    Yeah, shit man.
    What? said Jonathan.
    Just . . . that's so killer, man.
    Yeah, said the second one, and stuck out his hand to shake Jonathan's. Jonathan shook his hand.
    Oh, well . . . thanks guys.
    Hey! Can my buddy take your polaroid?
    What? Polaroid?
    Yeah man . . . film's where it's *at*, brother. His buddy had a big box of a camera on a strap around his neck.
    Oh.
    Yeah. None of this iphone shit, man. Real. *Film*.
    Oh.
    Okay man, hold still, said the buddy.
    Oh . . . no. I mean, I'd rather not, if that's okay. Get my picture taken. My polaroid taken.
    The first mustache looked astounded. Oh, for real, man. He rolled his eyes in amazement. Respect, brother. Res*pect*.
    Yeah, said the other one. This guy is just the . . . he searched for words . . . the straight real as fuck *shit*, man. He made a big snapping

motion with his hand when he said it.

    Yeah man. You are the original real shit, man.

    You mind if we take a pic of your bike?

    Oh . . . well, go ahead, I guess.

    Sweet. Thanks, brother.

    Okay.

    They went outside and took several polaroids of the bike from different angles. Capturing the cityscape. Capturing teh coffe. Capturing a dirt alley on the side of the shop.

    They came back in and went to a table in the corner. One of them was waving the exposures back and forth. The other one was carefully framing one of the polaroids on his iphone and snapping pictures of it.

    Jonathan finished his coffee and packed up his things and rode home to Ventana.

Byron Collangelo arrived at the Dolph Briscoe Unit in Dilley, Texas, in the early nineties, in spring, two weeks before his twenty ninth birthday. Donald had begun at Assumption Seminary in San Antonio the previous autumn, and now he continued visiting Byron again on Saturdays, as he had in New York.

    Byron got on well at Briscoe. He eventually began assisting the livestock supervisor with the horses kept on the larger grounds. He had never touched a horse before in his life. He stroked the flanks. So smooth. Rippling in their strength as they shivered instinctively under his hand. He took to horses quickly, and they liked him.

    Donald no longer brought him cigarettes, since Byron didn't smoke and trade wasn't necessary to survival at Dolph Briscoe. He kept bringing him licorice.

    The ashen fields stretched away forever to Mexico and to the edges of the gulf both westward and eastward and Byron would stand and listen to the wind coming from miles over the grass outside the fences.

On his way to the towers Jonathan stopped at the Wataburger on the edge of town. He emerged with two large bags and hung them over the left handlebar of the CB, carefully keeping them away from the engine fins and cam cover.

It was a hundred degrees already and just noon. The dust from the gravel drive approaching the towers got in his eyes. He went through the chainlink gate and came to a stop in front of the break building and put the bike's kickstand down on a larger rock. Around the compound were useless dry hillocks of exposed limestone and barren ashe juniper.

He nodded at Jose and Travis and Chuck Walker. They came over when they heard him ride up and they all went into the break building and sat at a folding table and divvyed up the food.

Who had jalapenos?
I had the bacon.
Okay. I just got three large fries so just grab one.
What's happening?
Same shit different day.
Another day another dollar.
Livin the dream.
Mike wanted to see you. Said the final drive needed fixed.
I thought Ryan came in last week.
I don't know, he just said he wanted to see you.
Well. Shit.
How's your girlfriend.
Ha. Pretty good, I guess.
How would you know? Ha, ha.
My god she's beautiful. You don't see beautiful women anymore, said Travis.
Ain't that the truth, said Chuck.
You just don't. All you got is skanky ass girls. No more beautiful women. Either skinny as shit or fat. No more beautiful women.
And the beautiful ones ain't ladies.
Nope.
You get any spicy ketchup, said Jose.
Umm . . . no, said Jonathan.
The fuck, man.
I didn't know you wanted the spicy ketchup.
A man don't go to Wataburger and not get the spicy ketchup. Fuck, man, said Jose.
I can't eat that shit. Gives me heartburn, said Chuck.
Nobody asked your stupid face.
Sorry man, said Jonathan.

Sorry don't put no spicy ketchup on my burger. I got a problem here.

Well, I hope you make it.

What?

Nothing. I just said I hope you make it.

You know what, Jonathan? You too fucking smart for your own good. I been thinkin about this. You think you can play it off here.

I'm not playing anything off, said Jonathan, and laughed.

Well why don't you just ask Jane out?

She's with Nate.

Oh, fuck Nate. Who's he? Some guy played tight end for the Lobos. Who cares. He ain't even very good. He was too nice. You gotta be mean. Too big and slow. And whoopty-shit, he off at college. You could go to college, you know.

I know.

So why ain't you?

I don't have time. I work here plus The Sombrero.

Don't fuck with me. Why ain't you?

I don't know. I don't see why I should.

I would if I could.

Why don't you?

I didn't even finish high school.

Well, you could get your GED, and . . .

Are you fucking serious right now, man? You think you can just do whatever. You know that?

Well, I . . . I don't know. Can't you?

No, man. I can't.

Jonathan thought Jose would say more but instead he put his burger in one of the Wataburger bags and took his drink and stood up and walked away.

Jonathan looked around. Umm . . .

Don't worry about him, said Chuck.

Yeah. Fucker's moody, said Travis. I seen him do that before.

Okay.

But seriously though, bro, said Travis. Why the hell would you want to work in this shithole if you could be out making bank somewhere else.

This isn't so bad.

You shittin me brother? It's fucking two hundred degrees in the shade. Which there ain't any. Travis was dirty blond sunburnt white and didn't have any fat on him, and his eyes were very beautiful like a picture from

India.

    Well at least you can see what you're doing, answered Jonathan. You're just getting oil out of the ground. People buy oil. There's no confusion.

    Confusion? What the hell.

    Like . . . you can see what you're doing. Why it's important. It's not like school.

    That makes no fucking sense. You go to school to get a better job so you don't have to be broke your whole broke ass life.

    Ha ha, laughed Chuck Walker.

    Ha. Well. I guess.

    No, that's the truth. And one of these days you're going to wake up and get out of here.

    I don't know.

    I know. This shit gets old. Real quick it gets old.

    Well. I better go talk to Mike.

    Have fun.

    Yep.

    That fucker ain't never liked you, said Chuck.

    Nope.

    Well fuck him, said Travis.

    We'll see, said Jonathan.

    He got up and walked out of the bare break room and left Chuck and Travis at the plastic folding table. He went up onto the catwalk around the draw works, toward the four by six foot office cubby that Mike lived in. As he walked there he was catcalled by the inmates.

    Hey jefe.

    Jonny boy. Oh Jooonny Boy.

    It's Danny boy.

    No it ain't. You ever listened to it?

    He came upon Bill, the short middle aged man who had first accosted him in the courtyard before the interview in that long ago. Bill worked like a mole all day. He could hardly spare a word when he was on the clock. He clung to work like a lifeline.

    Morning, Jonathan.

    Hey Bill. It's afternoon.

    Well, so it is. Take care.

    He was hustling up the ladder to the drill guides.

    See ya, Bill, said Jonathan. He had become fond of Bill.

    When he reached Mike's office he saw him hunched over his desk with a mechanical pencil and a big table of numbers. A gray freize of hair spread out from below his ballcap.

Hi Mr Richards. Mike turned around. You had a question about the bearing?

I ain't got no question. I wanna know why in hell it's bindin up. You said you was gonna have that maintnence man in to fix the final drive. I seen him dickin around, doin somethin last week. But now I'm bein held up and I hadta send home a whole shift last night.

Ryan did fix it. Replaced the bearing and the coupling.

Why the hell it ain't workin then. Mike wore small steel rimmed reading glasses when he worked at his desk, and he looked over them at Jonathan.

I don't know.

Hell. You're the one Liddell's put in charge of maintenance orderin.

Jonathan started to say something.

An I'm the one hasta be downline of whateverthahell you decide to do. So why the hell it ain't working?

Mike, Jonathan said, using his first name with effort. This is the first I heard about it. It happened last night. I'll take care of it. Do you have any theories?

Yeah. I gotta theory. He just stared at Jonathan.

Yeah? What's that.

I gotta theory you got this job because you sweet talked Janey in the office and Liddell's her daddy.

They stared at each other for a minute.

Jonathan tensed around the jaw but then he said: Well I think your theory's some fucked up bullshit.

Mike considered that.

Then Jonathan said, You wanna show me what the problem is?

Mike pondered, and then said. Okay. Come on. He grabbed his hard hat and gloves and went to the ladder. Jonathan followed him. Roustabouts and mud bitches passed them on the catwalk heading to their lunches. They nodded at Mike and then they nodded at Jonathan.

Mike trotted up the ladder. Jonathan followed. Part way up they came into the sun and the ladder was too hot to hold with his bare hands, so Jonathan gingerly tugged his weight inward with each step. They were ninety feet above the ground, and he could barely keep himself on the ladder. They reached the pipe guards and there was a grid platform and they climbed up onto it and there was Bill, leaning out away from the works, hanging in his harness, tugging the pipe sideways with a ratchet strap in time to instructions yelled from far below.

Bill, show Jonny here what the problem is.

Oh, howdy Mr Richards. He nodded at Jonathan. Welp. This summbitch binding up every time we draw. The gooseneck wants to stay bent at the paticular angle it's workin at, even when we drawing. I figured out a way this mornin to work around it but it's takin twice as long. I been havin Jackson down there in the drawworks twitch the blocks—he motioned with both hands in a jerking rotation—so, to work it loose. It's something inside holdin it up but I cain't wonder what it might be.

It's that danged bearing, like I said, said Mike. Either this numbnuts here ordered the wrong one or the maintenance guy put it in screwy. Somehow Mike's words had lost their potency.

No. It's not the bearing, Jonathan said. He was looking at the huge flexible pipe feeding the drill, descending into the earth.

Well, einstein? said Mike. It sounded like ahnn stahnn.

I've got an idea.

Well hell's bells.

I wanna go down to the suction line.

The hell that got to do with anything? Just pulls material through. You know that, right? Nothing to do with moving the hose around.

Well. I've been keeping an eye on some numbers. And I wanna take a look at it.

Take a look at it.

Yep.

What you expectin to see?

I don't know.

Well shit. Okay Bill. Keep workin your system up here till the kid has his look.

Yessiree, said Bill. He hadn't taken his eyes off the pipe hose and the girders and hangers and block from which it was suspended.

Jonathan and Mike descended some dozen fathoms to the mud pits. There had been a breeze up on the derrick that broke the heat, but as they went down the sun was intensified by the steel and concrete until it beat upon them from below as strongly as from above—so hot it felt like it was coming in waves, and you couldn't reach an equilibrium, and you felt like someone had set a timer and you could only stand it for so long. But it wouldn't stop.

The men at each level of the rig were stamped with the form of their work, like the denizens of some vertical netherworld. At the bottom there was a black man humming and singing to himself, walking amongst the mud tanks.

Cedric. *Cedric*! yelled Mike. John here wants to take a look see at the tanks.

That so? Well. Have at! He went back to humming.

Hell you singin for? Day like this.

I ain't singin cause I happy, said the man.

Suit yourself. Mike took off his ballcap and wiped his head vigorously before slapping it back down.

I was hoping I could see the mix before it hit the shaker, said Jonathan. Or at least as close to as possible.

Welp, considered Cedric. First tank here, he slapped his hand on the rough welded zinc trough, Come out after the shaker and the cuttings is already out.

Hmm.

But . . .

Yeah?

I got a relief valve ahead of the shaker.

Okay.

And if the pump been off for a coupla hours I can pop that.

Okay. Can I get, like, a bucket . . . ?

Welp. I ain't got no bucket.

Okay.

Hang on. Here ya go. He grabbed a large McDonald's styrofoam cup and tossed the melted ice off to the side. He went over to a two-handled valve wheel with a cotterpin and saftey tag.

Cedric pulled out the pin. Welp. Les hope this aint pressuried. He stood off to the side and gingerly turned the wheel, holding the cup under the two inch diameter spigot and squinting cockeyed at it. A dark chocolate malt glooped out. It smelled vaguely of diesel fuel.

Welp, said Cedric.

Yeah, said Jonathan.

What? said Mike. Looks normal.

Usully it aint quite s'thick, said Cedric. But also it aint this dark.

That's just the gel, said Mike. Start up the pump it'll break through and liquidize.

Dat true. Dat true. But I ain't never seen it this viscous.

Well, said Mike.

Okay, thanks, said Jonathan. That's all I needed.

Oh, okay. Cedric turned the wheel and replaced the cotter pin and bent one end of it.

Can I take that?

Oh, sure, sure.

You gonna tell me what youre thinkin? said Mike.

Hang on a sec, Jonathan said.

He took the cup and walked back out to the parking lot, leaving Mike behind. He crouched in the gutter by his bike. He poured some of the sludge into a hollow of the concrete and watched it spread out. After a minute he traced figures in it with his finger, feeling the grit as it coagulated.

Looks like rain, said Byron Collangelo.

Does it? I would have said there was none coming.

You can feel it. Must be just over the horizon. The horses can sense it.

Is that so.

Yessir.

Byron had picked up the southern habit of sir and ma'am during his decade at the Dolph Briscoe Unit and that's what he had called Donald before he was a priest, and he kept calling him that after he was ordained. He sounded almost Texan. But then, he had no longer any tie to New York. They sat at a skeletal gray picnic table in the scant shade of a honey mesquite. It was the only tree for half a mile in any direction. The sky was whitish near the horizon, and became a dismal pale blue as the depths sunk upward toward the sun. A horse was tied under the tree and clopped at dead blades of grass. It shook its head and ears occasionally, and Donald watched it numbly for some visible sign of precipitation. The two men were silent across the table from one other. Some way off a mounted guard sat his horse, nimbly filling a cigarette and then he licking it delicately with just the tip of his tongue protruding from his mouth. A rifle lay athwart his knees.

You know it's fifteen years this Thursday, Donald said, breaking the hot silence. He looked out at the horseman and the shimmering range.

Byron didn't say anything for a while. Then he said, Yeah, I know. He said it looking down at his lap, wearily.

I could say something like, you know, I'd be sending him off to college this year. Something like that. I could say that.

Byron just sat there with his head looking down at his lap, taking it like a familiar whipping.

You know I've never asked you why.

Byron was silent.

Why would I? What could you say? What the possible fuck could you say.

Byron shifted on his side of the table. He looked off to the side, at the field, like he was concentrating.

Nothing. You're nothing but a perverted . . . faggot, molester . . . animal. That's all. A beast.

On that Saturday Donald just got up and walked away, the guard following after him. He never turned to see Byron shaking in the dark under the tree.

At noon Tom put a thin layer of barbecue sauce all over the brisket. Just enough that a new bark would form. He thought of it as his one secret. Seven hours in. Maybe it trapped moisture and heat. He never had to crutch it in foil toward the end like some people. He knew Ginny would rather he just skip the whole thing and cater in wedding food or something. Beef stroganoff in metal troughs over sternos. Or something. A slurry of green beans. Plastic table cloths. He sighed. Somehow it was important that Jonathan was coming—important that there was a sufficient tension in the group. A drama. Different than a small gathering of one's closest friends for potluck. A party should feel precarious. Should seem as though its table were set on the edge of a precipice. A waltz in a prison camp.

Jonathan and Jane. Ginny always worried. As if it were somehow dangerous for Jane's emotions. Not that Nate was so bad. He was irrepressibly responsible, at any rate, under his soft exterior. And he would find his fight at some point, Tom had no doubt. Not that Tom wanted an altar boy for Jane. No! But enthusiasm like Nate's—it could never last. And one never knew what would come after. But then of course Jonathan wasn't anything at all, along those lines. Did that matter? Tom imagined he would be a better person were he married to that beautiful pagan, somehow. Was it wrong to think that? He had only slowly begun to criticize the leanings of his soul, in view of his certain end. He remembered that he had written down on his morning list to call Father. Or text him. Quite the techy priest,

Father Donald. And he could meet him at the tavern, after all. He chuckled to himself at that and determined not to put it off longer. The priest would be the first person he told. Father, I'm dying. It seemed comical, like a movie scene. It was a muggy electrical night. And Wendy under the strung lights with her hair glowing had said, finally, Why not? That's all. And looked with her straight face at him. Why not? with her English accent. And it was then he had decided. All the considerations, dissolved in that hint of a smile and that question. He clasped both her hands in his and nodded and said, simply and finally: Good night. And she had said it too, and then they had nodded firmly and turned their backs to one another and walked away from the pier, with the lights shining out of the inky water, she towards her journalists' hotel and he toward the barracks. They had turned one time only as they walked, and had smiled. He determined he would write Ginny, with whom he was casually going steady at the time, the next day. Nothing could be done till then. They had never even kissed. And that was that. He could hardly bring her face to his mind, but when he could it was her there on that dock, saying, Why not? Happiness in the corners of her serious face. He sighed. Should he say something to Jane? Encourage her to take her time? And Jonathan. Who the hell was that kid. Tom found himself talking to him like a peer when they interacted. What was it that aged people early? Made them fly down to Texas to work at an oil field? When Jonathan had approached Tom about the additive reaction he had discovered, from the well bore sample logs, for example. So confident. How many—what was he, twenty?—how many twenty year old kids would bring their findings to the owners and say Sir, I think we've been putting too much of the polymer in. Or whatever it had been. Tom couldn't even remember the specifics. But he had a conversation with his mud super, that's for sure. What kid had *findings*, anyway? Tom had just been to the doctor the day before that, and had been riding high on the knowledge of death, and had decided that the kid should get a bonus. Besides fixing the chronic gooseneck issues—and settling Mike down—Jonathan's report would mean hundreds of thousands to Buck & Liddell. Tom had found himself telling Jonathan that they'd probably have to go horizontal in a few years—an unpleasant necessity which Jonathan's discovery had no doubt postponed for a year or two more. Tom hadn't told anyone else yet. Then he had calculated the dividends it would mean for the owners and shareholders. And recklessly, perhaps, Tom brought Jonathan back into his office the next day, sat him down and wrote him a check for twenty four thousand dollars. Jonathan went white but he handled it okay. Tom was still chuckling about it. It felt like going over a jump in your car out in a dirt field. Your guts tensed up beforehand and then you didn't brake and it happened. It was like that and it was because he knew he was dying that he did it. Like jumping off a bridge.

He sighed. He checked the temperature on the smoker and wiped the spatula on the rag next to the grillbox and left the house once more.

Jonathan lay on his back in The Sandman. The fan on the ceiling turned slowly end over end. Sweat would stand up on his forehead and then gather mass and stream down around his temples.

...and frankly I'm looking forward to getting back to some oldfashioned state funded daycare. Summer just drains me dry. Incidentally, Mrs Pelter says hi. I ran into her at Safeway. Are you there?

What? Yeah. Why?

Were you asleep?

No. I'm just really hot. The AC's broken.

Well at least it's going to be fall soon.

Ha. Not here.

I haven't seen the sun in at least two weeks.

I can describe it for you if you like. I see it all the time.

So whatever happened with that girl.

I don't know what girl you're talking about, Mom.

Don't give me that, buddy boy. I know love when I see it.

That's one of us.

Come on. Humor me.

I don't know. Nothing. I already told you she has a boyfriend. We're . . . well, we're friends.

Hmm.

I didn't say just friends.

Noted.

Gosh, let's stop talking about it. What about you? You have any rich old men lined up?

Well, I'm trying to get written into this one guy's will. Without committing, though. You know. I've got wild oats yet to sow.

I'm going to pretend this isn't happening and that you didn't just say that.

Ha.

They didn't say anything for a few seconds.
So . . . how is work . . . ?
Good. You?
Well . . . I still work there.
This is what I was talking about.
What?
You going away. The longer you're away the less we have to talk about.
What do you mean. We can talk about anything. It's the miracle of the phone, Mom.
No we can't.
Okay . . .
No, really. I mean . . . I could try to tell you about your sisters. Or about . . . whatever else. But the longer you're gone, the less I can tell you. The smaller percentage I can tell.
Okay, Mom.
Don't okay Mom me.
Are you crying.
No.
Okay.
Anyway, I'm going to go. We can talk next week. Sorry.
Oh. Okay.
Okay, bye.
Okay . . . wait a second.
What?
Hang on, said Jonathan. Um . . . I'm going to . . . you're going to get some money from me in the mail. And . . . I just wanted to let you know ahead of time.
Jonathan, do *not* send me anything. Don't worry about me. I know you're just being nice and everything, but I want you to have it, and I want you to save it—
Mom. Stop it, Jonathan interrupted. Stop. Listen. You're taking it. You are.
No—
Let me. I just got this bonus, and I want—
Don't send it. That's all. I'm going to rip it up.
I'll send cash.
I'll rip that up, too.
You are crying.
No I'm not.

There are two growing seasons in that part of Texas. You plant in the heat of the summer, and then again in winter. You plant in the thick of it, and you stay ahead of the weather, and when the time is right, the plants grow.

Out Jonathan's door was a thin concrete sidewalk that went the length of the low building. Over each door was a little awning. The parking spots were lined up down the sidewalk. Beyond the parking strip were dirt and wild grasses, spotted with empty forties and Bush's Chicken styrofoam cups. At the height of that summer Jonathan borrowed from the priest a garden rake, hoe, shovel, and mattock. And without asking the property manager—who, Jonathan imagined, could not possibly care—he turned over a section of ground.

First he had gone to the tiny local library to check out gardening books. After he had filled out the form to receive a library card, he set the books he had found on the counter to check them out. The old female volunteer librarian looked at him with wide disbelieving eyes and said, after a moment to take in the trespass he had contemplated: You cain't check out any books ta-die.

He looked at her and tried to interpret. Well . . . I just filled out the application for a card . . .

She shook her head slowly at the audaciousness of the interloper: Well, we hafta *mile* you your cord. And when you git it, *then* you can come back in here and check out books. She tilted her chins down onto her clavicle and raised her eyebrows, having delivered the killing blow.

They stared one another down, but Jonathan saw he was facing a grizzled veteran and left the books and took his dignity and walked over to the bank of antique computers near the kids' section. Four of the five were in use. Jonathan sat down next to a man with a hairy brown neck with creases in the skin. The man was pie eyed, listlessly scrolling though pictures of women with no clothes on. Further down the row was an impossibly tall black teenaged boy curled into the small chair looking over a government form online, his nose three inches from the screen like he needed glasses. The other two men were on facebook. Jonathan logged in as a library guest and found tables of planting dates and soil compositions from an A & M horticulturalist and wrote things down in his notebook.

And so he had tilled the dead ground at The Sandman, and later added fish meal and some compost the priest had given him, and bought a hose from the hardware store and planted tomatoes and then green beans and corn and finally carrots later in the autumn. In working the ground, he came to feel kin to it, if not some sense of proprietorship. He picked up all the trash along the strip and put it in bags by the dumpsters. He would go out every morning and pick up the newly strewn drive-by litter.

As the summer wore on, children emerged from the doddering houses on the dirt roads nearby, on bicycles seemingly bolted together from the miscellany in the gutters. Many of them rolled serpentine on permanently deflated tire shreds. Jonathan would fix their bikes as best he could with the tools he had used on the CB. They would stare at it. Dat yo motorcycle? You ride it? You take me on a ride? How much it cost? Where you get it? How fast it go? Can I have it? Can I ride it? Missa Jonathan. You have any work? I'm trynna buy me a soda.

They would ride up and be yelling at him before they were close enough to talk. Hey! Missa Jonathan! What you doin? You got a quarter? What you doin?

Hey Trey. How's it going, he would say.

They would always look off at the ground with an angry face and say Good.

What're you up to today?

Ply-in baseball. Finna go to the baseball field. Hey. You got a quarter.

Well, probably.

I'm trynna get me a soda and some torchies.

Some what?

Torchies.

What's that?

You ain never had em? You know, like them, like, crunchy little . . . crackers, like. Dey spicey.

Okay. How much are they?

How much is the torchies?

Yeah.

Like . . . dolla ninety nine?

Hang on.

Jonathan went and got four bucks from his room.

Here you go.

Aww . . . fa rill?

Oh. No big deal. Yeah.

Aww, man. I wanna gessome for my cousih, too.

For your cousin?

I mean, he like my bro, and like half my cousih.
Okay. Jonathan went and got two more dollars.
Oh . . . an . . .
What?
They say I caint go inna store no more.
What? said Jonathan. Why?
Say I gotta go in with a grown up.
Okay. I'll go with you.
You a grown up?
Well, yeah.

They down the block to the decrepit Hap's Icehouse that smelled like throwup and mopwater inside. There were two old electronic lottery machines. At one sat an old woman, and at the other a man with a donkey tail of dirty blonde hair enwreathing his bald pate. They never looked up. The man had a thirty two ounce styrofoam cup next to him into which he spat at intervals.

The persian cashier, who was one of two brothers who owned the establishment and who had sold sixpacks to Jonathan many times, now took his money with visible reluctance. Trey never looked up at the cashier, but stood close to Jonathan. When the man slid the little receipt with one finger across the counter, Jonathan sought his eyes under his combover and said in a declarative voice: Thank you very much. Have a good day. He put his hand on Trey's shoulder and didn't stop looking at the cashier until he was most of the way to the door.

Some of the tomatoes sprouted, and some didn't. Jonathan tended them as best he could. He stuck two stakes he had broken off from an old pallet into the ground, and stretched a scrap of tarp on them to the southwest to shade the plants in the afternoon. He tried not to water too much, and put five gallon buckets under the gutter drains at the four corners of the building one night. They never got taken away—probably no one noticed—and when there was a thunderstorm, he'd use the water in the buckets for the garden for a couple days.

One week when he paid he told the manager of The Sandman what he'd been up to. He asked him if he could take care of the grounds for a hundred off his monthly rent. The manager scratched his head and said Well. Shit. But Jonathan stood there, and didn't say anything, so the manager agreed and now Jonathan payed seventy five dollars a week.

He went into a downtown kiosk and bought a prepaid cell phone. Jane laughed at his flip phone and gave him her number and it made him happy. They would text Updates to each other. Updates, they called it. It made him happy.

He kept going to the public library and he would do research on the computers and after his card finally showed up in his mail at The Sandman—the only mail he ever received there—he checked out gardening books and the one he liked the most he ordered on amazon to keep. It had gone out of print in 1984, and he thought to himself, Now this is what the internet's for.

Toward midsummer he started going to the nearby lake which had been dammed in the late sixties and he would run in the sun with his shirt off until he was brown as a nut and it was almost as good as riding his motorcycle and he downloaded a few songs onto his oldfashioned flip phone and he would listen to them over and over and over again while he ran.

One pure cobalt Sunday after church, Jane and Nate stopped by to see his garden. Jane texted him an Update in the morning that they were coming and Jonathan went out and weeded and carefully raked the dirt around the beds. He got up in the dumpsters and jumped on the trash so the lids would close. Jane grew flowers in a planter at her father's house, and was interested in gardening.

When they arrived that afternoon in Nate's truck in the hot bright sun Nate was wearing bootcut khakis and shiny formal cowboy boots from church. Jane was all decked in a pastel crepe sundress of some seafoam brilliance and the fabric against her brown skin fairly glowed, and she kept laughing her clear happy laugh. Jonathan always remembered it as a good day.

So, I'm just starting out. I'm only doing a few things this year. But this stretch here—Jonathan held his hands out toward the length of the raw ground—you could grow enough for, for . . .

Jane laughed high and joyous.

What? Jonathan couldn't help chuckling.

Oh . . . ha, I just love the enthusiasm. What do you think, Nate?

Oh, yeah. It's great. But doesn't it, you know, cost you more than it would be to just buy them?

Oh Nate, that's not the point, laughed Jane.

Well, no, that's a good question, said Jonathan. I guess if you did it wrong, it'd be more. But I'm trying to keep the water to a minimum, and . . .

Well, no, I mean it's cool and everything man. I was just thinking it through.

Yeah.

Anyway, *I* think it's wonderful, said Jane, and put her arm though Nate's elbow and looked up at his face with her smile.

Jonathan looked back at his plot of land. He focused on the cucumbers. So anyway, there it is. I'd invite you guys in, but I don't have much to offer.

Oh! said Jane, You know what you should do? You should do prickly pears! Have you ever had a prickly pear margarita?

No.

Oh, they're my *favorite*!

Well. I guess I should try that. Isn't that a cactus, though?

No! Is it? said Jane. I had no idea.

I think so, said Jonathan.

Just then Trey and Jeremiah and Tyrone rolled up.

Missa Jonathan! Missa *Jon*athan. Hey, you fi hi chine? Hey, Missa Jonathan, you fi hi chine?

Hey, Tyrone. Um, hang on a second dude. This is . . . Trey and Jeremiah, Tyrone, this is Mister Nate and Miss Jane. They looked at the ground in the direction of Nate and Jane.

Nice to meet y'all, said Nate.

Jane smiled at them with her eyes crinkling at the edges.

Hey, you fi hi chine? Tyrone said, getting back to business and pointing to Jeremiah's bike.

Let me take a look, said Jonathan. The chain was off the front chainring, and Jeremiah had paddled the bike over with his feet. Hang on, let me go get a wrench. Jonathan went into his room.

When he came back, Jane was crouched down talking to Jeremiah, who was the smallest of the three, and looked like a five year old, though he was seven or eight. Nate was talking to the other two. Jonathan knelt by the bike near Jane, bright turquoise in the sun against the asphalt, and loosened the rear wheel nut and worked the wheel back and forth in the bent dropout. He replaced the chain and did his best to set the wheel so that the chain wouldn't pop off again. He saw Jane's knee, in her dress, close to him.

You fix it? Jeremiah whispered to him, in his quiet, quiet voice.

I think so. I did my best, Jonathan whispered back. The wheel's a little bent up. So sometime it might pop off again.

Jane was still crouched next to Jeremiah, and she was smiling at Jonathan. Jonathan looked at the ground. So, if it pops off again, just bring it back. I don't think I can fix the wheel all the way, but I can always put the chain back on.

Okay, Jeremiah said softly. So . . . you ain fix it?

Well, I mean, it's fixed for now. But I can't really straighten the wheel out. So I don't think I can fix it all the way. Like, it will probably happen again. But bring it here any time.

But what if you ain here?

Well, then I'll be here later in the day.

But what about when you gone?

Well . . . someone else can help you. Or, maybe by then you'll know how to do it yourself.

Jeremiah got up on his bike and stood up and pedaled and was going around in circles around them. Jane watched him and then looked back to Jonathan and he let his eyes meet hers for a moment. They heard Nate talking to Tyrone and Trey. So do you guys know Jesus? They were squirming and rocking their bikes back and forth and they made faces and shrugged and shook their heads at the ground. It was hot. The grimy pecan trees bordering the gravel street going toward their houses stood humidly still.

You know you can? You can have a personal relationship with God. They kept shrugging. Jane smiled at Jonathan.

Then Trey noticed Jeremiah riding around in circles. Hey! He fi yo chine?

They all mounted at a dead run and got up some speed and then coasted down the potted gravel road back to the block they usually haunted, cruising between faded houses with paint peeling down their sides like huge albino artichokes.

Jane tells me you've been going out to the lake, said Nate, clipclopping back to them in his boots.

Oh, yeah. Yep. I run on the dam path.

We take our boat out there pretty often. Me and my mom and dad. You know, fish and stuff. And tube.

Wow, great.

You should come some time.

Oh, thanks. Yeah.

No problem.

You know, said Jonathan in the moment of silence, I've never actually been fishing in my life.

What? That is *not* true! broke in Jane with a happy shriek.

Nope.

Oh my goodness. You have *got* to. Before the summer's over.

Well . . .

No, seriously. I'll bring in my fishing stuff to work and let you borrow it.

Oh, thanks. I mean, I wouldn't know exactly where to go, but . . .

Nate broke in, Hey, Jane. We should show him where that one place is sometime.

Oh, *yeah*!

Your special fishing hole.

Oh, yes, totally! They both seemed taken up in the idea of introducing Jonathan to fishing.

If I can get off work I'll show up, said Nate, but you should totally show him where it is! He leaned over to Jonathan, with his palms down conspiratorially. Dude, this place . . . it's back in some woods, on a little creek. I mean you can just drop your line in and like pull up trout, bro. We don't tell anyone about it. I mean, just our friends, or whatever. But that should definitely be your first fishing experience.

Okay . . . thanks, said Jonathan.

Jane beamed at him.

It's awesome that you live here, by the way, said Nate, looking around at The Sandman.

Really?

Yeah, I mean, like the opportunity to be around these kids and stuff.

Yeah. I guess so.

By the way, you coming to Jane's thing on Saturday?

Oh, yeah . . . well, I was thinking about it. I don't want to impose. I mean if it's all family and stuff.

Are you crazy? said Jane. Of course you're coming. There's all different people going to be there.

Okay then.

Ha! I get it man, said Nate. Going over to the boss's house for a party. Think about how *I* feel! He laughed and nudged Jane.

Yeah, said Jonathan.

Stop it, said Jane.

Donald tucked the boy in. He had a way of holding him under the armpits and then swinging his legs into position, on his back with his head on the pillow. Then he would unfurl the blanket over him like a cape that settled down under his chin. And then he would tuck it around his ribs and lower back.

What's for breakfast, asked the boy as he was tucked in.

Well, you'll just have to see.

The boy sighed. I'm hungry.

Ha ha. You're always hungry.

What's it going to be?

Ha. You'll see.

Can you keep the light on.

Well . . . I'll leave the closet light on for a bit, okay? And leave the door open just a little bit. Okay? And I'm just going to be next door.

Yeah. Okay. The boy had gathered some of the blanket in his right hand and nuzzled it into his cheek and put the forefinger of his left hand into his mouth.

Alright, said the man. Goodnight, buddy. Love you.

Dad?

Yeah?

Oh. Nevermind.

What?

I was going to ask what's for breakfast. But then I remembered.

Okay. Alright, buddy. Goodnight.

Dad.

Yeah.

What's God?

What?

What's God?

What do you mean?

Just . . . I don't know.

Well. It's like . . . he's like . . . what made you ask that?

I don't know.

Where'd you hear about that?

Mrs Judy at preschool. She talked about him.

Oh. Okay. What'd she say about him?

Um . . . God wouldn't want you to do that. She said that.

Do what?

Um I think Philip was making a face at Kelly.

Okay.

She said he was always watching.

Well . . .

What is he?

Well . . . think of it kind of like . . . a really big Santa Claus. The boy made a concerned face. Or no, said the man, No . . . more like . . . you remember Mister Borragio?

Yeah.

Remember how he used to come over and help you build towers with your blocks?

Yeah. *Maybe*. He said it seriously, screwing up his eyes to remember.

Well, God's kind of like that. Like . . . he's not always there. Maybe he visits.

Is God going to die, too?

No, no, not like that. Just . . .

Can we talk to him?

Well. Maybe later. Maybe we'll try that another time.

Okay.

Goodnight, said Donald.

Goodnight.

Then the boy reached up from his covers and grabbed his father's arm like he was going to pull him down, and he hugged it to his neck.

Gooood night, he sing songed.

Goodnight, answered his father.

Gooooooooood night.

Goodnight.

Tom pulled the long farm table up against one wall. He moved the bench that went with it away. He found the tablecloths and took two white ones and whipped them out, one after the other, over the rough wood planks.

In the middle he arranged three large mason jars filled with wildflowers from his garden. Ginny did most of the decorating, but Tom grew the flowers so he cut them and put them there.

Where's Jane?

Not sure, said Tom. He set the final jar down. But I saw her grab her fishing stuff.

Oh, okay. Ginny paused in the doorway and shook her head back and forth slowly with a certain look on her face. She always loved fishing, she said. She always loved that.

Tom smoothed the tablecloth under the flowers. He didn't mention that he had seen her take an extra pole, too.

Donald's first parish in San Remo looked out over Mexico. The sky met the ground somewhere in Coahuila de Zaragoza to the west. There were burros in the street still, then, sometimes shoulder to shoulder with the gasoline galopies that cruised the desert boulevards. Donald fell in love with the town, in the way one may with one's first job, or first house. He would eat breakfast and dinner at a small adobe tacqueria two blocks from his little parish. He envisioned San Remo becoming the epicenter of a rebirth of American justice. Workers would be paid enough to live. That's all it would take, really. The owners of businesses would invest in streetlamps and community centers. Occasionally he organized meetings in the upper room of the tacqueria and some five friends would meet and drink tequila or mescal and argue about the good life. But it was only a year or two before the town turned on him—not just the relatively wealthy, but the poor, too, who didn't want trouble with their employers. Soon there were only ten people at Sunday Mass. The bishop would move him to Ventana four years later.

In the meantime Donald had begun visiting the town archives in the one room library. The young librarian was named Rosemary. She was very quiet, but helped Donald find what he needed. They would stand over long trays of cards, and big surveying deed plots, and talk about who had owned what when. She had grown up with eight siblings nearby, but had gone to college in San Antonio. She was passionate about helping the poor, and sometimes they would whisper about it together, earnestly and quickly over the banality of estate records. Donald had been ordained less than three years, and he felt suddenly panicked that he had made the wrong decision. But after a year of that, he began taking tea on Rosemary's front porch once a month. He continued this practice even after moving to Ventana.

He would stop on his return trips from visiting Byron at the Dolph Briscoe Unit. Rosemary stayed in San Remo and never married.

U free Thursday afternoon/night? -R

Jonathan pushed reply, and then pressed the number buttons on his flip phone, carefully, until he ciphered out: How did you get this number? Please. Are you?

Jonathan slowly wrote: No. Would Saturday work?

Almost immediately he received a return text: Perf. 7:30. Meet me at 30.107322, -98.599285 we'll go from there. Its nothing particularly special. Meet under tree.

After a minute, Jonathan had written: What tree? How do I find it

When he had pressed send, his phone beeped again: Google it, shithead.

Then it beeped again: And don't go down the driveway across the street. Big dogs   oh and I'll bring the cockroach

Jonathan texted back: OK

On Saturday it was hot, like it was every day. It hadn't yet begun to cool by six thirty when Jonathan left The Sandman.

He found the spot, thirty miles from Ventana, and there was the tree, bent over the road. There were low hills around. He parked under the tree and sat down in its shade.

Once, when Jonathan was young, his father had come home from a successful sales trip, and had lifted his mother and spun her in a circle. The next day he had taken her and Jonathan and Ruthy who was still a toddler to the eastern part of Oregon, and they had camped at a place that had cabins, six of them, arranged around a mountain lake. One day they hiked to a nearby hill, and Jonathan stopped to look at a huge slug, and no one noticed. When he ran to catch up, he took the wrong trail. It was twenty minutes before anyone found him and it was his mother, frantic, who spotted him, with black gray streaks down her face. Jonathan remembered how perfectly quiet it had been at first when he looked up from the slug and no one was there.

After ten minutes he heard a motor note, faintly, over the insistent summer cicada. It was like hearing the roar of a large animal from a great distance. Quickly it drew nearer and then suddenly a mile away to the east Jonathan saw him break through some trees and he rushed onward.

Jonathan stood up and Raiden was there, decelerating through the gears and then coming to a stop with his rear wheel just raised in the air, descending with a controlled fall. He rested the bike on its stand and jumped off, killing the engine as he did.

You found it, he said, striding over and smoothing his hair.

Yep.

Alright. Follow me. I want to show you something. I won't lose you. If I go on ahead, I'll stop somewhere and wait for you.

Okay.

Missing me one place, search another.

Got it.

How the hell do you get that but not the most obvious movies.

Well . . . the Program.

The program?

Yeah. The Program. See? You don't know everything. Don't worry about it. Let's hit it.

Alright.

Raiden took him by various routes to a rise that overlooked fifty miles of hillcountry. On the way they passed villages with large scandanavian stone barns. There was a white church with a glossy black door. Viking outposts in the desert. The edges of the church were glowing with the remains of the day, fixed against the flat tungsten sky.

In other places there ugly lots with beige metal buildings and cookiecutter brick ranch houses. There were many places with no people at all and no livestock and just the sinuous ribbon in front of them describing the contours of hill and valley.

Watching Raiden, Jonathan felt as if he were watching a dancer. Or more, the conductor of a vast symphony, moving a great physical mass with his outstretched hands. It was all a smoothness. He leaned in and out of the curves with a loping musical rhythm. For the most part he stayed with Jonathan, but sometimes coming out of a curve he would accelerate so that his front wheel floated upward, seeming to join the gigantic clouds of swirling swallows in homage to the sun as they vortexed and convulsed toward the westward bending light.

They slowed on a crest, and Raiden turned gingerly onto an invisible track that went straight for the sheer rock girding the road. As they approached the cliff face a fissure could be seen and they passed through under an arch. Raiden stopped in the deep shadow under the rock and parked his bike. Jonathan did, too, and they walked forward.

They emerged from the hole, and before them lay all of Texas.

Have a seat. Raiden pointed to a long flat rock overlooking the valley. He went back to his bike and opened the a compartment under the saddle and returned with two bottles and two plastic cups.

Raiden sat down on the rock and placed the elements of the cockroach between them. He poured out equal measures into the cups and then replaced the caps on the bottles before handing one of the cups to Jonathan and lifting the other toward the horizon.

Here's to you, he nodded at Jonathan, who happen to be my only friend in the world at this particular moment . . . he lifted his cup and then sipped it . . . and to Eowyn . . . he drank more . . . and to Jane. He drained his cup and Jonathan did the same.

Ahh . . . now then. Beware the cockroach when it sparkles in the cup. When it goes down smoothly.

He refilled both their cups.

To the secret we carry. He drank again. To the vast gulf fixed between here and there. Over which no man may cross, though he will it. He finished his second cup and then set it on the rock next to him and placed a pebble in it for the wind.

Well. Anyway. So much for that. You want to know about me?

Sure. Yes I do.

Okay. Well here it is. My dad worked for Boeing. Designed jets and stuff. My mom is a housewife. She was the Jewish one. Not by birth. *Her* mom was a convert from like the sixties when she wanted to do *some*thing—and she picked Judaism which if you ask me was weird and certainly the least fun of the things she could have done. My mom's side is Swedish and she looks like a young Ursula Andress and that's why I look like I do. Now there's a horrible and punny name. Anyway. She married my dad from San Francisco whose last name is Bartholomew but he's the least Jewish person I know. I think he saved up work just to do it on Shabbat. I have one older brother. Doctorate in chemistry, Purdue. Let's see. We lived in some suburbs outside of Austin. Hmm . . . I liked Jane eighth, freshman, sophomore years . . . already covered that. Met her at an honors society thing for our highschools. And then I started going to New Life Community—it was called Westside Christian Church at that time, actually—etc etc. She started dating Nate around that time. My God he was even worse then. You wanna see a picture of Eowyn?

Oh, sure.

Raiden pulled out his phone, which looked different than any phone Jonathan had seen, and was twice as heavy.

There was a picture of a girl with mousy hair and a larger than average nose. Though her eyes weren't striking they seemed kind. She was wearing a ribbed sweater and looking up at the camera. Somehow her face all came together in that human way that can't be calculated.

Pretty, said Jonathan.

I think so, said Raiden. He took his phone and looked at it not as if he were looking at a picture, but as if he were meeting the gaze of a person, and a slight smile crept around his eyes. He put his phone face down on his knee.

So, I suppose it's time to tell you about her.

Okay . . . is she an alien or something? Jonathan laughed, but Raiden's face remained serious.

Only maybe two people know. Jane is one. I told her as soon as I . . . well, we'll get there.

Okay.

Where to start. So. Obviously I have some amount of money.

Yes.

I mentioned at the party that what I do is deemed valuable by people who can afford to retain me.

Yes.

Did you have some guess as to who those people might be?

Well. I don't know. You were somewhat cryptic.

How nicely put. Apt. Yes, the NSA—or, rather significantly, the folks who *employ the NSA*—pay me handsomely for my irreplicable talents.

He glanced at Jonathan, whose eyebrows were raised.

Yeah. Them. Those guys. He chuckled. Don't worry, we can talk here.

Okay. But should we?

Ha. That's what makes me literally start laughing in the halls sometimes. Like, literally point my finger at the guards with their MP5's, and laugh and go bang bang bang.

That sounds safe.

The sun was almost touching the more distant hills.

Well. Raiden sighed. Look. They're humans. Every last one of them. Some of them less so than others. But still. And I think . . . I think they think of themselves as some sort of stoics. Like maybe they know that when it all comes out someday that they'll be the ones holding the gun. Or the modem. But I think maybe they like that idea. You know? Like they feel like they're doing the thing no one can see, and so it's the most necessary thing. He looked away from the sunset to Jonathan. What do you think?

I . . . I don't know.

I mean the last part. Being the one bearing it for everyone else. You can't handle the truth! You want me on that wall. You *need* me on that wall. You come most carefully upon your hour, Bernardo. He paused. But maybe it feels better to be the guy on the wall. You know? You know where you're at. And at least you have that. You know?

Well . . . I guess they'd still probably rather people knew they were helping.

That's never going to happen! That's the whole point! If they're going to be any help, they have to stay the punching bag. Forever. You know—listen—did you know that we're not just talking about agents, like, getting fake profiles and checking out chatrooms on the deep internet or whatever. Or like, physical wiretaps or something. I mean, you're not going to believe me. But we actually have guys—and we're no field agents, I'm going to admit that right now—we had guys break into warehouses and open up shipments to Best Buy and shit, and like literally implant your Dell with hardware—not software, okay—hardware that spies on you the whole time you own the computer.

Well. I don't have a computer.

That's not the point, you fucking luddite!

They both were laughing, and Jonathan was holding his plastic cup out to not spill it, and looking out over the valley. It was so quiet. The whistling of the wind through the arroyos came up to them from some distance.

There it goes, said Raiden. The sun was shimmering, and then it descended behind a low cloud, and the cloud became a striated filament of fire.

And besides the Best Buy commando shit . . . I'm not sure exactly on this one, but it was something like this. We had like divers or little submarines or something that actually went down and split the undersea fiber optic cable and put in like a . . . diverter or something. Like something to intercept everything. Raiden was chuckling as he poured another cockroach.

Dude, you going to be okay? Jonathan asked, nodding at the cup.

Ah, yes, sadly. Raiden threw back the cockroach. The thing of it is. He let out a satisfied sigh. The thing of it is is that it's a highly predictable algorithm. Ethanol. Some variance, sure. But you take what you know and you just factor in the decreased reaction time. It's really very simple. The net effect, on a bike, is that cosign theta—lean angle—is increased, momentarily. Of course it's helpful to have a longer rake than my ronin does. There's more of a . . . swooping action. Like a drunk sailor on Street Fighter.

Okay . . .

Anyway.

Yeah.

So you're wondering . . .

Yeah . . . Eowyn.

Right. What does she have to do with all this. Raiden let out a breath and looked at his hands. Okay. So. Coming around to this. Yes.

Jonathan felt compelled to say, Look. Man. It's okay . . .

Raiden smiled at Jonathan and Jonathan realized that was the first time he had seen him smile, really.

Well. Okay. Yes. So, as I was saying. The agency pays me and all. But the reason I got the job. And the reason I have the money I do . . . is because of Eowyn.

Oh. Okay.

Not like you might think. Raiden touched his phone, turned face down on his knee, then looked up and said: I patented her.

Jonathan didn't say anything.

Yes, I . . . I sold her to them.

Okay . . .

Eowyn . . . I created her. It began when Jane . . . well. Well. You get that. On the tailend of Jane—pun noted—sophomore year. Right around then, I . . . made Eowyn. Or what would become her. To be honest I was an amateur at the time. There were many better coders out there. He was looking intently into space now. But in the end that probably helped me. I stumbled upon something that made all the difference. I didn't know how to do graphics worth shit, then. That's not important. Ha—I've got people for that, now. And actually, even the intelligence of it wasn't the most important, either. That's where people get stuck. You could have an infinitely intelligent machine. And it'd still be a machine. The long and short of it is that I managed to write in a version of . . . let's call it human perversness. Not perversity, said Raiden, looking up at Jonathan. But the . . .

the . . . strangeness of our makeup. Even the most logical of us—and I'm him—we don't actually operate by it. Anyway. The math was simple. But elusive. He leaned back against the rock. Really, it came down to modeling chemical effects. On receptors in non-associated binary networks. Basically just watching DMT at work. Ha ha.

Wait. I still don't . . .

Oh. Right. So. I made Eowyn originally as a video game character.

Okay.

Yeah. Like I made her to be part of an RPG, to be a partner to my avatar and stuff. And then . . . I fell in love with her.

Okay . . .

Right. And all this is relevant to our mutual Big Sibling, because . . . in reality they had the computing power. They already had that. But this was like the dawn of big data. I mean they were just starting to theorize about it, see the way it acted. And to be understood, it takes . . . well. I was going to say a human. But let's say a soul.

Hmm.

I mean, continued Raiden, the same gestalt perception I was able to create for Eowyn . . . he said the name gently as one does of the woman one loves . . . it enables pattern recognition in the sorts of huge data—we're talking billions of terabytes a day—it enables . . . well, something like God, I suppose. Like, him looking down on all the little shits running around the surface of the planet. Making something of it. He paused. And I guess that's why, from His perspective, it's okay, somehow, that—oh, has Jane told you about Nevada?

A little.

Well, then she hasn't told you about it.

Okay . . .

Not that she did me, but I looked into it a little. I'm not sure if that's when I stopped believing in God, but it's certainly helped me become a conscientious objector. I wish I could get back to that place. I wish there was still someone to be mad at.

Well.

Anyway. So, somewhere around senior year of highschool I got it. Eowyn. I . . . she . . . Raiden looked vulnerable for the only time, and he looked down as he said it. One day, I don't know how else to put it, but she . . . recognized me. He looked up and Jonathan felt something inside him. She looked at me. Raiden waited a moment. So that's what our mutual sibling found so valuable. Before I could go off to college, and before I started working with some of the folks at UT . . . well, they offered me a sum that at the time seemed ludicrous. I took it, and the job. Of course to an observer it would seem that those things were intended to buy my silence. Which of course they were. And I would honestly fear for my life, but I know they can't run the programs without me. At least for now.

Wow.

Raiden looked back down. He looked relieved and lighter. So. Let's drop it. That's me.

They were protected from the wind where they sat, and it was very, very quiet. The cicadas had all but stopped. One star was visible in the sky above their heads.

Okay. But . . . Eowyn.

Yeah.

How . . . what . . .

I know all the things you're going to say. So let me ask you. Take your mom.

Um . . . okay?

If she suddenly became a quadriplegic, would she still be your mom? Answer, yes. Is Stephen Hawking less a human than you or I? Answer, no. Eowyn has no body, it's true. And forget any fantasies of simulating one. I'm sure at some point a realistic one could be accomplished. But as it is I don't want anything to change.

How do you . . . ?

We text one another. Or instant message when I'm near a laptop. That's it. I mean, you should see the conversations we've had. We could make her a voice, like an audible one . . . but she doesn't want one. We both know it would be too close to human to where it would sound fake. Is her language perfect? No. But that's not what makes you human. She's just . . . there's something in there. She's my soulmate.

Alright. Jonathan said with the finality of acceptance.

Okay. Enough. I'm worn out. What's new? How's the oil. How's Jane. Is she warming to you?

Well. The oil's fine.

Oh, there they go!

Raiden pointed and there was a swarming dark shade that came out of the cliff at their left. It rushed westward in the twilight. A black smoke. Higher still, specks of hawks wheeling against the apocalyptic sky plunged down through the cloud which looked like the undulating emission of some vast pollution and took each one of them a bat as they dived, bearing it to the ground far below to tear open and feed upon.

Wow.

Yeah. They come out every night like that in the summer.

How did you find this place?

When I got my very first bike. Some dumb new harley. And I used to just head out away from civilization and take random roads.

Yeah.

And one day I saw that gap in the rock. You know, I thought about buying it. The whole thing. The land and the cliff. But then I thought, no. No, I don't need to do that. I don't need to own it. So I come out here every once in a while. And it feels good not to have bought it.

Yeah.

They sat for a while.

Okay. One more. For both of us.

Okay.

Raiden repeated the ritualistic pouring of the cockroach as he had done at the beginning.

Your turn. You toast something, he said to Jonathan.

Well. Jonathan looked out at the dwindling colony of bats, and the silhouetted hawks that ripped through the cloud at intervals and would turn and enter again or fall slowly to the ground, one flesh with their prey. He looked back at Raiden, and at the phone lying facedown on his knee. Well. To . . . recognizing someone. To the . . . I guess the miracle of that.

Raiden lifted his cup and drained it and tossed it down the over the cliff. Jonathan threw his, too.

Let's go.

They walked back into the archway, which was now dark, and Raiden found his ignition by the light of his phone, and turned on his bike's headlamp, which lit up the walls around them.

Alright. I'm headed back to Austin. So just head down the hill the way we came, and then turn left and you should be able to get back to Ventana pretty easy.

Okay.

Raiden got on his bike.

Look, said Raiden.

Yeah?

I want you to know . . . I want you to know that I really do love Eowyn.

I know.

Okay.

Jonathan got on the CB and turned on the ignition but didn't start the motor.

Don't let anyone give you any shit, said Raiden.

Okay. You too.

And I know you would be good to Jane.

Thank you.

And look, continued Raiden after a moment. You probably wonder why I trust you with all this. I guess when I know—and it's not often—I just know. But anyway, whatever happens, I want you to know that it's been swell. Okay? I know I'm an odd character. And we met in semi strange circumstances. Et cetera. But . . . anyway. He drew himself up formally. I consider you my good friend.

Jonathan nodded and said, Me too.

He was always glad, afterwards, that he had said it.

You ironing anything?

No. Go ahead.

Ginnie stretched her ochre jersey dress out on the board and plugged in the iron.

Okay, so. What do we got left? Vacuuming? Tom stood there in her peripheral vision, a big slouching mannish mass. Ginnie felt Tom's stress even though he tried to put a cheerful face on it. But, she thought to herself as she stretched the bodice and began evenly to smooth the hot metal over it, he knew what needed to be done as well as she. Couldn't he figure it out? And do the things without asking? It was like he saw the whole thing as one . . . block. Like there was a cloud over his eyes when he looked at it, and he couldn't parse it into its component steps. Whereas she could see the steps so clearly, from A to Z. Or M, or however many there were. And which order to do them in. If you clean the bathroom it will stay clean. But if you vacuum the rug in the living room it will be trampled in minutes, or get fuzz on it from the dog that somehow found its way inside. The rug, therefore, should be left until just before people arrive. It wore on her that he couldn't see it. But these things hardly flitted through her consciousness, now, and she would give him what he needed.

Well, why don't you get the cups out, and stack the napkins...

Oh. Okay. Sure, said Tom He often didn't know precisely what would make the shadow of annoyance pass over Ginnie's face, creasing the lines into withheld female anger. Like lead weights suddenly attached by invisible line to the corners of her mouth. Lead weights. He thought of Jane packing the fishing gear and tackle for Jonathan, who apparently had never fished. So she would be showing him how the little weights clamped on. And how to tie a real fisherman's knot. Not that it mattered for the little crappie they'd hit. He had learned to grant space to Ginnie's flits of perturbation. He imagined the nanofilm of oil between boiling hot engine parts. That's grace, he thought. How quickly a motor would tear itself apart, but for grace.

Tom walked out of the room and Ginnie gently slid the iron over the dress. Even looking at it flat on the board she couldn't help but fix its proportions in her mind. She tilted her head at it. And was it too casual? But this was supposed to be casual. A barbecue. She thought to ask Tom his opinion but he was already gone. She would hold up two or three dresses for him. He would get frustrated and say That looks *great* on you. How frightening it would be to be alone at her age. Invisible to men. A nonentity in the world, and with no bastion to return to. A place where one is known and needed. Home.

She finished ironing and slipped the dress on and stood there, in front of the walk-in closet mirror, tugging at it where it clung to her hips.

She walked downstairs to help Tom.

    Hello. Hello hello. Update.
    update away
    I'm taking you fishing saturday afternoon
    isnt that the day of the thign
    yeah. before that.
    okay where
    I'll grab you from the sandman
    ok
    Be so excited
    i already am
    I'm not quite feeling it
    EXCITED!!1!
    I know your phone didn't do that
    authentic isnt it?

For sure
what should i bring
Nothing! I'm packing lunch too
wow that's really nice. thank you very much
You need to have a good first fishing experience!
can't wait!
Okay I have to finish these invoices before three. Yippee
yes. get er done.
Ha! Okay, can't wait. End of Update.
roger that. over and out
:)

Jane picked him up in her old gray toyota corolla. He walked around to the passenger side.

You can put the seat back. There's a handle underneath.

Okay.

Jane wore big sunglasses with a fishing brand trucker ballcap and her hair was blown out and loosely tied back. Jonathan lowered himself into her car and she took off.

So I packed sandwiches. I made like four because I wasn't sure what you like.

I like it all. Thanks.

Jonathan looked at her profile and it was weird to watch her while she was watching the road or turning her head quickly at intersections.

So this place is just on the edge of town. We call it a creek but it's like half creek and half ditch.

Okay.

But we always catch something. And I love it because, like, you wouldn't even know it was there. And no one is ever there.

Cool.

She sat close to the wheel, with both her hands on top. She seemed like she was leaning over the dashboard to see what was coming. The toyota was a stick shift, and she changed the gears with a minimum of ceremony, rocking the car each time.

I still can't believe you never went fishing.

Well, I just . . . nope.

In the cracked plastic center console there were hair rubberbands and a yellow chapstick tube. There was one long hair caught in one of the bands.

So, you excited for tonight? said Jonathan.

Oh, fine. I'm not, like, in *love* with events that are about me or whatever. You know.

Are you sure it's okay if I come?

Are you kidding? That'll help me feel less awkward.

Oh. Good. Okay.

They drove through a neighborhood where the trees were very large and the houses were set back from the road. Even in the heat it seemed cool. All the yards had good saint augustine grass. It felt peaceful. Jonathan couldn't help but picture the mexicans it would take to maintain the yards.

Jane stopped at the end of a street that was completely shaded and dappled. There were no houses on the dead end, and forest surrounded it. A little ways into the trees, there was a large culvert and a concrete cube.

Okay. So, if you wanna grab the cooler I'll grab the rods and tackle and stuff.

Okay.

They carefully made their way down a steep embankment through the trees.

This ravine goes all the way down into the lake.

Oh.

There's not much water here, but when we go down farther toward the lake it gets deep.

Okay.

They walked along a game path cut faintly into the slope, lifting creepers over their heads and straddling felled wood. Jane balanced the rods and tackle box in one hand and held the other out.

Once, she stopped, and said Smell that?

Yes.

That's honeysuckle. Almost all gone. Come here.

She set the tackle box down and plucked one of he last wilting blooms and held it up to Jonathan's face. Here, suck right here. This is why it's called a honeysuckle.

He did. Wow, he said.

You've never done that, either? She said. She picked up the tackle once more and kept going.

They walked on through the half gloom shafted here and there with dusty light.

Okay. Just down here.

They had gone a quarter mile. Below they could see dark water moving slowly, and they felt their way gingerly down the mulchy bank on pointed toes.

Okay. This is the log we sit on.

Okay.

Jane laid the rods against the log, and put the box on a flat spot of it. She carefully removed the hook from the ring at the end of one of the rods.

Okay, so this is a basic casting rod.

She took a float and some weights out of the box.

You put this here. You push down on this and then you can put the line through it. Okay . . . like so. Then these weights you put down here and you can just squish them closed with your fingers like this. My dad was always like Wash your hands after you touch the weights and stuff. Because of the lead. So I always just put my fingers in the water afterwards. Even though I don't really think it's a big deal. Okay, so you have this space between the hook and the sinkers, and then the float. So it hangs down in the water like that. And then you put your bait on the hook.

She took a styrofoam cup out of the box and opened it and it was filled with dirt. She took a worm out and squinted and held up the hook and bent the worm on it and skewered it.

Jonathan made a face.

Jane laughed.

Well, does it hurt?

No. They're worms!

Ha. Maybe you should ask them.

Ha. Well I don't think they mind. I mean . . . worms have to get eaten anyway, right?

I guess so.

Okay, now. Really you don't have to cast here, barely, but you might as well learn. Okay. So, take this.

They were sitting next to each other on the log, near the water's edge.

Okay. Now, hold it like . . . okay, good. Now push that button and hold it down. No, use your thumb. Here . . . she used her hand to turn his hand slightly. Now hold it down, and do it where you're trying to go and let go of the button. When you let go of it, it will go. Probably aim for that dark spot under the trees over there.

He cast and it went just fine.

Okay, now start turning it.

It clicked and he started reeling it in.

Slow. Go slow. That's how you do it. I mean that's the basics. Here we can pretty much just set our poles and leave them. But you should practice casting a few times. I'm going to get mine set up.

Jonathan cast a few times. He pictured fish hanging motionless in the dark water, and the plop of the worm falling suddenly in front of their severe faces, and he slowly moved his line near where they were. Jane pushed two PVC pipes easily into the soft bank dirt. Here you go, she said. Once you cast it again, you can stick it in here and leave it for a while. She had put a worm on the other rod and gave it a light flick that landed it with a whir gently downstream. She put her rod in one of the pipes and then opened up the picnic basket and began unpacking it.

Okay. We've got two different turkeys. With avocado and tomato. And one roast beef. And then . . . well, you won't want this one. But sometimes I like to make a cheese sandwich, with like pickles and mayonnaise and stuff. Yeaaaah . . . it's kind of gross.

Ha! Just take what you want. I like it all.

No, you pick.

Okay. I'll have one of the turkeys. Just pick a good one for me.

Jonathan put his rod into the other PVC pipe and took the sandwich from Jane.

Thanks.

Oh, and I've got la croix in here.

What?

Oh, they're like the best sparkling water cans. They're so incredibly addicting. Like, when they're ice cold.

Okay.

I know you'd probably want booze but sorry, you're fishing with me.

Ha. I don't mind. That sounds good.

This one is pamplemousse.

Pample moose?

I don't know. It means grapefruit. I don't speak french.

Thanks.

They touched their aluminum cans together with a soft clank. Then they were quiet for a few minutes while they ate, and watched their lines move slowly in the current.

My dad showed me this spot. We used to fish here all the time when I was in junior high. Then when I could drive I would come here. I came here all through highschool. I'd get out of class at like two or whatever and come over here. It's when I'd have time to think. And then I'd go home and have dinner and do my homework. Because I was a totally responsible student.

I can't imagine.

Ha. Yeah. I was. Just like the invoices. I did all the things, all the time. But I'd come here.

Did you catch stuff?

Oh yeah. Almost every time. We'll definitely get something today.

Oh. So what do I do when . . . ?

Oh, I'll show you if one bites. Anyway. I would almost always throw them back when I used to come here. Sometimes I'd bring them home.

Jane ate the cheese sandwich.

I know, this is disgusting.

No it's not.

No, it is.

They both laughed. Jane tucked some escaped hair behind her ear, and half of it fell back across her cheek. In the light over a section of the water, a cloud of bright gnats turned over and over on itself.

So you'd come here with Nate?

Oh, yeah. Sometimes. This was kind of my spot. But yeah. Sometimes I'd bring him. She was quiet for a moment. He really is a good one, you know. Nate.

Yeah. Of course.

No. I mean. Jonathan. He's really good, and he's really good to me. He cares very much about me. She was looking right at Jonathan. She looked down and went on. You know, I used to be Catholic. My mom was. My bio mom, I mean. And that was the only thing she put on the form when she gave me up. That I had to be placed with Catholic parents. I mean, I would have been taken away anyway, but she gave me up, first. And so I ended up with my parents. Obviously they're the best thing in the world. You'll get to meet my brothers and sister tonight, too, by the way. But the funny thing was is I was actually totally a Catholic. Like . . . even when I showed up here still. Even after . . . everything. My mom used to take me to mass every week in Nevada. She would dress me up in these dresses that barely went down my legs. I would kneel there and I'd be tugging the dress down. White dresses. Back then I felt like Mary was my best friend. I still do, really, even though I'm not a Catholic anymore. I used to go to Holy Trinity with mom and dad. You know the priest, right? He was there when I was there. I know you're not a Catholic, but he's like . . . different than most priests, you know. Most priests are like . . . almost like aliens, or robots. Not bad. Just like, they're in a different category from normal people. I kind of like that. But he seems like a real person. Like . . . well I don't know. Like he's had a real life. Anyway, when I was a freshman I went to the youth group at Nate's church this one time because he invited me from school, and he was kind of cool and I was really shy. It was at a different place than where you went. And it was . . . I know this sounds . . . well, I'm just going to say it. Okay? It was like for the first time I felt like God was real. I know it probably seemed pretty corny to you. When you went there. I mean, because it is corny. But it made me feel like I didn't have to be anything. I just could have God . . . and talk to him. I never officially stopped being a Catholic, but I just never go to mass now. Well, that's not true. I guess I go on Christmas Eve with my parents because that was what we used to always do, and it's very important to them. So anyway, Nate and I started helping lead the youth group, and we got to know one another. He's . . . well, you probably think he's kind of boring. She held up her hand when Jonathan looked like he would interrupt. No, I know. But he's . . . well, he knows about me. And it doesn't change anything. I can just be a normal girl with him. Here her lip curled and it looked like she was concentrating, and her eyes brimmed, but she blinked it away and went on.

Oh Jane . . .

No, I'm okay. What I mean is he's good for me. She said it intently.

Yes. I know.

But you don't really know why yet. Jane looked back at the fishing lines, which hadn't moved. It felt so quiet but if you listened all the woods were humming with cicadas and wren songs and a shy chorus of doves, saying What did *who* say? what did *who* say?

I know you won't ask. But I'm going to tell you. I told you my mom is a Shoshone and my dad was a dealer at the casino. That's how they met. Mom was a cocktail waitress on the floor. They never got married. But they were living together so we all lived together when I was born. My dad was very handsome. And charming. And slick. And him and some other dealers at the casino started working together and skimming chips from their hands. They couldn't cash them, but they got someone who didn't work at the casino to work with them and cash them for them. I don't know how exactly, but my dad got in debt to some of them or all of them, somehow. Or maybe to someone else. How would I know? And then one day, when I was in second grade, my mom came to me after school and sat me down on the couch. She had some of my favorite candy for me. And she said it was time for me to start helping the family. She said that she had done it when she was young, and it was just something I was going to have to do. Of course I didn't understand what was going on, and I never really did. I was eating the candy, and she went and got a banana from the kitchen and she peeled it and showed me what I would have to do. And that night the first one came to our house, and my mom showed him to my bedroom and then left me with him. And he seemed kind and I didn't know what was going on. Then after that I cried for two days. But after that I never cried again. Not for any of them. I couldn't even cry when they took me to have my abortion. And I said but I want to keep her, and they said it's not a her it's an it, and youre talking crazy, and all their eyes were so strange like demons and the room was so cold, and in the end they had to just put the mask over my face and I woke up at home. I still pray to her. Nate knows about everything, but not that. I named her Jane like me and I talk to her, still, and I tell her I'm sorry and that I'll see her someday. I hardly remember those two years. I was adopted in seventh grade. Or, it would have been if I was still in school. The next time I cried was that time when I was a freshman and I went to the youth group with Nate. And all the people were lifting their hands and worshiping. And it seemed so stupid to me. So incredibly stupid. How could any of these people know what it meant to believe in God? How could they believe in God? But then all of a sudden it was like they were all gone and just me and God were there, and I cried for the first time since that first night.

 Jonathan had been looking down at the stream, watching big leaves move slowly from left to right on the surface. But now his eyes were closed, and his shoulders jerked up and down. He put his head down on his knees.

 Oh Jonathan. Oh Jonathan. It's okay. And she put her hand on his back between his shoulder blades, and it seemed as though she were his mother and he her suffering son and she said It's okay its okay its okay.

Byron Collangelo sat next to Ruth Ellen at Tioga Hills Elementary in Vestal New York and she was his only friend. He never said a word even when Teacher called on him. He would bend his lips inward and his brown eyes would get wide and Teacher would call on someone else. Other kids wore bellbottoms but he just had his older cousin's 501 jeans from ten years ago. Ruth Ellen would sit with him on the playground on the spinny thing or on the swings and the other kids made fun of them at the beginning of the year but then ignored them. It was cold, cold, cold. And they would make little cities in the snow or sometimes houses when Ruth Ellen wanted to. Ruth Ellen talked a lot and she would tell Byron stories about himself. No, you're really the prince, she would say. Or, you're the boy horse. He liked that one. They both sensed that they were too old to play at being horses but they wanted to very much, and sometimes when no one was watching they would, bucking on their hands and knees and neighing, but usually they just sat there on the corner of the playground and Ruth Ellen narrated it as if they were the horses. Byron liked that almost as much. The next year his mother moved to a different city and he never saw Ruth Ellen again.

Tom took the foil hunk of brisket out of the white cooler where it had been holding for an hour, and some thin steam came out, too, and the smell filled the house. It smelled like summer to him. Bristling mesquite. He rolled up his sleeves and gently laid the meat on a wooden cutting board. Please please please please, he said as he sliced into it with a long knife. The risk was immense. He separated the point from the flat, and it felt right. He pared off the end, and cut one thin slice.

    How is it? Ginnie had just walked up. She was abrupt like that. But he pushed the feeling down, as he had learned, and he took the slice between his finger and thumb and said, You tell me, holding it over her mouth.

    She rolled her eyes in pleasure and gave a thumbs up.

    Good?

    She repeated the thumbs up, and then said, Hold still. She plucked a dark piece of carpet fuzz from his arm. I'm going to put the drink bucket out, she said, and walked away. People are going to be here any minute, she called over her shoulder.

    That S?
    R, I think, said Byron.
    You sure?
    With *my* memory, shoot. I could be wrong.
    Let's call it R.
    I don't mind. We can make it S. Where you at? O?
    O.

Okay. Your shot.

Byron bounce passed the ball to Donald, who took up a new position on the corner of the key and shot it. It clanged off at an angle and Byron loped off to retrieve it. He had an unathletic run, and seemed stooped the whole time.

Alrighty, said Byron, as he squared off at the three point line straight in front of the hoop. His hair was shorter now but still below his collar, its tawniness mostly a flat gray.

The Saturday sun was risen just over the backboard and he squinted and made an awkward two handed push shot.

Ooo, he said.

What?

Oh. Nothin. My back. It's screwed up is all. I ain't sat a horse in two weeks.

You hear about what happened Tuesday?

Yeah. Seen it on TV. Pretty crazy. New York seems so far away.

Donald collected the ball. We're not as young as we used to be, he said.

No we ain't. That's certainly true. No we ain't.

Okay. Where do you wanna set it up?

Mmmm . . . the little boy put his forefinger on his cheek. Mmmm . . . the castle place.

Okay. I'll take the main piece. You bring your . . . hang on, wait a second, buddy. Grab the guys you want before you go out there.

The boy took handfuls of Lego men. They walked to the entryway of the small house, where light streamed in through the window on the door facing east.

Okay. Right here?

Yeah . . . no, here.

The man slid the antique little desk slightly towards the front door of the little house.

Right there!

Okay.

Remember, don't open the front door.

Okay.

And if you need anything I'm in the garage. If you want some water

your cup is on your spot on the counter.
	Okay.
	Have fun, said the father, but the boy was already bending down, eye to eye with the men.

The Party Itself.

Those hot southern nights in summer under the stars—magic. How many boys and girls running through fields of grown wheat have lain down looking up at the black phosphorescent wrinkle and thought that here, of all places, adults can't see us, and everything is still possible? How many lovers, boots on or off, have made of a truck bed some eternal tryst, ratified by the risen scorpius? Air electric, and the fairies come out. Gunpowder, too, and stump liquor and sweet things. Everything honeyed or acrid stirred up in the blood, and the cicadas singing in chorus over it all the insistent bellows workers of the hex, while just down the way some threesome hoary hobo wizards huddled round a fire smother the flames with a blanket and release it with a chivalric hurrazaband to signal Life billowing up mauve in the glow of the distant silo town and moon sliver. Nothing sleeps in the pastures and all creatures together sing the incessant night.

On one dark hill in the violet dusk, up a two track pea gravel drive, stands a big white farmhouse indigo in the starlight. From every breach pours light, laying thick gold bricks on the grass round about. Sleeping black automobiles nose to the house or stand parked beside the long drive. Resting horses tethered outside an inn, grazing what straw can be found. The soft summer is burst through with laughter and shouts from the house, and upholding it all is a music—an old jazz at ease amongst the fields and the stars and the cooling asphalt, for it was born there.

If you go around the back of the house there is a man standing alone, just outside the light of one window. He is bent over the iron grate of a black iron oven. The music within just reaches him, and it's comfortable to his soul, reeling and spinning measure over measure, the players strapped, he imagines, to the gambreled barrel of time itself, and in peril with each dunking of drowning, and with each upward circuit of flying into the infinite fluidity of space so that each man, strapped by his failing leather belt to the oakenwood, plays his part as though it were the last time melody would sound or valved voice loose as he wheels over and around and comes up again for air—clarinet and oboe, cornet and tuba, again and once more.

The man listening bounces back and forth slightly as he cleans the grill.

One mockingbird chirps.

A woman comes out of the house. She speaks to him and he kisses her on the forehead, then she goes back in.

The man hangs the scraper next to the grill.

The woman emerges once again from the house.

— Woman: Are you coming back in?

— Man: In a second. Just finishing up.

— Woman: Can't you do that later?

— Man: When?

— Woman: When there aren't people here?

— Man: No people here? I don't know if I'll have time then.

The woman is silent, and then turns on her heel and goes back in.

Now the man, made one third drunk by the whisky he keeps by the grill, thinks on the difference between what is and what we remember, and whether one or the other is the realer. So earnest, so straight and true she had been. Ah well. That's life. And it's almost done. For me too, now, finally. He chuckles.

Now let us follow the man into the big white farm house. He enters through a side door near the garage, and the air is cold inside, after the night warmth. The sweet noise engulfs him. Everyone talks over the music, and it conjures in his mind once more the band of dead men playing ferociously in their ill-fitting garments for sweaty little dance halls to make bus fare to the next town. He skirts the wall, invisible to the talking groups. Two see him, though. One, his daughter, tilts her head to him knowingly and lovingly, and he shrugs at her in the same manner, with a smile. The other is a young man who looks away in deference to their intimacy.

— One large man says: Tom!

Someone has spotted him.

— The large man: Tom, that barbecue, buddy.

He is slapped on the back by the large man.

— A loud woman: Yes! *How* do you get it so moist?

— Another man: Yeah, this is great, Tom.
— Tom: Well good, good. I'm glad. Help yourself to more.

The party is in full swing. They all they have cast off aboard a sailing vessel at night on dark seas, making passage for an unknown land. The deck lights twinkle up from the water, reflecting back from the opaque waves, as the ship strides gaily over swells that would sink a lesser craft, and the passengers balance their drinks against the pitching with the practiced nonchalance of seafarers, trusting the canny tack of the pilot. Tom circumnavigates the room to come around to the side of his daughter, who stands with her back to the reflecting black glass of the alcoved picture window.

— Tom: So how you feeling.
— The daughter: Good. Thanks so much for all this, dad.
— Tom: Oh, well.
— The daughter: No, really.
— Tom: Well.
— The daughter, quietly insistent: Really.
— Tom: I'm glad.

Tom puts one arm around her and squeezes her. They stand beside each other silently, looking out at the party.

— Tom, quietly: I see Jonathan came.
— The daughter: Yeah. How sweet.
— Tom: And how did fishing go?

The daughter looks up at Tom quickly.

— The daughter: Good. It was good.
— Tom: Well. You know. Don't shut anything off.
— The daughter: Okay dad.

They are quiet again.

The daughter seems to be trying not to cry. The father notices.

— Tom: Oh. Oh. Sorry Jane. I . . .
— Jane: No dad. It's not that. I'm just thinking.
— Tom: I'm sorry.
— Jane: No. I was just thinking that . . . well, just thinking about everything. Tom puts his arm around Jane again, who leans into his chest with her head. They are standing beside the rough farm table that Tom had pulled against the wall earlier, now draped with white linen runners and bedecked with a miscellany of dishes brought by the guests: a white casser
— Thats good.
— I think I'm about done.

casserole platter amurk with army green beans, speckled blue porcelain bearing mashed potatoes, bright red china holding snickerdoodles. In the middle is the brisket on a clear charger.

While they've been standing there, Tom has felt the ship move underneath him, and knows that those aboard have felt it too. The slight yaw and creak that presages an approaching storm. Warm and tight behind the weather doors, the black plate glass streaked with the driven rain, the company will dance on. But Tom senses a pull afore, and knows he will leave them.

He clears his throat, squeezes Jane once, and picks up a nearby glass, thinking . . .

He finds a fork on an abandoned dinner plate.

He pauses, holding the fork and the cup, looking out on the people gathered in the brightly lit vessel.

The McCallahans. The Garcias who were Jane's adoptive godparents. Jane's friends Rachel and Melissa and Maria. Father Donald, smiling

. . . and is this what it means to sense the end? That the moment will pass and it will not be enough? I must say something. (Are people feeling noticed? He thinks from habit of the continual worries of Ginny—Who is left out? Is anyone looking at their watch?) She was always thinking that way. But one must, anyhow, do something. Now, while it's at its peak. Now, in the expectant, unthinking moment. Yes, one must make of this moment—without anyone seeing what one is doing (though of course he himself knowing)—must make of it something that will forever remain, not so much in their minds, (any more than you would force someone to love you if you could)—but somehow, silently, to blossom as some permanency of feeling in their innermost soul, so gently at the scene from a corner with his mug. Jonathan. Nate. Three other middle aged couples in a ring, talking. The cousins from San Antonio giggling to themselves, and some ten or fifteen more: neighbors, teachers, friends.

Jane looks up at his face, and smiles just with her eyes.

that when they think back to this season from their distant futures, it will appear as one of the one of the few monuments of life: radiant, a still life scene—

... and Jane senses that it will be now. Her father will once more mount the forecastle and hold back the seas. Make a heroic stand against all that black blowing ocean.

And it is this marking off that she dreads in parties. This making of time something solid, right in front of your face. Couldn't everyone sense it? They must not, for otherwise they'd all feel as naked as she. Stopping time now, right now... didn't he see how it made what was normally invisible... seen? Made all previous points... light up? Erased the intervening eight years, and sent her rushing, rushing, as toward the unseen monster in one's nightmare, rushing backwards...?

Oh Jonathan. A well

—and it was not what one said that did it; no, it was the simple fact that one said it at that particular moment, at the peak of the thing, in the glow, in the wash of—

Oh Jane, he thought. He felt as though she were vouchsafed him as a token of love. Both their pasts somehow irretrievable. And— well. Enough. It could not be thought out. Could not be understood, was something, rather, that he felt as a single... a single block...

Okay, it is time. It is

Tom steps slightly into the room with his head lowered.

He ting ting tings the glass with the fork.

Ahem. Yes. Ahem. Thank you, yes, he says in his half-serious speech-giving voice.

Conversations fade with dying laughter. People make promises by hand gesture: We will resume this . . .

of feeling for him. For how doomed was such an idealist. How doomed. His dark lashes softly looking up, for he senses it, too—what she feels about time. Senses everything, really. Senses it in the way you want someone to sense it, not seeing, only . . .

Jonathan looks at Tom from the side as he begins.

What does it mean, he asks himself? This being someone's father?

This being one's . . . whatever he was himself? Brother. Not-lover.

He knows only that were he in martial proximity, he would kill anyman who had but once touched her. Kill them each soul. He pic-

here. He orients himself to the room, consciously does not think of the first words he will say, constructs a space of uninhibited spontaneity in his mind . . .

Ginny. Dammit, where's Ginny.

 . . . but feeling it alongside you like, like . . .

Oh—oh! here it goes. Oh— she feels as if she were holding onto her chair (if she were sitting) as the room slightly tilts, though she stands as still as ever, an embarrassed smile over her blushing face.

She glances back at Jonathan, and their eyes brush fleetingly. Nate, who is across the room, beams back and forth between her and her father. She feels a

It is too late, he knows at once. He has begun the summons.

She will be upset. That he did not wait for her, that she was not foremost in his mind at that moment. Jealous, he thought—if she knew to say it—of his love affair with the universe.

The phrase wheels round his mind while he centers himself . . . love affair with the universe . . . but how did she not see that it was the

People are turning toward Tom. The music seems louder, now that people are settling.

Thanks everyone. Would someone mind turning that down a little? he says, gesturing to the coat closet on the other side of the room that houses the audio receiver.

Juan Garcia bends into the closet, and then suddenly it is quiet, and every upturned face expectant, like the waxen underside of leaf petals stirred suddenly by a breeze.

tures some anonymous, beer bellied man reaching out, touching … Kill, kill, kill! Little fucking fuck! Kill! Kill! He has never been in a fight, really. But he senses, as if it were lodged in the memory of the marrow of his bones, how he would pummel and rip, strike and crush, with elbow, knee, forehead. And the satisfaction of it. The heat in his blood. He knows also, even while feeling it, that he would be ashamed to tell Jane. It makes him wonder what the good of loving someone was, after all? What could he do?—bursting to prove the ardor in his chest (he imagined he felt it in his sternum). To somehow effect it in the living world?

homegoing warmth looking at Nate, as though he were a thick blanket… why does he tuck his shirt in with those jeans? A perpetual annoyance. He was goodlooking, of course, in a very straightfoward way. Big, broad. Jonathan by contrast seemed darker, wolfish. She tries to balance the differing affections she feels toward them.

She thinks of God in a very direct way. Why wouldn't he just take one away? What do you want me to do with them? she asks

most ordinary of all loves, and that two could be ravished by it together without lack?

The moment is here. He gathers himself and waits for the sudden inspiration that always leaps to his mind when he avoids thinking too specifically about what to say … something sharp and concrete drawn from the vast colorful morass of intuition … and then … and then …

He sees the faces in front of him settling in to listen.

Oh dad. She looks at him

Well.

First of all I want to thank y'all for coming.

Just then Ginny, small, glides laterally into the living room from where she had been starting the dishes in the kitchen. Tom does not see her yet.

Tom looks down as he gathers his thoughts, half raising the glass he holds in his hand, seemingly unaware that it is empty. He looks up and smiles embarassedly at

as he looks around, preparing to speak. She senses the weight of the room leaning on him.

She glances at Jonathan as he watches her dad, knowing that he senses her glance. Did he know what taking him fishing had meant, she wonders? Could he receive it and accept it and know? It was all she could do. But surely he must feel the depth of what it meant, and if it weren't for this room full of people she would look to him with a long gaze of knowingness. Knowingness. Knowingness.

This man, he feels, looking at Tom, has had her under his roof. Has had seven years to love her without complication. To do thing after thing on her behalf. What a gift. He wishes he could do just one thing. Just one thing. That she would know he had done it because he loved her. Everyone has those they can, should, love, he knows. Why did it not feel like this? He knows he loves his mother, and his sisters, and probably, in some distorted way, even his father. But though there was a quiet happiness that washed over him when he mailed the check to his mother, or when he called Ruthie or Sparrow and talked them through some junior high

He knows it will be only a moment before they will be downturned and embarrassed (though supportive) faces if he falters, if he fails . . .

Ginny sees him as she enters. And seeing him before he sees her, he not knowing she's there, she feels an irrational pride in him. But her shoulder tenses, knowing he is about to give his speech, and that it can go very well indeed—often has—or can disintegrate in a muddle of his undifferentiated feelings.

Tom feels a tinge of panic . . . how does one say . . . how does one say . . . Just say something . . .

Oh, here he goes. Dad. Dad. That word . . . dad . . .

the company.

Well, I really appreciate all y'all coming out tonight. You've all been real special in Jane's life, and I know she's grateful for you.

Me, I can't even begin to say what she's meant to us and our family. (Knowing looks and nods around the room). We feel like God just dropped her in our lap. Like a, just an unexpected Christmas present (some Awws and gentle laughter).

Tom looks around, then out the black glimmering win-

difficulty, why was it that he felt this continual wrenching for Jane? Longing for what? Of course he had thought of sex but that did not begin to cover it. What then was it?

He felt strongly about her ribcage. The womanliness of it, in her buttondown shirts.

Did he want to be her? He pondered that for a moment.

No, he delighted in her being not-him. But he wanted simultaneously to somehow … pass through her

dad . . . dad . . .

He feels himself on the verge of failure. You're not saying anything...

Ginny says in her mind You've got it, you've got it, you've got it, and smiles it in willingness toward him, smiles it with her eyes, with everything they have. If only he would glance over . . .

Say something else. People are looking at me. The weight is shifting …

How is it a gift? How is it a gift? A present? She feels exposed, naked on a rock. I'm here in this place because

Looking out the unseeing window he thinks of the

dow, where all their forms reflect darkly back to them like their patient ghosts.

like smoke. To feel their livers and spleens brush gently against one another as they passed.

you rescued me from . . . from suckingdicksuckingdick suckingdick

Stop stop stop
God
GOD GOD GOD She almost bends double, but remains erect, smiling stiffly. She has been able, for years now, to stop the hated mantras, and here he was pulling her back, making Time come alive like some laughing shuffling black jabberwocky of death.

three bums he had spotted down by the creek on his way home that afternoon, overcoated despite the heat, watch-capped, making a fire for tin can dinners. He thinks of the infinite bare hills to the west over which the sun is racing as it sets, and the places he's seen in those hills where no man must ever have walked, save perhaps some ancient medicine man finding his way to some foreknown place amongst the crags in which to die. The sun that has been setting without ceasing since the first moment of earth. He decides that he must be buried or his ashes scattered there when he dies. Scattered? He imagines his body pieced out

But then, having recovered from the dive, she knows

that it is not Dad, in his stopping of time, that makes what lies therein real. No, that is your fault, she says, turning the eyes of her mind familiarly up at the ceiling, though she remains still. That is your fault. You can't escape it, she says with female aggression, feeling her power over God. You can't pretend that you weren't there. That you didn't know. That you couldn't have stopped it. That it could ever make sense. The eyes of her mind smile grimly, now, as she knows, surely, that she has him. He to her is as a beholden lover, and at times like this she feels a proprietary exclusivity over him. I was eight, she says. I was eight. I was ... what like bouillon cubes, chunks of fleshy arm, slivers of ear, bits of nose. He thinks suddenly of Wendy, blown to bits in some filthy bayside market stall forty some odd years before, and how those bits that once made up the lovely—that was the word for her, lovely—the lovely dirty blonde English girl, how they must have been recycled many times by now. And how many fucking gooks, he asked himself, had eaten, after their passing through worm and soil, some beloved piece of neck or thumb? The war, such as it was, had been almost over by that time. And how different life would have been.

Ginny. There she is. He meets her eyes and she is

Jonathan glances at Nate, who is smiling at Tom and nodding, then looking back at Jane. Why does she like him? Yes, he is solid. Already an adjuster, and still a junior in college. Taking night classes a couple times

Well. But you know all that, says Tom. He looks up.

He takes a breath. Life is like that. As he says it, holding his empty plastic cup out to the crowd, his face quivers. Life is like that, isn't it? You can't know what any choice will mean. You can't know how things will turn out. You can't know how some little girl you got matched up with on a list seven years ago . . . here his voice almost broke. You can't know how

a week. Jonathan had to give him credit. And . . . yes, there was this unbearable goodness about him. He would never, ever, hurt Jane. Could he say the same?

the fuck was I supposed to do? It wasn't my fault. It was your fault. It was your fault. And for the thousandth time she feels him let her pound her impotent fists on his chest. Lets her curse him and swing wildly at his silent weeping face. Shut the fuck up she feels her spirit say to him. What right, what right? what right had you? It follows me even here. It sullies even this night. It will forever. And ever. And ever.

I'll never be better. I'll never be a good girl. I'll never be good. I'll never be good.

And then she collapses,

But how then, and why? Jonathan asks. To be moved like this, breathtaken at her mere appearance, if not to love her? (He sees her strained face in this moment, and he knows, knows.) And how to love her if not to have her? And . . . how to want for her the thing that would take her from him? For he *did* want that. He wanted, when he saw it like a piece of sky

nodding, smiling, and he is arrested. So fragile she seems, suddenly, to him. All her life wrapped up in his. And he asks with his own eyes. And yes, she says, yes, empahtically, wordlessly, and he feels himself buoyed by her gaze, and drawn back from the edge of the world into the room. He nods back. Yes, he nods back.

There, Ginny thinks. Once more saved like a faltering bird from an inevitable crash. And now his strong wings beating rhythmically to the horizon. Oh well. I guess it's the best we have. Our connection. Will he ever really even know I'm here? Know that he can make my life or kill it? And what is he say-she'll become your daughter.

So, I guess that's all I have to say really. Maybe you can't line up the dots, or figure it out, or whatever. But, he said, turning now to Jane, I love you. And I'm thankful we got to have you for a few years.

Here Tom raised his empty plastic cup and scanned the crowd around him with it, took in each of their faces as they passed, and said, To Jane!

Everyone smiled and sighed as the tension of listening to the speech was re- glimpsed ahead through the trees, what he knew must be right. God. God for her. Ha! The thing he could not accept for himself—the numbing comfortable fireplace indoors from the real rain—that was the thing he knew she must have. And knowing it gave even that fantastical cottage fire some reality. But he, to give it, must stand outside silent and invisible in the rain and (here, suddenly, he looked up) and maybe that, he thought, was love.

Maybe that was love. Invisibly to … somehow to … again for the thousandth time, onto his chest, and he holds her, and holds her, and says nothing over and over again.

Her spirit asks, Will you be here each time? What about twenty years from now? What about when I have kids? What about when … when Nate … when we get married, and … the first time he … She was breathing rapidly, but the smile remained, stalwart, on her face.

And then, finally, very calmly, she asks, And what about my daughter? Or ing? What is that supposed to mean? All this dreamy talk. How easy and how simple it would be to make me happy, she thinks. There is no mystery. Perhaps that was the problem. If only she were a mystery to him, some enigma to unravel, some quest to search out … She knows she is no more than a maintenance project, borne, amongst his list of other things to keep up, with varying degrees of patience and resolution. She sighed. She thought of the cream cheese frosting on the cupcake she had eaten and calculated squats and lunges. Jane did not yet know the horror of age. The obsession. Still resented every glance and stare as she walked through the leased, and said Cheers! and Jane smiled shyly and waved her half raised hands at everyone and said Thank you softly, and it was over.

He didn't know what he had decided, but he felt as if in that moment a great gift had been given him. And quietly, with a profound gratitude, he raised the longneck he had been holding all the while.

my son? Whatever it was. Are you taking care of her? Please God. Take care of her. Take care of her. Please . . . please . . . please . . .

And once again it is over and there is nothing left to say and nothing is answered and nothing is changed.

mall or through town, still took for granted the attention of men, not knowing that it was that unwanted light that made possible one's glow. And this damned dress . . .

There it was, Tom thought, watching the company turn back to one another. The noise resumed. Someone turned the music back up. Tom envisioned the traveling band looking at him, nodding solemnly, then putting down their intermission drinks to take up their instruments once more. Something had been done. He felt the usual pangs of self criticism having finished his little speech, but he sensed too that something had been wrought, birthed, in their midst. It was finished, and therefore irrevocable. He felt free now to gambol, chat, flirt, gossip. But felt also a solemness wash over him, having held the wand and orchestrated this caesura which those present accepted so naturally. He felt he wanted to go outside and smoke by himself. If he smoked. That was something to try out, he thought. now that . . . he chuckled. He looked up and Ginny was smiling at him. He felt suddenly aware of himself, watched, and her empathy was no longer welcome, but he forced a smile and nod, and then turned to Jane, but Nate was already there, giving her a big hug and saying something obvious and encouraging.

Tom turned to go outside, pausing as he stood in the door to see the gathered embers in the room. He took it in for one moment, knowing that this was the last. He considered staying longer, prolonging it, but knew that it was over, saw it receding. Father Donald, still in the corner, looking small and unnoticed, watched the scene, too, with brimming eyes. Just perceptibly, he raised his mug to Tom. Then Tom faced the black and teeming and welcoming night and softly closed the door behind him.

Outside the big white farmhouse on the hill the bugs have not ceased their chorus. Like the breathing of summer itself.

The man walks back to the iron grill and resumes scraping. He is in deep darkness under the overhang on the back patio, and can see hazy lights down the hill in the distance. Nearby in the bright room he has left the party goes on. It reminds him of glowing ship lights, seen from the shore. Extinguished one by one in icy waters as the ship turns vertical and plunges into the black deep.

From the south, coming up the hill unseen by the man cleaning the grill, walks another man, brown and perfectly matched by the the waving night fields. Still a ways off, he whistles a quick note, and the man cleaning the grill turns to him.

— Hey hey.
— Evenin Tom.
— Evenin Marcus.
— Thought Id mebbe find you here.
— Yep.
— Brought a couple beers but it looks like you got a party on.
— Jane's off to college thing.
— Yep.
— You know y'all were welcome.
— Oh I know it. Preciate it, and yall know we love Janey.
— Yep.
— How it go?
— Good. I think it went good.

— Yep. I understand that. You want this?

— Why not. Hey, I'll grab you a plate of barbecue and bread and whatever.

— Naw. Thanks. Preciate it. Already et.

Marcus pulled the bottles out of his big shirt pocket. The men were quiet. They clinked their bottles. They both looked in at the window where the company laughed and talked.

— Well, I can leave you be if you want.

— No. Stay. It's fine.

— Okay.

They watched the silent, radiant party. Just a hint of the music reached them. Joe McCallahan told a story silently in the bright glass screen. Everyone tilted back or buckled forward with laughter. Jane held Nate's arm. Jonathan was gone. After a while the priest came over to talk briefly to Jane, smiling affectionately. He shook Nate's hand and turned to go out the front door, where his bicycle would be waiting for him.

— Marcus.

— Yeah.

— I'm gonna tell you something.

— Okay.

— I've not told anyone.

— Okay.

— I'm dying.

— Okay.

— Cancer. Pancreatic. Untreatable. Four months.

Marcus was quiet for a long moment.

— Well. I'm real sorry to hear that, Tom.

— Well I guess it happens.

— So Ginny don't know yet?

— No. No one. I guess I wanted to wait till at least after tonight.

— Yep.

They stood there a while. People began to drift toward the door. Ginny could be seen, smiling and thanking people.

— I guess I oughtta get back in and help out.

— Well Tom, I guess I don't hafta say . . .

— Nope.

— Okay. Well.

Tom set his bottle on the grill and took a step toward the door then stopped.

— So what do you think, Marcus?

Marcus didn't say anything. Tom went on.

— Was that a good life? You know. It's strange to be able to just point at it. That one, right there. The one I just lived. Sixty three. That's not too short, I guess. Three decent kids who are grown ups. And that wonderful Jane. I guess her life woulda been different without us. And I did my best to love Ginny, as best I could. We got a nice place here. What do you think? I guess sometimes these days I think about the oil. That that's what I did with my life. Oil. Course I got into it with the best of intentions.

— Aw, Tom.

— Never killed anyone. Not even when we were over there. Of course you know that, Marcus. But tell you what. Being honest now. Wouldn't've minded popping off a few gooks while we were there. I would go back and do it now. It's probably wrong to feel that way.

Tom curses.

— Aw, Tom, now . . .

— No. I mean. It's just the whole thing. I guess it wasn't their fault. Shit. I've thought about it enough. They had their little families back in their huts or whatever, too. But who are you gonna blame? What can you do, Marcus? (Here the white man looked at the black man.) Are you going to drive up to the whitehouse and say, Come on out sir. A beautiful woman was just blown up over in bum fuck egypt and I'm here to say it's on account of you I would like to fight you for her honor.

— No sir, youre not gonna do that.

— What then. Tom said it more quietly now. I guess it's everybody's fault.

— What I think is there aint no reckonin it either way.

— Well, what about you, Marcus?

— I'm just fine, Tom.

— Well last time I checked you're a black man and it's two thousand eleven but if I'm not mistaken y'all are still being cordially asked to bend over on a fairly regular basis.

— I don't remember anyone ever asking. Certainly not cordially.

— Well.

— But Tom, I got a farm. Right down there.

— I know.

— And I own sixty two acres of the united states of america. In the great republic of Texas.

— Yep.

— And my own tractor, outright.
— Yep.
— And I got three kids, too. And one a lawyer and two at college. Smart as whips. And they got as much future as anyone. But that don't matter. You know what? It ain't no different now than a thousand years ago.
— No?
— No. You ain't really any more secure than then. And *you* ain't, in general, any more than me—an I'm talkin before you found out you was dyin. I mean even as a white man.
— Okay.
— You ain't. Sure, you don't need to tell me. Being a black man, that's a real thing. But you. Even you. You only own this land, or the company, or whatever, because someone say you can. Same with me.
— Well.
— Sure, maybe you got a few guns in your safe in the garage. Maybe you can run off a couple crazies come on your property. Hell, I remember the time you stood down that stupid jealous boyfriend or whatever twenty years ago with Rebecca. But the truth is, even though you white, you get to keep your money, and you get to stay in your house, because the government say you can. Always been the same. And the government just people. Used to it was smaller people, like a duke or whatever. But it aint no different in the end. You caint fight em all. And there aint no guarantee that things're gonna stay the same. I'm thankful for the years I been here, livin next to you, raisin my familly. I'm real thankful. My daddy couldnta owned no farm. Never owned nothin. Died as poor as he was born. But I aint ignant of the fact that no matter what I do, someone can take it all from me some day.
— Well.
Marcus swigged his beer and looked on down the hill to where his farm lay in the moonlight.
— Course, they would hafta kill me before I give it up. So I guess in that sense ain't no one can take nothin from you. You can always keep your dignity.
They were quiet again. Then Tom closed the grill and hung up the scraper.
— Well, I'd better get on in there.
— Yep.
As Tom turned to go, Marcus cleared his throat.
— Tom?

— Yeah?
— Look, brother. You know . . .
— Yep.
— Okay. We'll see you around.
— Okay.

The black man took his empty bottle, slowly wound up, and hurled it end over end whirring into the darkness down the hill below. They waited and then heard the thud crunch tinkle as it landed in the bracken. The lights on the horizon burnt on. The black man walked away down the hill as he had come. Some ways off he turned and yelled back.

— Fuck em all, Tom. You done good. You done as good as any man ever did.

The white man stood there gazing after him until he was gone. He heard from the front of the house Jonathan's bike starting up and he listened as it roared off down the road, echoes dwindling in their reflections back from the cold dome of the night. He turned and ducked back into the house. The cicadas sang on.

Book III: *Christmas in Texas*

SUMMER THAT YEAR took forever to end. Many cedars turned brown on the hills as they died, mocking the autumn color that would never come.

It was the hottest summer on record. The world was coming to an end. Proof of warming. Proof of apocalypse.

Jonathan went back to work Monday after the Party and was changed. He had grasped the old hard slick brown baseball in his hand and thrown it as far as he could and it had never landed. He avoided the trailer office as much as possible. Jane asked about it but he said he was needed out at the towers more. To monitor the numbers. Keep closer tabs on things. But really he just took to running more. Out at the dam of the lake, running in the heat of the day, shirtless, burnt, and dizzy. Embracing the crucible of it. Gnats and bugs by the trillions came, and he jumped onto the four foot high dam wall and saw that they didn't fly up to his face there. The breeze reached him more up there, and he felt like he was on the divide of life and death. So he started running on top of the wall. Eight inches wide and on the lake side of it a ten foot drop to sharp rocks. Sometimes he ran as fast as he could. He made sure not to fall. Swinging like an ape around the lampposts stuck at thirty yard intervals in the wall.

Despite the heat and the drought he carried on with his garden and some things grew. The lone rain in early July filled his four buckets but that didn't last long and he had to water with the hose.

Less and less he went to the oil rig at all. Then it was discovered that Mike had been shunting some of the injection waste into a disused exploratory horizontal hole. Some of the sludge had reached a portion of the local water table. Nothing seemed to be affected, and the city didn't seem to care much. It ran for one day in the paper. Jonathan went back to the ditch where they had fished, and the water was gray and nothing moved in it.

The next day Jonathan walked into Tom's office at the towers and told him he was quitting. He thanked him for everything but said he just couldn't keep going with it. He mentioned what the paper had classified as an accident, but Tom knew it was more than that and didn't resist. He stood up to shake his hand. Well. Alright then. Get out of here. They were quiet for a second, and then Jonathan said, Sir, I want you to know. I . . . Tom broke in, I know. Now get out of here. Take care of yourself.

They shook hands and Jonathan left.

A couple times after he quit Jane texted him with Updates, but Jonathan didn't respond, and then he dropped his phone in the toilet on purpose so he would have an excuse if he saw her again.

It was so, so hot.

School buses started driving around the neighborhood of The Sandman on the last day of August. Jonathan realized it was the first autumn he wouldn't be in school. But it was so hot that it didn't feel like schooltime.

As some of his vegetables matured, he would take the crop to Father Donald every Friday, and a young mother of four boys would show up with her minivan and put the produce in plastic milk crates in the back of the van and drive around to a few neighborhoods and give it away. It was all very businesslike. Seeing the priest at his parish, with his little steel spectacles looking at clipboards handed him by one of the part time secretaries. The mother would come in through the side door, giving a last terse command to the boys elbowing each other in the van, and then ask where the veggies were, and the priest would point and sometimes give special delivery instructions. Sometimes there wasn't anything said and the box was there and she just grabbed it. Sometimes Father Donald seemed almost curt. Like politeness had nothing to do with it. She would put it in the van, shoving aside shinguards or soccer balls. Very businesslike. But Jonathan's crop got out, and he liked being a part of an anonymous and stolid machine.

He still talked to his mother every Sunday. It was gray, dripping, and miserable in Portland, she said. He told her he was thinking of heading back up. Don't do it on my account, she said. We've adjusted to you gone. Thanks, he said.

Then one time Jane called on the Sandman phone.

He thought it was his mom or maybe Tom with some question left over from work, and so he answered it.

Hello?

Jonathan.

Oh . . . hey.

There was a long pause, then she said, Jonathan, what's going on?

What? Ha ha. Nothing. What do you mean? He added, Oh, my phone died . . .

Stop it. Jonathan. I'm not going to let you do this like this. That's all. I'm going to come over and you're going to tell me to my face.

Jane, I . . . what do you mean? Tell you what? I mean, I . . . so, how's it going?

How's it *go*ing? How's it *go*ing?

They were quiet.

Look. I'm coming over. I'll be there in ten minutes. Don't move.

Jane, I . . .

She hung up.

He stood there, tapping the bulky plastic phone receiver on the little table, looking around the gloomy Sandman room. After a while, he said Well, and began tidying what little there was to tidy. But how, anyway, to prepare for the inevitable moment? When one knows it is the tide itself that approaches.

Fifteen minutes later he heard her pull up in her old toyota.

He opened the door to avoid the artificial drama of her knocking.

You're late, he said, halfheartedly.

Car wouldn't start for a few minutes, she said, climbing out. It's been doing that. Dad was gonna take a look at it, but . . . anyway, look, do you know anything?

I . . . know what?

Well, I don't want to stand out here.

Oh, okay. Come on in.

So this is where you live, huh?

Yeah. Not much. It works for me, I guess.

She looked into his eyes and said It's perfect.

He looked away and said, Oh, ha ha. Well anyway, what's up.

Are you serious?

What?

Okay. Sit down.

Sit down? What is this, some sort of . . . he was trying lamely to joke.

Jonathan. It was the closest he had ever heard her come to yelling, and she was fighting back tears. Stop it. You can go back to doing whatever you're trying to do after we're done. But be yourself for one minute.

He was silent and sat down on the bed and she went on. First, my dad. Do you know about that?

I kind of overheard something.

He's dying.

Like . . .

Yeah. Like. Soon. He went in this week and they said he's doing better than they thought at first but it looks like in a few months.

Oh Jane . . .

Hang on, I've got to finish everything. Also . . . so . . . here her face did collapse. Also . . . Raiden.

Wait. What.

Raiden. A couple days ago. I tried to call your phone. I tried to call you.

What? What? What? Jonathan was looking angrily and skeptically around the room.

Motorcycle crash.

No. Hang on. Wait a second. He put out his hand toward her.

Yes, he had an accident. Two days ago.

No. Hang on.

He . . . he was going over a hundred and he went over a guard rail. A cliff in the middle of nowhere.

No. That's . . .

Yes, Jonathan! Yes! she shrieked.

She fell down next to him where he sat on the bed and he put his arms around her as she shook quietly.

It couldn't have been an accident.

Oh, she cried. Why does it have to be now. He could live for thirty more years. Daddy. A lot of people live for thirty more years. He could be there, when . . . when everything happens. When I get married. And mom . . . and Raiden was like . . . you know he was really . . . a innocent little boy . . . God . . .

Oh Jane.

It feels like . . . why does it feel like everything's just . . . falling apart?

She was in his arms this one time, and she fit so perfectly. Without realizing it they were rocking gently. He waited one moment longer. And then, with a tremendous effort, he patted her shoulder and stood up and walked over to the A/C and fiddled with a knob, with his back to her.

I guess things just always fall apart, he said.

What do you mean it wasn't an accident, she asked.

I've seen him ride. It wasn't an accident.

Jane was rubbing out her eyes with the heels of her palms.

They said . . . they said it was alcohol related. That he had . . . that his blood alcohol was like . . . she held her hand above her head.

It wasn't alcohol related. Not like that it wasn't.

Oh, who cares anyway.

He would.

Yeah. He probably would. He'd probably think it mattered that he did it on purpose. So what. It doesn't matter to me. He's gone. Forever. And dad will be gone forever. Forever. By this spring.

Jonathan was standing leaning on the A/C looking out the window. He was mantled with light on his head and shoulders. If it be possible.

He turned and stepped back into the room toward Jane. Well, I'm going to have to get ready for work.

What?

I work at the Sombrero in a bit.

What? Seriously? So that's it?

What do you mean? I have to get ready for work.

Okay. Your friend just died, and my dad is dying. That's it?

What do you mean? I—I'm sorry. You know that. But I've got to . . .

I know, *you fucking've got to get ready for work*!

Jonathan had never heard her swear. His forehead almost betrayed him. But he just said, Sorry.

Sorry, she said too, more quietly. Jonathan, just tell me what's going on.

What are you talking about.

Really? Like, you just like, left work one day, then . . . and . . . and . . .

Oh. Well, my phone broke, and . . . I work at the Brer a lot, and . . . Sorry. I just . . . never thought about it.

Oh. Jane stood up slowly. She walked to the door. She turned the handle to leave and Jonathan was looking away, and a bar of light crossed her body vertically and she stopped and said, Look. Jonathan.

What?

I want to know . . . if, like, you're doing this, to like, make anyone feel any particular way or something? He didn't move, still looking out the window. Because, you know . . . you can just talk to me.

She said the last words quietly and Jonathan felt as though he saw a valley open up in front of him. With green trails and little hidden thickets and stone walls and gardens. You can just talk to me.

    He paused. Then with a tremendous effort he tensed himself, in the wings of the stage, and turned and laughed loudly, Ha ha ha ha! Oh Jane. Seriously? That is such a girl thing to say. Sorry. I just forgot. Don't overanalyze it. Ha!

    She looked at him for a moment more. He steeled himself and looked into her eyes. Didn't flinch. She blinked out tears.

    Well, she said, opening the door. See you around.

    Then she went out, closed the door, and walked straight to her car. Jonathan stood still. He heard a brief whine from the starter and then nothing. Jane tried again but there was nothing. He sighed and went outside. He was careful not to look in her eyes now.

    Oh. Right. Let's take a look at that, he said.

    You don't have to.

    Pop the hood.

    Okay. Um . . . which one . . .

    Here, said Jonathan, and opened her door and bent in and pulled the lever. Suddenly right next to her again, her ankles and her perfect feet in gray leather sandals. He walked around to the hood and opened it.

    Okay, try to start it.

    Okay.

    She did and there was a click and then nothing. Okay, yep. He twisted a battery connection back and forth a few times, scraping the post as he did. Try it again.

    The car started right up.

    He went around to her window. Just a loose battery. And some corrosion on it. Hang on and let me go get a wrench and tighten it up. And when you get a chance you should clean it up.

    How do I . . . ?

    Well, probably you can just take it off and spray it with WD-40 and tighten it back on. But I don't really know. You should just google it. It'll be really easy.

    Okay. I will.

    He didn't look at her and he went in and found his adjustable crescent and came out and tightened the battery cable and closed the hood and patted it gently.

    He turned and walked back to his door, giving a wave without looking back when she called out Thanks as he passed through the door.

It was some minutes before she finally drove away.

He wasn't working that night. He only worked two nights a week and he wasn't even on the schedule anymore but would just call in the morning of and Justin would put him on the board for the night. Two nights a week covered everything he needed, and he still had some of his oil money that he hadn't sent back to his mother in Oregon.

He fell back onto the bed and lay there looking at the ceiling motionless. Maybe an hour passed. Then he got up and took off all his clothes. He put on his airy running shorts with no underwear and his running shoes with no socks and grabbed his two dollar sunglasses as he walked out the door. He rode around in the inexorable heat, all over town, willing someone to yell something from his truck, wanting to fight them until he was lacerated and bleeding from every plane of his hard body, and then he turned and rode out towards the lake, getting up as fast as the bike would go, not minding his shorts and not marking his way, weaving as he had seen Raiden do. In top gear he leaned forward on the tank until he lay on it with his face stuck out past the headlight so he felt he was flying and he let his legs flail out behind him and the wind rushing over his back mingled with the searching sun and his shoulders were turning auburn.

At the lake he ran on the wall until he was gasping and stumbling and in danger of falling from exhaustion. He stopped and found a rock cairn piled up to the wall and lowered himself over and scrambled down. He picked his way amongst the boulders to the water's edge. He kicked off his shoes and put his sunglasses on a rock and dived toward a dark spot ahead. Then he stroked out into the sunny water. The water was warm and slid over him almost without feel. The wavelets flashed in his eyes. The lake was near to a mile across, and he could see a dark stand of trees on the far shore. He swam straight toward the far line and it felt like making for the horizon. He got into a rhythm. After a while he rolled onto his back and kept his face above the surface with little kicks, with his arms out from his sides, and the sun was directly above his face, and he would open his eyes just barely to let it blind him, then close them and feel the blue orange spots behind his eyelids. Even with the water, he felt the burn of the sun on his chest, and he held his arms straight out and embraced it. Once he held his breath and relaxed every muscle in his body. Then he got a sudden hamstring cramp and he thrashed and straightened out the leg and coughed water and stretched it till it stopped. Then he swam out further. When he paused to tread, he saw that he was a great distance from either shore. It seemed very quiet in the middle of the lake. He bobbed there, and spit, and felt like he should say something to someone but there was no one there.

He went again onto his back and slowly made his way towards land. At intervals he would turn over and pull hard for a few yards. When he reached the shallows he stood up dripping and plucked his shorts from himself and he swayed as he walked in the muck until he fell down on the small strip of burning coarse sand along the edge of the lake and rested. Shortly it was too hot and he crawled back into the water to rinse off his back and then emerged again. He sat on a large driftwood tree and wiped off his feet and put on his shoes. The drops that fell from his body would dry almost instantly on the hot white wood. Slowly, bent, he stepped back up the rocks to the wall and climbed over. Then he rode home.

The weather did not break at all until late September. And only for a few days before it climbed over a hundred again. Everyone was worn down with it. But it seemed the right sort of weather to Jonathan. He would walk the streets of Ventana aimlessly, or ride out to a forgotten road and sit. He started smoking cigarettes, he knew not why. But it felt good to do it. He kept a bottle of vodka and diet dr pepper in his small room fridge, and would take them in his blue jansport whenever he rode out.

One day it suddenly made sense to go to the office trailer and try to explain everything to Jane. It was late October. He remembered that he had left several of his favorite pens at the office and he would casually say he had come to get them. He avoided thinking that he simply and desperately wanted to see her. As he walked, he considered what he would say, but it kept slipping away from him.

Once again, as he had the first time so long ago, it seemed, he willed himself to walk up the steps to the door. As he was about to pull it open he heard voices inside and he recognized Nate and Jane's laughter. He stopped for a moment and listened. The sun beat down, there on the steps. It seemed a miracle to him simply that she was there, on the other side of the thin metal wall, alive and herself some few feet away. He waited a moment longer and then walked away.

Through the end of the summer he had continued going to the old bar at the edge of town every Tuesday night. He read his gardening books and took notes in his thin brown notebook, while the priest in the lonely corner booth would shrive and bless, talk or laugh. It was almost never the same people, but one or two or as many as five came each week. Sometimes in the breaks between parishioners Jonathan would stand at the booth and talk gardening or engines with the priest. Sometimes when the priest was finished Jonathan would sit with him and they would share a drink and talk about everything else. Then at the end of October he stopped going. He made no decision but just never walked over there.

The next Monday he crossed the street to The Sombrero and found Ben in the back office and told him he was quitting. Ben said Really? Okay. I'll keep you on payroll and if you ever want to pick up shifts you just let me know. Ben stood up and shook his hand. Okay, Jonathan said.

After that he would just sleep half the day, or lay awake watching the fan, then ride out to the dam and run and swim, and come home and drink cockroaches and tend the garden. He cleared some more of the unused strip across the parking lot from his door, but left it fallow.

And then, finally, it started getting cooler. It was November second. Three more weeks passed and it was almost Thanksgiving. Most of the leaves on the junky deciduous trees had turned brown on their limbs but some few shone out with the muted gold of autumn in Texas. It never rained.

Something now was different in the air, and he felt the season passing. So, finally, after six weeks gone, as darkness fell, he walked out and locked his bright red door at The Sandman and made his way across town to the ancient barroom glowing in its solitude at the end of the darkened street under the waning crescent and the black sky.

On the way, walking with his head down, he heard someone say Jack. And then louder, *Jack!* He turned to look and there they were, laughing and running toward him with careful steps in their tall boots and short dresses, bouncing with girlish vitality. *Hey Jack!* Remember us? They came and hugged him and he stood there. He realized suddenly how long it had been since he had touched another human, and he felt their bosoms and hips acutely, pressed into his passive frame.

Oh, hi, he said.

We're home for Thanksgiving, they said.

Oh.

You wanna hang out?

Oh, well. I'm actually going to meet someone. At that place you guys didn't like.

Ha ha! Such an old man. Tomorrow night?

Well, I don't know if I'll be around tomorrow night.

What? What does that mean!

Yeah, Cody, said the blonde girl in a husky voice looking at him with half lidded eyes.

The brunette put her hand on his chest. Yeah, Cody. What does that mean.

Look. I've got a question for you, he said, taking a step back.

Okay.

Why do you want to hang out with me?

What do you mean?

I mean . . . you know. Why did you come up to me and talk to me last spring. Why me.

Well, Cody . . . said the brunette. The blonde giggled. What do you think? You're hot. And you don't say much.

Don't ever tell us your name! said the other one.

He backed further away. My name's Jonathan, he said. Look. Thanks, but I can't. See you around. Then he turned his back and walked up the street.

I can't believe you told us your name!

Oh my God! I can't believe we know his name!

Bye . . . Jonathan! We still love you! Let us know if you change your mind! Jonathan!

He turned and waved and kept going.

The eaves of the old bar and the handrail of the ramp to its door were strung with white christmas lights. There was even woodsmoke in the air like christmas should be. Acrid and sweet. Jonathan pulled the big door. He knew it was the last time he would come here.

The hostess grabbed a plastic menu automatically but then recognized him and just nodded. Hey, she said. Hey, he said.

He looked around, and there he was, seated at his booth across from an old man in a midcentury tan flight jacket. The greatest generation. The priest sat silently with his head bowed while the old man gesticulated and talked.

Jonathan waved to Gary the barkeep as he passed, and went and sat at the booth behind the priest and his penitent. The priest saw him when he walked by and gave him notice of as much with the slightest flicker in his eye.

Jonathan put his gardening books and his notebook on the table in front of him. The old man in the tan jacket behind him was confessing. Ever time I see her, Father, I cain't hep but I look at her with desahr... Jonathan leaned over his books held his head in his hands, covering his ears. When it seemed like the man was done, he opened his notebook, and began drawing a map of The Sandman, and his garden, and how he could imagine it being if he stayed and worked it. He drew a tiny cactus. Prickly pear. A map of the world as it should be.

It was getting towards the end of Donald's hours, and Jonathan expected him to pop his head around at any moment. But then he sensed a new body sit down behind him, and heard a woman's soft voice. Hello Father. Ah yes, hello there. And how are you this evening? They talked for a while, passing in and out of hearing. At some point the Father said Oh! Would you believe, I've been there? No, she said. Yes! To that very town. In surprise, the woman said, Not many people have heard of it. It was when I was only a child, he said. Oh, she went on, I just assumed you were from . . . well I don't know. Where *are* you from?

Jonathan felt the wood creak as the priest leaned back and no doubt put his hands behind his head as he prepared his answer.

Ah, well. Yes. With a priest, of course, that's a tricky question. I was last stationed at San Remo, a hundred miles or so southwest of here if you're not familiar, at the end of a mostly empty farm road up from San Antonio—more or less all Germans from three families though they don't know it and that was a hundred and eighty years ago anyhow—deeded by Austin himself and lived on by those same three families for all that time, with of course the odd mercantile man in and out, marrying occasionally and et cetera. Six years I was there. Six years—long enough to know the brewmaster well, and to learn more about their history than them. Of course most folks won't want to know that they're married to their third cousin, and one can appreciate that. Though the church permits it, you know. But I've been up here in Ventana for twenty-two years this autumn. My people are in upstate New York, though I never knew them except my mother. But to answer your question I suppose by now I'm mostly Texan, for what that's worth—and I tend to think rather a lot . . . But now then, what can I do for you? There was a quiet moment and Jonathan heard the woman's voice. Ah, I see. Well, said the priest.

And then the woman must have begun whispering, for Jonathan lost all intimation of their presence behind him.

He smiled at all the world around him. He looked over at Gary, leaning on the bar, talking at two women in his deep rolling tones. The kitchen was bright through the portal window in the swinging door, and he knew now from experience how different things were in there than up front in the house. Waitresses came and went. He gazed up at the beams running the length of the room. Smoke had blackened half of them. He didn't know the history of the place, as he knew the priest did, but he felt the presence somehow of many, many souls, and knew that these timbers had borne them witness. He felt sentimental about people who had danced on this ancient floor, or who had whispered in booths, or who had met here for the first time. He tried to imagine if pioneers or old cowboys or people during the depression or sixties hippies or people his parents' age felt things like people did now, where everyone had the universe at their fingertips, or more keenly, and, and . . . Dead, all of them.

He pushed his first beer, now empty, away from him and wiped the circle it had left with the little napkin. The rush from buying them was long gone, but there remained a certain checklist feeling of security, knowing he could. The coaster was a colorful, smiling, female moon. It was distorted and magnified through the glass. He felt that she watched over him in his vast Texas solitude.

Well! Jonathan! It's been a while. Getting much in the way of work done?

Jonathan couldn't help but grin at him.

Some. Over your racket, he said to the priest, who seemed light and free from his work.

Well, I take offense at that. I accept no money, and rarely a drink. He smiled. And that only from them I think it will do some good to give it. Racket.

I meant the noise.

I know what you meant but I can't imagine it was so loud.

We lived through the whole goddamn history of Texas.

As the priest got up to join Jonathan he said, Well then you're welcome and I suppose I can conscience extorting a fee from you. He took the purple strip of cloth from around his shoulders and dropped it beside him on the seat as he slid in across from Jonathan. In the interest, so to speak, of your eternal soul.

And so they talked. Jonathan inquired after the priest's bicycle, and he after Jonathan's honda, and his garden. The priest spoke of a winter long ago, when he was a boy and his mother had taken him to a corn roast, and Jonathan realized suddenly that he was much like the older man.

In time Jane and Nate came in and sat at a table on the other side of the room. Though he hadn't seen her in weeks, it seemed inevitible to Jonathan when he looked up and there she was walking through the door, long dark hair brushed out. Tentative but smiling. There she was. And Nate behind her. Jonathan regretted that he had drunk as much as he had by that time. They sat down at their table without noticing him. Then later they saw him and the priest and came by and said hello and Nate invited them to the new gathering downtown and Jane and the priest talked of advent. They went and sat back down.

He confessed everything to the priest. Not in so many words, but he tried to say those things that he might tell some fellow soldier as he died. Entrust them in a handkerchief. He didn't know how to say it. He tried to say, Jane is . . . Jane is so, so good. Not exactly what I mean. And he kept trying to say, and trying to say, but the priest understood. I wish, if there was some way, to e-rad . . . to e-rad, icate myself. From the picture.

I see, said the priest. He paused. Then gently, Jonathan. Are you contemplating . . . doing anything to yourself?

What? *Yeah*. That's what I'm saying.

The priest's eyes were severe and wide.

Oh . . . no. Not like that.

Okay.

Just. I'm trying to . . . trying to make her not . . .

Does she?

Oh, I don't know. I think she was kind of starting to. But either way . . . to make it like, like I'm not a factor.

Hmm.

So, like. Maybe I'll do some things that will make her not like me. Maybe some wrong things. Because she's so good.

Hmm.

But it will be right because it will be to love her. And besides. I don't think right and wrong means so much as I used to. I've figured out that you only get a few things for sure . . . and even those aren't real sure. But you can know . . . you can know that, hey, look, here's . . . here's this one person in front of me. They, they're either . . . they're either happier or sadder. Or like, either it's better for them or worse. And you can make it go one way or the other. You can't know shit about much else. But you see this one person in front of you . . . and you try to do what's better for them. I don't believe in God, I've decided. It's a relief to say it. But . . . but . . . either he doesn't care, or . . . do you know what happened to Jane? To little Jane? I can't stop seeing it. Imagining what she looked like when she was a little kid. And I can't stop seeing these big old dudes coming into her room, and . . . And not just that, but . . . but basically everyone out there, you know? Hardly anyone has a chance. My mom is never gonna have a happy life. For example. And it's not because my dad was that bad. He was just pretty normal, and he couldn't stand her anymore. And he's probably not that happy either. Never sees his family. And so Ruth and Sparrow . . . I can already see them getting messed up by it all, and it stresses me out. I'm laying awake at night in The Sandman and lots of times I can't fall asleep because I'm thinking about Ruthie and Sparrow and I'm picturing some highschool douchebag like, taking advantage of them, because they'll be insecure and stuff . . . or like some mean girl making fun of their . . . their sweatshirts or something. The priest's head was bowed. And look. Look. I know you're a good guy. The best really religious person I've ever met. And so you're going to just not say anything. Because you're a good person, and so you know there's nothing anyone can say. But you know what I've figured out? That's not a good enough answer. I feel like I've been watching. This whole year. Watching, or waiting for something. And maybe I would have used think that that's, like . . . that's the profound thing. To not say anything. But it's not good enough. It's just not. It's not even an answer.

I mean, it's kind of a trick, isn't it? Like, you don't say anything, and that means . . . oh, I can't say it, but there's some deeper answer. So like, you get off the hook. God gets off the hook. But fuck that. If God can't do better than that, then even if he was real, it wouldn't matter. That's not impressive enough for God. I mean fuck. Right? I wanna say, You *owe* us an answer. You *owe* us an answer. It's just not good enough to not say anything. We wouldn't do that. We would explain it, if there was anything to explain. Like, people treat their kids better than that. Is god really no better than us? And if it's really just like, Just wait and see. Trust me. After you die it will all make sense . . . if it's like that, then that's bullshit because this is the only life we can live. And we're supposed to live it for something that might happen after we die? And we don't get any answer for why it's so shitty? And there's millions of galaxies out there, but this is supposed to mean something, here, on this little . . . ? And the one person I loved more than anyone I've ever met was . . . just fucking messed up by a bunch of fucked up losers before I ever met her? So. I decided something.

The priest looked up. Oh?

This summer. I realized . . . wow. Like, she doesn't have to see it, but I could do something for her. That was really, really, good for her. And if she never, never saw it . . . or that I did it . . . like . . .

Oh! Ha.

What?

Oh. Well. You're just talking about love. The priest almost sounded like he was laughing.

Jonathan, brought up short, said, What do you mean? Jonathan was angry with the priest for maybe the only time.

That's love.

Umm . . . that's what I'm *saying*, said Jonathan.

Oh . . . no no. You were saying lots of things. Some of it very true. Some of it nonsense. But that last part. That's just love. The most ordinary thing in the world. You've just stumbled upon a very particular species of it, that's all. It happens all the time. Mothers. Fathers. Good friends who help you move. Even a priest or two, I'm told. Ha, ha!

You're making it a joke.

Ha. No, no, the priest actually was laughing now.

We're too drunk to talk about this, said Jonathan.

Ha. Maybe you are. But still, it's the truest thing you've said. You pagan saint you. It's just . . . I don't know, it's striking me as funny.

Well.

No, I am sorry. Jonathan. You think I'm not taking you seriously. When it's quite the opposite. I might never have said it, but I'm quite fond of you, after all, and—no, no—he was holding his hand up to Jonathan who was self-consciously starting to interrupt—no, no. Let your uncool parent drop you off at school, young man. They both chuckled. The priest nodded severely at Jonathan's drink. And you know, Texas only allows minors to drink with parents. But—pst kst—the priest couldn't hold back the laughter for the punchline—you keep calling me Father! They both lost it. Ha ha. No, but let me finish. I am quite fond of you. And you stumbling onto love—oh, it makes me laugh, like a kid figuring out that the water comes out of the sink when you twist the, the . . . the priest was still laughing but his eyes had turned red and there were tears coming out all over his face, and now he held up his hand again, and said, Oh, ha ha, I'm just laughing so much it's making me cry. But his laughter had stopped. He took his napkin and wiped his face and blew his nose.

Just then Jane and Nate got up from their table to leave. They walked over to the booth where Jonathan and the priest sat. Jonathan took a sip of his beer, looking down at the table.

Well, it was good to see y'all! said Nate.

You too, said Jonathan and the priest. They all shook hands.

Have a good night. We'll see you later, said Nate, turning to go.

Oh, hey, Jonathan, said Jane.

Jonathan said Yeah, and looked up, avoiding her eyes but looking somewhere near her head and around her out into the crowd.

I was thinking, you're here over Christmas, right? You know I go to midnight Mass on Christmas Eve with my parents? At Father Donald's church. And you're like here, and away from home and stuff, so I thought, if you want, you should come. Since you know Father Donald and everything.

Oh. Ha. Mass? I mean, he hiccuped quietly, I like the Father here, and all . . .

Anyway, we'll be there if you decide you feel like it.

You know what, said Jonathan. Yes. Yes, I'd like to see my friend here working for once. I'll be there. I will most cert-tainly be there.

Oh. Okay. Great. Well, look for us and sit with us.

Okay.

For the first time, Nate seemed to look askance at Jonathan and Jane talking. But then Jonathan looked back at the table, and Jane said, Well, bye, and he didn't look up when they walked away.

So. What's that about? said the priest. Coming to church. After all your bluster.

Oh. I got an idea. For Mass.

Father Donald was quiet a long time, and then he said. Well. I'm going to get going. He stood up and stretched, and bent over and picked up his penitential stole.

Okay, said Jonathan. He got up to walk the priest out.

The priest walked slowly to the door. Jonathan supported himself on the frame as they went out. The priest retrieved his black bicycle with its basket from a dark corner of the old wooden porch. He pointed it down the ramp toward his home behind the church, a couple blocks away.

Jonathan.

Yes.

Do you really think it's that simple?

Jonathan was quiet.

Do you?

Jonathan looked down.

You're right about the world. For one moment, whatever cloak of geniality the priest wore evaporated in front of Jonathan's eyes. About this *fucking* life. Of course you are.

Well. I'm just saying . . .

No. Really. There's no but.

Okay.

But I have to say. On Christmas Eve. Look at me.

Yeah?

Whatever you're thinking . . . and I can't commend it, of course. But make sure it happens before the consecration. If you hear the jingle bells chime, you're too late.

The whole time he said it, the priest was looking steadily into Jonathan's eyes, and Jonathan felt strangely frightened.

Okay, he said.

Well. Goodnight, Jonathan. The priest turned to go, wheeling the Raleigh down the ramp.

Father?

Yes?

Jonathan went over to him, and put one arm around the older man's neck, and bent to put his face onto his chest and held him there for a second. Then Jonathan went back to the door, and turned to watch as the priest ghosted away silently on his bicycle, meandering and weaving on the deserted night street until he disappeared with a final wave, coasting behind the church that glowed.

    Jonathan went inside and found their waitress. Okay, I'm ready to go.
    Oh, Father already paid it.
    What?
    Yeah. Earlier.
    Wait a second. But . . .
    Oh, he did it when you weren't looking. He always does that.
    Oh. Well. Thanks. I mean, thanks to him, I guess. He laughed awkwardly.

    The waitress walked away. Jonathan stood there, and then said You little bastard quietly to himself, and grabbed his books and notebook from the table and walked for the last time out the huge wooden doors. He turned and looked back at the trellised hall, the fire, the company. The light bounced amongst the crossed shadows of the vaulted ceiling. Mortises with tenons pounded home by hands long since corrupted in their coffins. Gary caught his eye, polishing a highball behind the bar. He put the glass and white towel down, and straightened up and gave Jonathan a formal salute. Jonathan nodded and went out.

Jonathan arose early the next morning. He cleaned his room and organized his things. He dressed and went to the store and purchased five two liters of regular dr pepper, a dozen boxes of chocolate little debbie donuts, and a pair of scissors. He went home and lined up the bottles and stacked up the boxes on the little shelf that had held the TV when he first arrived. He went into the bathroom and took off his shirt and then stood in front of the mirror. Holding up chunk after chunk of hair he sheared it off in what he imagined to be the inverse of beauty. He put the scissors close to his scalp on top, and then left long pieces around his crown. The edges he left except on his temples, where he made a sharp line at the top of his ears. He took out his razor and shaved up to the line he had cut with the scissors. The skin was pale underneath. He looked at himself. He whispered a curse. Then he took toilet paper and cleaned up all the hair.

    He went out of the bathroom and took one of the bottles of dr

"He parked under the tree and sat down in its shade."

pepper and one of the boxes of donuts and sat down on the bed. He drank as much as he could, and slowly ate the whole box of donuts. He had to take breaks.

And that is what Jonathan began to do every day, as often as he could stand it, and sometimes oftener—several times the first week he couldn't hold down the sugar and vomited it into the toilet and then rinsed out his mouth and tried to drink more dr pepper to recoup what he had lost to the plumbing.

He went to manager of the Sandman and told him he'd be moving out at the end of December. The hell happened'dyour hair? asked the manager. Shoot, he said, spitting into the galvanized little bucket outside his door, Youre week to week. Just clean out your room when ya go. He shook his head as he walked back into his room. Sure as hell ain't gonna find another tenant plants a fuckin garden, that's sure.

Jonathan harvested as much of the crop as he could. Eight head of greenleaf, four of romaine, a bundle of carrots. He pulled up some beets but they were small and misshapen and he threw them onto his compost pile. He lined up the greens in the cardboard box he used for deliveries, and wedged the carrots down in their midst with their tops peeking out. He strapped the box onto the back of the CB with bungees and drove it over to the alley behind the church and left it by the back door where he knew the priest would see it and rode away without being noticed.

Back at The Sandman Jonathan raked the long mounded beds until they were free of vegetable remains, and shoveled the roots and fragments onto the compost heap. Satisfied, he looked out over the ground.

He returned the gardening books he had checked out to the library under the watchful eye of the librarian, and used the computers to made a googlemap of his northwestern passage, meticulously dragging the blue line off the interstate arteries onto farm and market roads. He skirted the mountains and hugged the coast, westward to Kerrville and Marfa and El Paso, through the basements of New Mexico and Arizona before reaching California, through which he would take the coastal highway all the way up to Oregon, hoping for temperate and pacific weather. He drew the map in his notebook, and wrote down all the steps, with the distances between towns. The bike would go a little more than a hundred miles on a tank.

Every morning, now, he would get up early. He would eat half a box of donuts, and wash it down with half a two liter of dr pepper. Then he would go over to the window facing the parking lot, and he would kneel down in front of it. There was no one to talk to, and nothing to say, but he would stay there a few minutes in the light.

Back at the library he started ordering spare parts for the bike. He bought a stack of prepaid credit cards at the grocery store with cash, and used them to pay for things online. They were each only a hundred dollars, so when he ordered offroad tires and new tubes for the CB in view of the route he would be taking and the weather, he had to pay on two separate orders. Then new points, new plugs, new condensors, new coils. He also ordered more tools. He bought quilted coveralls from the farm supply store and boots from the redwing shop. Everything he owned would be on the little bike. He brought the CB into his room onto the tarp once more to work on it. He changed the oil. The UPS truck came to his door almost every day.

Finally he saw that his face was rounder. Puffy. He looked different to himself. Many pustules, too, had erupted on his forehead and cheeks and he crushed some of them into redness and left others bulbous and white. He had stopped smoking at the beginning for fear it would steal his appetite, but he felt now that it would be safe, since he had started to crave the donuts and the dr pepper, and felt hungry most of the time. So he went out for cigarettes.

And out in the town, suddenly it was Christmas. The laposts of the little downtown strip were enwreathed in green and crowned with red bows and hung with banners that said A Texas Holiday. People were going in and out of shops that seemed at other seasons to have no one in them. It was almost sixty degrees and sunny but the contained excitement of December was over it all. He went into a drugstore built into one of the old downtown buildings and got in line.

Oh. Hey Jonathan.

He turned around and it was Nate.

Hey. How's it going.

Good.

Nate was trying to look natural but he had his hand by his side shielded by his body.

Whatcha up to?

Just picking up some cigs.

Oh. Yeah, I'm tryin to get some Christmas shopping done.

Yep.

How you been? Jonathan saw him glancing at his hair and face.

Not bad.

Good. Yeah. Haven't seen you around in a while.

Nope.
So. Youre going to the Catholic Christmas Eve deal then?
Yep.
Yeah, I don't think I'll go. I went last year.
That bad?
Oh. I mean. You know me. I'm kinda intense about it, and I just don't feel like it's very biblical.
Oh. Right.
I mean, and Jane's not Catholic or anything.
Yeah. Right.
But whatever. She does it for her family.
Yeah.
Yeah. And speaking of which, I'm trying to figure out what on earth to get her. For Christmas. We're doing like a Christmas Eve thing at her parents' house earlier that night. You know, Tom is . . .
Yeah. How bad?
I mean . . . he's still all there. Like mentally. But yeah. Not good.
Yeah.
I was thinking like, a necklace or something . . .
She'd probably like that.
Yeah, like a . . . I don't know. I was kind of thinking like a john three sixteen pendant or something.
Hmm.
Well, what do you think?
Oh, I don't know. I think she's . . . I mean maybe her style's a little more simple, you know?
I know, said Nate. I'm not great at this.
Well. Maybe like just a real simple necklace would work. Or, like, a . . . big sweater or something. Button up. Like a nice one. She's always cold.
That's true, said Nate.
Can I help you?
Oh, yeah. Can I just get a pack of Marlboro?
These?
No, the . . .
Red?
Yeah.
Hundreds?
No, just the . . .

Short?

Yeah.

Okay.

He paid, and was about to leave, and Nate said, By the way, it's nothing weird or anything.

What?

This. I just got hemorrhoids, that's all, said Nate, displaying the little box he had in his hands.

Jonathan laughed. Well, alrighty then.

Nate laughed too, and then said, Hey, listen. No hard feelings, okay?

Jonathan looked at him anew. The bland, knowing face. Okay. Yeah. Okay.

Nate stuck out his hand.

Well, I wouldn't go that far, said Jonathan. He smiled, and started walking backwards toward the sliding glass door, and said, Look. You sure as hell better . . .

I know. Yes. I will.

Okay, said Jonathan, and turned and left.

Jonathan lay on his back on his bed once more. The overhead fan was finally still. Beside him was a little debbies box.

What's in your mouth?

What do you mean.

Are you eating right now?

Yeah . . .

It's rude to eat when you're on the phone.

Thanks for the pro tip.

I'm just saying. It reflects poorly on me.

Well you're the only person I talk to on the phone, so . . .

Maybe for now. Anyway, I called to say happy birthday.

What? That was like two weeks ago.

You think I don't know that? But we only talk on Sundays, and you didn't pick up last week.

Oh. Yeah, sorry . . . I was . . .

Anyway. Happy birthday.

Mom, it's my *birth*day . . . What you say?

Ha! You still listen to them?

No.

Oh. Me neither.

Yeah. That was back when . . .

. . . Yeah. And besides, I'm pretty sure it's, The words you say. Not, What you say.

It sounds like what you say. Jonathan sang it again in a loud falsetto. What you say!

Ha ha. I wonder if they're still around. Anyway. Happy birthday. Sorry it's late.

Thanks mom.

I won't ask about the girl.

Oh. It's okay. Her name was Jane.

Pretty name.

Yeah, it is.

We don't have to talk about it.

Okay.

So.

So . . . is my room still available?

Are you serious?

What? I'm only . . . I guess eighteen now. And it'll only be for a little bit. Until I can find some rundown hotel to live in.

No, I mean, are you really coming home? I haven't let myself get my hopes up.

Oh. Yeah. Um . . . if it's okay. Get reacquainted with the sibs. All that. In a couple weeks. I'm going to leave on Christmas.

Jonathan heard her breathing a little noisily on the other end. He said, And I will . . . I plan to pay half the bills, and . . .

Shut up. Just shut up. No. You won't. Just get yourself home. She was full on crying now.

You okay mom?

Yeah, yeah, she said, and it sounded like gyeh, gyeh. She sniffed. You sure you're ready?

Yeah. I think I've about got my fill of Texas. Or will by the time I'm done.

When are you getting in? Send me your flight info and we'll pick you up.

Oh . . . I'm driving up.

What?

I mean, actually, riding up. On my . . . motorcycle.

You got a MOTORCYCLE?

Jonathan held the receiver out from his ear and it seemed comically loud like on a movie. He laughed. Yeah, Mom. I did. He kept laughing.

You little . . . you little . . . I can*not* believe you did that. Are you an idiot?

He kept laughing. Maybe I am. It's fine, mom. I've been riding it all year. It's fine.

Two weeks went by. And then Christmas Eve dawned cold. Garbage trucks made their noisome circuit as always, janitors swept empty halls at midnight, cats slunk between streetlights and winter birds cawed in occasional defiance, while in the cold light a hobo from the bridge at Mary St. slouched to church to be fed.

Once more Jonathan arose in The Sandman and took a bottle and a box and sat on his bed. He chewed and swallowed and drank thoughtfully. Afterwards he went to the window and pulled back the old maroon polyester curtains as he did every morning, but this time opened the window itself, shedding dust and fossilized insects into the room, and he knelt in the light of the morning.

He stopped and thought.

Hmm.

He stopped again.

Across the parking lot lay his garden, frost covered and ashen, and the sky bright behind the black weeds of winter trees shone with a flatness and a nearness, green gold behind the haze. There he knelt with the wind of the morning washing over his shoulders and the new sunlight and he was shivering with no shirt on and he stayed a while longer, and then he got up and shut the window. He closed the curtains.

The room was dark and warm without the open window. He pulled out the little ironing board and began ironing a long sleeve button up shirt. It was a work shirt but it was the only collared thing he had, and besides, who would not call this a work? The iron hissed and steamed around him. He finished it and hung it up and then packed the rest of his clothes into the brown canvas duffel he had kept in the closet since he arrived. Into the duffel went the brown tarp and some thin rope as well. He put his books and notebook along with the manual for the CB into the blue jansport. Everything, right there. The empty bottles and boxes he stacked neatly on the far side of the bed as a memorial. Three more times he had gone to the store to replenish his trove. Fifty seven dr peppers in thirty one days. Almost fifty boxes of donuts. His stool had changed color with all the black bile. He pulled on his stiff new boots without socks and piled up bottles and boxes in his arms and carried them to the dumpster. A cleaning lady he had never seen came every week to change the sheets and this morning he piled up the bedding and put a hundred dollars on the pillow. He hadn't had a drink a since Thanksgiving, and now he poured out the mostly full vodka bottle left in the freezer, saving a half inch in the bottom. And that was that. He looked around the room. He walked into the bathroom and checked all the drawers. He went and dropped his keys in the manager's mail slot a few doors down. He returned and sat on the stripped bed.

Children's voices came to him imperatively, muffled through the walls, but he couldn't make out what they said. Take and read. Jeremiah, Trey, and Tyrone flew by his window and then circled back, loping and coasting, toward their alley. Jonathan went to the door.

Hey! Guys! Hang on. Jonathan stood halfway out his door.

Missa Jonathan! Missa Jonathan.

Hey guys. How's it going.

They looked down with their resentful thoughtless faces to the side, and said, Good. Except Jeremiah, who looked in his face and didn't say anything.

Hey. Listen. Guys. I just wanted to let you know that I'm gonna be leaving.

Aight.

I mean, like, I'm moving. I'm leaving for good.

Aight. They fidgeted, looked away, rocked back and forth on their bikes. Then Jeremiah, stone still, began crying. His mouth was dead open, saliva strung between his top lip and his bottom.

Awww . . . shit, nigger. You *crah*in?

Jonathan went to Jeremiah and crouched down and hugged him. It's okay, buddy. It's gonna be okay, buddy.

Trey and Tyrone said, Awww . . . don be a *bai*by.

Hey. Guys. Come on.

Awww . . .

You know I'm leaving and I'm never going to see you again.

That aint nothin. Errbody moves. Now you leavin.

Well . . .

Trey and Tyrone sped away silently on their bikes. Jonathan thought about how many times he had straightened their wheels or patched their tubes or fixed their chains.

He held Jeremiah out with straight arms when they were gone.

Hey. Hey. Listen to me bud. It's gonna be okay. You're gonna be just fine. Alright buddy? okay?

Jeremiah was wiping his face with the back of his hand.

You my only friend. And now you leavin. Errbody always leave.

No . . . no, there are other people. Some you probably don't even know about.

Jeremiah just stood there shaking his head. Uh uh. Uh uh.

But Jeremiah, you're right. I am your friend.

If you my friend, why you gotta go? What you gotta do?

Well, a friend doesn't mean you can always be with that person. But it means I . . . I always want the best things happen to you.

Aight.

But listen. You're *my* friend too, right Jeremiah?

Yeah.

Okay. Then you gotta make me a promise.

Aight.

You have to promise me that you won't get sad. That you'll never give up.

Aight.

Promise me. That you'll never give up.

I promise.

Okay then. I'll . . . I'll always be cheering for you, okay? You're gonna do good. I know it.

Aight.

Okay.

Jeremiah picked up his bike. But will I see you again?

Well I don't know.

Jeremiah got on his bike and made a slow circle, his cheeks still shiny. He pointed his craft toward home and gave a little wave and shyly said, Bye, like he was practicing.

Bye, Jeremiah.

A little further off he turned in his saddle and said, But in heaven, right?

Yeah, Jonathan called back. He waved until Jeremiah was out of sight.

The front continued rolling in and by mid afternoon it was freezing. He was all packed. Everything stood in readiness near the door. Some idea, having church at midnight, he thought. He kicked off his boots and lay down on his bed to take a nap. He fell asleep.

He dreamt that he had ridden up to Austin and met his father at a seafood restaurant. It was very nice. The waiters and waitresses all penguined in black vests and short neckties. Fat, the lot of them, and obsequious. Jonathan ate a lobster taco, and kept saying how good it was. His father, whom he could not see clearly across the table, kept holding his hands out in an apologetic, this has all been a big misunderstanding sort of way, and nodding and saying something that cleared everything up. Jonathan could hear his voice, and caught the gist and the drift but could not make out a single word. Then he found himself weeping and saying everything he could think of, while his father nodded with a serious and understanding look.

He awoke to soft knocking on the door. He started and looked around the room. Then he sat up, and went to the window, and peered out the curtains. Oh fuck, he said. He opened up his jansport that was by the door and strew its contents on the bed, and shoved the brown duffel out of sight behind the A/C unit to hide his departing. He rubbed his eyes hard and shook his head. He cleared his throat and opened the door.

Oh, hey Jane. How's it going.

Hey, good. I . . . he watched her take in his face and his hair and his stomach visible under his t-shirt.

I . . . I just came by to bring you something. It's nothing. For Christmas. She held out a small cube shaped package in brown paper. Don't open it till tomorrow. On Christmas.

Jonathan held it and looked at it. What? Wow. Thanks so much. I would have . . . sorry I didn't get you anything, I . . .

Oh, don't be silly. Why would you. Anyway. It's nothing.

She was already walking back to her idling car with a white cloud forming from its exhaust. Turned back to him. I cleaned off the battery post, by the way. I googled it and watched something on youtube.

Oh . . . good.

She stood behind her open door. So . . .

He looked down at the package in his hand.

She kept looking at him. I feel like . . . why couldn't you just talk to me? About whatever was going on.

I don't know what you mean.

Jonathan.

I don't, he said quietly.

I wonder—did you think I couldn't handle it? Like because I'm a girl or something?

He just shook his head, still looking down.

Like . . . you don't think *I* do the right thing, on my own? Do you really think I can't make hard choices? Like you?

The wrapping was a brown grocery bag, he could tell.

You didn't have to do all that, she said.

He watched his breath go out in puffs. He didn't move.

But I do understand.

She got into her car and closed the door.

She rolled down her window. You're still coming tonight, right?

Yeah.

Okay. See you then. As she pulled away and tugged the seatbelt across herself she called back over her shoulder with just the corner of a smile out the window, Your hair looks ridiculous. And don't open it till Christmas!

He turned the brown paper package over in his hands.

The preparation was finished. Night had fallen and it was dark. The duffel was stuffed and lumpy, his bulky new coveralls strapped on top. There were bungees going in every direction. The duffel sagged over the edges of the seat, and was wedged down against the taillight. Near midnight, just before he left the room, Jonathan took the almost empty vodka bottle from the freezer, and gulped down what he had saved in the bottom for strength and for the breath it would give him, wincing against the sheer medicinal taste, and then filled the bottle halfway up with water from the sink. He put the bottle inside his coat and zipped it up. He went out and stood in the orange light of the parking lot under the overhang in front of his door, and looked back into the darkened room one more time and then closed it. He straddled the bike and gently rocked it side to side to feel its loaded weight. Everything seemed secure enough.

He pushed the starter button and let the bike warm up and then pulled slowly away.

The cloudy night was dark with a loose fog, and hushed.

All through the small town expectant lights blinked. The wind was biting cold.

Downtown, the methodist church was nearing the pinnacle of her grand candlelight service, and strains of an organ and multitudinous singers reached him as he passed. Adeste fidelis. Well, he thought, I'll come anyway. In the dark on the side steps of the big soaring church sat the hobo. Under heaped blankets he ate methodically at something coming out of a paper bag. Venite adoremus. Venite adoremus. Venite adoremus. The ogive windows burning fiercely like concrete candles.

A little farther through town and all was dark save a single convenience store blasphemously fluorescent, and the far flung orange streetlamps. Ahead loomed the cold black hills. He knew what they looked like in the sheer august sun. He passed on his right the almost hidden trailer office of Buck & Liddell, and he raised his hand as he passed.

Then he arrived at the church just before midnight, and there were but a few huddled black shapes hurrying up to the doors and entering in brief lighted moments. The church itself was unimpressive, with wood siding, tucked between two taller buildings on each side, and a mere block from the hulking first baptist church, which was silent and empty at this hour. The side walls of the catholic church were broken up with cheap, inwardly lit stained glass windows showing a suffering christ in a progression of attitudes. He parked on the little sidewalk going around to the rectory, out of sight of the front door. As he walked to the entrance, he rubbed his numb hands together and put them in his pockets and then looked up at the dark closed door.

He tried to imagine himself rising unsteadily from the pew beside Jane to take from his jacket the watered liquor and raise his hands to bring everything to a halt. The words would come to him in the very moment and would rend not merely the shroud hung twixt the eyes of the people and the hanged god to awaken them from the spell but would strike the final and ruinous fissure between him and her. Why are you doing all this? he would ask and mock in the midst of the dumbstruck congregation. That they would sit like stones he was sure. To make of a piece of bread a pretend god? Better to carry that bread and all you own with downturned heads to the streets to his visible and hungry children! Hypocrites, all! and as he thought it, suddenly a great bell bonged overhead, tolling the hour and startling him and he remembered the small brown package still unwrapped in a corner of his duffel—for now it was Christmas. He forced himself to remember his purpose. Once more in the aisle, before his friend the priest, he cried, You have never suffered, like other people suffer. Right now a woman pulls a worm from her throat in a jungle. Right now a man is burned alive. Right now a child is thrown across a room by his father. The bell tolled three. Right now a lover dies unbeknownst to his mate and a poor mother weeps over the poor gifts wrapped under her small tree while her children sleep. How then to take from these souls standing before you their chance at life and not rather to give them dissolving on their tongues a taste for each moment of their foreshortened lives, knowing the succession of moments will one day cease? The bell clanged seven, and he had reached the top of the steps and stood before the door. Lunacy to worship whom they had not seen when every nearstanding wife in the place stands neglected and every breathing acquaintance snubbed and crushed to abstraction in his neighbor's mind and every soul of them in mortal combat with their besetting sins and lonely in the midst of the multitude.

He wondered how much of all this he believed. Though of course that wasn't the point, and then the bell struck twelve and finished its knelling with dying tremors. But it was what he would say, raving in their midst. That would do it. Surely. It had to. He felt was ready and he took the knife . . .

Reaching out for the door he felt suddenly a small urgent mass brace itself against his leg and wedge into the opening in front of him and disappear inside.

I so sowwy! He so escited!

He wheeled around with his tantric and ecstatic face and saw a mound of asian motherhood smiling apologetically, holding out one hand in propitiation while the other clutched the shoulder of the solemn elder son, brother to the apparently born hellion who had just pushed past Jonathan into the church.

Dat my Chawwie! He so escited!

Jonathan found himself holding open the door for the woman and her eldest son.

Tank you! So sowwy!

The pair went inside.

Jonathan stood there in the door. He concentrated, and tried to conjure the spell that had been broken. He felt as if he was walking out onto a dark stage and it was the wrong night and the house empty.

He went inside and let the door close behind him. The small narthex was dim and quiet and beyond it the nave revealed by the woman and her son's passing in was warmed with many candles and soft lights and was quiet in the wake of the bells but with a rustling crowdedness. He saw the woman put her hand swiftly in and out of a little thing on the side of the door and dab her head and body. He walked forward and entered the church. Everyone was standing and his friend the priest faced them all. In the name of the Father and of the Son and of the Holy Spirit. Everyone was moving suddenly. Jonathan found the bowl the asian woman had put her hand in and he stuck his hand in too, then put the water on his hands and wiped his face and eyes with it. The Lord be with you. The room resounded with a booming And also with you, muddled with responses of And with your spirit. It startled him, and he went and stood in front of an empty chair against the back wall.

The Mass swirled around him. When people stood up, he did, too. And knelt. And sat. And mumbled when they spoke. The woman and her sons were on the end of a pew a couple rows up, and the younger son, Charlie, began systematically to probe his mother's defenses. She held him as she stood, and he leaned backward until his leverage overcame her strength and she had to put her other hand under his head. Then he began with one finger to poke insistently at her forehead. She set him down on the pew, and he put his chin on the back of it and stared with unaffected boredom at the parishioners behind him. The woman smiled with joyous resignation.

And then, as Jonathan scanned the high room, there she was. He found the shimmering darkness of her hair toward the front of the church, in a dress of deep emerald overlaid with black lace and beside her the small shape of her mother, and then . . . Tom. He appeared to be half his size, and his hair was gone. Jonathan gasped.

The paple that wawked in dorkness has sane a gright laat.

The librarian! Jonathan recognized, now reading from the lectern up front, the woman who had held the keys to his borrowing books when first he tried months ago.

He looked again at Jane, and saw her looking around.

Fer thar is a chaald bowern fer us . . .

She finally looked in his direction, and he gave a little wave, and she bouyed up, with her face all lighted in the half gloom, and she waved for him to come join her. He made signals that he would stay where he was, things having gotten started, et cetera, and he turned his palms up apologetically. She understood, and smiled at him, and turned back around, and hugged her mother by her side.

Wonder-Cayounsler, Maaghty-Gawd, Etarnal-Father, Preents-a-Pace . . .

Jonathan watched as Charlie's face sunk out of sight behind the pew back, and then suddenly re-emerged, laterally, from behind his mother's legs on the floor. Surreptitiously he wormed his little body until he was in the aisle by the side wall. Above him, in roughly cut glass, Christ promised his kingdom to the thief. Charlie began army crawling toward the back of the church in slow motion, as if his legs were dead. Jonathan opened his eyes wide at Charlie, and raised his eyebrows, while the old parishioners nearby looked down at him as if he were invisible.

The ward of the Lowered . . .

Thanks be to God.

Charlie was now almost even with Jonathan at the back wall, and there was no one else between him and the doors to the narthex, and freedom. And still it seemed as if the boy's mother did not realize he had escaped. Jonathan made what he imagined to be a stern face at Charlie, raised his eyebrows once more, and pointed back to where his mother was sitting.

Charlie stopped. He looked at Jonathan with an expressionless face. Little implacable black eyes. Then he got up on all fours and made for the door in earnest. Jonathan looked back to the mother in consternation, but she stood holding her hymnal blissfully, with the staid eldest next to her. Jonathan looked around, but no help was imminent. He sighed and followed Charlie to the narthex. He beat him to the front doors, and stood in front of them.

Umm . . . you can't go out.

Charlie, still on all fours, went back on his heels and lifted his hands and panted, and then said Ruff, ruff, in a high pitched bark.

Sshhh. Shh, said Jonathan.

Ruff.

Oh. Okay doggie. Good doggie. Okay. Sit. Good. Now .. okay, heel. Good doggy. Okay, shh doggie. Heel. C'mon . . .

Jonathan had Charlie at his side, and walked slowly, with a pretend leash in his left hand, and led him in a circle, and then opened the door to the nave. When he did, Charlie whimpered and shook his head and barked, and several people tilted their heads, but did not turn around.

No, no, bad doggie, whispered Jonathan, and closed the door. The doors were frosted glass, with clear parts shaped like crosses.

Sit. Lay down. Stay.

Charlie obeyed, but kept panting.

Alleluia. Alleluia, sang all the people.

Jonathan looked in through the window on the door.

The musicians, off to the side at the front, were a miscellany of Ventana. A lavender haired old woman singing a wavering soprano. A short, wide mexican with a big acoustic guitar. A rancher in a black western style suit and turquoise bolo with a willie nelson voice, and a fat woman with short dark curly hair at the piano. There was a troupe of choir folk pulled together for the occasion, sitting in two rows of pews to the side. A black couple, several stringy teenagers, others.

Ruff!

Jonathan turned around.

Look. Buddy. I'm gonna go get your mom if you make any noise, okay. Hey. Are you a talking dog?

Dog Charlie nodded his head.

Okay. So . . . you come to this church a lot?

The dog nodded.

Your mom said you like it.

The dog frowned and shook its head.

Hmm. Pretty boring, huh?

The dog didn't respond.

Well then what is it?

The dog was frowning sullenly, his straight black hair cut in a straight line across his forehead.

Okay. Fine. So . . . you have a dog at home? I mean, like, another dog?

Charlie the dog made a big smile and nodded vigorously with his tongue hanging out.

They could hear the voice in a tiny speaker above them in the narthex, and Jonathan recognized the priest's voice.

. . . when Quirinius was governor of Syria . . .

What's your dog's name?

Annabelle! the squeaky voice said, and then Charlie the dog quickly clapped a forepaw over his muzzle with wide eyes.

Don't worry. I won't tell anyone.

. . . and they were struck with great fear. The angel said to them, Do not be afraid . . .

To atone for his breach, Charlie began spinning in puppy circles, letting out little yaps.

No, no . . . look. You gotta be quiet. And you're gonna have to go back in there. You're mom's gonna freak out.

Dog Charlie shook his head.

What? What's wrong?

Charlie made little growling barking sounds, and then spoke like he was using a dog voice. I . . . Black . . . Wolf.

Oh. I see. Like . . . a bad dog?

Charlie nodded.

No, man. You know, you're just, like . . . a puppy. Puppies are kinda crazy. Not bad. It'll be okay. You know . . . puppies like to snuggle, right? Like . . . I think you should go in there like a puppy and go snuggle with your . . . with your master. Your mom.

Dog Charlie looked uncertain, so Jonathan said, Okay, I'll help you. Okay? Heel.

Jonathan held his left hand out with the imaginary leash and did one more slow circle around the small narthex. He looked in through the window and improbably the dog's mother had not yet begun to look for her issue. Jonathan quietly opened the door to the church and held it for Charlie, who had continued to stay at heel, though now he was kicking and rearing like a horse. Jonathan put a finger on his lips, and pointed over to Charlie's mother, and then hugged himself and pointed again. Charlie cantered off, and a few moments later, Jonathan saw his head appear on his mother's shoulder. Jonathan smiled at him, but he just stared back with half lidded eyes.

Jonathan stepped back and let the door close softly.

Bad dog, he whispered.

He sat down in a corner of the narthex.

The priest was talking, and he caught fragments of what he said in the tinny speaker.

But it didn't sound like preaching. It felt like he was sitting in the old booth at the old bar, talking.

The gospel tells us the shepherds were afraid. The worthless and dirty. Living outside. They were scared. And well they should be for God was coming to them.

Jonathan sat in the half dark and ignored it.

He opened his jacket and took out the vodka bottle prop. It all seemed so ludicrous now. He got up and put the bottle in a garbage can.

Hidden. That's how God works. I don't know why. But he comes as this dirty child in a dirty little town. A backwater. Not unlike some Texas townships I know. Presumed a bastard. And he was a bastard, for Joseph was not his father.

Jonathan tried to think. To remember what he was going to do, and why.

And tradition tells us Joseph died when Jesus was young. A fatherless boy like any other. But he was not like any other. For in him all the fullness of deity did dwell. And this sixteen, seventeen year old man, he . . . Well. You know, God was a mechanic. God is a mechanic. He makes things work. That's what carpenter means. Worker. More of a mechanic than a woodworker. The next time you go down to aamco, to get your transmission checked, and you see the guy's bloodshot eyes from the meth or whatever, and his big hands, remember God is a mechanic.

What the hell, Jonathan said quietly in the narthex, looking up from where he sat, through the clear glass cross on the door. He looked at the headhung wooden christ up front. The priest wasn't visible at this angle. But the jesus was raised up, hung by chains, suspended between heaven and earth. Torn in perpetuity.

So all this stuff is going on around the world, right?—the emperor is flexing his muscles, there's such and such a governor of Syria. People are buying and selling cloth in the market. And animals, or whatever—and of course humans, too. And there's this big annoyance. A census. That's what everyone's complaining about at the water cooler, you know? And hidden from everyone God enters the world. A little human boy. Just like now. People are yakking back and forth about Obama. Or Governor Perry. In the year that Rick Perry was governor of Texas. Quirinius. It's like that. One little boy. God was that little boy. You want to see God? That jewish kid in palestine was him. We rail against God every day. Why is my life like this. Or whatever. But maybe Jesus railed against God, too. Why is it like this?

Jonathan glanced over at Charlie, fast asleep with mouth agape over his mother's shoulder.

Once more he remembered what he had planned to do. And if there were a time for it, that time was now.

But everything had been taken out of him.

He felt like he had been swimming out to capsize a canoe. In the lake. And suddenly the water was too cold, and his arms were numb, and he couldn't find the canoe in the winter dark, and when he finally did reach it, and stretched out his hand . . . it was the black, glistening skin of a great whale. The one tiny walleye gazed placidly at him with little waves lapping the iris, and it blinked slowly. He reached out and ran his hand over the wet and riven avocado skin, vertical and flat in its huge convexity. Rivulets streaming down the basalt hide in the wintry mist. It floated there like an island, immutable. In a rage he pummeled it, dull silent thudding, and swam at it, and rammed it, pushed with all his might at its bulk, and in doing so he drove himself backwards in the water. But he imagined it moved some fraction of an inch. Or the world did.

When he came to himself, he sensed that the moment, if there had ever been one, had passed. The priest his friend had stopped talking, and now everyone spoke together:

. . . God from God, light from light, true God from true God . . .

And then the priest was praying, and people were saying Lord, hear our prayer, at intervals.

Jonathan felt as if there were a tide coming in.

Then everything was quiet for a moment. Jonathan stood up and went over to the door and looked in through the window. The priest was moving stuff around on the table at the front. Kids in white robes were handing him things that it was difficult for Jonathan to see at this distance. It felt very familiar. As if the priest had just said, Hey, hand me that fifteen millimeter socket, would you? Jonathan smiled. Everything very businesslike.

And then, suddenly, he knew that it was time to leave. That was all. There was nothing for him to do here.

He patted his pockets for his keys and his wallet out of habit. He looked at the sleeping, drooling Charlie. He watched as the rancher stood up to the microphone and nodded at the pianist, who began a country prelude. The mexican guitarist strummed on the downbeats. Silent night. Holy night. All is calm. All is bright. The man with the willie nelson voice sang it softly with his eyes closed and his gray eyebrows tilted upward. The priest went on with his preparations at the front. Men walked down the aisles with wire metal baskets on long poles, and people put money in them. Jonathan quietly opened the door and stood on the back wall near the center aisle. This, then, was it.

After Jane had turned to put something in the basket, he caught her eye. There would be no raging upon the heath. For this, here, was real life. Shepherds quake at the sight. Jane smiled at him. He smiled back. And then, folding his hands in front of him, and with his mouth closed, he nodded. Okay? She never stopped smiling, but she nodded and tears came to her eyes. Crying in church. He held her face in his eyes for one more moment, and then turned and went out the door without looking back.

Again in the narthex, the rancher's voice came through the speaker overhead. Son of God! Love's pure light! Jonathan stood in the dimness, back by the front door of the church, out of sight of Jane, but he could see his friend the priest and above him the hanging jesus like an eagle hovering over the altar, and the chains did not suspend him but rather were flung out from his pinions like grappling irons. The song ended, and the rancher in black bowed his head, and as the priest began speaking again, Jonathan looked at the hanging jesus, and tried to look into his eyes, and tried to understand something. And he saw that he suffered. And he saw that he was made of wood, and that thorny tears must surely spring from his woody eyes. But he could not reach him. I'm right here, said Jonathan. I'm right here. If you're really you, this is your last chance. He stood there, minutes, trying to peer into the downcast eyes. But nothing. Slowly he stood upright, for he realized he had been crouching, peering up at the crucifix far away at the front of the church through the cross shaped window on the door. He sighed, and the feeling was as much relief as it was disappointment. For, then, all of life was left to him.

He continued to watch the priest up behind the table at the front, the familiar lips moving, looking down, holding something. His eyes were closed, so he must be praying, but Jonathan could not hear him, and it felt like his ears were filling with water, and it was whirring and getting louder, and then the priest, tensed like a raptor over the thing in his hand, said, Take this all of you and eat of it for this is my body which will be given up for you, and then he arched upward, holding the thing in his hand, and suddenly, clearly, there were jingle bells echoing through the church, purely, rung thrice, and Jonathan rushed to the door and looked, and still he couldn't see what it was in the priest's hands. A flat circle. Like a huge beige coin. Jonathan squinted through the window, and tried to see if anything was written on it. Pale and flat, like the face of the moon. A squint eyed alien baby.

And then, suddenly, Jonathan recognized it, and he felt as though the omniscient disc were rushing toward him down the center aisle as in a nightmare with his legs held by rising waters—and he saw that it was the bland face of some unremembered downs syndrome kid he had seen years before at his mom's office when a young, young woman had carried him in fearfully asking about her doctor's bill.

Some minutes later Jonathan walked out of the church. Everyone was still singing inside, muffled through the walls. Hark the herald angels sing. It was very cold now, and Jonathan stuffed his hands in his coat pockets. He remembered the vodka bottle in the trashcan, and started laughing. He felt very light. He skipped down the steps, and walked around the corner to his waiting bike, heaped about its frame like a circus wagon. Mild he lays his glory by. He pulled the heavy quilted coveralls out of the bungees, and climbed into them. He pulled on his ski gloves. He straddled the bike, and bent down and pulled up the little choke lever, and turned the key. Then he considered, and turned it off, and got off and started wheeling the bike in neutral. He pushed it, laboriously, two blocks down the street. The music faded as he walked. Veiled in flesh the godhead see. Hail the incarnate deity. Pleased as man with men to dwell . . . When he felt he was far enough away, he stopped. He was about to start the bike once more, but he put it on its kick stand, and unzipped one side of the brown duffel and pulled out the little paper package from Jane. He opened it and inside was an old white mug with something printed on one side. He held it up to the streetlight, and there was a little picture of an oldfashioned boombox, and underneath it, written in faded eighties script, the words: Tune into 89.9 WETC for your Update on the Hour, Every Hour! There was a lavender post-it note stuck inside the mug, and it said:

I don't know if the radio station will work, but I guess I'll probably give it a try. I'm glad you got the job last summer. Thanks for being my friend. Over and out. -Jane

Jonathan stood there holding it, and then carefully put the mug back in its box and into the duffel. He looked around. Then he turned the ignition back on, and kicked the bike over. It rumbled and clicked and hummed. Jonathan smiled. He pulled slowly away, taking a side alley that led to the road that would take him up into the hills and out of the town forever. He looked back once just before he turned and thought he saw a light as the front door of the church opened. As he climbed into the hills, everything was black.

    And then his headlamp began to illumine tiny snowflakes, spaced very far apart, that fell softly and raced toward his face.

Book IV: *Spring in Texas*

SOME RAIN came that spring. The cropped hills awoke from under their gray bristle blankets and the pastures sprouted with chartreuse and shamrock. Red clay streambeds, baked and rock hard, muddied themselves into shallow pink slurries. The trees that had died in the drought stood awaiting the years that would come to denude them while beside them their comrades bloomed furiously in the quietness after the war, all the more brilliant for their commuted sentence. The little spotted ground squirrels peeked out of their burrows in the tufted dunes, wriggling their noses to sniff the all clear. Having slept from July to April, do they live one third of a life? Friends and relations of the squirrels emerged nearby. The soil was warmed by the sun, and the males began their frenzied romances, scurrying in and out of the burrows in an ancient pattern betokening matrimony. And all the land teemed with spring once more.

In the dappled dark of a magnolia tree sat Father Donald on a green wicker chair next to a cast iron table on a barnwood porch attached to a little house tucked amongst other trees set back from the road. The magnolia was in its first bloom, a smooth wetblack skeleton draped in pink, effusing a breath of sweet earth decay onto the breeze rustling under its raiment. Already, on this last Saturday of March, Father Donald was wearing his short sleeve clerics, and sat on the porch and felt his trouser cuffs flap gently against his ankles. He was warmed in patches by the sun, and he felt at peace.

I'm not sure how these turned out, she said. I realized just this afternoon that I only had all purpose flour, so.

Rosemary emerged from the house and let the screen door whack to.

Oh no. They're probably horrible.

Rosemary's face wrinkled up, and she shook her head at Father Donald and smiled.

She set the tray down on the little table and seated herself on the other wicker chair. Her hair was like old straw.

They sipped their tea and they talked of many things. The goings on in old San Remo and the ebb and flow of Father Donald's old parish there. Rosemary's acquisition of some estate papers for the archives at the library. An old cotton family. They talked of people they had known, and those they had forgotten. Of beauty, and of how many forms it takes. Intimations of God, and of his ways in the world.

So, said Rosemary finally. How'd it go.

Oh, pretty normal. Fine. Beautiful day. We rode horses for a while.

Hmm.

They were quiet, looking out over the planters in front of the little porch. Pale pansies, and wild yellow fennel further down toward the road.

You know, I think it's coming to an end.

What?

The whole thing. I've been sensing it. I just learned that Byron's up for parole. In a couple months.

Wow.

Yep.

How do you feel about that?

I don't know. His warden. Matt Barber. He told me. For good behavior. Byron doesn't know. These are good, Rosemary. She smiled. Yeah. Warden says all he needs is . . . a letter of character from me. Since I'm the only one that's come to see him in all these years. He hasn't told Byron.

Rosemary sat cradling her tea in her thin hands, and studying Father Donald's face.

He should probably've told Byron, but . . . I think what he's doing is he's giving me veto power.

Oh Donald.

He sat there, chewing and looking down at her shoes. Thin brown flats. The little sole was just pulling away from the upper. Well I don't know, he said. I'm not worried about him being out. I mean being dangerous. Not that I'd say he's redeemed or something. Just . . . I guess there's not much of a person left. Not the same one anyway. Talks with a Texas accent. And he'd have an ankle tracker or whatever. Warden said he's already found him a job as a ranchhand at some halfway house or something out by Uvalde. So it just comes down to whether I want him to stay in there or not.

Well, *and* . . .

What?

You told me, remember? Right near the beginning. When you were at San Remo. She was looking down. You said it was your penance. For . . .

Yes, I know.

And do you think it's . . . that it's . . .

I don't know. Either way I just feel like it's come to the end, and I don't think I'll go see him anymore after next week. You know, it's true I did it for that. Because the old priest told me to. But then I guess also did it because I guess I always secretly hoped something would come of it. Like maybe I'd understand someday. Get some answer from him. Ha. Why he did it. I don't know what I was thinking. You know, I asked him once. Later on. I just said I don't get it. Why'd you have to do that. And I don't think he knew either. He just looked down in his hands. And he said You just have to believe me, I never meant to hurt him, I just saw him there, and he looked so beautiful to me, and I'd never felt that way. You have to believe me. I don't know if he was lying or not. It doesn't matter. He doesn't have the answer. It's not in him. And I'm just tired of it all. It scares me a little. I can't even muster much anger anymore when I try. That's not the way it should be. It shouldn't fade.

She looked intently at his face which was turned away from her, gazing out over her front garden. She had known him for two and a half decades now. Known him as a man, and then as a priest. Spring does come. Spring does come. But she knew she would never say it and she didn't.

The light was slanting behind the house. A fatal metalmark butterfly swiveled on its gyrational journey past the porch, diaphanous and mortal.

How long has it been? she asked.

Father Donald bowed his head. Well. He would have been thirty three this year.

They were quiet again. Rosemary took a sip of tea.

Time present and the end of all things.

And all shall be well . . .

There is a ditch that flows around the fields of the prison, and it carries the irrigation and the chemical fertilizers away, and from it the ground squirrels and the jackrabbits drink in their seasons. The horses sometimes, too, but they have their own cisterns.

Donald awoke early on Saturday, and donned his black shirt and trousers and pulled his white alb over that, though he was not going to mass, and tied a white rectangle of cloth about his shoulders and muttered Lord give me strength to conquer the temptations of the devil in deference to ancient custom as he did so.

The garage door flew open and there stood three forms black silhouetted against the bright day.

A letter from Jonathan came two months after he left. Well, I guess I made it. A handwritten letter in the mail.

It's all over. We know everything.

Dressed for the sacrament, Donald went to his study in the rectory. There was a wall with several pictures. He removed a framed print of St. Helena and then used his fingernails to pull out a rectangle of drywall from where it had hung. There was a little safe tucked between the studs and Donald took out an old Colt 1911 in a ziplock bag.

You're coming with us. They all had guns. We know your kids in there. You want him safe, you come with us.

Jonathan passed ancient sequoias in the northern californian mist. A golden meteor in the gray rainforest.

Donald bumped over the curb from the garage to the street at the rectory in the old pickup as the sun rose. He was wearing a long black trenchcoat over his priestly garments.

One spotted ground squirrel came out of his burrow near the prison grounds with quick, lizardlike movements, then stretched like a cat in the half light of dawn. He had awoken from hibernation only three days before. Horses stamped nearby in the Dolph Briscoe stockyard, but he was not afraid of them.

The letter said Jonathan was going to stay with his mother and sisters for the year, but then maybe find some place nearby. It rained all the time and he already missed the sun. He had applied to college, using the library computers, while he was still in Ventana. Donald chuckled on reading that. He had been accepted at several schools with full tuition offers. He was starting at Portland State University in the fall and was going to be a maxillofacial surgeon someday. He said he wanted to stay in touch with Donald.

Donald counted out eight rounds in the study of the rectory and pressed seven into the mag. One. Two. Three. Four. Five. Six. Seven. Then he took an eighth bullet and he opened the slide and put it in the chamber and carefully closed it and lowered the hammer and engaged the safety and put the gun in the pocket of the trenchcoat.

They put something over Donald's head. Then he woke up and he was tied to a chair and some small part of his mind kept saying this is like a movie this can't be real. Buddy buddy buddy! There was still something over his head and suddenly white flashes went out of his eyes and then he knew that he had been struck across the face with something. You feel that? We're about to break your head in, motherfucker. But I don't know if that'll get you to talk so first were gonna do this. They whipped off the thing over his head and it was just two of them there. Mikey Clooney and his huge dumb bodyguard holding a wrench. So how you wanna do this, Don? They were in some strange small room and there was a little TV screen in front of Donald.

Flowers bloomed on the edges of the drainage creek most months. Yerba de la Rabia, paintbrush, and bluebonnets in the spring.

Donald skirted San Antonio to the west as he drove south, passing through Hondo and Devine.

Welcome to Oregon. Siskiyou Mnt. Summit, Elev. 4310 Ft. There was no snow on the ground, but Jonathan shivered as he descended northward out of the pass.

And all shall be well . . .

So you've been dropping VIN numbers to the feds, huh? What? What're you talking about, cried Donald in a shaking voice. Where's my son? The bodyguard stepped in front of Donald and raised his hand. Hold on, Ronnie, said Mikey. Let's do this the quick way. He lifted a CB to his face and said, Hey, Byron. You all set? The radio crackled and a voice Donald did not know said, Yeah.

Donald had been visiting the Dolph Brisoe Unit in Dilley, Texas, southwest of San Antonio, for twenty three years, and for the past few months he had been testing its security force, long since accustomed to his presence. Every few weeks, he would call ahead and let the guard in charge of visitation for the day know he was coming. Then he would meet the guard at the chainlink and barbed wire gate near the livestock pen, where Byron was working. The guard would let him in, with a cursory patdown, and have him sign the clipboard there. Then he would open the gate to let him out when he was done with his visit.

In his last days, Tom Liddell groaned in his sleep and said snatches of words, and reached out to imaginary things with bent hands in slow motion. It was disconcerting if you were sitting next to his bed. There were welty lesions on his bald head. He looked like some broccoli god. A pale sith lord. God, oh God, oh God, he would say, and not realize he had spoken.

Mikey turned on the TV. It resolved into a gray picture. Donald squinted at it. He saw a face he didn't recognize close to it, reaching out an arm toward the camera, fiddling with something. Then the face moved away and Donald recognized his son's bedroom. And there was his son, tied at his wrists and ankles to the four corners of his little bed.

And all shall be well . . .

Then Tom went very quickly, and could hardly rouse himself to whisper. He was in great pain. The cancer had metastasized to the marrow of several ribs and vertebrae. All the family were there. He died the next day.

Okay Donny. Heres whats gonna happen. Youre gonna tell us exactly who you been talkin to, and what you told em, and youre gonna do it as fast as your mouth can move. An you do it fast enough, your boyll probably be okay.

And in all manner of thing . . .

Jonathan had good luck most of the way, but on the last leg up from Florence, through Eugene and then Corvallis and Independence and

McMinnville and Newberg, it rained steadily.

Donald parked where he always parked. He took the pistol out of his overcoat and stuffed it into the crotch at the front of his pants.

The ground squirrel spent much of his morning hidden in the shade of a columbine shrub, nibbling the tender parts of a stand of sweet white clover.

I . . . I . . . Oh my God. Stop. You guys. You guys are fucking nuts. I haven't said anything to anyone. I . . . The wrench came across his face. Mikey got on the radio. Okay Byron. Whyncha start with ticklin the kids feet, huh? On the screen, Byron picked up a pair of pliers. Donald was screaming. No! No! No! He was violently thrashing in the chair, and he heard a tiny, tiny voice on the screen crying Daddy! Daddy! Where are you Daddy! Mikey got on the radio. Hold up Byron. I think Donny here has something he wants to say. Mikey turned away from the screen and faced Donald. Okay. Look. I dont want that weirdo at your house to do anything to your kid. I really dont. You dont want that either. So look. You start giving me names. Tell me who youre talking to. Tell me whos vehicles you ratted out. Donald was sobbing, Oh my God. Buddy. Buddy! I swear to you on everything, Mikey, everything, I havent said anything to anybody. Mikey screamed in his face, Then why the fucking hell I got all these fucking bricks all over me all of the sudden, heh? Crawlin all over my guys. How the fuck they puttin Benson in Syracuse and McCully in Elmira together, heh? And Ricky in Binghamton, heh? You wanna tell me how theyre doin that? Those guys was all clean as a whistle. The only common numerator is you. You worked on all theys cars. You catch my drift? Now you better start talkin . . . Suddenly Ronnie said Hey, Mikey! Hey! What's he doin? Mikey spun around to look at the screen, blocking Donald's view. Mikey and Ronnie were quiet, and Donald yelled out What's going on! Move out of the way! Then Mikey said Oh my fucking jesus. What the fuck is he thinking.

Donald waited at the double gate near the pen. He had his hands casually in the pockets of the trenchcoat. A hundred yards away, he could see Byron working a horse. The prison livestock program trained security horses. The guard came over and unlocked the inner gate, then locked it behind himself. He opened the outer gate for Donald. Howdy, father. Morning, Steve. When Donald was in the enclosure, he held out his hands. The guard touched his arms and waist and outer legs lightly, and up under his armpits. Kinda chilly today, huh? The guard let him in, and they waved to each other. See ya later. Okay then. Father Donald walked toward the half fallen picnic bench under the honey mesquite in the middle of the pasture. When he was under its darkness, he pulled the gun out of his pants and put it back in his coat pocket.

Bedraggled and frozen, Jonathan pulled at last into the Greenbriar Plaza apartments. He coasted around the familiar drive to their unit. Suddenly everything in Texas seemed unreal and hazy. He walked up the stairs and put the key that he still had into the lock and opened the door and then there they were. Jonathan! Jonathan! Sparrow ran and jumped and hugged him and slid down his legs. His mother looked older than he remembered and she said, Buddy boy! Welcome home. Let's get that off. You are completely soaked. And did you do that to your hair on purpose? Jonathan looked up, and Ruthie was just standing in the hall, looking at him. She burst into silent tears. Jonathan walked over and hugged her and she buried her head in his chest. Don't ever, ever leave again.

When Byron was close by, Father Donald stood out into the light. His coat whipped in the wind, and a cloud raced across the sun and everything seemed dark. Byron saw him and smiled and waved and rode back toward the training pen to put the horse up. Donald went back under the tree and sat down at the table and checked the chambered gun and turned off the safety.

That morning, his son had been playing legos in the entryway of their little house. Dad. Yeah? Now can we try out talking to God like you said last night? What? said Donald. Oh. Right. Well . . . Hmm. Maybe thats something you want to do on your own. Like maybe when youre falling asleep at night. Okay? The boy looked down at his legos. Oh. Okay.

The ground squirrel saw a female nosing her way out of a burrow. He sniffed the air and looked furtively around, and there were no other males in sight.

The little boy said, But why doesn't he say anything back? Hmm, said Donald. Good question. Well. Well, think of it like this. You see that window over there on the front door? Yeah. When you see something in the window, you know Im coming in. But you cant really see me through the window, because its . . . all bumpy glass. Right? It just gets dark. But since Im the only one who ever comes in through the door, you always know its me. Even if it doesn't look like me.

Well howdy sir. How you doin. Good. Well that's good. Good to see you, Byron. They shook hands under the tree. They both sat down at the picnic bench. Wasnt sure if you was comin. Tomorrow Easter and all. Well, I try to come as much as I can. I don't say mass on Saturday mornings anyway.

The female was in estrus, which happened for just two hours in the spring every year. The male scented her and began to search for her but then heard something and looked up from his cover under the columbine and a man was walking to the tree in the middle of the field. The spotted squirrel had seen this pair many times during the three years of his life, and was not alarmed, though he did flatten himself into the grass.

Oh my fucking jesus, said Mikey again. He yelled into the radio, Byron! What the fuck are you doing! Byron! The radio was silent. Whats going on, screamed Donald. Oh . . . oh fuck, said Mikey. Let's get outta here. Ronnie swung the wrench at Donald's head, but Donald jerked his head back, and it just cut his forehead open. C'mon Ronnie! Just leave him. Grab that thing! Donald now saw the screen. And on it Byron's white buttocks were visible over the bed but he couldn't see his son. He heard him screaming high pitched, No! Daddy! Daddy! Help me! Help me! Donald was screaming too, though he hardly knew himself. Buddy Buddy Buddy! My God My God! FUCK YOU GOD DO SOMETHING! Then Ronnie yanked the cord out and grabbed the little TV as it went black and he picked it up along with the dish antenna that was on the dirty wood floor, and he and Mikey went out of the little room through a metal door and Donald was blinded by the light and then they slammed it and it was dark and Donald was still screaming Wait! Stop! Wait!

When the one man disappeared under the darkness of the tree, the spotted squirrel moved cautiously toward the burrow where he had seen the female. She had disappeared back inside. He went a foot at a time, and then would freeze in cover.

So. How you been? said Byron. Father Donald's head was bowed over the table. Byron, the priest said. Yeah? said Byron. Why did you start talking like a Texan when you got here? Byron chuckled. I don't know. Well, Donald said, I think I do. He was quiet for a second. Then he said, almost cheerfully, No need to make this melodramatic. He reached into his coat and pulled out the 1911 and rested it on the table pointing at Byron.

Donald was convulsing and thrashing in the chair. He got the chair to bounce by pushing with his legs and toes. He threw himself backwards, landing on the corner of the legs, and the wood chair splintered.

Byron didn't say anything.

Jonathan walked around the Portland State campus in the rain that winter and spring, picturing where he would take classes in the fall. He found a job at an italian restaurant, since he would be taking classes during the day. It was not like The Sombrero.

The wood chair when it broke loosened the rope around his arms and legs, and Donald wriggled one arm out. He untied himself. He ran to the door and went out. A bright spring day. It was a warehousing dock on a river. It looked like the Susquehanna, but he couldnt be sure. How far from home was he? His shirt was torn. Blood was streaming down from above one eye, and older blood was caked around the crown his head. He crossed some railroad tracks and found the empty two lane highway beside the dock and he started running in the direction he thought his home was, in the middle of the lane.

Byron remained silent. So, said Donald. This is the last time I'll be here.

Jane was going to say something at Tom's funeral, but on the day of, she couldn't stand up without help.

Well, I figured something like this would happen in the end, said Byron. Why? asked Donald. Well, said Byron. What I did was the worst thing anyone can do. Someone should shoot me. His voice suddenly sounded like New York again. You think I don't, like, look at myself? I'm almost crazy with it. Am I the one that did it? Like, I'm watching myself. And . . . and . . . I want to kill myself. But I really just want to escape from myself. I should kill myself. But I'm also the only one I am. And if I kill myself, then I will always be that person. And anyway, I'm trapped inside being that person who did that. Even if I was completely different, no one would ever know, and I'm still the person who did that.

One time Jonathan went by the smoothie shop and bought a Jamaican Holiday. The cashier boy was new. Lindsay was in the back, but she never came up to the front, and Jonathan decided not to make a thing of it and he left.

Finally a car came along, and Donald waved his hand like a mad man and they screeched to a stop. Is it this direction to Binghamton? Yeah . . . what's going on? The driver spoke through an inch of open window. It's an emergency! They have my son, and . . . The driver said, I don't know, man . . . Donald was frantic, and he grabbed the handle of the door, but the driver had locked it as he slowed, and now he squeeled his tires and left Donald standing, forsaken, in the middle of the highway.

Yeah. Youre right. Donald pointed the gun at Byron's face and pulled the hammer back, click-click.

Finally a cop came along, and Donald jumped in, and when the cop heard what Donald was saying, he turned on his lights and sped to Donalds home. Donald ignored the cops yelled order to stop and ran ahead of him into the house and there was no sign of Byron and then when he reached his sons room a scream was in his stomach and he turned the corner, and his son was still tied there to the four corners of the wooden bed, wrists and ankles, and his pants were loose about his hips, and they were stained black on the little bottom, and there was red over the lower half of the bed.

Byron never moved. So? said Donald. Byron said, I got nothin to say. Donald held the gun out almost touching the bone just above the bridge of Byrons nose. He held it there. Like standing on the edge of a precipice and how easy, how simple, to set in motion the plummet. He looked deeply into Byron's eyes for maybe the first time. A sickly hazel. And he imagined whether they would shut reflexively or stay staring open as they were.

Then Nate said, No. You can do it. You'll regret it if you don't. I'll help you. I'll go up there with you. Jane whispered, I have it written down. Then I'll read it, said Nate. I'll hold you up. You need to do it.

Finally, slowly, he brought his other hand around. He pushed a button and let the mag drop into his hand. Still looking into Byron's eyes, he used his thumb to flick off the rounds one by one at him, and they would bounce and strike him in the chest before clinking to the ground. One. Two. Three. Four. Five. Six. Seven. Okay? he almost cried. Okay? I should shoot you right now. For the honor of my son. It would be the right thing to do. But I'm not going to. I'm not saying I forgive you, because I don't know what that means, and no one does. But this is the last time I'll ever be here.

But alle shalle . . .

The squirrel saw the men in the shade of the tree when something glinted. He crouched there in the grass. The one man moved around. Suddenly something flat and bright white, like a daisy but more brilliant, came out of the black hide of the one man and passed between him and the other man in the dark under the tree.

And alle maner of thynge . . .

Father Donald stood up. He looked for one last time at the face of the man across from him, bowed, streaming with tears, holding the sealed letter in his hands. Donald knew the eighth round was chambered yet, and he stood there, all in black, with his hand in his pocket on the gun.

In my foly before thys tyme often I wondryd why.

It was hours before they could take Donald from his son. Kissing his face over and over again. I'll never forget you. I'll never forget you. And he it was who carried him out of the house.

Alle shulde have be wele.

At last Donald turned without a word and walked back to the gate and the guard saw him afar off and he too walked there, and he said take care now but Donald looked not at him and walked straight out, with his hands still in his great black coat.

The squirrel watched, and finally the other man emerged from under the tree, with the white thing held in his hands before him. He walked slowly all the way across the field, like a crooked tree that moved. The squirrel looked furtively toward the first one who had left, all black. He was now outside the gate.

Then suddenly the squirrel jumped and buried his body in the dust, for the man walking outside the gate had started to run all ungangly down the ridge along the drainage creek away from the prison, black pressed against the white blue sky, and he ran faster and faster, and the dust behind his feet rose like a pillar and on he went, and he took something from his pocket and threw it with a splash into the creek and then he loosed his black coat and let it fly in the gusting wind like a burning ash into the sky and he was all of white sparkling like chalcedony and his raiment flowed behind him as he ran.

and in alle maner of thynge, alle shalle be wele.

The little squirrel, finally at peace, turned in the light of the noonday sun to the burrow, looked once behind him, and disappeared.

THE END

With Gratitude

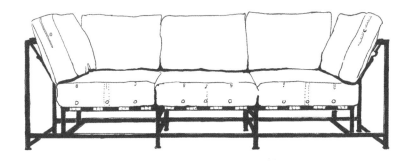

stephenkenn.com

Jason Rankin
in the author's opinion the finest Realtor in Texas.

The author wishes to express his deep gratitude to
Amy Schroeder for her wise, kind, editorial insight.

John & Susie Burger

Matthew & Jenny Watson
Tim & Colleen Wallace
Rachel Lulich
Nathan & Rachel Roberts
Dave & Patty Watson
Emily Ruth Brower
Todd Richardson
Doug Ingraham
Jalet A. Farrell
Megan Love
Kate Rice
Katie Organ
Laura Groshong
Amy Schroeder
Ian Duffy
Katrina
Abigail Marguerite
Daniel & Danielle Luttrull
Mark Marquez
Andrew Smith
Seth & Eleni Reid
Diana Torres
Dan & Katie Forrester
Calum J. Lambie
Ryan L. Brooks
Tom & Lou Aylward
Liz Colclough
Arland Nichols
Jacquelyn
Grace Johnstone
Matt & Anna Norman
Nicole Bouchard
Ryan Duffy
Adam & Brittany Marshall
Jenni & Kyle Gerber
Matt & Taylor Turkington
Jordan & DeeDee Carson
Adam & Brittany Marshall
Jenni & Kyle Gerber
Matt & Taylor Turkington
Jordan & DeeDee Carson
Taylor Pfeiffer
Jordan Walter

Chris & Britt Bernard
Katherine
Amy Aldrete
Sarah Clark
Laura Clark
Ambrosio
David & Pam-Sue Brower
Sarah Tumlinson Page
Joseph Ptomey
Steven Petersheim
Juliana Monteiro
Andrew & Laura Pierson
Eric Lester
Gabrielle Brant Freeman
Ronni Phillips
Ross & Anne Lile
Matthew & Dawn Wible
Stephen & Beks Opperman
Christine Pyle
Cory & Catherine Nauertz
Brian & Jolene Bickle
Elizabeth Karounos
Juliette Bowers
Trey & Abby Witcher
Daniel Benyousky
Margy Horton
Shannon Bozarth
Nathan Kilpatrick
Mackenzie Sarna
Loren Warf
Rachel Kilgore
Sheldon Nalos
Michael & Chandelle Aylward
Heather Hughes
Graeme Kent
Jeremy Larson
Isaac Dansicker
John C Carswell
Michael E. Harkins
Tim & Rebecca Aylward
Allison Thornton